GALPA

GALPA

SHORT STORIES BY WOMEN FROM BANGLADESH

Edited by
Firdous Azim and Niaz Zaman

SAQI

British Library Cataloguing-in-Publication Data
A catalogue record of this book is available from the British Library

ISBN 0-86356-567-0
EAN 9-780863-565670

This first edition published by Saqi, 2005

SAQI
26 Westbourne Grove
London W2 5RH
www.saqibooks.com

Contents

Introduction

Putting together a collection of short stories by women from Bangladesh has been both an exciting and a daunting task. Combing through old journals, conferring with young writers and discussing amongst ourselves about what could or should be included were the exciting aspects of the editors' tasks. At the same time we had to keep asking ourselves how representative our choices were, both of the authors and of the times in which they wrote, and indeed of the country itself. At moments of intense optimism (and ambition) we thought of this collection as tracing a hundred-year history of writing by women in Bangladesh, a showcase where all our best writing would be displayed. However, we had to clip our wings, constantly reminding ourselves of our self-imposed limitations, among which that of genre – short stories only – was the one we perhaps felt the most, as it led to the exclusion of poetry and novels. Women's poetry is a rich field in Bangladeshi literature, but this was definitely outside our purview.

Women's writing from Bangladesh – or from anywhere else, for that matter – brings to the fore issues of identity, both regional and gender-based. The old debates of women and difference or of the special sphere of women's writing surface yet again. We will try to see whether this debate has a different resonance in the Bangladesh context.

We decided to start our collection with Rokeya Sakhawat Hossein's

'Sultana's Dream', published a hundred years ago in 1905.[1] We have used this piece as a beacon – a guiding light – for women's writing in the region. 'Sultana's Dream' is a utopian vision and opens a limitless world for women to explore, to occupy and to represent in their writings. This vision takes us far beyond the conventional limitations that circumscribe women's lives, opening up the windows of the mind to wider and wider vistas, describing a boundless space where dreams, visions and ideas can flower and proliferate.

It is also interesting that this utopian vision was expressed in the English language. Rokeya is well ensconced in the annals of Bengali literature, and her occasional English writings, including her correspondence, prove how adept she was in both languages. By writing 'Sultana's Dream' in English (a piece she herself later translated into Bengali) she seems to want to open up the imaginative world of Bengali women to a larger readership. At the same time, the fact that it is written in English enables 'Sultana's Dream' to be placed within the European modernist tradition, so that the literary historian or critic may read it alongside the writings of Virginia Woolf or Kate Chopin, for example.

Written in both Bengali and English, Rokeya's work also highlights the issue of translation. This collection of stories contains both original writings in English and short stories translated into English from Bengali. Hence the task of translation was central to our concern as editors of this volume. We were dogged, as can be expected, by the larger questions surrounding the task of translation, questions regarding the faithfulness of the translation to the original as well as about the status of translation, of whether the re-rendering of the text is tantamount to a re-writing. We gave practically the same importance to the selection of translators as we did to the selection of writers, as is borne out by the fact that some of the translators appear as writers in their own right.

Also and crucially, the need for translation of women's writing was at the forefront of our concerns. Women need to read each other's writings, as much within their own cultures and languages as worldwide. Contemporary global culture is defined by and dependent on the new media industry – on film and TV – which is guided and controlled by

---

1. 'Sultana's Dream' was first published in *Indian Ladies' Magazine* (Madras) in 1905. It was published in book form by S. K. Lahiri and Co., Kolkata, in 1908.

financial conglomerates, and in which women's own voices hardly find a place for expression. We need to carve out other spaces where women can speak and hear each other, forging the path towards the formation of a transnational feminist arena. Women's writing, with its long history, is perhaps less mediated than other global forms of cultural expression and exchange, and efforts such as this one are guided by the need to create autonomous arenas for women. Debates such as the one regarding the special nature of women's writing can thus be held within broader parameters, where differences and commonalities between women can be understood and appreciated.

At the same time, especially in post-colonial cultures like ours, translation brings into focus the dual linguistic and literary traditions that our writers draw on. Writing in Bengali can be seen to traverse into and draw on other linguistic and literary traditions, and is thereby enriched. The inclusion of writing originally in English in this collection illustrates the easy access to both English and Bengali that our writers enjoy.

***

Rokeya stands as a beacon introducing our collection of short stories by women from Bangladesh. The next piece dates from the 1950s. This gap of a few decades in between is for generic reasons, as that period seems to be marked by a concentration on poetry. Sufia Kamal (1911–1999) started her literary career during the 1930s, going on to become a leading poet in the country, adept also in the art of prose fiction. After much debate, however, we felt that her pieces do not represent the true spirit of the writer.

The real flowering of women's writing in this region is visible from the 1940s, partly thanks to the establishment of *Begum* as a woman's literary magazine in 1947 in Kolkata. In 1950 *Begum* moved to Dhaka. It continues to be published, though somewhat irregularly. In the early decades of the newly independent country (when Bangladesh formed the eastern wing of Pakistan), *Begum* provided a springboard for many a woman writer. It also helped to create a women's readership. Most of us have fond memories of the weekly arrival of *Begum*, for which our mothers and grandmothers waited avidly. *Begum* uses cheap newsprint,

especially unattractive to look at, and it can in no way be mistaken for the
glossy products that are the staple women's magazines today. It covered
the political issues of the day, talked about health matters, introduced
scientific debates, such as those about the uses of nuclear energy, and most
crucially provided space for women's essays, short stories and poetry. We
have gone through the pages of this magazine, selecting stories that we
think are representative of the age in which they were written. The 1950s
and 1960s were marked by a social realism in prose, but we have also
found humour and satire within the pages of *Begum*. For us, the editors,
these stories represent a world that perhaps our mothers inhabited,
and in that sense trace women's history through women's writing. The
writings of Razia Mahbub, Helena Khan and Rabeya Khatun are taken
from *Begum*.

The relation between women's reality and women's writing has been
the main feature of feminist literary criticism. To this can be added the
validity of a women's literary tradition. Is there such a thing, in the words
of Elaine Showalter, as 'a literature of their own'? Is there a strand that
needs to be followed, an insight into writing and culture that needs a
special women's vision? While putting together this collection, however,
the question that seemed to come to our minds is that of mother-daughter
connectedness. We wondered whether drawing a literary history would
enable us to examine intergenerational links between women, whether
women's voices from the past echo within our own lives.

***

It was only after 1971, when Bangladesh emerged as an independent
nation after the War of Liberation with Pakistan, that writing from this
region reached a full flowering, whether it was writing by women or
by men. The main bulk of our collection comes from this period. We
have incorporated work by well-known writers such as Selina Hossain
and Makbula Manzoor, as well as short stories by lesser known writers.
We have tried to give prominence to younger writers such as Shaheen
Akhtar, Audity Falguni, Papri Rahman and Jharna Rahman, who are
already making a name for themselves as writers in Bangladesh. A story
by Dilara Hashem, who lives in Washington DC, represents writing from

outside Bangladesh. We have incorporated stories by women writing originally in English, such as Niaz Zaman, Shamim Hamid and Shabnam Nadiya. The bilingual literary corpus, though perhaps not as well-known (or as prolific) as in other countries of South Asia, nevertheless lives on, and we felt that including these stories gives another dimension to this collection, bringing to the fore post-colonial literary issues and the question of the authenticity of literary language. Bangladesh can perhaps be differentiated from other South Asian countries on the basis of its linguistic national aspirations, as the country itself is based on linguistic considerations and Bengali is recognized as the only language of state. English writing from Bangladesh therefore needs to be put under a different kind of microscope from the other post-colonial nations in the region, and, although as editors we were mainly concerned with the richness and diversity that English writing lends to prose fiction, we need to look at the tenacity with which English cultural and literary forms persist in our literary traditions.

It is interesting to note how contemporary women writers take their place in the literary sphere. Today *Begum* seems to have lost much of its influence. Women seem to be more individualistic, striking out on their own. The literary pages of daily newspapers have since emerged as a strong launching-pad for fledgling writers, and women writers have not lagged behind in publishing in these pages, be it poetry or fiction or literary criticism. Literary journals abound, and women publish along with men in them. However, while we do not seem to need a special platform for women's writing any more, women writers do seek to formulate a separate identity for themselves. Women writers as a group are discernible in literary discussions and circles, and older more established women writers can now be seen as an influential group with the ability to promote and help publish the works of their younger women colleagues. Writers also double as editors at times, thus providing a special avenue for the publication of women's writing.

It is thus not only in reading but also in writing and publishing that an inter-generational – a mother-daughter – relationship can be seen to be emerging. And again, while we celebrate this relationship, its fraught nature surely finds expression among writers themselves (see, for example, Nasreen Jahan's short story 'Different' in this collection – perhaps for us a cautionary message about drawing comparisons too easily). How enabling women are for each other is a matter for debate, and women writers are of necessity equally dependent on their male peers for literary recognition.

Among the stories from the 1970s to the present, the variety of themes is significant. We introduced this volume with a piece of utopian fantasy, providing a space for the playing out of dreams, as well as fun and humour. We followed it with pieces of domestic realism from the mid-twentieth century and stories with variegated themes from post-independence Bangladesh. Our writers seem to belie the usual accusation that women's writing is too limited in vision and theme, is too confessional, is locked within domesticity and so on. Most of the writings in this collection do delineate women's lives, but not necessarily the lives and experiences of the writers. Our largely middle-class women writers – literate and literary – seem to be mainly concerned with lives of poor women, of sex workers, of women living on the margins of society. How do we explain this preoccupation with lives of 'other' women? Is there a privileged voyeuristic position that these women writers are exploiting? If not, how do we explain this turning away from describing their own lives?

In analyzing the leap of imagination that the writing of such stories entails, we felt that our women writers were performing an act of solidarity, in trying to speak for women who have no voice in the literary arena. This act is definitely neither voyeuristic nor privileged, but one that requires great compassion, imagination and a sense of solidarity with the subjects that are portrayed. This is amply borne out in the stories by Selina Hossain, Shaheen Akhtar or Jharna Rahman. These writers perhaps find an echo of their own position as women writers in the stories they choose to write and in the lives they opt to represent. They too have to carve out their own places within the literary arena, at the same time sticking to their positions of being on the edge, of edgy writing from the margins.

Social realism has by now acquired a new dimension, domestic realism giving way to the broader examination of social inequities. Portraits of displacement, marginality and poverty become even sharper when emblematized through the figure of a woman. Our women writers explore all kinds of issues, such as political corruption, migration or ethnicity, to name only a few. Along with this array of themes, our writers display boldness in their experimentations in literary style. The stories play along with the properties of prose both in English and Bengali, going much beyond the parameters of direct realism, to the world of magic (in Audity Falguni) to exploring the stream of consciousness (in Shaheen Akhtar) or to abstraction (in Papri Rahman).

***

Mahasweta Devi, the well-known Indian writer in Bengali, once commented during a talk in Dhaka that she had stopped reading novels because she could not possibly read another description of the vagaries of the lives of the Bengali middle class. This rather harsh comment reflects the connection between the class status of the writer and the world that is described in the writing. The identity of the writer and the writing are intermixed.

'Short Stories by Women from Bangladesh' – the subtitle of this collection – will provide an insight into the lives of women in Bangladesh. We hope that the collection goes beyond that and becomes a way of introducing readers to women's writing from Bangladesh. This writing exists not only as women's writing, but also in the general sphere of Bengali fiction. We found that the most important question is perhaps the way in which women enter into the literary arena, rather whether women writers concentrate on special themes or deploy a special woman's language. We have also found it important to see whether women carve out a special niche in the readership, and whether there is a different relationship between women and the literary tradition. Women have certainly created special spaces for themselves: Rokeya by means of the establishment of her school for Muslim girls in early twentieth-century Kolkata, or the offices of *Begum*, which provided a meeting ground for literary women in mid-century. Today there are associations such as the Lekhika Sangha that offer such spaces. Women's journals such as *Annanya* recognize women's writing by honouring women writers. But what we discovered more and more is that women do not seem to need these women-only spaces to such an extent any longer.

On the issue of difference in theme, we may ask whether women write more or even exclusively about women. Not only do women writers not have the luxury of sitting back and writing confessional pieces about themselves – they have also taken on the onerous responsibility of representing the nation of women to their readers. This seems to be true even in the case of a Bangladeshi woman writing from overseas, such as Monica Ali in *Brick Lane*.

Male writers appear to share this sense of responsibility. Indeed, contemporary fiction in Bangladesh can be said to be involved in the task of 'writing the nation', in the sense of narrating it and exploring it in all its aspects. Literature in Bangladesh, along with other forms of cultural production, seems to be seeking a distinct voice, creating a distinct language. While urbanization proceeds at a hurtling speed, our writers seem to be drawn to rural settings. This provides a wonderful opportunity to portray the changes that the country is undergoing, not only in its urbanism but also within its rural heartland. The rural in this formulation is not a site for a comfortable retreat: there is nothing pristine or idyllic about it. The rural becomes the site where change can be studied, and our stories are not just annals of rural-urban migration, but a record of the changes in the rural itself.

Mining rural Bengal for its themes also provides our authors with the opportunity of exploring the many forms of spoken Bengali. The variety of this spoken language when introduced into writing creates a new form of literary language, as colloquial and regional versions of Bengali occur not only in the form of dialogue but also within the main narration. It has been very difficult to reflect in translation this fluidity and elasticity of differing linguistic registers, and has been more successful in some pieces than in others.

As we have seen, women share with their male colleagues the task of 'writing the nation' as well as of fashioning new forms of literary Bengali. Where they may perhaps differ is in the description of the female body. Representations of the female body have played a crucial role in literature, providing an aesthetic space that is potent with meaning, a space that echoes our fears and desires. How successful women can be in manipulating and reshaping this image is one of the main questions that guide the debate on the difference of women's writing. Do these figures remain the passive repositories of a culture's fears and desires or are they active autonomous agents? Are women's voices – in all their diversity – heard through these stories?

***

We hope that this collection of stories brings to life the changing nature of women's writing and the way in which the authors choose to write about women's lives. We also hope that we have been able to reflect the roles that women writers have ascribed to themselves – that of guide and teacher, that of chronicler of lived experiences or that of narrator, who brings a nation and culture to life.

Putting this volume together has been a rewarding process for another reason. As we set about collecting stories, we came across many women who were willing to help us with suggestions, sharing the excitement of something they themselves had read. We want to thank all who associated themselves with this process, making us realize that women's writings do have a special place in the hearts of women readers.

Special thanks go to Selina Hossain and Maleka Begum. Selina Hossain has helped to enrich this volume by organizing a discussion with young women writers and publishers. Maleka Begum generously shared her research on *Begum* magazine with us. This warm and generous cooperation from fellow writers and researchers has been of immense value in the compilation of this volume.

ROKEYA SAKHAWAT HOSSEIN

Sultana's Dream[1]

One evening I was lounging in an easy chair in my bedroom and thinking lazily of the condition of Indian womanhood. I am not sure whether I dozed off or not. But, as far as I remember, I was wide awake. I saw the moonlit sky sparkling with thousands of diamond-like stars, very distinctly.

All of a sudden a lady stood before me; how she came in, I do not know. I took her for my friend, Sister Sara.

'Good morning,' said Sister Sara. I smiled inwardly as I knew it was not morning, but starry night. However, I replied, 'How do you do?'

'I am all right, thank you. Will you please come out and have a look at our garden?'

I looked again at the moon through the open window, and thought there was no harm in going out at that time. The men-servants outside were fast asleep just then, and I could have a pleasant walk with Sister Sara.

I used to have my walks with Sister Sara when we were at Darjeeling.

---

1 'Sultana's Dream' is taken from *Rokeya Rachanavali* (*Writings of Rokeya*), published by the Bangla Academy, Dhaka, in 1973.

Many a time did we walk hand in hand and talk light-heartedly in the Botanical Gardens there. I fancied Sister Sara had probably come to take me to some such garden and I readily accepted her offer and went out with her.

When walking I found to my surprise that it was a fine morning. The town was fully awake and the streets alive with bustling crowds. I was feeling very shy, thinking I was walking in the street in broad daylight, but there was not a single man visible.

Some of the passersby made jokes at me. Though I could not understand their language, yet I felt sure they were joking. I asked my friend, 'What do they say?'

'The women say that you look very mannish.'

'Mannish?' said I, 'what do they mean by that?'

'They mean that you are shy and timid like men.'

'Shy and timid like men?' It was really a joke. I became very nervous when I found that my companion was not Sister Sara, but a stranger. Oh, what a fool I had been to mistake this lady for my dear old friend, Sister Sara.

She felt my fingers tremble in her hand, as we were walking hand in hand.

'What is the matter, dear?' she said affectionately.

'I feel somewhat awkward,' I said rather apologetically, 'as being a *purdahnishin* woman I am not accustomed to walking about unveiled.'

'You need not be afraid of coming across a man here. This is Ladyland, free from sin and harm. Virtue herself reigns here.'

By and by I was enjoying the scenery. Really it was very grand. I mistook a patch of green grass for a velvet cushion. Feeling as if I was walking on a soft carpet, I looked down and found the path covered with moss and flowers.

'How nice it is,' said I.

'Do you like it?' asked Sister Sara. (I continued calling her 'Sister Sara' and she kept calling me by my name.)

'Yes, very much; but I do not like to tread on the tender and sweet flowers.'

'Never mind, dear Sultana. Your treading will not harm them; they are street flowers.'

'The whole place looks like a garden,' said I admiringly. 'You have arranged every plant so skilfully.'

'Your Calcutta could become a nicer garden than this if only your countrymen wanted to make it so.'

'They would think it useless to give so much attention to horticulture, while they have so many other things to do.'

'They could not find a better excuse,' said she with smile.

I became very curious to know where the men were. I met more than a hundred women while walking there, but not a single man.

'Where are the men?' I asked her.

'In their proper places, where they ought to be.'

'Pray let me know what you mean by "their proper places".'

'Oh, I see my mistake, you cannot know our customs, as you have never been here before. We shut our men indoors.'

'Just as we are kept in the zenana?'

'Exactly so.'

'How funny.' I burst into a laugh. Sister Sara laughed too.

'But dear Sultana, how unfair it is to shut in the harmless women and let loose the men.'

'Why? It is not safe for us to come out of the zenana, as we are naturally weak.'

'Yes, it is not safe so long as there are men about on the streets, nor is it so when a wild animal enters a marketplace.'

'Of course not.'

'Suppose some lunatics escape from the asylum and begin to do all sorts of mischief to men, horses and other creatures. In that case what will your countrymen do?'

'They will try to capture them and put them back in their asylum.'

'Thank you! And you do not think it wise to keep sane people inside an asylum and let loose the insane?'

'Of course not!' said I, laughing lightly.

'As a matter of fact, in your country this very thing is done! Men, who do or at least are capable of doing no end of mischief, are let loose and the innocent women are shut up in the zenana! How can you trust those untrained men out of doors?'

'We have no hand or voice in the management of our social affairs.

In India man is lord and master. He has taken to himself all powers and privileges and shut up the women in the zenana.'

'Why do you allow yourselves to be shut up?'

'Because it cannot be helped, as they are stronger than women.'

'A lion is stronger than a man, but it does not enable him to dominate the human race. You have neglected the duty you owe to yourselves and you have lost your natural rights by shutting your eyes to your own interests.'

'But, my dear sister Sara, if we do everything by ourselves, what will the men do then?'

'They should not do anything, excuse me; they are fit for nothing. Only catch them and put them into the zenana.'

'But would it be very easy to catch and put them inside the four walls?' said I. 'And even if this were done, would all their business, political and commercial, also go with them into the zenana?'

Sister Sara made no reply. She only smiled sweetly. Perhaps she thought it useless to argue with one who was no better than a frog in a well.

By this time we had reached Sister Sara's house. It was situated in a beautiful heart-shaped garden. It was a bungalow with a corrugated-iron roof. It was cooler and nicer than any of our rich buildings. I cannot describe how neat and how nicely furnished and how tastefully decorated it was.

We sat side by side. She brought out of the parlour a piece of embroidery work and began sewing a fresh design.

'Do you know knitting and needlework?'

'Yes: we have nothing else to do in our zenana.'

'But we do not trust our zenana members with embroidery!' she said laughing, 'as a man has not patience enough even to pass a thread through the eye of a needle!'

'Have you done all this work yourself?' I asked her, pointing to the various pieces of embroidered teapoy cloths.

'Yes.'

'How can you find time to do all these? You have to do the office work as well? Have you not?'

'Yes. I do not stick to the laboratory all day long. I finish my work in two hours.'

'In two hours! How do you manage? In our land the officers – magistrates, for instance – work seven hours a day.'

'I have seen some of them doing their work. Do you think they work all the seven hours?'

'Certainly they do!'

'No, dear Sultana, they do not. They dawdle away their time in smoking. Some smoke two or three cheroots during the office time. They talk much about their work, but do little. Suppose one cheroot takes half an hour to burn, and a man smokes twelve cheroots daily; then you see, he wastes six hours every day in smoking alone.'

We talked on various subjects, and I learned that they were not subject to any kind of epidemic disease, nor did they suffer from mosquito bites as we do. I was very much astonished to hear that in Ladyland no one died in youth except by rare accident.

'Would you care to see our kitchen?' she asked me.

'With pleasure,' said I, and we went to see it. Of course the men had been asked to clear off when I was going there. The kitchen was situated in a beautiful vegetable garden. Every creeper, every tomato plant was itself an ornament. I found no smoke, nor any chimney either, in the kitchen – it was clean and bright; the windows were decorated with flower garlands. There was no sign of coal or fire.

'How do you cook?' I asked.

'With solar heat,' she said, at the same time showing me the pipe through which passed the concentrated sunlight and heat. And she cooked something then and there to show me the process.

'How did you manage to gather and store up the sun's heat?' I asked her in amazement.

'Let me tell you a little of our past history, then. Thirty years ago, when our present Queen was thirteen years old, she inherited the throne. She was Queen in name only, the Prime Minister really ruling the country. Our good Queen liked science very much. She circulated an order that all the women in her country should be educated. Accordingly, a number of girls' schools were founded and supported by the Government. Education was spread far and wide among women. And early marriage also was stopped. No woman was allowed to marry before she was twenty-one. I must tell you that, before this change, we had been kept in strict purdah.'

'How the tables are turned,' I interposed with a laugh.

'But the seclusion is the same,' she said. 'In a few years we had separate universities, where no men were admitted. In the capital, where our Queen lives, there are two universities. One of these invented a wonderful balloon, to which they attached a number of pipes. By means of this captive balloon, which they managed to keep afloat above the cloud land, they could draw as much water from the atmosphere as they pleased. As the water was incessantly being drawn from the atmosphere by the university people, no cloud gathered and the ingenious Lady Principal stopped rain and storms thereby.'

'Really! Now I understand why there is no mud here!' said I. But I could not understand how it was possible to accumulate water in the pipes. She explained to me how it was done, but I was unable to understand her, as my scientific knowledge was very limited.

However, she went on, 'When the other university came to know of this, they became exceedingly jealous and tried to do something more extraordinary still. They invented an instrument by which they could collect as much heat from the sun as they wanted. And they kept the heat stored up to be distributed among others as required. While the women were engaged in scientific researches, the men of this country were busy increasing their military power. When they came to know that the female universities were able to draw water from the atmosphere and collect heat from the sun, they only laughed at the members of the universities and called the whole thing "a sentimental nightmare"!'

'Your achievements are very wonderful indeed! But tell me how you managed to put the men of your country into the zenana. Did you trap them first?'

'No.'

'It is not likely that they would surrender their free and open-air life of their own accord and confine themselves within the four walls of the zenana! They must have been overpowered.'

'Yes, they have been!'

'By whom? By some lady warriors, I suppose?'

'No, not by arms.'

'Yes, it cannot be so. Men's arms are stronger than women's.'

'Then?'

'By brain.'

'Even their brains are bigger and heavier than women's, are they not?'

'Yes, but what of that? An elephant also has a bigger and heavier brain than a man has. Yet men can enchain elephants and employ them, according to their own wishes.'

'Well said, but tell me please how it all actually happened. I am dying to know it!'

'Women's brains are somewhat quicker than men's. Ten years ago, when the military officers called our scientific discoveries "a sentimental nightmare", some of the young ladies wanted to say something in reply to those remarks. But both the Lady Principals restrained them and said they should reply, not by word but by deed, if ever they got the opportunity. And they had not long to wait for that opportunity.'

'How marvellous!' I clapped my hands heartily.

'And now the proud gentlemen are dreaming sentimental dreams themselves. Soon afterwards certain persons came from a neighbouring country and took shelter in ours. They were in trouble, having committed some political offence. The King, who cared more for power than for good government, asked our kind-hearted Queen to hand them over to his officers. She refused, as it was against her principles to turn out refugees. For this refusal the King declared war against our country.

'Our military officers sprang to their feet at once and marched out to meet the enemy. The enemy, however, was too strong for them. Our soldiers fought bravely, no doubt. But in spite of all their bravery, the foreign army advanced step by step to invade our country.

'Nearly all the men had gone out to fight; even a boy of sixteen was not left at home. Most of our warriors were killed, the rest driven back and the enemy came within twenty-five miles of the capital.

'A meeting of a number of wise ladies was held at the Queen's palace to advise on what should be done to save the land.

'Some proposed to fight like soldiers; others objected and said that women were not trained to fight with swords and guns; nor were they accustomed to fighting with any weapons. A third party regretfully remarked that they were hopelessly weak of body.

'If you cannot save your country for lack of physical strength,' said the Queen, 'try to do so by brain power.'

'There was a dead silence for a few minutes. Her Royal Highness spoke again, "I must commit suicide if the land and my honour are lost."

'Then the Lady Principal of the second university (who had collected heat from the sun), who had been silently thinking during the consultation, remarked that they were all but lost; and there was little hope left for them. There was, however, one plan which she would like to try, and this would be her first and last effort. If she failed in this, there would be nothing left but to commit suicide. All present solemnly vowed that they would never allow themselves to be enslaved, no matter what happened.

'The Queen thanked them heartily, and asked the Lady Principal to try her plan.

'The Lady Principal rose again and said, "Before we go out the men must enter the Zenanas. I make this prayer for the sake of purdah." "Yes, of course," replied Her Royal Highness.

'On the following day the Queen called upon all men to retire into zenanas for the sake of honour and liberty. Wounded and tired as they were, they took that order rather for a boon! They bowed low and entered the zenanas without uttering a single word of protest. They were sure that there was no hope for this country at all.

'Then the Lady Principal with her two thousand students marched to the battlefield and, arriving there, directed all the rays of the concentrated sunlight and heat towards the enemy.

'The heat and light were too much for them to bear. They all ran away panic-stricken, not knowing in their bewilderment how to counteract that scorching heat. When they fled away leaving their guns and other ammunitions of war, they were burnt down by means of the same sun heat.

'Since then no one has tried to invade our country any more.'

'And since then your countrymen have never tried to come out of the zenana?'

'Yes, they wanted to be free. Some of the Police Commissioners and District Magistrates sent word to the Queen to the effect that the Military Officers certainly deserved to be imprisoned for their failure; but they never neglected their duty and therefore they should not be punished and they prayed to be restored to their respective offices.

'Her Royal Highness sent them a circular letter intimating to them that "if their services should ever be needed they would be sent for" and that in the meanwhile they should remain where they were.

'Now that they are accustomed to the purdah system and have ceased to grumble at their seclusion, we call the system "murdana" instead of "zenana".'

'But how do you manage,' I asked Sister Sara, 'to do without the police or magistrates in case of theft or murder?'

'Since the "murdana" system has been established, there has been no more crime or sin; therefore we do not require a policeman to find out a culprit, nor do we go to a magistrate to try a criminal case.'

'That is very good indeed. I suppose if there were any dishonest person, you could very easily chastise her. As you gained a decisive victory without shedding a single drop of blood, you could drive off crime and criminals too without much difficulty!'

'Now, dear Sultana, will you sit here or come to my parlour?' she asked me.

'Your kitchen is not inferior to a queen's boudoir!' I replied with a pleasant smile, 'but we must leave it now, for the gentlemen may be cursing me for keeping them away from their duties in the kitchen so long.' We both laughed heartily.

'How my friends at home will be amused and amazed, when I go back and tell them that in far-off Ladyland, ladies rule over the country and control all social matters, while gentlemen are kept in the murdanas to mind babies, to cook and to do all sorts of domestic work; and that cooking is so easy a thing that it is simply a pleasure to cook!'

'Yes, tell them about all that you see here.'

'Please let me know how you carry on land cultivation and how you plough the land and do other hard manual work.'

'Our fields are tilled by means of electricity, which supplies motive power for other hard work as well and we employ it for our aerial conveyances too. We have no railway nor any paved streets here.'

'Therefore neither street nor railway accidents occur here,' said I. 'Do you not ever suffer from want of rainwater?' I asked.

'Never since the "water balloon" has been set up. You see the big balloon and pipes attached thereto? By their aid we can draw as much rain water as we require. Nor do we ever suffer from flood or thunderstorms. We are all very busy making nature yield as much as she can. We do not find time to quarrel with one another, as we never sit idle. Our noble Queen is exceedingly fond of botany; it is her ambition to convert the whole country into one grand garden.'

'The idea is excellent. What is your chief food?'

'Fruits.'

'How do you keep your country cool in hot weather? We regard the rainfall in summer as a blessing from heaven.'

'When the heat becomes unbearable, we sprinkle the ground with plentiful showers drawn from the artificial fountains. And in cold weather we keep our room warm with sun heat.'

She showed me her bathroom, the roof of which was removable. She could enjoy a shower bath whenever she liked, by simply removing the roof (which was like the lid of a box) and turning on the tap of the shower pipe.

'You are a lucky people!' I exclaimed. 'You know no want. What is your religion, may I ask?'

'Our religion is based on Love and Truth. It is our religious duty to love one another and to be absolutely truthful. If any person lies, she or he is – '

'Punished with death?'

'No, not with death. We do not take pleasure in killing a creature of God – especially a human being. The liar is asked to leave this land for good and never to come to it again.'

'Is an offender never forgiven?'

'Yes, if that person repents sincerely.'

'Are you not allowed to see any man, except your own relations?'

'No one except sacred relations.'

'Our circle of sacred relations is very limited; even first cousins are not sacred.'

'But ours is very large; a distant cousin is as sacred as a brother.'

'That is very good. I see Purity itself reigns over your land. I should like to see the good Queen, who is so sagacious and far-sighted and who has made all these rules.'

'Very well,' said Sister Sara.

Then she screwed a couple of seats on to a square piece of plank.

To this plank she attached two smooth and well-polished balls. When I asked her what the balls were for, she said they were hydrogen balls and they were used to overcome the force of gravity. The balls were of different capacities, to be used according to the different weights that were to be lifted. She then fastened to the air-car two wing-like blades, which, she said, were worked by electricity. After we were comfortably seated she touched a knob and the blades began to whirl, moving faster and faster with every moment. At first we were raised to the height of about six or seven feet and then off we flew. And before I could realize that we had commenced moving we reached the garden of the Queen.

My friend lowered the air-car by reversing the action of the machine, and when the car touched the ground the machine was stopped and we got out.

I had seen from the air-car the Queen walking on a garden path with her little daughter (who was four years old) and her maids of honour.

'Halloo! you there!' cried the Queen, addressing Sister Sara. I was introduced to Her Royal Highness and was received by her cordially without any ceremony.

I was very much delighted to make her acquaintance. In the course of the conversation I had with her, the Queen told me that she had no objection to permitting her subjects to trade with other countries. 'But,' she continued, 'no trade is possible with countries where the women are kept in the zenanas and so unable to come and trade with us. Men, we find, are rather of lower morals and so we do not like dealing with them. We do not covet other people's land, we do not fight for a piece of diamond though it may be a thousandfold brighter than the Koh-i-Noor, nor do we grudge a ruler his Peacock Throne. We dive deep into the ocean of knowledge and try to find out the precious gems that Nature has kept in store for us. We enjoy Nature's gifts as much as we can.'

After taking leave of the Queen, I visited the famous universities and was shown over some of their manufactories, laboratories and observatories.

After visiting the above places of interest we got again into the air-car, but as soon as it began moving I somehow slipped down and the fall startled me out of my dream. And on opening my eyes, I found myself in my own bedroom, still lounging in the easy chair!

M. FATEMA KHANAM

Chamely

Chamely, who was fond of playing with boys and wearing boy's clothes, just disappeared one day. The neighbours said, 'What do you expect? Her mother's a cook and she is friendly with all the *mastans* of Mirzapur. How can you expect her to observe purdah?'

The younger mistress of the house said nothing. Chamely's disappearance had hurt her terribly. She had not given birth to her but she had brought up little Chamely as if she were her own daughter.

The younger master of the house rode his motorbike up and down the lanes of Kolkata for several days looking for Chamely. The wheel of time ground on irrevocably and gradually almost everybody forgot Chamely.

Salmu had a ten-taka note in one hand and a balloon in the other. Playing his bamboo flute, he came up to his mother and said, 'Mother, Chamely has sent you ten takas.'

'Where is Chamely? Go and call her quickly.'

'Mother, she's gone.'

'Get lost, you little rascal! You got the flute and forgot everything. Why didn't you bring her with you?'

'She didn't want to come. She disappeared down the lane in front of Potol's house.'

'Didn't she say anything to you?'

'Of course she did. She said, "I have got my salary – go and give this money to mother".'

Malek had been Chamely's friend from childhood. Along with Chamely he would smoke, play cards, wander about here and there and talk nonsense. Many other naughty boys of the neighbourhood also joined them.

One day a *waz mahfil* was announced. It would be chaired by a Moulvi of the neighbourhood.

Chamely's gang said, 'Let's go listen to the *waz*.' The Moulvi recited a verse from the Qur'an and explained, 'The noblest task is to show the right path to those who have lost their faith in Islam and are wandering down the wrong path.' Malek passed his eyes over Chamely, who was sitting beside him.

He thought to himself that he must make this errant Chamely, so fond of swaggering about in *punjabi* and *dhoti*, return to the fold of Islam again.

The youthful *adda* came to an end. Chamely disappeared. Malek became the film operator of Madan Company. Many a charming actress flashed before his eyes, each of them as daring and bold as Chamely. But the words of the Moulvi had etched themselves in Malek's heart.

One day Chamely appeared again along with two or three of her male companions. She had opened a shop selling paper boxes on the corner of Chapa pond.

Offering Chamely the *bidi* he was smoking, Malek said, 'Chamely, why did you stop working?'

'Why? Who wants to do a clerical job for a measly salary of fifteen taka? So, I opened a shop and am quite independent. I earn twenty to thirty taka per month.'

'Oh, that's why you went to Darjeeling? To get orders!'

'Yes. But why only to Darjeeling? I've also visited Delhi, Lahore, Ceylon and many other places this year.'

Rather seriously, Malek asked her, 'How long will you live like this, Chamely? Please get married.'

Chamely burst out laughing. 'Who is going to marry me?'

'Why not me?'

Chamely replied rudely, 'Marry you! Why? What for? Am I not a man? If you speak such rubbish again, I'll kick you hard – and with my shoes on!'

Malek went away disappointed. Chamely was no longer just wearing male garments. She had started to think she was a man.

'Mother, oh Mother.'

The younger mistress of the house looked up at Chamely. There was a small bundle in her hand. There were two cauliflowers, a kilogramme of mutton and a *ruhit* fish head inside the bundle. She hadn't eaten a home-cooked meal for a long time – today perhaps she would.

'Chamely, you've come! Why did you run away from me, daughter?'

The boys stood around her. 'Dear sister, please don't leave us,' they said.

To Chamely their words sounded like the rattling of the iron chains of a prisoner. Her mother stood in front of her, looking at her affectionately. Chamely touched her mother's feet quickly and left.

'Chamely, wait a bit. Eat something before you leave.'

Chamely did not pay heed to her mother's word. She was soon swallowed up by the huge crowd on Harrison Street.

Chamely fell ill. She was confined to her bed for three weeks. When she regained consciousness, it was to find Malek sitting beside her bed. All her other friends had left. Only Malek sat patiently by her bed, day and night, while she struggled with death.

After another two months Chamely completely recovered. She started to do the shopping herself in the morning. She also cooked. When Malek sat down to eat, she did not grab the choice pieces of food for herself. She filled up his plate with the larger pieces of fish and meat.

While eating, Malek told Chamely, 'Don't cook any more, Chamely. I do not want you to fall ill again.'

Chamely did not respond. It seemed as if she were Chamely no more, but somebody else. After eating, Chamely did not smoke the half-smoked cigarette offered by Malek. Instead she threw it away.

Malek said to her in surprise, 'You've thrown the cigarette away, Chamely!'

'I'm not going to smoke any more.'

Malek was surprised when he returned home that night. Chamely had discarded her life-long masculine garb for a woman's dress. She had covered her head with her sari *anchal*. She was wearing flowers in her hair and round her neck and wrist. It seemed as if she were a bride seated in her nuptial chamber.

'Chamely, you're dressed like a woman! How beautiful you look! Will you dress like this every day, Chamely? Tell me that you won't dress like a man again.'

Casting a quick glance at him, Chamely said softly, 'Will you be happy then?'

Looking at the quiet darkness outside, Malek nodded his head, 'Yes.'

Translated by Md Jamal Hossain

RAZIA MAHBUB

Troubles

What constitutes troubles? Sarkar Sahib tried thoughtfully to broach the subject, but before he could do so, ten china plates fell from the hands of the servant and broke into a thousand pieces. At once, with the shattering din of the broken plates, came the sharp voice of Sarkar Sahib's wife. 'You have done it now. Is this your common sense, to utter early in the morning the inauspicious word "trouble"?' She shouted at the servant, 'Shameless idiot, good-for-nothing, layabout.' Dumbfounded, Sarkar Sahib tried to twist the ears of the servant, but the servant cried out, 'Oh mother, oh father, you are killing me.'

Fortunately, this was the city, and so no one came to interfere. But the real problem remained. Sarkar Sahib withdrew his hand without touching the servant, but the servant put together his belongings and found this an opportune time and excuse to go. Nobody could prevent his going. Sarkar Sahib's wife collected the fragments of the plates and said, 'Very good; you have done well. No one works, but everyone increases the amount of work to be done. No one brings in the slightest amount of money, but everyone can destroy. I want my ten plates by the afternoon.

And furthermore, give that bastard his salary and send him off so that he can never set foot in this house again.'

The eldest daughter was married. The younger daughter came and said, 'He has broken so many plates, why are you giving him money?' The wife said, 'No, why should he? Go on, create more trouble. I have said so many times, no one should mention the word "trouble" early in the morning, or bring out money before the house has been cleaned. But no one listens to me. You are all like your father.' Before the wife could turn on her husband, somebody knocked on the door. The wife said, 'It is the washerman early in the morning.'

'Washerman? Are there washermen these days?' asked Sarkar Sahib, setting off another barrage from his wife.

She said, 'Where can you find washermen, when you have turned them all away? You are all busy serving society: when do you have time to help in the house? The servants have all become gentlemen and the sons have become nawabs. No one takes soiled clothes to the washerman.' The elder son meekly replied, 'Where are there washermen these days? I take the clothes to the laundry.' His mother taunted, 'Laundry or foundry. I have managed to keep the washerman, paying him with great difficulty, at double the usual rate.'

Sarkar Sahib sighed, 'Then you must be happy at seeing him. No wonder I can hardly make ends meet.' He opened the door to see not the washerman Rajab, but Rajab Ali, his nephew who lived in the next flat. He had in his hands a yellow and a white paper.

Sarkar Sahib asked, 'What is the matter, Rajab Ali, what has happened?'

'Why should anything have happened?'

'He must have come to telephone, another trouble,' said the wife. 'Last night, at midnight, the telephone rang. I hurriedly got up to take the call. A good-for-nothing young boy said, "Have you seen the beautiful moon in the sky?"'

Sarkar Sahib said, 'When did this happen? Which scoundrel? I would have given him half of the moon. Why did you not call me?'

His wife said, 'Rubbish, you could not have done a thing. You couldn't have thrown dirt on his face through the wires of the telephone.'

'Well, since you have come, go on, use the telephone. Where are you calling? Don't call your girlfriend and cause us trouble.'

'No, I have not come to phone,' said Rajab Ali in a soft voice. As he said this he blushed, because Shumi, the youngest daughter of the house, had appeared. And Rajab could not help but stare at her.

'Then what?' said Sarkar Sahib's wife.

Rajab Ali replied, 'Chachi Amma has sent me to check your electricity bill.'

'Our electricity bill? Why?' The wife became furious.

'There's nothing wrong with you. It's just that our electricity bill has somehow jumped from thirty-five to forty-five.'

The wife said, 'If you use more electricity, then it will jump.'

Rajab said, 'But in flat number six, the bill comes to only ten taka. That's why Chachi Amma is angry. She says there is something fishy about it.'

Shumi said, 'Ma, our bill has come as well.'

Her mother replied angrily, 'It has? Then why did you not give it to me? The rebate date has probably expired. I don't know what to do with all of you grown-up children.'

Sarkar Sahib said, 'Oh, why are you scolding her so much so early in the morning? So what if she forgot? Bring it to me, dear.' Sarkar Sahib was an important man, an important social worker, respected and heeded by the people of his neighbourhood. He had a cool head on his shoulders. He had to be cool, and no, for this he did not need any special herbal oil.

The bill was brought.

But what did his wife see? She could not believe her eyes. Eighty-five taka! 'Look, dear, isn't that eighty-five?'

Without looking at the bill, Sarkar Sahib said in an extremely irritated tone, 'What did you say? Can't you say it in Bangla? Eighty-five!' He couldn't quite seem to understand.

'That is what I said,' replied his wife, 'Eighty-five taka.'

'Today is the last date,' said Shumi.

Her mother's fury fell upon Shumi, and the girl turned away her face in the nick of time to escape the slap that was meant for her cheek.

'Stupid girl,' said her mother, 'you hid this trouble from us. Just wait and see. I am sure there's some mistake. Calculate the bill again. Correct it and pay the bill.'

Sarkar Sahib went out immediately. He understood that the morning's trouble would not end all day. He had not had a chance to explain to his wife that he was himself in trouble. And he did not feel at ease without telling his wife everything. After all, he was a peace-loving man. He was not in the habit of doing anything thoughtlessly or haphazardly. He did everything after due thought and deliberation. No matter how many faults his wife had, she was the pilot of the ship of their marriage. Without her steering the ship, Sarkar Sahib could not have managed things on his own. Why he alone? It was the same with all men. Other men were cowards and did not admit it as openly as Sarkar Sahib did.

Meanwhile, a handsome man turned up at this moment to create more trouble. 'In whose name is this house?' he asked.

'Whose name?' The wife turned to look at her oldest son for assistance. But where was he? Only once had he shown his face and then gone back to sleep again. It was impossible to keep him awake the whole day. She turned to the man. 'What does it matter in whose name this house is? Who are you?'

'I am an agent,' he said.

'Agent? You mean a broker?' she said.

'Why should I be a broker? We do not work with deeds. All is by word of mouth and on trust. We want to serve you,' he said.

'Good,' she said, 'will you do my grocery shopping for me?'

'Of course. But, madam, this house is in your name.'

'Perhaps it is, but does this mean that you would not do anything for me if I were not the landlady?'

'No, that is not it. Can I sit for two minutes? I will explain everything to you. If you are the owner of the house, then we will spare you from the harassment of handling tenants. And if you are the tenant, then we will help you face the arrogance of the landlord. You will get the same service, the only difference being in the rate we charge. We always consider tenants first. From them we take twenty taka to twenty-five per hundred, and from owners we take thirty-five to fifty taka. If you want us to go to court, or be your lawyer, or find something to quarrel about between tenants – we will do everything. In fact, we can even find a low-rent house for you to live in and rent this house at a higher rate.'

This time, the wife was truly astonished. What sort of trouble was this? She said, 'Shumi, send your elder brother to me and ask him to bring the shopping bag. This gentleman is a well-wisher. He will teach my simpleton of a son to shop properly.' Then she said to the man, 'But, be warned, it is noon now and if you bring rotten fish, I will see to it that your brokering is finished. Buy some vegetables as well. You have already wasted an hour with your idle chatter.'

Rumi announced from the next room, 'Bhaiya has gone to take his bath after his exercises.'

The wife said to the man, 'That means one more hour. You may as well come tomorrow. Put this shopping on the list of your various businesses, and it will help everybody.'

The man insisted, 'But whose house is it?'

'My father's,' said the wife in anger. 'Whose house? Certainly not yours. Get out, I say, get out!'

The young man thought her half mad and quickly went out.

All these troubles. But more troubles were to follow. It was only noon, and events would continue till midnight. Rumi reminded her that the day was Saturday and everything closed at two p.m. Tomorrow was Sunday and everything would be closed too. Therefore, Rumi's friend's wedding present had to be bought today and she needed approximately twenty taka.

'Twenty taka? Does money grow on trees? After this morning's loss, I cannot give you any money.' But she was compelled to give her fifteen taka. Her children were ashamed to go without anything nice.

In the meantime, the head of the household returned. 'Oh my, what has happened to your knee?' cried the wife.

'Nothing, I had a narrow escape.'

'Meaning?'

'Meaning, the rickshaw.'

'The rickshaw? Do you mean the rickshaw overturned?' The wife almost burst into tears.

'What are you getting so upset about? The rickshaw tilted a bit. Can't you see I am all right, except for the bruise on my knee?'

'That's all right, but you should buy a car now,' said the wife, wiping her eyes. 'If you are not here, what will I do with all your money?'

'Really, father,' said her son. 'You must buy a car. Not buying a car is a mistake.'

Sarkar Sahib said, 'What is the matter with all of you? A car! As if having a car would save us all. The fault was the rickshaw wallah's, and the gentleman driving the car got such a beating for nothing. If the police hadn't come, things could have taken a terrible turn.'

The wife said, 'Rubbish. Both the rickshaw wallah and the gentleman should be thrown into jail.'

Sarkar Sahib said, 'It may have happened already.'

By this time Shumi had brought Iodex to rub on her father's knee. The wife also sent the son to fetch the doctor.

But the son returned almost immediately.

'What's wrong? Why have you come back?'

'Bad news.'

'What bad news?' said his mother. 'Who has died? For the past few months I have heard bad news and nothing but bad news about friends and acquaintances.'

'No,' said the son. 'Nobody is dead. My friend has divorced his wife.'

'Divorce? What a scandal!'

For the first time Sarkar Sahib seemed agitated. 'The whole country is falling to pieces.'

'This is why I am not getting married. Marriage means divorce.'

His mother said, 'Oh, what a statement. Employment means slavery, so you enjoy the free life. I can see very well what you are doing. No accounting for young people these days.'

The son said, 'So you begin your nagging again. This is why I don't want to stay home. I want a little peace.'

Shumi cried out, 'Bhaiya, don't go, have your lunch first.'

The mother remarked, 'Honestly. Shumi is my only hard-working daughter.'

The son said, 'I don't want plain rice and lentils.'

Shumi said, 'Why only rice and lentils? There's fried egg and mashed potatoes too.'

Her mother asked, 'Where did you get potatoes and egg?'

Shumi began, 'Rajab Bhai from next door ...'

Speechless, the mother stared at her daughter. Her face seemed flushed. Her dark daughter seemed to be glowing. She thought, let them do whatever they wanted. She couldn't cope any more.

In the evening, after the day's troubles had subsided, the wife sat on the open roof. She sat there every evening. It was her habit; she would not change. Before the evening meal, she had to rest there awhile. Limping, Sarkar Sahib came to sit beside her. He did this very rarely, because he was busy most evenings with the various meetings and social activities of the neighbourhood.

Startled, his wife said, 'You could not go out tonight, but why are you here with me?'

Sarkar Sahib said, 'Yesterday, it was too late when I returned and I did not get a chance to speak of it. Can you see the one-storey house in front? The one that Mr Ali's new tenants have moved into? Mr Ali is having a great problem with them.'

'Why? They mind their own business, they do not seem to bother anybody.'

'No, they do not do that, and they pay the rent regularly, but still it is not possible to let them stay there.'

'Why?' cried his wife anxiously.

'It is a tremendously scandalous affair.'

'Scandal? They are the parents of two children. How can they be involved in anything scandalous?'

'What if they do have children? They are not even married.'

'You are mad,' said the wife. 'How can such thoughts enter the head of such a respectable person?'

'Then why can't they show us the marriage deed?'

'Marriage deed? Do *you* have one? Can you show it? Why, we who have been living together these last thirty years, what proof is there that we are really husband and wife?'

'Why, who does not know it? It is the truth ...'

The wife did not let Sarkar Sahib finish the sentence. She said, 'How do you know that they are lying?'

'People are saying ...'

'Which people?'

'That Mr Ali could not say. He only said that some people of the locality are saying that they cannot be allowed to live here.'

'Have they heard that?'

'Yes.'

'What did they say?'

'They said, "We did not have a court marriage with a deed we could show to everyone, and even if we did, what does it matter to anybody?"'

After a while, Sarkar Sahib said, 'The problem is right there. The gentleman is a bit hot-tempered. He works for a company where no one bothers or interferes with anyone's private life. But can one live with just one's home and office? One has to live with the people of the locality, talk to them politely, have tea with them, exchange good and bad news. But he won't do this; he is absolutely unsocial.'

The wife said, 'Forget it. This town I see is worse than the village. Why are people so greedy? Don't they have enough to eat at home?'

'I said as much, and yesterday we had a meeting about the matter, but everybody is of one opinion. No one is even listening to Mr Ali. Mr Ali is such a nice man. He almost wept and said to me, "Sarkar Sahib, tell me what to do".'

The wife said, 'When you help him, why tell me? Is it so easy to uproot the tenants? Won't they go to court?'

'No, because already people are throwing pieces of bricks and stones at the house. These missiles will drive them away. Honestly, the unsocial couple have become exhausted with the ghostly visits every night. And now this scandal. Ali Sahib will try tomorrow for the last time. If they do not agree to go, then Ali Sahib will probably go for litigation. But, before that, they will probably leave. The neighbours say they are packing their belongings.'

Suddenly, the wife realized, the tenants' daily routine was not being followed today. Unlike other days, they were not sitting close together or playing with their children. A still sense of foreboding enveloped the house, yet they were busy. Unlike on other days, their affectionate squabbles were not visible to her eyes, and that is why she did not have to look away. Perhaps she was thinking of them. What had changed them? Looking at them, hope and belief filled her heart. There was still love and trouble-free happiness in this world. She decided she must carry the burden of their happiness. She would not let others break up the nest of one loving couple.

Next day, everyone heard in amazement the way Sarkar Sahib's wife had gone over to the couple's house and scolded them openly. 'I may be your distant aunt, shameless girl. I cannot look after all my relatives. But

I was there at the wedding. Maybe my present was not so nice. Is that any reason not to look up your aunt?'

'Auntie,' the girl burst into tears.

'Never mind, dear, your uncle was abroad, and your husband would not know me after seeing me for only one day, but would I throw you out? There is nothing to fear. Let us see what anybody comes to say now.'

On returning home, Sarkar Sahib said, 'You should have told me earlier. I feel so foolish.'

His wife said, 'I did not feel the need. I can hardly bear all my troubles, how can I bear the troubles of my nephews and nieces?'

'But you have, haven't you?'

'When the need arises, one has to do it. You don't have any idea how many gossip-mongers and troublemakers there are who cannot tolerate the happiness of others.'

Sarkar Sahib said, 'Tell me truly, are they related to you? Do you know them, or are you doing something irreligious?'

'Irreligious? Don't scare me with your religion. Black-marketing, profiteering, usury, breaking up someone's daughter's marriage, or making someone lose a job, not recognizing merit, denying people their true rights, where is religion in these activities? Let Allah judge. As a social worker, can you not be open-minded?'

Ashamed, Sarkar Sahib left. In his heart, however, he could not help praising his wife. He himself had been uneasy over the breaking up of a household and had wanted to stop this great misfortune from happening in the couple's life. As he was leaving, he heard his wife say, 'No one can light the lamp of peace in a house, but everyone wants to blow it out. I know, I felt it when the plates broke early in the morning that some people were trying to break up the peace of the world. Do you hear me? From now on, that girl is not only my niece, she is my adopted daughter. Tell everybody to ask me if they want to feast at their wedding, but no one should try to create any more trouble.'

Sarkar Sahib stopped in his steps. He realized that his poorly educated, absent-minded, superstitious wife had a beautiful affectionate heart. He wondered why other mothers, other daughters didn't have a heart like hers.

Translated by Rebecca Haque

HELENA KHAN

Projection

They like the gentle breeze of the afternoon and the mild quiver of the rickshaw very much. A lock of Husna's short hair tumbles down over her forehead again and again, sometimes covering her lotus-like eyes. Her dark blue sari flutters in the gusty breeze.

Casting a glance at her, Rakib says, 'Hello, beautiful lady. I am afraid that somebody might be tempted seeing your beauty. Please lower your veil. Otherwise, how will people understand that you are my wife?'

Husna pulls down her veil, 'Rubbish, how can I control my veil in this wind? How irritating you are! What does it matter now what people think?'

Rakib keeps staring at Husna's dreamy eyes. Then he says, 'The fact is, I do not want people to see my treasure.'

A dark shadow falls on Husna's eyes. She says, 'That's strange. Who will cast a glance at your worst asset?'

'Who won't?'

Husna likes Rakib's possessiveness. It suggests his love for her. Husna is entirely Rakib's. Yet Husna does not understand what pleasure Rakib derives saying this again and again.

The rickshaw passes through the rows of green trees flanking the road.

They cross the park. Both of them are suffused by a feeling of happiness at each other's closeness.

Rakib takes Husna's soft hand in his own. Both are silent. Maybe they are absorbed in their feelings. It is the rickshaw-puller who speaks. 'Didn't you say that you would get down here?' he says.

'Oh, yes.'

Consciousness returns. They get down. Rakib pays the rickshaw fare.

They walk along one corner of the park. As they walk side by side, they sometimes bump gently into each other consciously or unconsciously. They look at each other and smile. There is a bush of flowering *jhumkalata* in this corner. There are also fewer people here. Rakib says, 'Let us sit down right here.'

They sit down touching each other. It is a pretty environment to recall the early days of their acquaintance. Rakib says, 'We used to be very afraid to sit like this just a few days ago. We were so afraid that somebody would see us. And today?'

'I know. My heart used to beat so fast. Mother knew about you. But she did not like my roaming around with you, going to the park, going to the cinema.'

Husna seemed lost in the romantic world of the past. After a moment she said, 'Do you know hectic preparations for my marriage with Professor Alamgir were going on?'

After a brief silence, Husna again said, 'It was my determination that won in the end. Mother said, "Rakib is better than Alamgir as a bridegroom. But how can we offer our girl unless the bridegroom's party proposes?"'

'Well!' Rakib asks suddenly, 'What would you have done if you had been married to Alamgir?'

'Ah, what would I have done? I would have tried to forget you.'

Glancing at him, Husna realizes that Rakib does not want to hear this. The muscles of his face grow taut and grim. The shadow of a crooked frown darkens his forehead.

Husna understands that Rakib has taken what she said to heart. Drawing closer to him, she says, 'Ah! You don't understand jokes even! Could it ever have happened? The music of my heart had merged with yours.'

Rakib does not speak for a long while. When he does, his voice sounds like the rumble of distant thunder. 'Did you like Alamgir?'

Now Husna becomes vexed. There was no question of her falling in love with Alamgir. She had been madly in love with Rakib. Naturally human beings are attracted to beautiful flowers. They look at them. She did not have an opportunity even once to see the handsome Alamgir properly. She had seen him briefly, from a distance. But she had not felt any attraction. However, she had not disliked him either, but she could not say that to Rakib today.

Touching Rakib's shoulder, Husna says softly, 'What nonsense are you talking? Would I have cried as I did to prevent the marriage if I had been in love with him? It was you who occupied my mind.'

But the cloud in the sky of Rafiq's mind does not clear away. They do not talk in the rickshaw while returning. Husna is surprised at her husband's jealousy. For whom is this hatred? Is it for Alamgir? Alamgir had been selected by her parents. Husna had not even talked to him. And was Alamgir still waiting for her after being rejected by her family? He had married the beautiful Nasrin long ago. They were a happy couple. Does Rakib not know that? He knows it very well. Why then does he behave like this? Husna feels very sad. Why has Rakib unnecessarily destroyed the romantic atmosphere today? Husna's eyes droop in anger.

It is ten o'clock. Rakib and Husna go out together after locking their bedroom. There is a duplicate key. Rakib will go to the Secretariat. He has a long way to go. He has a fairly good job now. Husna's school is very near – at Azimpur. From their house they can even hear the bell ringing in the school. The warning bell has rung. Today Husna has line-duty.

They start walking. When they near the school gate Rakib says, 'Today I will bring two tickets for an evening show.'

Husna realizes that Rakib is ashamed of his behaviour yesterday. He is trying to make up. She pouts and says, 'I am not interested. I'm not going to the cinema. You go alone.'

Rakib likes that offended face very much. He smiles and says, 'Wow, the lady can be in a huff! And she looks very pretty when she is angry.'

Though Husna turns away her face, she cannot help smiling. Rakib too smiles as he resumes walking.

There is a huge crowd in the theatre. As they push their way through the crowd, Rakib is separated from Husna. There are people milling around Husna. For a moment she doesn't know what to do. Then two people help to clear the way for her and she is able to rejoin Rakib.

'My God, what a crowd! How could you walk so quickly leaving me behind in such a crowd? I was lucky that those two helped me!'

Casting a glance around them, Rakib sees that the two persons who helped his wife have already boarded a rickshaw. They are handsome. Looking at Husna, he asks, 'Did you know them before?'

'No,' replies Husna casually. But the muscles of Rakib's mouth grow taut.

In the rickshaw Husna chatters about the movie. Rakib is silent. Tapping him with her left hand she asks, 'Didn't you like the film? I liked it very much.'

Rakib looks displeased. She holds his face and turns it towards hers. 'Before we went to see the movie, you were so happy. Why are you upset now?'

Rakib does not speak. Hurt, Husna says, 'I won't ever go to watch a movie again.'

'Why should you? Go alone. You'll have no lack of companions.'

But she cannot continue to be angry and bursts out laughing. 'You think so? How childish you are!'

Husna's school is closed on Friday. Rakib also does not have to go to office. On this day Husna takes care of domestic matters. As long as she is inside the house, she likes to do household tasks. She tries to keep the small house neat and tidy to create a happy atmosphere.

Today Husna will cook *bhuna khichuri* and spicy meat curry. She had set a pot of yogurt last night. Husna tells the boy servant, 'Lalu, prepare the spices and put up the chicken. I am coming after I have cleaned the next room.'

Tucking the end of her sari around her waist, Husna starts dusting the house. She will cook after she has finished cleaning. She hears a knock at the door. Rakib has gone to the house of one of his friends.

'You have returned so quickly!' But it is not Rakib. It is Shuja – Shujauddoula – at the door. He used to be the best student in their class.

He was not only good at his studies but also at sports. She had known him quite well as she too took part in sports. Untucking the loose end of her sari from around her waist, she draws it round her shoulder. She says, 'You! Why are you here? Please, come in.'

Entering the house, Shuja says smilingly, 'I am going to Karachi. I have got a good job. So I came to see you before leaving. Where is Rakib Bhai?'

'Please sit down. He should return soon.'

Husna sends Lalu to call Rakib.

Shuja and Husna used to be classmates and often Shuja helped her with Psychology notes before the examination. Once Husna had asked him, 'Both Soheli and Sarwari want to meet you so much. Why do you avoid them?'

Shuja spoke shyly but clearly, 'I don't want to have anything to do with them. I run away from ladies who want to be friendly with me. Besides, mother has chosen a girl for me.'

'And you also like her very much, don't you?'

Shuja nodded. Husna felt she was more than a friend to him. Otherwise he would not have told her about his fiancée.

Husna asks him, 'When are you planning to leave?'

'Tomorrow, in the afternoon.'

'My goodness! When will you have a meal with us? Have lunch or dinner with us, whichever suits you.'

'You will have to excuse me. I'm already booked for several meals.'

Slightly hurt, Husna says, 'You didn't remember us before, did you? You really are something!'

Shuja tries to defend himself, 'No, no. I was late returning from Comilla.'

Husna is curious when she hears of Comilla. Shuja's village home is in Comilla. It is there where the bride chosen by his mother also lives.

'Of course,' Husna laughs.

Shuja also laughs. 'I just went to meet my mother. But everyone insisted on the *aqd* – the marriage vows. The marriage ceremony will take place after I finish my IA.'

Shuja waits for about half an hour, chatting after snacks and tea. Then he gets up to leave.

'No, I'm just not fated to see Rakib Bhai. I've got a lot of things to do, visit a lot of places. Do tell Rakib Bhai that I am sorry to have missed him.'

Shuja leaves.

Rakib returns after a long time. Husna is cooking. Rakib enters the kitchen without making any noise and stands behind Husna. Husna does not see him. Rakib observes her. He likes this mood of Husna's very much. He puts his arms round her waist.

'What are you doing? The food will be ruined!'

'Let the food be ruined. You look very nice.' Husna turns smilingly towards him and asks, 'How do I look?'

'No, I won't tell you. You'll become vain.'

Glancing at the flat opposite theirs, Husna gently pries her husband's hands loose. She pours water into the rice and pulses. Placing the piece of firewood under the pot she tells him, 'Let's go into the sitting room. Do you know that Shuja came? He waited for you for a long time before he left. He said that he is leaving for Karachi tomorrow. He has got that job. Do you know ...?'

Husna's chatter suddenly stops as her glance falls on Rakib's face. There is a raging fire in his eyes. It seems that he will burn Husna to ashes with that look. Husna doesn't understand at first. She asks, 'What's wrong with you? Why are you looking like that?'

'No, why should anything be the matter? Why did Shuja come during my absence? Do you think I don't understand anything?'

Husna stands stock-still. She can't speak. Then she asks painfully, 'What are you saying?'

It seems to Husna that all the light of the world has gone out in shame, hatred and embarrassment at the meanness of her husband. She seems to be standing in an obscure and limitless space. Her head starts to throb. Somehow she manages to reach her bed and lie down on it. Rakib does not bother about her. He must find out the truth today. He must make Husna confess her guilt. He says, 'Before marriage many people have affairs. But why do you want to continue even after marriage? Forget what you have done before your marriage.'

'Ah! Please keep quiet.'

'Why? Why did he come to you when I was not in?'

'Did he know that I was alone? And so what if I am alone? You know me very well. There was never anything between Shuja and ...'

'Don't try to hide it. I know everything. Everyone knows with which of his classmates Shuja had an affair. I knew it too, didn't I?'

Finding herself falsely accused, Husna becomes very angry. She goes up to Rakib and rages. 'Did you then? So you knew everything? Why were you mad enough then to marry me if you knew everything?'

Rakib is silent. What has Husna said? Did she love Shuja?

So his suspicions were true. She really was in love with Shuja. Is she telling the truth? The real truth? Suddenly Rakib feels very depressed. It's as if an inflated balloon has sprung a leak. He grows numb and quiet. Opening the door, he goes downstairs.

Standing under a tree in the front yard, Rakib goes over what has happened. His beautiful day has been ruined. It is the only day of the week that is a holiday. Husna devotes herself to her household chores. She cooks the meal herself and serves it to him with so much love. She makes the dull moments of noon interesting. They go out after taking tea in the afternoon. They discover themselves anew every day. The black clouds of his suspicious mind have darkened the day.

Rakib asks himself again and again: has Husna really confessed that she was in love with Shuja? But can he be happy knowing the truth? He insisted on making Husna say it, yet he can't believe that Husna can roam about with an innocent, pure smile. Why doesn't he trust Husna? When his friends say to him, "Rakib, you are lucky," instead of being happy why does he start suspecting her?

A piece of dim memory, an almost forgotten memory, begins to prick him. Is it this that is making him unhappy? Has he poisoned Husna's life too along with his own?

Why can't he forget the sad memory that has been swept away by the touch of remorse? To everybody Rakib seems a good man. He is good-looking and attractive, leaves a trace in everybody's mind. Perhaps for that reason he can't get rid of his fears.

It happened eight years ago. His father was supposed to be transferred from Rangpur to Faridpur. His examination was ahead. He had always been very good in his studies, and his headmaster was unwilling to let him leave. As there was no hostel in the school, his headmaster proposed that Rakib should stay at his house. Rezina was his elder daughter, a beautiful young woman of eighteen. Even now, thinking of her, he feels disgusted. How can girls be so wicked? They used to study together. She was preparing for her SSC examination as she had failed twice before. She would visit Rakib's room frequently. No one suspected anything, as he was a good student. She would come on the pretext of learning mathematics. At first Rakib failed to understand. He would say, 'No, Rezina *apa*, you can't learn mathematics. You are very absentminded.' Casting an angry look at him, she would say, 'What? Why do you call me *apa*? Can't you call me Rezi?' Abruptly touching his chin, she said, 'Do you think I am your superior? Do I look very old? Look at me.' Rakib looked at her ... she was beautiful.

He forgot her age. An excitement ran through his youthful veins for the first time in his life. He became curious to know – what was in that secret and beautiful world of a woman? He kept staring at Rezina's mysterious female body. He did not understand what had happened to him. Rezina felt overjoyed at her victory. She could distract a saint.

One day Rezina entered his room with a plate full of pudding. Rakib was engrossed in mathematics. Rezina sat down, touching him. Rakib felt embarrassed. Rezina attempted to feed him. 'Do your sums,' she said. 'I shall feed you.' Rakib could say only, 'Don't be silly!'

'I see he is a little boy!' Pressing his cheeks, the girl left the room but as she did, she cast a wicked look at him and said, 'I shall come to learn a lot of sums from you this evening. Today there will be no one at home, do you understand?' Rakib did not know what to say. He only felt hot and sweaty.

Rezina came later that evening. She was a strange, sensual creature. How beautiful she looked with make-up! Was she a fairy or a nymph? Her fine sari, her made-up face, her strong perfume and the wreaths in her hair all created an irresistible Rezina! The youthful Rakib felt aroused. He grew very afraid. Closing his books, he advanced to the door. 'I have some work outside – I'll return soon.' Rezina caught hold of his hand. 'Are you a man? Have I come to see the four walls of this room?' She came close.

Rakib forgot everything. He only heard the echo of 'Are you a man?' The magnet in front pulled him to her. He could not resist that magnetism. In a fit of passion, he embraced Rezina. But then the heavens fell. The headmaster returned suddenly. Rezina moved away quickly. The shameless, false woman cried out, 'Father, see what a viper you nourished in your breast! I was going to Janu's house. The boy called me, "Rezi *apa*, come and look at this sum." He seemed so innocent. How was I to know of his evil intentions. Fie! Fie! I am so disgusted. I want to die.'

Furious, the headmaster took off his shoes and beat Rakib mercilessly. Then he wrote a letter to Rakib's father telling him about his wicked son's activities.

Ashamed, afraid and insulted, Rakib had not gone back home for several days. Then he had finally written a letter to his mother telling her everything that had happened. His parents believed him.

Rakib could not sit for the final examination that year.

After his marriage Rakib recalled that buried bitter memory. The discomfiture he had felt returned to plague him. Black clouds of suspicion covered the new clear sky. Was Rakib the first man in Husna's life? It couldn't be so. Didn't Husna charm anybody before she charmed Rakib with her enchanting smile?

Inwardly doubts burn him up. Sometimes he analyzes himself. He becomes upset. But he asks himself, 'What? What happened to me in the past? Nothing happened.' But his conscience continues to prick him. That is why he cannot be happy, and to counteract his own feelings of guilt he turns his suspicions on Husna. He tries to compensate his own failure by questioning her morals. Today's incident is nothing but the expression of his doubting and deformed mind.

The blazing flame of rage inside him burns no more. The quivering fire of doubt goes out. Only the ashes of remorse remain. He suffers a sense of repentance. He advances with slow steps.

Today his misbehaviour to Husna has gone beyond the limit. Husna is his beautiful white jasmine. Why should he, her husband, misjudge the simplicity and sincerity that are admired by all? He has discovered the answer to this question. He admits that his suspicions regarding his wife are unjustified. He is also tired. He cannot deny that he has wronged Husna several times over.

Yes, he'll apologize to Husna. He'll approach his wife with his confession. Rakib wants to wipe out all the darkness from his mind. Rakib wants to get rid of all his internal confusion. That's why he must tell Husna everything today. He'll accept his punishment humbly. He can't tolerate the sadness of his self-deception any longer.

Rakib knocks at the door softly. Husna opens the door and stands before him. Her eyes are swollen – there are traces of tears. Rakib feels a mixture of repentance and affection. Seeing him, Husna bursts into tears. She goes into the bedroom and, covering her face with a pillow, continues to sob. Rakib can't say anything. He only caresses her head. Some silent moments pass. Finally Rakib says quietly, 'Please don't cry, my love. I have been wrong.'

Only two words. But Husna's pain and grief come to an end.

Taking Husna's hand, Rakib says, 'Do you know, when I was young I fell in an evil trap. You'll be sad to know it. You'll hate me. But ...'

'I know everything,' says Husna gently.

Rakib sits down in surprise. 'What? How do you know? When did you know?'

'I knew it before we got married. Such things can't be kept secret.'

'In spite of knowing that you married me!'

'Yes, why shouldn't I?'

Husna looks at her husband with her eyes wide open. Coming close to him, she says, 'You're really good. That was such a small incident and it happened long ago. Why do you still remember it? You're suffering the pangs of conscience.'

'Not only that, I've been trying to impose my fault upon you. I have suffered from the deadly poison of doubt, and I have not spared you even. Please forgive me.'

Rakib embraces Husna passionately.

At that moment a pair of *shalik* fly across the front window.

Translated by Md Jamal Hossain

RABEYA KHATUN

Obsession

As the wintry evening sky darkened, the guests began to leave. It was bitingly cold outside even though it had not snowed. Inside the house, however, it was warm and bright with the conviviality of the party. The remaining guests were lingering in the cosiness of laughter and friendly gossip.

Mrs Mollick's plump cheeks were still flushed. She puckered her brows as she said, 'Are you talking about Shahanara, the chain-smoker's wife?'

'Yup, about that future cancer patient's smart better half. Have you noticed the way she walks? She claims it's her personal style! Let me tell you it's the way ...'

'The way the gypsy women walk here,' interrupted Mrs Khan, trying hard to suppress her annoyance.

Mrs Moin laughed. 'Ah, let the ignorant remain in bliss. But have you noticed what Asad's wife has been up to? She's approaching forty, yet she wears bras like a teenage flirt.'

'Pity. She should stop dressing like a teenager. I find her most charming when ...'

'She's playing mother hen – is what you were going to say. But who will tell her so?' Expressing the general disapproval of Mrs Asad made Mrs Naim suddenly conscious of the voluptuousness of her bare neck and midriff, and she quickly drew the *anchal* of her sari over the offending bits.

Just then, the hostess, Mrs Amin, stepped in to safeguard the geniality of her party: 'Let's forget about these unpleasant matters.' She always tried to be very hospitable and was on the lookout to prevent malicious gossip among her guests. The other ladies, however, ignored her entreaty. They knew they would have done the same thing when they hosted their own parties, but now they were enjoying the gossip way too much.

But the conversation came to a stop when the two chief guests of the party stood up behind the stuffed, long-haired Persian cats. Mrs Bokhari and Miss Burton from Chaklala's Boy's Line and Wavell Line came out of the shadows to say goodbye. A Buick and a Cadillac were waiting for them.

After seeing these two ladies to the cars, Mrs Amin returned to the drawing room with a worried look.

Mrs Moin remarked, 'Oh dear, I hope they didn't mind. Our talk about age and ...'

'Who knows?' Mrs Amin tried to seem indifferent.

But Mrs Moin saw through it. 'I think it's time we went home.'

Mindful of social etiquette, Mrs Amin insisted, 'No, it's still early. Stay a while longer. Especially since they are no longer here.'

'If you are thinking that everything has been sorted out, then you are wrong, dear. Not all husbands are like yours in taking charge of the household when the housewife is out. At least not in my case. I will return home to find my husband off to Zero Point; the kids up to some mess instead of studying; and the cook snoring away, having forgotten to light the stove.'

'You don't say.' Mrs Khan laughed and everyone joined in. But the earlier harmony had been broken, and the new mirth could not recreate the party spirit.

One by one they walked past the Belgian glass cabinet fitted over the Persian carpet and filled with numerous figures. They all left except for Nasira, who huddled by the tape recorder. She knew she should have been the first to leave because she had a long way to go, and she had no car or male escort to take her home. Yet she did not get up. The pleasure of a room packed with guests having fun was now replaced by another delight, an even more intense one, that of the stillness of a splendid room.

Her presence was superfluous and unremarkable among the crowd. But now in her solitude she was the centre of all attention. The figurines behind the Belgian glass were all smiling at her. She smiled back. She relaxed at last. She had spent the entire afternoon watching the changing acts of the ladies' tea party.

In the early afternoon everyone had arrived in a good mood. They kept up a casual conversation limited to mundane topics of the weather and refrigerators and televisions. At one point, Mrs Naim tried to change the tempo with travel stories, but Mrs Mollick could not tolerate the other woman's enjoyment. She had snapped, 'What's the big deal about Murree? It's so close to home and you just went there last summer. So why go on about it?'

She then began to describe her visit to Swat and Malkanda. It was a clever ploy to take the floor from Mrs Naim and draw attention to herself. The trip west was off the beaten track as well as expensive. Only a few Section Officers of Islamabad had been fortunate enough to go there.

Mrs Naim, however, didn't give up so easily. She challenged Mrs Mollick. 'Are you trying to say that because we have not been to Swat, it is more beautiful than Murree?'

'It is really picturesque,' went on Mrs Mollick in a careless and affable manner. 'In addition to recent newspaper articles, foreigners have also acknowledged that Swat is the Switzerland of the East.'

Once again Mrs Amin neatly stepped in to break up the imminent Murree versus Swat fight. She diverted everyone's attention to her own stories about her two-year stay abroad in the Far East and the Middle East.

'Please do stop, you are making me envious,' giggled Shahanara.

'Don't worry, I believe your names have been placed on the foreign list.'

'Well, yes, that's true.'

Mrs Mollick smarted at Shahanara's happiness. She put an end to the giggles with the gibe, 'What with your and your husband's talents at home and work, the foreign posting will definitely materialize.'

'Well, before all that why don't we all go to Murree for a day trip?'

'My goodness, in January? It will be snowing.'

'But that's why we should go off-season. We have all seen the scenic side of Murree in full seasonal bloom.'

'The roads are dangerous! Go, if you wish. You will have to turn back half way.'

'Why?'

'The GTS Bus has cancelled all services from today. One side of the Murree Highway has collapsed. Didn't you see it in today's papers?'

'So you have not looked at today's papers yet?'

'Is that so? And I heard you were a walking encyclopaedia.'

Satisfied with this dig, Mrs Mollick decided she could end her put-downs for the time being. But Shahanara continued to look miserable. She had not imagined the older woman would take advantage of her seniority to humiliate her in front of so many people. She had often thought that Mrs Mollick disliked her; now she suspected the woman was jealous of her as well. Mrs Mollick was the wife of a man who had grown old and grey before he could become a Section Officer, whereas Shahanara's youthful husband had began his career directly from this coveted post. To make matters worse, Shahanara's husband was more likely to be promoted than Mr Mollick. No wonder the woman's bitterness and hostility slipped out at the slightest provocation.

Mrs Amin had noticed the change in Shahanara's mood. Being the ever-graceful hostess, she did her best to perk up everyone's spirits with racy anecdotes. Among all her guests, Nasira drew the most comfort from Mrs Amin's lively prattle. Even if the others were not amused, Nasira was immensely relieved to have the threat of ugliness removed by the vision of a sparkling and elegant high society. It had almost hurt her to imagine that petty and mean feelings could tarnish this beautiful world. There were times when she feared she would have to confront precisely what she was trying so hard to avoid. Why, just this afternoon on her way to the party, she had had to witness an unpleasant scene. One of those itinerant buyers of old papers and bottles, who frequent the A-type Peon Colony and the D-type P.A. Colony, was actually here in this area. Mrs Naim was bargaining with this man with repeated '*Keya*? Just because I am a Bengali you are trying to cheat me! *Bengali paya hay*? You had better not short-change me!'

In spite of the warmth and light of the afternoon sun, Nasira felt cold and lost. She was momentarily confused whether she was in the First Class Officers' Colony or had lost her way in the F-type Colony.

The clink of pencil heels on the cold floor roused Nasira from her reverie. Mrs Amin, back from bidding her guests farewell, reclined on the divan with a sigh.

'Do you have a headache?' asked Nasira gently.

'No, just extremely tired.'

'Then I think I should leave now.'

'What, so soon? I have not even had a chance to talk to you.'

'Well, talk to me.'

Taking her hand off her temple, Mrs Amin hesitated, 'Ah ... I'm sure you can guess.'

'Go on,' encouraged Nasira.

'It's the third week of the month. Then there was the expense of this party ...'

'Oh, I see. Will tomorrow do?' Nasira asked hurriedly.

Mrs Amin smiled at seeing Nasira's usual diffident response. She answered, 'It will have to do. Anyway, the car is at the garage, otherwise I would have dropped you or even sent Simki with you.'

Thank goodness the car was not home, thought Nasira. She didn't have any money left at home to hand over to Simki or whomever Mrs Amin sent. But if money was short why had she been extravagant and thrown a party?

However, Nasira did not utter the thought aloud. In fact, she quickly suppressed it. She became anxious to fulfil Mrs Amin's desire. Why shouldn't she, who was so wretched and undeserving, give something back?

Nasira kept staring at Mrs Amin. She was mesmerized by the vision of the elegant and striking woman whose appearance matched the decor of the beautiful room. Rare Middle Eastern wall hangings and paintings were artfully placed on the red and blue walls of the room. Mrs Amin had decorated her open living and dining area with great sophistication. She had balanced colours by offsetting the gold of one corner with the green of another; the souvenirs from her extensive travels were tastefully strewn around the room, with one stand holding a classical white marble Eiffel Tower and the mantle over the fireplace displaying a landscape of African jungles.

It was also a very opulent room. Besides the tape recorder, there was a new television set. Nasira still had not been able to overcome the nervousness and fascination that she experienced when she first encountered this sumptuous room and the well-heeled family who owned it. She had initially come at the invitation of Mrs Amin's daughter, her student. When she was struggling to make small talk with the mother, Mrs Amin put her at her ease with the suggestion that they listen to music, 'How about a song?'

It was a wonderful idea, not only for the joy of music but also as a release from tension and fear.

That day Mrs Amin had served dry fruits with coffee in tiny cups. She had astounded Nasira by asking, 'How do you like your coffee?' As far as Nasira knew, one only asked about sugar in tea. She later observed that Mrs Amin drank her coffee black, and her daughter Simki had hers with cream.

She had also been introduced to Mr Amin, who was wary of her modest background. He was unable to relax with the lowly teacher of a government school. His wife, on the other hand, was cordial and generous to Nasira, who in turn was overwhelmed by and grateful to Mrs Amin.

Then one day while Simki was running around excitedly on the lawn because she had just won first prize and second prize at events in the school Orange Race, Mrs Amin asked for a loan. It was for a considerable sum, more than half of Nasira's salary. But she could not say no. She justified her generosity by arguing to herself that she didn't need that much money. It was true that she had to send money to her mother. But Mother could wait a few days longer, couldn't she? Meanwhile, the Amins were implicated in a matter of prestige. And, it was a loan that would be soon returned. Also, Nasira felt honoured rather than annoyed to be called upon for a favour.

But the loan was not repaid the next month. She was handed excuses of sudden extra expenditures requiring huge amounts of money. She accepted these explanations as things that happen once in a while. She wrote to her mother, 'I can't send all of the money. Please manage this month somehow.'

The next few months also passed without any repayments. Not only did Mrs Amin never raise the topic of the loan, she even sent notes through Simki seeking more money. She borrowed almost each month, and she never repaid any of the sums. Meanwhile, the family held Nasira in great esteem. She became a regular guest at nearly all their events. She was there every week for a family afternoon. Then she was always included at celebrations and festivities. In return, she happily went on lending more money and writing to her mother, 'This month too ...'

Yet this month was different. There was something wrong. The month was not even over; it was only the third week. The question kept pricking the bubble of her contentment.

Out of the blue, she heard Mrs Amin's aged cook asking her, '*Keya Mem Saheb, keya hua?*' He had been walking behind her and had been taken aback to find her walking towards Islamabad's undulating highway. His words forced Nasira to notice her surroundings. To her amazement she found that she had strayed from her short-cut home through Abpara. She stared at the white building of the GTS bus stop and then at the lights of Murree Hills beckoning her like stars inviting earth-bound humans to far-off galaxies.

In contrast, the silent darkness of the road mocked her. All the lights of the shopping centres and offices of the capital's new suburb were turned off. Although night had just fallen, everything was closed, and the small populace of Islamabad had gone home, leaving behind a desolate and dark place.

Nasira became angry with herself for having loitered. She should have told Mrs Amin that she didn't have the money. But somehow she had not. An enigmatic reluctance had prevented her from doing so. When the elderly cook had finally seen her safely home, she called him back abruptly, '*Suniyay!*'

Obediently he turned back; however, the speech that she had prepared for Mrs Amin got stuck in Nasira's mouth. She could only mutter with embarrassment the cook's dismissal, '*Kuch nehi, aap ja saktay.*'

As she entered the room where she lived alone, she switched on a lamp. Its faded blue shade was torn in one corner. To her dismay, the entire room appeared decrepit and bleak. Everything was falling to pieces. It was a harsh reminder of her penury. Her unbearable excruciating poverty!

She agonized over her dreary existence. Alone with her thoughts in her tiny room, she hauled herself over the coals. True, she could not go on shopping sprees at Rawalpindi's downtown, Mati Bazar, Raja Bazar or even New Market to pick costly accessories for her home. Still she could have bought a few pretty things from the neighbourhood market. Why didn't she even try to decorate her room?

Of course she could have. But whenever she had the urge to indulge herself with good food or any comfort, she remembered her mother and younger brother and sister. The memory of hardships of their village home killed any desire to make her life better. Her dream of luxury scoffed at her.

Deprived of the beauty and well-being that she craved, she took refuge in the school. She satisfied her thirst for aesthetic relief with the flowers and trees in its chocolate-box garden. If only she could pass the miserable time after school hours at Mrs Amin's marvellous drawing room, she would be ecstatic.

The thought of Mrs Amin soothed her troubled mind. On contemplating her regal graciousness, Nasira at last drifted off to sleep.

Alas, the tranquillity did not last till the morning. She woke distraught and upset. The postcard that had arrived from her mother four days ago was still lying on her table, and her distress grew. At school she approached her colleagues for money. Unfortunately, everyone was in the same boat. It was the end of the month and their meagre salary hardly stretched to the entire month. She felt desperate.

In the afternoon, Nasira looked out of the window in despair. It was a bright day with a strong sun. Cars had poured out on the rolling highway of Islamabad. In the horizon of the clear sky, Nasira could make out the peaks of the far-off Margalla Hills. Suddenly, the spark of an idea appeared in her mind. She would take the risk and see Sharmin's mother. She would ask for an advance.

Nasira changed her sari to go to the G-Type house facing Rawalpindi. It had an exquisite garden that was patently not the creation of the office gardeners but achieved with the help of a private gardener. Unlike the regulation petunias, zinnias and other seasonal flowers of most gardens, this was unique, with its manicured verdant lawn and masses of rare yellow roses, magnolias and gladioli. Nasira gazed in rapture at this delightful sight.

She saw Sharmin's mother standing on the lawn with a hose in her hand. The lady appeared a bit surprised to see her daughter's tutor at this unexpected hour. She asked nonchalantly, 'What's this? You have been thinking of your student?'

'Actually I came for something else.'

'Sure, come in.' Sharmin's mother ushered her guest into the drawing room. Nasira meanwhile had broken out in a sweat. She had not realized it would be so difficult, otherwise she would not have never ventured on this expedition.

Her hostess kindly offered. 'Would you like some tea?'

'No, thanks.'

'Well, then, how can I help?' Sharmin's mother inquired with a smile. It gave Nasira courage, but, at the same time, made her more nervous. Since it would be impolite to waste more time, she plunged in with a desperate cry. 'There is an emergency ...'

But she could not continue. She lost her voice, and the sentence remained incomplete. Sharmin's mother just said, 'No problem. It's almost the end of the month. Let me get the money.'

With the money in her hand, Nasira departed feeling calm and peaceful. She glanced back once to see Sharmin's mother smiling again by the sweet sultan sapling. She was a very good woman, a kind woman.

As she walked on, Nasira was depressed again. Why did she take advantage of this decency? She remembered her mother. She thought of her younger brother and sister ...

However, Nasira did not go to the post office, instead she went to that splendid drawing room. A wave of serenity passed through her as she entered. With her eyes closed, she sensed a wonderful lavish world and was almost intoxicated by the heady exotic music. Oh what joy!

'What's the matter? When did you come?' demanded Mrs Amin. The soft polite voice had never sounded so harsh. Her behaviour was odd as well. Nasira decided not to say anything.

For the first time, Nasira could see the cracks in Mrs Amin's painted mask. She saw the real face under the veneer of polished manners. She experienced the chill of the soul underneath. Simultaneously, she heard her inner conscience telling her – Mother needs money.

'What has happened? Are you okay?'

'Uh huh.'

'Then?'

Why was the lady so harsh? Or was it the sound of her own

apprehension and despair? She heard once more 'So, did you make any arrangements?'

Her hands were shaking. Nasira was not sure what was happening; she had never come this far. Perhaps she would lose her power of speech or she would accuse or slander her for no reason. Again she heard Mrs Amin speak. 'Do you want a cup of coffee?'

'No, thank you. Here, take the money.'

She took out ten crisp ten-rupee notes from underneath her *anchal*.

Mrs Amin fiercely snatched the cash and got up. Before leaving the room, she casually said, 'Stay a while. Don't go out in this scorching sun.'

By this time, Nasira was drooping from exhaustion and tension. She lounged on the sofa until murmurs drifting into the drawing room made her sit up suddenly. A male voice said, 'You took a loan again?'

'What else could I do? The money is almost finished.'

'But why? It's almost the end of the month.'

'Didn't I say that my doll exhibition is starting this month? Cash is like Aladdin's lamp but you were not able to give me any.'

'Even then, why from that teacher?'

'Who cares about the teacher? What will she do with the money? All she does is wear cotton handloom saris and eat rice just with *bhajee*.'

The rest of Mrs Amin's words faded away. Perhaps she had left the guest room and walked down the passage to the master bedroom. She was probably scheming about what to do with Aladdin's magic lamp and making plans for her upcoming exhibition. She was submerged in dreams about her dolls.

But why was there a pounding sound in Nasira's head? She was nauseated and dizzy. She could not face the army of dolls standing to attention inside the Belgian glass cabinet.

Nasira rushed out of Mrs Amin's house into the sweltering afternoon. She ran and ran till she reached Islamabad's main highway, where she wandered about in a daze. There were trees, or rather saplings, recently planted in the new capital, which gave no shade. But the stunned Nasira was oblivious to the heat and the glare of the unpitying sun.

Translated by Zerin Alam

KHALEDA SALAHUDDIN

Relief Camp

Jaigun lights the earthenware stove. When she came to the relief camp, Jaigun had somehow managed to salvage a few battered pots and pans, some patched clothes wrapped in a quilt, a couple of rusty tins of powdered milk and her old earthenware stove. The stove had given her good service during storms and monsoon rains. People like Jaigun have to move frequently. Sometimes the police come and break up their shanties. Sometimes during heavy rains the low-lying roadsides are inundated. Their temporary shelters are flooded. Cellophane and sacking can no longer give them refuge. And sometimes there are floods, as this time. This is no ordinary flood. It is a deluge. Everything is inundated. Even a small flood is bad enough to uproot them, send them looking for a dry shelter. But wherever she goes, Jaigun is careful to take her earthenware stove with her.

As soon as the floods started, several parts of the capital Dhaka were submerged. Relief camps were set up in areas that remained above flood level. Jaigun came to this relief camp with her pregnant daughter Batashi and her ten-year-old son Abul.

This is a primary school. Many people have taken shelter here. Many have come with their entire family, others have come alone. The place is crowded. It doesn't matter. They are safe from the deadly reach of the flood. They have a place to rest their heads at night. It is true that perhaps they have only one full meal of *khichuri* or bread each day. If they get something to eat for lunch, they might not get something for dinner. But it does not hurt them too much even if they get nothing for dinner. They are used to having nothing to eat. Sometimes they miss one meal, sometimes both. Here they are getting at least a meal a day. Of course, they have only had either *khichuri* or bread for several days and they are all longing to eat rice. Yesterday afternoon some people distributed relief materials. They brought a huge truck full of bags of rice, lentils and small packets of salt. They also gave them some candles and matchboxes. Those people were really kind. They had crossed the black floodwaters to bring them so many things. How much sympathy they had for poor folks!

Deep in her thoughts, Jaigun takes two more scraps of paper from the bundle that Abul has brought and feeds the stove. The flames brighten. She also throws in the broken leg of a bench. She is cooking rice after such a long time. Batashi is nearing her term. She should be delivering any day now. Before the floods came, Abul used to carry lunch-boxes to offices. Now all work has stopped. How is he going to wade through these waters to do anything? He is such a little boy. Batashi's husband is a rickshaw-puller. When the floods came he just disappeared one day – and has not returned. Jaigun's husband was also a rickshaw-puller. He used to suffer from asthma. Towards the end, despite his illness, he had to continue pulling in order to feed his family. He died a couple of years ago of asthma. Jaigun managed to carry on working as a daily woman in several houses. She has the added responsibility of her pregnant daughter now. She can't even go to work now because of the floodwaters. What can she do? Everything is God's wish.

Jaigun washes the rice and puts the pot on the stove. The girl asked for rice the other day. She said, 'Mother, I don't feel like eating *khichuri* any more. If only I could eat some rice.'

Jaigun gave her a good scolding. 'Rice, rice, rice! Where will I get rice for you? If I could go to work I could get a little rice for you. But isn't it enough that you are getting some *khichuri* and bread to eat? It isn't in your destiny to eat rice, so how do you expect to eat it?'

After getting the rice yesterday, Jaigun thought of cooking it for dinner, but she was too exhausted to do so. They had to be satisfied with a little left-over *khichuri* for dinner. Today she will cook some rice and lentils and give it to Batashi as soon as it is ready. After all, she is pregnant. And there are so many things one wants to eat in her state. Jaigun rues her fate. Not to be able to satisfy her daughter's craving! She heaves a sigh and returns to her cooking.

Jaigun's family used to live in a Rayer Bazaar slum. They had been able to find some shelter on the sloping banks of the dying river. When the floods came, their slum was inundated. During last year's floods at least their bamboo rooftops remained standing above the floodwaters. This time the black, swirling floodwaters came so rapidly that, even before they knew it, their entire slum was inundated. The slum-dwellers hurriedly moved to the higher ground near the tiled house. They raised bamboo shelters to keep their humble possessions: patched quilts, bundles of clothes, pots and pans, a few tins of powdered milk. Jaigun also kept her mud stove on the bamboo platform. No, the waters could never reach this high. In a couple of days they would be able to return to their old homes. But that very night the floodwaters covered the bamboo platform and all. Much of Dhaka was by then under chest-deep water. Boats were navigating the main streets. Jaigun's family had to carry their bundles on their heads and wade through shoulder-high water to reach this relief camp. People had come from all over for shelter. So many people, so many faces. There was a small field in front of the schoolhouse. On the east was a spreading mango tree. Rahima Bibi from Rahmatganj laid out her betel leaf and areca nuts under the tree. She managed to earn a tidy sum selling betel. Naimuddin from Keraniganj sold lentils and potatoes. He used to have a small grocery shop in Keraniganj. The flood inundated his shop.

Karim Sheikh came to the camp with his wife and four children. He used to sell baked and steamed rice cakes. He had managed to save some ground rice and molasses from the floodwaters. Finding a dry spot on the footpath, he carried on with his business. Some buying and selling still went on.

Chan Bibi came from Kamrangirchar. Driven from home by the flood, she had finally managed to make her way to the relief camp. Her two-year-old was suffering from diarrhoea. A volunteer group came with some packets of oral saline, which she gave the toddler.

All of Bangladesh seems to be floating on a raft. Dhaka is floating. People are floating. But life goes on, slowly recovering from its close embrace by the deadly cold waters of the great flood.

Setting down the rice pot, Jaigun calls out to Batashi. 'Come here a moment. Wash the lentils and put them on the fire. It is quite late. Abul will come and start shouting, "Give me my lunch, give me my lunch." How can I manage everything all by myself?'

Batashi, with her bloated body, is sleeping in one corner. She isn't feeling at all well. Hearing her mother, she sits up somehow. She rolls up the torn mat and sets it upright behind the bundles of their clothing. Then, covering her head with the edge of her sari, she goes and sits beside her mother.

'What is it? Aren't you feeling well? How are you feeling?'

'No, I'm not feeling well. Since morning I have been having this strange pain in my back and stomach.' Her face is distorted with pain.

'That's nothing,' says Jaigun comfortingly. 'Go and sleep. I'll put the lentils on myself.'

'Give me the lentils. Let me at least pick the lentils. I'll manage. It won't be any trouble.' Batashi takes the packet of lentils from her mother and pours the grains into a chipped enamel pot.

Suddenly, hearing a lot of shouting outside, everyone hurries in the direction of the noise. Sonaban, the wife of Karim Sheikh, is shouting at the top of her voice.

'You son of a devil, how dare you steal my ground rice? I'll chop off your head and throw it into the floodwaters. Do you understand, you beggar's son? Have you never seen a rice cake? Hasn't your beggar of a mother ever given you any to eat?'

'I'm warning you. Don't insult my parents,' Abul protests shrilly.

'Why not? What will you do? Let me hear. The beggar's son doesn't bother about his parents when he's stealing, does he? Just wait. I'm going to hand you over to the police.' Sonaban tugs at Abul's hand with all her might. A little powdered rice and molasses fall to the ground.

Hearing Abul's voice, Jaigun leaves her cooking and runs out.

Like a hawk, she snatches Abul from Sonaban's grip. Immediately, all hell breaks loose. Jaigun starts shouting at the top of her voice. 'You bitch! You want to hand over my Abul to the police! I'll send you to the dock before you can do that. Who stole my red towel? Do you think I don't know?'

'Who's a thief? I? Say it, say I'm a thief.' Sonaban pulls her sari tight around her waist and leaps forward.

'Well, if you haven't stolen my towel, your son has. Haven't we seen your son with it? I can still see with both eyes. I have not gone blind.'

'You beggar! My husband bought my son the towel. Who said that that was your towel? God will not stand such blatant lies. Do you hear?'

'Huh, his father bought it for him. Just because you say so, that doesn't mean anything. You'll say all sorts of things now. Who took my towel then, you whore?'

This time Sonaban lifts both hands and starts shouting, 'Oh my God, this woman is accusing my son of stealing her towel. How could she tell this terrible lie?' She approaches Jaigun and gesticulates wildly. 'God will punish you. Your tongue will fall out.'

By now a crowd has gathered to watch the fight. Sometimes they put in a word or two to fan the tempers. Sometimes they anger Jaigun, sometimes Sonaban.

Rahima Bibi has by now stopped selling her betel goods and come up panting. 'Oh Sonaban, oh Jaigun, why are you fighting? Stop your shouting and screaming. Relief is coming, relief. I went to the roadside. That's how I know.'

On hearing the word 'relief' the furore dies down. The battlefield is soon empty. Everyone quickly collects whatever they can from the schoolroom – chipped pots, pans, dishes, trays, plates, tins, mugs.

A narrow, unpaved lane runs south of the school to meet the elevated concrete street. Some of the destitute rush to see whether relief is really forthcoming. Yes, a group of relief workers are approaching the camp. A truck with a red cotton banner across its bonnet rolls down the street and stops at the head of the narrow lane. A jeep has also accompanied the truck.

Naimuddin runs back and scolds everyone, 'Why are you crowding around like this? Queue up – queue up. Make a queue and sit down, all of you. If you all behave like this, the sahibs will not give any relief.'

No, this time the relief workers have not brought *khichuri* but cans of milk powder and packets of oral saline. The relief has come from the National Children's Welfare Association. In a little while, the organizers of the relief camp make their appearance. The milk powder is dissolved in three large red plastic buckets that the volunteers have brought with them. As soon as the distribution starts, the video camera that the relief team have brought starts rolling. It is necessary to document the unhappy plight of the people affected by the flood. In about an hour's time the distribution of the packets of oral saline and the milk is completed and the work of the relief workers satisfactorily recorded by the video camera.

Jaigun and Sonaban have completely forgotten their quarrel in the scramble for milk and oral saline. It is quite late in the afternoon. Time has passed so quickly in quarreling and collecting relief that no one has had any time to eat.

Jaigun doles out the rice and lentils in plates and then calls out to Batashi and Abul. 'Where are you? Batashi, come here with Abul. Come and eat. It is almost evening.'

'I haven't seen Abul. Who knows where he's gone?'

Jaigun is furious. The boy is really becoming a nuisance. 'Where are you, you rascal? You make my insides burn up.'

Abul is sitting quietly behind the schoolhouse. He has been upset all afternoon. Why did he try to snatch a handful of rice powder and molasses? Every day Karim Chacha peddles rice cakes. Who knows where he goes? After selling whatever he can, he gives the rest to his children to eat. Abul also feels like eating rice cakes. But how will he ever buy rice cakes? They have no money.

He is feeling very hungry. Very, very hungry. He left very early that morning to wade through the floodwaters to collect discarded scraps of paper. Maghbazar, Eskaton, Elephant Road, who knows where else? Those places have not been affected by the floods. Kalu, Habul and Mintu went with him. If they didn't bring paper, how would the stove be lit? Of course, several people had broken the chairs and benches of the school to light their fires. What else were they to do? Most places had been submerged. Where were they to get dry leaves or scraps of paper?

'Abul, where are you hiding? Won't you eat? Won't you have some rice?'

At his mother's voice, Abul rises in some trepidation. He hears the word 'rice', and his insides cramp with hunger. He walks quietly towards the verandah.

Most evenings the relief camp is dark. Unless there is some urgent need, the refugees have no light. They guard the half-burnt stubs of candle as zealously as the wealth of Croesus. Most nights people don't bother to cook. If there is some left-over lunch, it is eaten before nightfall. Only those who can earn a little despite the flood are able to have any dinner.

It is ages since Jaigun's family have eaten rice and lentils to their heart's content. Having eaten late, Jaigun doesn't eat anything. Before nightfall, she gives Abul and Batashi the milk that was distributed earlier in the day.

Night descends slowly. Like a woman covering her face with her sari edge before going to sleep, the relief camp covers its face with the black darkness of night. The mango tree in the corner stands like a ghostly sentinel in the night. The lane in front of the school is not a busy one. By nightfall, the place is silent as a graveyard.

Like the others, Jaigun's family lie down to sleep on a mat that has been covered with a quilt and wait for morning.

In the middle of the night, Jaigun is woken up by Batashi. Batashi is groaning with pain. 'Mother, mother, wake up. My back is paining. The pain keeps coming. Oh God!'

'What is the matter, daughter? Is it paining very much? It's nothing, it's nothing. Don't be afraid. You'll be all right. All your aches and pains will soon vanish.' Trying to comfort her daughter, Jaigun gropes in the dark for a candle and matches. She lights the candle and her eyes fall on Batashi's contorted face. Oh God, what is she to do now? Candle in hand, she wakes up Rahima Bibi who is sleeping in a corner of the verandah.

'Oh Sister Rahima, do get up. Come and have a look at my daughter. What am I to do all by myself? I am frightened.'

Rahima Bibi has always been a light sleeper. She wakes up immediately. She's sixty years old, with greying hair. But she is still firm and strong. In her village she often assisted at births, and she likes to tell stories of those days. All the wives and mothers of the village were extremely fond of her. Remembering those days, Rahima Bibi is overcome with emotion. Nevertheless she had to leave the village when the river devoured her home. Like many others of her village, Rahima Bibi joined the floating population. Even then she was able to stand on her own feet. She was able to earn her own living.

Roused from sleep, Rahima Bibi rubs her eyes. Hearing Jaigun, she says, 'Don't be afraid. Aren't I here? Back in my village, I helped deliver countless babies. Don't be afraid.'

By this time several people have woken up. Chan Bibi emerges onto the verandah from her room. Seeing her, Rahima Bibi says, 'I'm going to sit with the girl. Go and heat some water, will you? Jaigun, hang up a sari this side. Don't let anyone come in.'

Rahima Bibi takes full charge of the situation. On one side of the verandah a sari is hung to give some privacy. Batashi is made to lie down on a mat that has been covered with a quilt. A number of candles are collected for light.

Everyone shares Jaigun's anxiety. What is going to happen? Everyone stretches out hands of sympathy. All of them are after all one large family. From the other side of the curtain, Naimuddin asks, 'Oh Sister Rahima, will we have to take her to the hospital?'

'Let us wait a little. If I see any problem, of course I'll tell you all,' Rahima replies.

Batashi is groaning in unbearable pain; her heart-rending cries rend the darkness of night. Roused from sleep, Abul is terrified. Clapping his hands to his ears, Abul runs outside. His eyes streaming, Abul sits on the school steps. He prays desperately, 'Dear God, please save my sister. Please save her, God. I will never steal again, dear God.'

All the waters of the Ganges and the Jamuna flow from Abul's eyes. His little heart seems to drown in the tears.

Finally, the night comes to an end. The soft touch of dawn lights up the horizon. The mango tree blazes resplendent in the early light. A gentle rain falls lightly on Abul's cheeks and on his dry, tousled hair. From a distant mosque floats the call to prayer, '*Assalatu khairul minan naim*'. The sudden cry of a newborn lights up the eyes of the camp-dwellers.

'Batashi, see, see, what a lovely son you have. Oh Jaigun, fill your eyes with the sight of your grandson,' Rahima Bibi cries out joyfully. She is happy that she has been able to help Batashi in her hour of need. Rahima Bibi's heart fills with satisfaction.

Jaigun's tired old eyes are streaming like the Brahmaputra. Her heart brimming with joy, she says, 'You were a great help, Sister. Without you I wouldn't have been able to save the girl.'

'What rubbish you talk, Jaigun. God is the one who saves. How much could I have done? And what did I do, after all? Wouldn't I have done the same for my own girl? Isn't Batashi like my own daughter? What do you say?' Rahima Bibi's eyes shine with joy.

'After all, we are all one family. Is Batashi an outsider?' Chan Bibi comes forward. Jaigun, Rahima Bibi, Chan Bibi and Anwara carefully clean mother and child. The men have been waiting outside on the lawn. Now Naimuddin comes forward and says, 'Oh, Jaigun, don't you need the *azaan* to be said in the ears of your grandson?'

'Yes, yes, but who will do it?'

'Why, I will do it. In my village didn't I give the *azaan* five times a day?'

Jaigun, Rahima Bibi and Anwara have a wash and then sit down in the verandah to rest. They have had a tiring night. The birth of a human being is not easy. Pain and toil attend it.

No one notices Abul entering and sitting down beside the newborn. He stares wide-eyed at the baby.

'What are you staring at like that? You are very happy, aren't you, to become an uncle?'

Abul looks up, startled. So do the others. Sonaban is standing there smiling with a plateful of *pithas*.

'Abul, wipe your tears. Today is a happy day for you. Here, sweeten your mouth with a *pitha*,' Sonaban says, stuffing a *pitha* into Abul's hands. Then she puts the plate in front of Rahima Bibi. 'Here, sweeten your mouth as well. For the first time a child has been born here. It is a happy day for all of us.'

Jaigun is sitting silently a little further off. Sonaban goes up to her, holding out both her arms. 'Come, Sister. Come and eat a bite.'

Jaigun looks at Sonaban in surprise. Sonaban is smiling. Jaigun holds out her hands to Sonaban.

Translated by Niaz Zaman

Makbula Manzoor

On the Road

Lal Miah had stayed awake all night. For the past three years, he had lain awake for nights. Suppressed feelings had kept him awake through the long nights in the jail cell. Having been pronounced guilty and then transferred from the upazila remand custody to the district central jail, he had thought that he was finished. He would never be free again and would spend the rest of his life in jail. As he was being taken from the courtroom, handcuffed and with a rope around his waist, he had seen under the dark bushy mango tree the plaintiff's party smoking and gossiping. Rahim the chairman's brother, Nabu Miah, the tout Hamid Ali, and Badshah Miah's sycophant Bhulu had been talking together and laughing loudly. Seeing Lal Miah, Bhulu had stepped forward. He had bared his teeth and grinned. 'You wanted to lock jaws with a tiger, Lalu. Now go and spend some time with your in-laws,' he had said with a wink.

Lal Miah had ignored Bhulu. His eyes had desperately searched for Hashu. And for his own brothers. But no, no one had come to see him that last time. Yet they obviously knew that this was the day for the verdict. They knew that Lal Miah would not go free. His crime had been grievous, injuring the chairman's son. He would be convicted. Yet no one had come, not even Hashu – even though it had been for Hashu that he had been convicted.

Then he had realized that it was impossible for Hashu to travel the eight-mile-long road from their house to the court alone. Hashu did not even have a brother to accompany her. But Lal Miah's two brothers were strong and able-bodied and they lived in the same *bari* as Lal Miah and Hashu. They had not come even once to visit him in jail or at the Thana. They had not bothered to pursue the case.

Lal Miah had heard that a person who has no one has Allah and the government lawyer. Before coming to court, he had cried and pleaded to Allah in his cell, day and night. He had cherished the hope that, with the grace of Allah, the government lawyer would be able to save him from punishment. But it was not to be. Standing in the court, the thin-faced government lawyer had mumbled something in his broken voice. The judge had probably not even heard him. Lal Miah was sentenced to three years' imprisonment on the charge of attempted murder for attacking Badshah, the village chairman's son, with a *dao*. Badshah had received a deep cut on his left shoulder. If he had died, Lal Miah would certainly have been hanged. No one could have saved him – not even the father of the government lawyer.

Bhulu blew smoke into his face and said, 'Whom are you looking for – Hashu Bibi? There are a lot of people to look after her. Don't worry about her. Go, go, go to your in-laws. Remember, your cow will now be eaten by tigers. Just let Badshah recover a bit.'

One of the constables scolded Bhulu, 'Hey, you, what rubbish are you talking?'

In reply, Bhulu just laughed like a jackal. And Lal Miah was pulled forward by the rope around his waist towards the black prison van. Tears of rage streamed down his cheeks. At that moment, it felt as if he really had no one in the world. His brothers were poor and selfish. With Lal Miah in jail, they would without doubt enjoy the profits of his meagre portion of land. They would probably get rid of Hashu and take possession of his house. But where would Hashu go? She had no parents. She had somehow weathered the kicks and blows at her uncle's house. Her skin was soft like a new leaf, her body was tight and firm, her large eyes were deep and sorrowful. Lal Miah had fallen for those eyes. At the wedding, Hashu's uncle had given nothing, not even a *lungi* or *gamchha* – let alone a transistor or a watch. Lal Miah's brothers had not consented to the wedding.

The *bhabis* had been sarcastic. 'Choto Miah fell for those droopy eyes and face.'

Mejo Bhabi had wanted Lal Miah to marry her own sister. She was even more bitter. 'So, this is the beauty we heard so much about! Now I see that all she has are a pair of cow-like eyes and a body. How long does a woman keep her figure?'

Hashu Banu came from a neighbouring village. As a child, with her hair like a crow's nest, she would come to this village and pick *kalmi* and *helencha* leaves beside the pond and gather snails for her ducks. She would wear a torn sari tied round her waist or a dirty frock. This same girl – how she grew! Lal Miah saw her at his cousin's wedding and fell madly in love with her. At the wedding of Samir Munshi's daughter, Hashu was wearing a red and yellow printed sari. She was joking and laughing with all the other young girls. Her crow's-nest hair, styled with borrowed oil and comb, now fell below her waist. She had made up her eyes with kohl, her forehead with a *tip*.

Lal Miah lost his head. On enquiry, he found out that Hashu had, by virtue of this wedding, become a distant sister-in-law of his cousin. Therefore, Lal Miah and she had become relations by marriage and could share jokes with each other. Lal Miah got hold of cousin Hiru, and finally, with Hiru's help, but without the family's consent, he brought Hashu home as his bride last spring.

After their marriage, Lal Miah saw that Hashu Banu's heart craved good things. She had never eaten well or dressed well in her life. She had never seen anything worthwhile or good, not even a film. That is perhaps why she was never satisfied. She had hoped that with marriage her yearnings would be fulfilled. Possibly she had imagined that her beautiful face would ensnare a man who would be able to satisfy her wants. In the beginning, it seemed, Lal Miah was not so bad. Having borrowed some money, Lal Miah had given her as wedding presents two saris, a gold nose pin, oil, soap, a bunch of imitation bangles and a pair of earrings, as well as powder and nail polish. He had forgotten to give her a lipstick, but he bought one for her right after the wedding. Hashu Banu was happy, very happy.

With his new bride, Lal Miah was in a whirl for a few days, a little crazy in the head. His senses returned when he had to deal with the creditors who had lent him money for the marriage.

With his *gamchha* tied around his head, Lal Miah went out to work as a day labourer. Every dawn he left with a bowlful of *panta* rice in his stomach. He returned late in the afternoon, after the *Asr* prayer. Hashu would wait for him with hot rice on the stove. Upon his return, she would give him a clean *lungi*, serve him rice, sometimes with greens, dried fish paste or fish curry. Lal Miah felt completely satisfied. One day, his wife expressed a new demand. Why not go to the cinema one day? Many of the wives in this village and even in her own village would occasionally go to the town to watch films. Her sister-in-law had gone twice. Hashu Banu was the only one to have been deprived of this good fortune. Lal Miah felt dejected at Hashu's words. For the first time, his new wife had asked him for something. His sense of manhood compelled him to fulfil her wish. But the town was eight miles away. Could Hashu walk all that way and back? Hashu jumped with joy – yes, she could. It was hardly any distance. If they left at dawn, they could see the matinee show and come back before *Esha* prayer. They could even take a rickshaw back. Lal Miah felt happy. He and Hashu had not gone out together since their marriage.

One day, Lal Miah told Shukur Ali of this plan. Shukur Ali used to go to town regularly to buy goods for his shop. He knew very well which film was showing at what time at which hall. Shukur Ali said with enthusiasm, 'Take Bhabi this week. There is a new film at Laxmi Hall – it is a Shabana-Alamgir movie. Let Bhabi see it, let her learn how to idolize her husband.'

Lal Miah was fully aware of what all this entailed. His wife's first request in six months. But going into town, cinema tickets, some snacks, a rickshaw on the way back – all this could add up to about fifty taka. Lal Miah had borrowed a thousand takas for the wedding, of which five hundred was still owing. Nevertheless, Lal Miah was prepared to meet his wife's request.

Hashu Banu dressed up for the occasion. She got up early in the morning, washed and powdered her face. She made her large eyes even bigger and darker with kohl. She braided her long hair with a nylon ribbon. She pleated her sari in front – the wedding sari – the pink sari with the Rolex gold *zari* flowers on it. Lal Miah could not take his eyes off her.

They did not tell anyone in the house about their trip. If they heard about the film, his *bhabis* would make a long face and his brothers would say harsh things about their lifestyle. What Lal Miah said was that he was taking Hashu Banu to her uncle's house as the uncle had asked for her. Even that invited caustic comments from Mejo Bhabi. 'Choto Miah, it seems that you have finally got lucky. Your in-laws have invited you to eat *polao korma*.'

Lal Miah didn't go to the town often. He had seen only a couple of movies in his life. He was taken aback by the size of the crowd in front of Laxmi Hall. He could not figure out how to get the tickets – where could his wife wait for him? Suddenly, he heard a voice call out, 'Hey, isn't that Lalu? Have you come to see the film? With your wife? But why are you standing there? Have you got tickets?'

Lal Miah was surprised to see Badshah Miah in front him. Badshah Miah was the chairman's son and they had been together in primary school. That was a long time ago. Now that Badshah Miah was the son of the chairman, Lal Miah looked up to him respectfully.

Badshah Miah was extremely courteous to Lal Miah. He sent Bhulu to get the tickets for them. He did not let them pay for the tickets. 'What is this, Lalu? You are my childhood friend. You have come with Bhabi to see a film. At least give me a chance to be hospitable.' With lustful eyes on Hashu Banu's face, Badshah said, 'I had heard Lalu's wife was beautiful, but I had not imagined she could be this beautiful. She is far more beautiful than Shabana and Babita.'

At Badshah's words, Lal Miah was flattered and Hashu Banu pulled up her *anchal* and bowed her head. Badshah kept an eye on everything inside the cinema hall –whether Bhabi was all right, whether she'd have tea or drinks during the intervals.

After the show, Badshah insisted upon taking them to a restaurant. He offered them *parathas* and spicy beef. Then he put them on a rickshaw and quietly stuffed the fare into Lal Miah's pocket. Before getting into the rickshaw, Hashu whispered, 'Your friend, won't he come to the house?' Badshah replied, 'I'll go later. I have my motorbike. It doesn't matter if it is late at night. You two go. Lalu, I'll come to your house one day.'

On the bumpy ride home, Hashu observed, 'That man has a large heart.'

Lal Miah answered instinctively, 'Yes, if one has money, it is easy to be hospitable.' Privately he wondered about Badshah's intentions.

Thus it began. Badshah's frequent visits and growing intimacy became conspicuous. He would bring *paan* and say, 'Bhabi, I have come to eat *paan* from your sweet hands.' Sometimes, he bought hot *jelabis* and said, 'Lalu, come, let's see how much we can eat today.'

People started talking about Badshah's visits to the house. The brothers' faces grew angry, the sisters-in-law made sarcastic remarks. Finally, one day, the elder brother said, 'Look, Lalu, there is still time. Tell the chairman's son not to come here.' Lalu himself would have liked to ask Badshah to lay off. But he didn't have the courage. In response to his brother, he said, 'You are the head of the household, you tell him not to come here.'

His brother scoffed at the idea. 'Who respects me as the head? Why should I jump into the middle of the quarrel and create bad feelings between myself and Badshah? Badshah is such a terror, he might set fire to my house.' Lal Miah was scared of the same thing. Hearing of his fear, his elder sister-in-law, Boro Bhabi, spoke up. 'Your house is already on fire, Choto Miah. You are blind and cannot see. Now only the roof is left.'

Lalu went wild with rage at these words. He rushed into his room and said to Hashu, 'Why do you let Badshah come to our house?' His wife heard him out. Angrily she said, 'Do I let him come? He's your friend. Can you not stop him coming here? For a few days now he has been coming in your absence too and sweet-talking all the time. I am really scared.'

Lalu's eyes grew red. He screamed, 'If you hear the rascal coming, bolt the door and stay inside.'

At this instant, calling out, 'Friend, are you there?' Badshah entered the courtyard. He came in accompanied by Bhulu, and holding a glistening pair of *hilsa* fish dangling from a string. This was the first time that Bhulu, Badshah's assistant, had come to the house. Badshah said, 'I am going to Dhaka tomorrow. I'll be away a month or so. If you need anything, tell

Bhulu, Lalu. Go, Bhulu, go home and tell mother I shan't be home for lunch today.'

Hashu Banu trembled all over at hearing these words. It meant that this man would stay here till lunchtime. He would eat the rice and fish that she cooked, and spend the afternoon gossiping lazily and not leave until evening. That meant also that Lal Miah would not be able to go to work today.

Lal Miah wanted to fling the pair of *hilsa* over the wall or feed them to the dogs. But he didn't have the courage and, anyway, Badshah had said that he was going away to Dhaka for a month. Then, maybe, something or other could be planned or thought out. For the time being, they had to accept the pair of fish. The brothers and *bhabis* would be angry, but what else could one do? There was no one to bell the cat!

Lal Miah went about his work as usual. If he did not work hard, how would he repay his debts, which were mounting daily? Every morning, his stomach full of *panta bhat*, he left, not to return until late in the afternoon. This morning, he had gone to the neighbouring village to thatch Shomir Sheikh's roof and he had been working on it since early morning. The hot Jaishtha sun burned Lalu's back. His head throbbed like a pot of boiling paddy. The work was done before evening. Taking the *gamchha* from around his waist and wiping the sweat from his brow, Lal Miah turned his steps homeward. The sun was still strong. The intermittent breeze stirred the dust. The fruit of the mango trees had already been plucked, leaving them as naked as beggars. In the waist-deep water of the roadside pond, Shomir Sheikh's buffaloes soaked themselves. The air had a dank, rotting smell. Lal Miah's throat was dry and parched. The first thing he wanted to do on reaching home was to drink a deep draught of cool water.

As he entered the courtyard, it seemed to him that the entire house was strangely silent. Mejo Bhabi had gone to her parents' house to have a baby. Upon hearing the news of the birth of a boy, Mejo Bhai had joined her. Boro Bhabi always slept in the afternoon. The children had gone out to play. Only a pair of ducks was sitting under the lemon tree in one corner of the courtyard. The door to his room was ajar. Is Hashu also sleeping? Ah! The lucky lives of these women! Their poor husbands toil in the burning sun, while they sleep, sprawled out in comfort.

Pushing the door lightly, Lal Miah entered the room. His face turned ashen when he saw Hashu fluttering like a caged bird within Badshah Miah's imprisoning arms. Badshah Miah was rubbing his mouth against Hashu's face and breast. It was all over in a second, a blink of the eye! Badshah saw Lalu standing in front of him like the angel of death, Azrael, with a sharp machete in his hands. Before he could release Hashu, Badshah fell to the floor with a cry, his right side bleeding profusely.

Everything that followed happened so swiftly that it seemed to Lal Miah to flow like the images of the film he had recently taken Hashu to see. In a moment, from who knows where, like magic, people started to crowd into the courtyard. A group rushed Badshah to the hospital. Another group tied Lalu up tightly with a rope and sent word to the police station. Possibly the chairman also came with his mass of supporters. He said something in a threatening tone. Tied to a bamboo stake, with his hands tied behind his back, Lalu could only think, 'Where is Hashu?' He wanted to ask her just once, had Badshah forcibly grabbed her or had she willingly consented to his embrace? He would ask her, was this the first time, or had they been intimate before? But he could not ask anything. Like a mute, brute animal, he was dragged to the police station. No one paid the slightest attention to his pleas. Not in the station, nor at the court. At court, in fact, Badshah Miah's lawyer called Hashu a whore and blamed Lal Miah and his wife for their artful deceptions. And that is why he was sentenced to three years' hard labour in prison.

Yesterday evening, during roll call, Lal Miah had learned that he was to be released. He would be freed the following day. His fellow-prisoners looked at him enviously, and some congratulated him on his release.

Lalu couldn't believe it. Perhaps the *havildar* was joking with him. All night he tossed and turned, troubled by his own thoughts. From the *neem* tree behind the cell, a bird called out all night. The watchman's boots creaked. In the next cell, a half-mad prisoner howled in his sleep. At dawn, before roll call, the sentry took Lalu to the jail office. After Lalu had changed into his own clothes, the officer in charge pushed a document and some twenty-taka notes into his hands and said, 'Go, you are free. This is your document of freedom and this is the money you earned by your labour inside the jail. Now, be a good boy and go home. Don't commit any more murders.'

After saluting the officer, Lalu emerged from the prison in a daze. It was a large world outside – the pure sunlight dazzled Lal Miah's eyes.

'Hey, you woman, are you still here? Go, run!'

Startled by the sentry's harsh voice, Lalu looked round to see a woman with her head covered. Even though she was crouched on the ground, it was easy to see that she could not have been more than twenty-five years old. The sentry said, 'She was released yesterday. No one has come for her yet. She has been sitting here since yesterday morning.'

This girl has been sitting, waiting since yesterday morning? For whom? Lalu's silent questions were answered by the girl herself. 'Who knows, who will come? The jail authorities sent them a letter. But no one has come.'

Lalu asked her directly, 'Where will you go?'

'Nalka ferry *ghat*,' she answered.

Lalu was startled! Nalka ferry *ghat*? That was his first destination too and after that he had a long way to go on foot. 'I am also going to Nalka ferry ghat. Which village are you going to?'

'Chandidas Ganti,' she answered.

'Oh! That is very close to Nalka,' said Lalu.

The sentry laughed and said, 'Go, woman, you have found a fellow villager. Now go with him.'

The girl started walking beside Lalu. As they walked towards the bus station, Lalu asked how long she had been in jail.

'Eight years.'

'Eight years? So long? On what charge?'

'Murder. I murdered somebody.'

Lalu shuddered. This girl had committed murder? With this thin body and sad, frightened face? This girl had been in the women's section of the jail for eight years. Whom had she killed? Many questions were running through his head. At the bus station they heard that the bus for Surjoganj would leave in another couple of hours. The ticket would cost fifty-two takas.

The girl handed over her money readily. What a slim hand! She had killed with this hand? Her face seemed to contain the world's sorrows. How could this girl be a murderer, Lalu wondered as he went to buy the tickets. The girl, with her head covered, sat on a bench in front of a *paan* shop. On the way back from the ticket counter, Lalu bought some fried snacks for them. She had been sitting in front of the jail gate since yesterday morning. She must surely be very hungry! Such a thin face!

The girl's face brightened at the sight of food. Lalu had a couple of fritters, the rest the girl gobbled up quickly. Then they both went to the street tap to drink water. The way the girl wiped her mouth with her *anchal* after drinking made Lalu's heart thump. Hashu, just like Hashu! Do all women wipe their mouths in the same way? Where is Hashu now, who knows?

She must have gone back to her uncle's house. Must still be there despite their beatings. Lalu would go and bring her back. Immediately that old question gripped his mind. Yes, he would ask her first, then talk of other things.

Sitting on the *paan* shop bench, Lalu asked where the girl wanted to go. To whom? Did she have anyone to go to?

'Yes, I have a child. And the child's father. I left behind a child of six months eight years ago.' She wiped her eyes with the corner of her *anchal*.

'Did you really kill someone? Whom?' Lalu finally opened his mouth to ask the important question he had suppressed so far.

'My mother-in-law.'

'Why?'

'That old woman and her son both used to torture me. I have no father. My widowed mother worked at somebody's house to earn her livelihood. At my wedding, my mother could not give anything to my groom. That is why I was beaten regularly. My mother-in-law wouldn't even give me proper food to eat. She wouldn't even let me carry my own baby. One day, I had taken a small amount of *moori* and she tried to burn me with a red-hot brass spatula. In anger, I wrenched the spatula from her hands and hit her hard on the head a few times. The old woman died. My husband himself handed me over to the police.'

The girl was a little breathless after narrating her story. The sun was scorching hot that day. Lalu said after a long time, 'You are going back there. Will your husband take you back?'

'If I could only see my child once …'

'Of course. Go and see if you can. And then will you go to your mother's?'

'I don't know.'

They both boarded the departing bus. The girl sat in the women's reserved section while Lalu sat at the back. They could not see each other across that distance. But Lalu's eyes continued to search for the girl. What was her name? He had not asked.

On reaching Nalka ferry *ghat*, Lal Miah started to become impatient. It was afternoon. He wanted to get to his village before evening. The girl pulled up her *anchal* and started walking in the opposite direction, towards Chandidas Ganti village.

The sun had not set. As he entered the village of Modhukhali, Lal Miah met Shukur Ali.

'Hey, Lal Miah. When were you released?' Shukur Ali grasped him by the hand.

Lalu's heart leaped with joy and emotion. This village, these people – where had he been all this time without them? He pressed Shukur Ali's hand to his heart and said, 'Are you well, Shukur Ali? How is everyone else?'

'They – oh, your brothers? They are well, very well.'

'And Hashu Banu? Is she at our place?'

Shukur Ali was quiet for a while, then he said, 'You are back, that is good. Badshah and his father won't leave you alive if they see you here. But I don't think you will be able to stay.'

Lalu lost his temper. If they didn't let him stay in the village, he wouldn't. 'I'll go with Hashu to the town. I'll pull a rickshaw there. I will kick this village in the face.'

Shukur Ali laughed strangely and said, 'You will go with Hashu to the town? Your Hashu Banu lives in the town already.'

'She lives in the town? Hashu lives in the town?'

'Yes. Badshah keeps her there in a house he has rented. She is his mistress.'

Lalu felt the ground give way under his feet. He forced himself to ask, 'Did Hashu agree to live with Badshah?'

'What could she do but agree? You were in jail. Your brothers would not take responsibility for her. Hashu went to her uncle's house. Badshah Miah carried her off from there. Hashu, it seems, is very well these days. I saw her one day at the Laxmi Hall when I went to see a film. She had gone there happily with Badshah. She looks even brighter now.'

Lal Miah started to walk away before Shukur Ali had finished talking. Night fell as he approached the ferry *ghat*. In the dusky light he saw the girl standing by the ghat office. The same thin body, the *anchal* over her head. 'You!'

The girl jumped at Lalu's voice. 'Yes, I've come back. They did not want me there. My husband's new wife came to beat me. My husband dragged me by the roots of my hair and pushed me out on the road. How can he accept his mother's killer?'

'And your child?'

'He's dead. He died at the age of one. That's what the neighbours told me. Couldn't even go to my mother's place. She's gone too.'

The girl looked at the sky with vacant eyes. The light of innumerable stars lit up the sky. The bats flew about in the faint light of the crescent moon.

'So, where will you go now?'

'I cannot say. You?'

'I don't know. Let the bus come. It's such a large world. We'll surely find a place.'

In a short while, the bus arrived and came to a halt. After Lalu boarded the bus, he saw that the girl too was there. She looked around and then, with a strange confidence, she came and sat next to him. She did not know where she was going. It was only then that Lal Miah asked her name.

Translated by Rebecca Haque, Firdous Azim and Niaz Zaman

RIZIA RAHMAN

What Price Honour?

The sky was an ominous leaden colour. Leaden, splattered with white clouds. The wind whistled in gusts. On top of a storm-battled palm tree perched a lone eagle. The murky, leaden sky was pitiless. Gusty winds rustled through the leaves of the palm tree. The eagle screamed in tune with the wild rustling of the leaves. Halimun was afraid. She was also angry. She wanted to catch hold of the tuft of leaves and stop the terrible cries. She wanted to rend the pitiless leaden drape of the sky with a sharp *dao* and rip out the bright blue day from within. That would punish the sky all right. But below? The river water was rising rapidly. Land and water were indistinguishable. The ravenous, sluggish brown flood had devoured the land, had inundated all the paddy fields. The floodwaters dashed against the sides of the huts. The very posts tottered. Any moment now their hut would be washed away, leaf-thatched roof and all. And the water kept on rising. The only noise to be heard was the gurgling and swirling of the floodwaters. Halimun shivered, wrapping the frail rag of a sari closer round herself. She was cold. The gusty wind stirred up the dismal drizzle against Halimun, adding to her discomfort. The water bubbled up through the earthen stove in the corner of the hut.

The sides of the earthen stove dripped like rotting meat. Her empty rice bowl swirled about on the water. Seeing her bowl twisting around on the floodwaters, Halimun shivered again. Her stomach twisted with hunger. The pangs of hunger racked her like pangs of childbirth. Hunger. Which one could not glare at and subdue. What was nineteen-year-old Halimun to do to assuage that hunger? For a moment, Halimun forgot about the turgid waters and the leaden sky. The picture of a bowlful of bright, full-grained rice came to her mind, each grain plump and separate. Beautiful, white rice. And golden lentils. What else could any one ask for? No, nothing else. Just one bowl of rice and lentils. At this moment Halimun could ask for nothing more precious than a bowlful of rice and lentils. Halimun was hungry. She had eaten nothing for four days. The flooded ditches and canals, the inundated paddy seedlings, the collapsing mud huts, the washed-out garden – amidst all this Halimun was conscious of one thing alone: her hunger. She wanted rice. Just one bowl of rice. Her father, mother, brother and sisters had been killed by the army. The killers were not men, but bloodthirsty hyenas who had set their hut ablaze. They had not killed Halimun, then a sloe-eyed girl of seventeen years. Instead they had called out to her, Come here, little girl. We must get our fill of you first. Halimun had not understood their words. But she had understood the look in their eyes. The smirk on their lips. She had understood that more than her life was in danger. Spared their bullets, Halimun had leaped into the flames.

The soldiers had been disappointed to lose so fine a prey. When they realized what had happened, they fired some shots into the flames and then left the place. Strange! Even stranger was that Halimun had not died in the fire. Though singed, she had somehow managed to survive.

A girl who could leap into fire to save her honour was worthy of respect and admiration. At least in those days of enemy occupation. First the villagers and then, after liberation, relief workers had looked after Halimun and brought her food and medicine. Relief workers had built her a hut made of *golpata* leaves. Journalists had come from town to take pictures of the orphaned Halimun to print in their papers. But after that? What had happened after that? The young girl who had burned her feet started doing odd jobs in people's houses in order to support herself. No one volunteered to look after her any longer. That was when the whispers started. 'That girl was ravished by the soldiers. That is why she tried to commit suicide by jumping into the fire.' Halimun did not heed the whispers. She held her head high. No one had touched her. What did it matter that she had no roof over her head? What did it matter if she had no husband? She hadn't lost her honour. It was true that the fire had left her with one leg shorter than the other, but the fire had not disfigured her soul, it had not distorted her mind. She sustained herself by selling her labour, not by selling her body. How many girls could claim the same? That is why Halimun thought herself one of the most fortunate of women.

It had only been last *Kartik*. The relief contractor, the one who it was said had now become a big businessman at Rajarkhola: Halimun had spurned him firmly, had she not? The rascal. He had a wife and family at home. But in the middle of the night he had come knocking on Halimun's door. Through the hole in the bamboo wall, Halimun had peered at him, standing there in the fog-dimmed moonlight. No, he had not looked like those bloodthirsty-cruel wolves, but like a greedy fox trying to steal chickens in the middle of the night. Halimun had opened the door and flung a fish-cutter at him. 'Where are you, you son of a whore? Come here. I'll chop off your penis. Come here, you bastard. I'll satisfy your lust for ever.' Seeing the sharp fish-cutter in Halimun's hands, the terrified man had attempted to flee. He had looked like a fox with his tail between his legs, fleeing from dogs. Halimun had started to laugh, Hee, hee. Hearing that laughter, two bats were startled out of the dark trees behind the hut. The quietness of the winter night was rudely shattered. The man fled. Halimun went on laughing as she fastened the door of her hut. 'Why are you running away now? Why are you running, you son of a dog? If you come near Halimun once more, I will cut off your head.'

After this incident, Halimun had always slept with the fish-cutter next to her. The incident did not remain a secret. The villagers heard it and said, 'Oh mother, that is no woman. She is a jinn.' Halimun would merely smile and hold her head even higher.

Her stomach cramped up once more. From behind the hut, where Asmat Mullah had planted his chillies, came a strange squishing sound. Halimun pricked up her ears. Perhaps Asmat's widowed daughter was wading through the floodwaters, looking for some *kochur loti*, some river weeds, to cook. Halimun herself had collected some *kochur loti* and an odd assortment of leaves and boiled them to satisfy her hunger. She had mixed the wholemeal flour with water and eaten that, so that, in the end, there was not a handful of flour nor a single rice grain left in the house. Ants, cockroaches and frogs had taken shelter in the empty pots and pans. Whom could she ask for food? No one in the inundated village had any rice or paddy husk. And where was there dry fuel to cook wild greens?

The swishing sound came closer to Halimun's hut. Halimun raised herself to peer in the direction of the noise. Asmat Mullah's twelve-year-old son, Ramiz, was sitting in a large trough normally used for feeding cattle and paddling with his hands towards her. The 'boat' bumped against Halimun's hut, and Ramiz alighted. He held on to the trough with one hand and, with the other, he clutched the bamboo wall of the hut, but it collapsed and slipped into the floodwaters. Ramiz let go and fell into the water. Ramiz had girded a *gamchha*, normally used as a towel, around his loins. Getting up, he stood before Halimun in the rain, smiled and asked, 'Have you eaten, sister? Your hut will collapse any minute now. The hut on the east of our courtyard collapsed early this morning. Father and I cut down an areca nut tree and have propped up the big hut with its trunk. Come and stay with us, sister.'

Halimun shivered in the rainy gusts of wind. She glanced at Ramiz through eyes as dark as the floodwaters, 'Where can I go? Everyone is in the same condition.'

After a brief silence, she asked, 'Do you think the water is receding a little, Ramiz?'

Clutching on to the trough with one hand, Ramiz grimaced. 'So soon? First the army destroyed half the country. Then poverty added to our suffering. This time the floods have come like Azrael, the angel of death. The floods devoured the paddy and the betel leaves, now they will destroy our homes. Only then will the waters recede.'

Halimun was silent. She looked at the branches of the tall palm tree. Ramiz said, 'I have brought something for you. Will you eat it?'

Halimun was startled enough to turn her gaze quickly on him. 'What, what is it, Ramizza? Has Chachi sent some rice for me?'

Water plopped down from Ramiz's wet hair. It rolled down his lips, bluish with the cold. Wiping off the water, Ramiz laughed mirthlessly, 'Where will she get rice from? The day before yesterday we had porridge made of broken rice grains. For two days we have quelled our hunger with all sorts of rubbish. Today my older sister went to collect some greens from under the berry tree and found that a fat snake had twined itself around the tree.'

Suddenly Ramiz stopped. He bent down and brought out a handful of roasted jackfruit seeds from the bottom of the trough. Proffering them to Halimun, he laughed, 'Here, sister, eat. Mother roasted these yesterday. I saved some for you. You too have eaten nothing for the past few days.'

Halimun's eyes sparkled. She almost snatched the seeds from Ramiz's grasp. She peeled off the white membrane covering the seeds and stuffed them into her month. But it was as if *ghee* had been poured on to flames, because, after eating the seeds, Halimun's hunger only worsened. Her hunger turned into a hundred sharp knives and stabbed her stomach. Clutching her stomach, Halimun doubled over with pain. She groaned, 'Ooh, I can't bear it any longer.' Ramiz became frightened. He clambered up beside her. He shook Halimun's doubled-up body and said, 'Oh sister, what is it? Why are you behaving like this?'

Halimun groaned. 'Hunger, hunger, my dear. I can't bear this any longer. Ramiz, get me a handful of rice.'

Ramiz thought for a moment and said, 'Be patient, sister. When I was coming, I saw two coconuts floating beside the chilli fields. I'll go and get them.'

Halimun sat up straight. 'No, don't go alone. Who knows where snakes might be lurking. I'll go with you.' Halimun stood up. They lifted up the trough and put it on the roof, then waded through knee-deep water towards the chilli fields. The colour of the sky had become even more ominous. Had the sky ever been blue? It was impossible to believe that a bright sun had once shone in this sky. The wind was blowing even more strongly, and the rain stung like sharp needles.

Suddenly both of them stopped in waist-deep water. Where were the coconuts? There was nothing. Just the water, churning by rapidly. Dead leaves and pieces of straw floated on the surface. Ramiz looked around him, then said dejectedly, 'I saw them right here. Where did they go?'

Halimun started up angrily, 'If you saw them, why didn't you get hold of them then? Were they going to wait for you? Where did they go?'

Ramiz shouted abruptly, 'See, sister, see. There's a pot floating by. Wait here. I'll swim and get hold of it.'

Ramiz waded through the water, now up to his chest, towards the floating pot. Halimun looked at the red painted earthen pot floating by. It was pretty large. What was inside it? As if struck by lightning, Halimun's imagination caught fire. Maybe there was gold inside it. Maybe rice and lentils and wheat. Ramiz was halfway to the pot when he cried out, 'Sister, snake.'

Halimun's happy fantasies slipped and fell. Halimun asked in fear and despair, 'Where, dear? Where is the snake?'

Ramiz lifted his head above the water and pointed towards the pot. 'There, next to the pot. It is swimming alongside it.'

Halimun also saw the snake. Yes, there was no doubt about it, it truly was a snake. With its head slightly above the water and its body stretched out straight, the snake was swimming along with the current, next to the pot. It seemed to be guarding the pot. Halimun watched it go by helplessly. It wasn't striped. There were circular markings on its forehead. Most likely it was a poisonous snake. If they attempted to catch hold of the pot, they could not avoid touching it. Both of them watched the pot, brimming with possibilities, float by their helpless eyes. It was going farther and farther away. By this time they had been standing in water for so long that their bodies had become stiff. Halimun thought she might slip into the water any moment. She felt miserable. Then she threw caution to the winds and did something foolhardy. She dived into the water near the tail of the swimming snake. She reached out above the snake and caught hold of the pot. Then, holding the pot with one arm, she swam towards shallow water. Ramiz was astounded. Halimun laughed. She felt courageous, capable of doing anything. Maybe she remembered that in times of danger, snakes do not bite human beings. Or perhaps, not having eaten for four or five days, she was simply unable to resist grabbing a pot that might contain something valuable. At that moment Halimun was not thinking of anything. Her stomach cramps had turned into a fast-raging fire. Drawing the pot to the shallow water, Halimun opened the lid. She cried out in joy, 'Ramizza, come quickly and see what I have caught.'

Ramiz swam to her side quickly, 'What is it, sister? What is it? Money?'

'No, dear. It's *chira*. A full pot of flattened rice.'

'Let me see, let me see.' Ramiz bent over the pot.

Seeing Ramiz's joyful face, Halimun's mood changed. She snatched the pot back quickly from Ramiz. She would not give up her one hope of sustenance. Clutching the pot close to her breast, Halimun glared at Ramiz. No, she would not share this *chira* with anyone. If she kept the *chira* all for herself, she would be able to survive for fifteen to twenty days. By that time the clouds would surely disperse. The sun would start to shine. The floodwaters would start to recede. Halimun would get work again. Her bad times would pass away.

Halimun spoke in a cold, firm voice, 'No, I will not give you any.'

Ramiz was surprised, 'Why not, sister?'

'No.'

Seeing Halimun's angry look, Ramiz flared up, 'Give me some, sister. Give me the pot. There's enough for both of us.'

Halimun clutched the pot even more tightly to herself. She screamed violently, 'No, I will not. Never.'

Hungry and tired, Ramiz was too astounded for a moment to reply. Then he jumped upon Halimun. 'Why won't you give me some? Why not? Didn't I see the pot first?'

Halimun was unmoved. She clutched the pot tighter to her bosom. Ramiz was thrashing the water. He shouted, 'Give me the *chira*. Give the *chira* to me. I have eaten nothing. My stomach is empty.'

Ramiz's anger gave way to tears. Halimun held on to the pot with one hand, and with the other she held Ramiz by the hair. She pushed his head under the water. Ramiz thrashed about in the water. Even then Halimun did not let go of his hair. Nor would she release her claim to the pot of *chira*. This was her only hope of survival. Ramiz continued to struggle desperately under the water, flinging his arms and legs about. Several times Halimun was on the verge of slipping into the water, but she managed to keep her head above the water and at the same time to hold on tightly to Ramiz's hair. Suddenly Ramiz gave a violent kick to Halimun's stomach. Halimun's sari came undone at the waist. It floated away on the floodwaters. Even now, had she reached out, she would have been able to catch hold of it, but one hand was clutching the pot of *chira* and the other was holding her prisoner fast. Halimun started to tire. What was she to do? She tried to push her head forward and draw the sari back with her teeth. Just then Ramiz kicked her again. Halimun swallowed water. Lifting her head above the water, Halimun saw her sari floating beyond her reach. The only way to reach it now was by stretching out her arm. Her numb body was growing weaker. Halimun realized that she had to choose now between the pot of *chira* and the sari. She could not save both. At the moment the pot of *chira* was more important then her sari. But the sari? With her earnings she could perhaps buy some food for herself, but, in these days of hardship and inflation, she would never be able to buy another sari to cover her shame. She had no other clothes. Just this one torn sari. Which was she to save? She stumbled. Her hold on the pot of *chira* grew weaker. At the same moment, Halimun released her grip on Ramiz's head. Ramiz lifted his head above the water, gasping for breath. The pot of *chira* wobbled, filled with water and sank. Gasping for breath, Ramiz asked, 'What have you done? You have let the *chira* sink.'

Halimun was silent. She was aware of nothing at the moment but her naked body and her hungry stomach.

Ramiz shouted at her, 'Why aren't you saying anything?'

Halimun moaned weakly, 'I had just that one torn rag. I lost it because of you. How am I going to preserve my honour now?'

Ramiz screeched, 'What honour? Once you leaped into the flames to escape the soldiers. At that time you had food in your stomach. So honour had some meaning then. You have nothing to eat now, and you speak of honour? Go, hang yourself, you whore.'

Halimun did not respond. She simply watched her ragged sari being whirled away by the floodwaters. She could not drag her starved body through the water to save it. Was she to drown? But she did not even have the strength to do that.

Halimun turned around and stood up. Then she climbed on to the muddy slope, completely naked. She was tired and wet.

Standing in chest-deep water, Ramiz screamed, 'Where are you going? Where are you going to find fire to set yourself alight when there is water everywhere?'

Ramiz flung his torn *gamchha* at Halimun. 'Here, take my torn *gamchha*. Wear it and go and hang yourself.'

Halimun paused for a moment. No, she had no need of a *gamchha*. The floodwaters had not just swept away her sari, they had swept away all sense of shame. The only sense she had now was of hunger. Her imperative need now was for something to fill her stomach, to get rid of the cramps in her stomach. The home of the contractor was at the end of the path. There was a sturdy home there, supported by strong wooden poles; there was hope of food there, of rice.

Halimun said, 'Go home, Ramiz. I am going to the home of Shamsher the contractor. I will take up residence in the marketplace.'

Translated by Niaz Zaman

NAYAN RAHMAN

Bon Voyage

Nine o'clock. Already.

Another fifteen minutes to go.

Runu had never known a minute to be so long.

Shanu was getting impatient. Come on, Sis, hurry up. The programme will start before we get there.

Both sisters were studying in the same college. Shanu, the younger sister, had just begun college this year, which was why she was so interested in these college do's.

Runu kept looking at her watch. The astrologer she had consulted had told her – after making numerous calculations involving, among other things, her date and hour of birth – that nine fifteen was an auspicious moment for her. Nine fifteen, he had told her. If you leave your house exactly at nine fifteen, you will succeed in whatever you set out to do.

She had handed over a crisp new one-hundred-taka note for the knowledge. She had also bought an amulet from a *pir*. I am in trouble, she had told him. Bad trouble.

Runu left the house exactly at nine-fifteen. She got on a rickshaw with Shanu. She looked back once as the rickshaw pulled away from her house. Her father had been ill for the last two days. The doctor had come and ordered a saline drip for him. He was a little better today. Runu had cooked some rice broth for his lunch before she left. She was to return by two o'clock, to see to his lunch and his medicine. He was in bed now, lying still and silent. Runu's mother had been away at her brother's house for some days. She was taking care of Runu's grandmother who was sick. A telegram had just arrived saying she would be back within a day or two.

Runu left Shanu with her friends at the college hall. She came out alone into the merciless glare of the *chaitra* sky. Runu grasped the bound pages she held in her hands tightly – her class notes. Today was her last day at college. Her father didn't know that. Neither did her mother. Nor did Shanu.

Runu spent some time walking desultorily around the college. Then she took a rickshaw to Kamlapur Railway Station.

She wasn't wearing her college uniform today. She wrapped her *orna* closely round her head as she silently recited prayers in her mind.

Runu was sitting in a train compartment now. The Karnaphuli Express was going very fast. She could see the trees and houses outside, scorching in the sun. Runu sat there looking out of the window, her face turned away from the crowd of men standing in rows in front of her.

Her eyelids flickering, Runu blinked again and again, as she thought of her father. He would soon start glancing at the clock. Wondering why she was late. He would be surprised at first, seeing Shanu return home alone. After that he would begin to worry. And after that?

Runu had never imagined that she would have to leave home like this. She had decided to leave only two days ago. Pintu had come to see her about a month ago. He had said that he wouldn't be able to come like this any more. I'm in a bit of trouble actually, he had told her.

Runu had listened to his bit of trouble.

Pintu was a very bad-tempered boy. His friends were even worse. Along with his friends he had become involved in two murder cases. They had killed a grocer for practically no reason at all. Their second victim was a doctor. He was a small-time general physician. A friend of Pintu's had been dating the doctor's daughter. The doctor found out about their affair and cut up rough with Pintu's friend. So they killed him. Just like that. Runu was horrified when she heard all this. She knew that this time there would be no way to hoodwink her mother. And once her mother knew, she would never agree to giving her daughter's hand in marriage to a boy like Pintu. She would rather see her daughter dead.

Runu didn't want to die. Life was so precious. Pintu was more precious still. It was impossible to think of death while the memory of the warmth of his love remained with her.

The movement of the train, the heat and the stench of sweat were making her nauseous. She needed to go to the toilet. But how could she push through the solid wall of people that was blocking her way? She put her head outside the window and threw up. The woman sitting next to her helped her to make her way to the toilet. She washed her face and arms, and felt better. But then she vomited again, her body heaving as if her insides were trying to push out of her body.

Runu made her way back to her seat, the crowd crushing her. Her eyes met the eyes of a man standing right in front of her. He was regarding her with a steady, cold look. As if he was slicing her body into thin pieces.

He was the tallest man in the compartment. And rather thin. What was he? A pickpocket? A conman? A *mastan*? Runu turned her face away. She clasped the amulet hanging from a silver chain round her neck and kissed it.

Runu was a good girl. As their first-born, she held a special place in her parents' affection. They trusted her. And she had never done anything to betray that trust. Until today. She had left them. But she had no other choice. She had heard from some of Pintu's friends that Pintu was fishing around, trying to hook new girls. Pintu was gradually slipping out of her reach.

Runu's head began to reel. She had spoken with Pintu only yesterday. He hadn't seemed very interested in talking with her. Why don't you think it over again? There's plenty of time, he told her.

Runu knew that. They were young. They had time. But she also knew that her mother would never accept Pintu as a son-in-law. Neither would her father. No one would. His family had a social standing. But not Pintu. Without his family behind him, Pintu was nobody.

The train whistled on its way, stopping at stations before continuing on its journey. The light was fading. A soothing breeze had sprung up.

Runu realized that she should have had some food. A cup of tea, at least. It was proving to be a long journey. She hadn't thought that she would feel hungry. Or tired. She had thought that she would fly to Pintu on golden wings. In the blink of an eye. And there he would be, waiting for her, the platform lit up with his love. Pintu was very attractive. His smart clothes, his clever talk, his jokes, his laughter were enough to make any girl want him. He was also a school drop-out, he had not been to college. But his was the face that Runu's eyes longed for.

Pintu, I'll be with you soon. I've left everything behind me, a good home, trusting parents, a sweet and simple sister – I've left them all forever. Only for you. To be with you. I know what you are. I know you're obdurate. You're a murderer. You're ... But still you're beautiful ... to me ...

Hey, Miss, we've reached the station. Don't you want to get off?

Runu started and raised her head from the window grille. Had she dozed off, thinking of Pintu? Was their compartment empty already?

She stood up.

Where are you headed? Where's your luggage? Oh, you haven't brought anything with you. Running away from home, eh?

Runu left the train without answering the man.

Hey, hey, Runu, this way, over here. The train's half an hour late today. I've been standing here for ages. Pintu took her hand and pulled her along as he talked. He didn't give Runu a chance to say a word. He walked her to another train and helped her into a compartment.

Sit here. I had a talk with the ticket collector and he arranged this seat for you. It's very comfortable and you'll get a good view. Wait here. I'll get some food for you.

Runu was surprised at the way Pintu was behaving. What was he doing? Why was she in this train? She didn't even know where it was headed.

Pintu hurried back with some food in a paper bag. Here, take this. How about some tea? Wait. Let me get you some.

Runu took hold of his hand and made him sit down beside her.

Don't run around like that, sit down. You haven't even told me where we're going.

We? We're not going anywhere. You are. Back to Dhaka.

What?

This train is leaving for Dhaka in a few minutes. You'll get there tomorrow morning. Around seven thirty.

Pintu, I didn't come all this way just to go back. Runu stood up suddenly in her excitement.

Don't shout. There's no need to make a scene. Pintu stood in front of her, blocking her off from the other passengers. I'm leaving for Iran this week. I'll be back in two years. When I'm back, I want to see you ready to come away with me like this. Not now.

Why didn't you tell me this before? Runu's voice was shaking in helpless anger.

You can't be sure of these things beforehand, can you? Do you understand why I'm going to Iran? Because it'll probably be more beautiful than a prison cell. Don't you think it's a preferable destination?

Pintu, are you trying to insult me?

Insult me all you want after two years. Tit for tat.

It was time for the train to leave.

I'll phone Dhaka, so don't worry, Pintu comforted her.

Runu had been quite unconscious of the packet of food she was holding in her hand. Now, she threw it out of the window.

Get off this train, now. Get away from me.

Don't get mad, sweetheart. There was nothing else I could do.

Runu's eyes were smarting with anger, humiliation and sorrow. She couldn't tell when it was that her eyes flooded over like the river banks, when it was that a dry wind rustled through the dead garden of her heart making the dry leaves settle down in small, unmoving heaps. She dimly heard a whisper in her ear. So, that boy rejected you, did he?

Runu wasn't a bit scared to find the man with the cold eyes sitting beside her. She wasn't afraid at all. She took off the amulet she was wearing and tried to throw it out of the window.

The man beside her stopped her. Don't throw it away. I don't think your troubles are over yet.

Move away from me, Runu said in a low voice.

The man settled down comfortably, blocking her view of the window. He spoke to her so that no one else could hear him. Don't try to act so brave, sister. A night train holds worse creatures than me. You were hungry, weren't you, and you could still throw away that food, so throw out that scoundrel too, kick him out of your mind. Life is something great and grand and beautiful. What are you worried about? How you're going to go back? How you're going to face your family? You were brave enough to take an unknown journey. You must be brave enough to go back on the path you know. Even if everyone else slams their doors in your face. Your parents won't. Their door will always be open for you.

Runu didn't want to listen to his advice. She felt light-headed. Hunger, thirst, fatigue, the sound of the train chugging its way through the night, the train's whistle piercing the dark silence – all combined to deaden her senses. Father was supposed to take his medicine at ten. Shanu was afraid to sleep alone. The young boy who worked for them started dozing off as soon as it got dusk. Runu started to doze off herself with the steady swaying of the train. She did not know when sleep closed around her – sleep that calmed her frayed nerves, sleep that was like an endless sinking into a bottomless sea.

Runu wasn't sure where she was at first as she looked around in the pure light of the morning.

We've arrived at Kamlapur. Time to get off. Come on. I'll take you home.

Runu looked up at the man with a start. She thought of last night. She had thought of jumping off the train. Or the train exploding somehow. Or their car being overturned. Somehow. And her body would be there, torn to pieces.

But nothing had happened. What a beautiful day it was going to be. Calm and silent. The day ahead of her.

Come on. Let's go, the tall man hurried her. As if he were her guardian.

The long sleep had soothed away her fatigue. Runu stood up.

The man followed her. It was then that she saw that he walked with a limp. He called a scooter and climbed in beside her.

OK, so where are you going?

His question gave her a jolt. Where was she going?

You'll have to give me some sort of an address or I'll have to take you to the police, he told her.

What if I hand *you* over to the police? Runu suddenly asked.

The man laughed. I'm not a nobody, you know. Don't think I'm a bad person just because I'm lame, either. That's a legacy of the Liberation War.

The scooter was gathering speed. The road was empty, so it was going as fast as it could. The man was sitting a bit away from her, but Runu couldn't help bumping against him. But she didn't care any more. All she could feel was a cold rage hissing inside her heart. With knife and scissors, *boti* and *dao*, she chopped and hacked her traitor lover's face, eyes, nose, mouth, ears, whatever she could find. She tore his smart clothes to ribbons with her teeth and nails. Last of all, she doused him with petrol and lit a match over him. The fire blazed angrily. But fire makes smoke as well as heat. The smoke made Runu's eyes water. She was thinking all this with her head bowed. Now she raised her head and wiped her eyes.

She didn't notice that a pair of eyes kept glancing surreptitiously at her tear-drenched, rosy face. The scooter sped through the empty road awash in the glow of the early morning sun.

Translated by Shabnam Nadiya

SELINA HOSSAIN

Motijan's Daughters

Marriage gives a woman a certain kind of stature in the new household – she becomes a wife, and becoming a wife means the beginning of a new chapter in her life. She has a world of her own made up of joys and sorrows and so many other things, as well as control over the household – that is what Motijan used to imagine, but she could not understand her position in this household. She did not even know if there was any need for her at all in this household. She had a mother-in-law over and above her who was really in charge, and Motijan was no more than a superfluous addition to the family. Her heart was full of the frustration of being superfluous. The sharp words of her mother-in-law often scorched her soul. At such times Motijan felt totally sick at heart of married life. She wished she were a widow.

The mother-in-law's name was Gulnoor and her son's name was Abul. She had lost her husband when her son was just eighteen months and had been a widow for twenty-two years now. She had managed the house and whatever land her husband owned with an iron hand, looked after the family and brought up her son. She had never asked for help from either her husband's family or her own parents. The people of the village said of her: 'She's a very hard woman, mind you.' Gulnoor was proud of this. She felt that being hard was really a matter of pride and this hardness had a significance for her. As a result, whatever she herself thought or did was the right thing; it could not be anything else. Motijan had expectations from her husband, but she found that her mother-in-law had totally usurped her rights. Sometimes she thought that even Abul was superfluous in his mother's household. When she expressed her acute grievance at not being able to lead a contented family life with her husband, Abul simply escaped from the house. He told Motijan in clear terms: 'Don't tell me anything. I know nothing and can do nothing. Mother is all in all. She keeps my heart trampled under her feet.' As he said this through twisted lips, Abul waved his hands in the air and gave vent to his feelings in vulgar invectives. But his words failed to indicate the target of his obscenities. Motijan looked at her husband with her eyes wide. His appearance was always bewildered, his eyes bloodshot, and he was totally indifferent about family life. He had absolutely no interest in household affairs. He frequented a den where he smoked *ganja* with his friends. He was a regular ruffian and thought nothing of spending money on a woman named Rosoi who had a place in the market. Neither his mother nor his wife were of any concern to him. Realizing this truth, Motijan grew hard. She wanted to be as hard as her mother-in-law. Her mother-in-law's reproaches made her stubborn inside.

Nine months of marriage had completely opened her eyes, but no one could guess that. She pretended to look neither to the right nor to the left, neither below nor above. But she had eyes for everything around her; not even a tiny piece of straw could escape her vision. Did her life in this new household have a very good start, after all? In the beginning she hardly understood anything properly. Looking back upon the past few months now, she realized that not even the first seven days after her marriage had passed well. Her mother-in-law's attitude was sullen; she never spoke to her properly. Motijan could look at her face only with fear. She did not understand her husband even. He too did not speak to her in a normal way. He puffed at *bidis* the whole day and night and filled the room with smoke. It was impossible to take a long and relaxing breath in that suffocating air. Motijan could say nothing to him. The sultry atmosphere in the house always frightened her. She was scared to put her foot down anywhere, scared even to sneeze. At mealtimes her fingers would suddenly become paralysed while picking the bones of a piece of *ilish* fish. Raising a ball of rice to her mouth, she would glance surreptitiously at her mother-in-law and find her looking at her with eyes that made her tremble inside. Motijan's heart seemed to beat noisily, almost like the rumbling of the waters of the Mahananda during the monsoon, as though she could feel the sound of the waves touching her body if she listened carefully. When her mother-in-law raised the topic of dowry on the eighth day, she shrank in fear. She had just finished eating and the aluminium plate still bore the marks of gravy. Gulnoor spoke through gritted teeth, 'At the time of the marriage your father promised that he would give a wristwatch and cycle to my Abul. Why hasn't he sent them yet?'

Motijan remained silent. She drew lines on her plate with her forefinger. She knew her father's circumstances well: his household expenses were twice his income. He had made the promise without being sure of his ability to get the money for all those things. What was going to happen now?

Gulnoor spoke harshly again, 'Why don't you say anything?'

Motijan said tearfully, 'I don't know anything.'

Gulnoor burst out, 'Why don't you know? You must!'

Motijan began to tremble. Her fingers became motionless on the plate. She felt as though the rice she had already swallowed was choking her; any further shouting and she would simply vomit out all she had eaten.

'Don't snivel, now! Go and wash up the plates and pots.'

The order to work relieved Motijan. It gave her a wonderful chance to escape. She collected all the utensils and carried them to the pond. It was the middle of the day, blazing sunlight all around. Motijan sat on the edge of the pond, looking at the sunlight with unblinking eyes. She realized that nothing was smouldering, inside her, there was neither any burning feeling nor the pain of being scorched. She only felt like bursting into tears out of an acute sense of helpless anger against her father. She buried her face between her knees and sobbed quietly. Why did father have to make false promises? What harm would there have been if she had not been married off? All she wanted was to join Beli *bua* who worked with the village cooperative making *nakshi kanthas*, fine embroidered quilts.

She was bent upon earning her own living. But her father ruled that out. He would lose face and be utterly humiliated if he could not get his daughter married off. So he had to find a husband for her by any means. Why? Why? Motijan wanted to kick all the utensils into the water. What a mockery of a marriage! Where was the good life she had been led to expect? What about her husband? Was this the prestige her father valued so much? The honour and prestige of the poor depended on the food and clothing they had. Motijan kept on staring at the blazing midday sunlight without blinking. Before her eyes, her bedroom darkened with the smoke of countless *bidis*, seemed to turn into a coloured balloon, soaring higher and higher up in the air. She could never reach up and touch it. At that moment the bright day around her began to freeze into a solid mass within her. She thought, I too shall become a hard woman.

Days roll on, as is the nature of days, and Motijan's days also rolled on. She came to realize that although she had to live with Abul, he was not really a part of her life. He spent at least half the month with Rosoi at her place. In the beginning Motijan had tried to remonstrate with him and been rewarded with beatings. Now she no longer raised the subject; neither did Gulnoor bother about whether her son returned home at night or not. She supported whatever her son did. In fact, she felt quite comfortable when her son did not come. Then she could torture Motijan to her heart's content, which she could not do when Abul was present. She had to pretend to humour her son – at least for the sake of appearances. Besides, nowadays Gulnoor directly gave vent to her anger about the dowry. She shouted loudly at Motijan, 'Your father is a liar, a cheat. If he couldn't manage to deliver the cycle and the wristwatch, why did he promise?'

In her agitation Gulnoor was quite abusive and shouted loudly much of the time. Abul also followed his mother's example. One day Motijan could no longer remain silent, although she felt like choking. In a trembling voice she said, 'My father is not a cheat. He's poor. My father is not a liar. He doesn't have any money right now, that's why it's taking him all these days to buy the cycle and the wristwatch.'

'Shut up, you wretched girl! How dare you speak such big words!'

Gulnoor dragged Motijan by her hair and threw her to the ground. She put a rope round her neck and tied her leg to a post inside the room.

Motijan was not given anything to eat the whole day. She grew numb. She had no tears in her eyes, no sense of burning in her heart either. Her lack of feelings slowly began to turn into a hard core within her. She wanted to turn into a hard woman. In the evening Gulnoor dragged her by the rope to the pond-side and said, 'I can no longer feed rice to you. All you'll get now is grass. Go on, eat.'

Abul joined his mother in laughing at this terrible joke and then went off to Rosoi's place in the market. A little later Gulnoor brought Motijan out on the verandah and gave her a plate of rice to eat. Motijan ate the rice in stoic, dispirited silence. Then she went into her room and closed the door behind her to be alone in the darkness. She could not sleep for a moment the whole night. She tossed restlessly on her bed, rolled on the floor. She tried hard to remain calm but could not. She spoke to the darkness, Tell me, O darkness, how can I take revenge? How? At this moment of ultimate silence she felt the need of a companion, someone very close to her, someone to whom she could open her heart. She craved for a little joy now. No more this tortured life for her. She felt no responsibility at all for a husband who was a drunkard, a gambler, infatuated with another man's woman. She could visualize only one opponent before her, the one who was reputed to be a hard woman in the village. Motijan's fight was with her.

Days roll on, as is the nature of days, and Motijan's days also rolled on. Abul came home sometimes, sometimes he did not. When her mother-in-law became abusive about the missing dowry, Motijan listened in silence. She had not been to her father's house for such a long time. No one from her father's house could come to see her either. Her elder brother had come twice. Gulnoor treated him very badly. She had forbidden him to come again without the wristwatch and the cycle. No one else had come in the last six months or so. On his last visit, her elder brother had told her in private, 'Try not to be so unhappy. I tell you, Father and I are trying to get the watch and cycle.'

Motijan had scolded her elder brother with anger in her eyes, 'No, you must not trouble yourselves. Father has already been branded a liar and a cheat. So why should you worry about the wristwatch and cycle any longer? And I? I have turned into a cow. They ask me to live on grass.'

Saying that Motijan had burst out in ripples of laughter – her first uninhibited laughter after arriving in that household. Her brother looked on at her stupidly. From the verandah Gulnoor rebuked her sharply for such unmannerly mirth. For the first time Motijan ignored her mother-in-law and kept on laughing.

Made nervous by her abnormal appearance and the loudness of her laughter, her brother slunk away quietly. His escape made her utterly sad; her grief seemed to rend her soul into pieces. Silently, she went into the cowshed. She cleaned the shed and sat there late into the afternoon making cow-dung cakes to be used as fuel. She kept at that task until the blazing sunlight outside grew dimmer. From that time Motijan's power to ignore anything became stronger within her heart.

Very late that afternoon, when Motijan felt ravenous, she came back to the house to eat, but her mother-in-law stopped her at the door of the kitchen. Motijan understood that Gulnoor had sacrificed her midday nap in order to guard over the food. She wanted to punish her for her impudent laughter earlier in the day.

Finding her way blocked, Motijan said in a cold voice, 'I want to eat. I'm hungry.'

Gulnoor said, 'There's no food.'

Motijan shouted, 'Why not?'

Gulnoor bared her teeth in a snarl and raised her hands threateningly, 'I won't give you any rice. You can have nothing but grass.'

'I do my share of work in this household. I earn my food – I don't just sit idle and eat. You have to give me food. Hasn't a servant got the right to demand food?'

Motijan stepped past her mother-in-law and entered the kitchen. She rummaged through the pots and pans but found no food. There was a covered plate in a *shika* hanging from the ceiling. As soon as she reached for it, her mother-in-law rushed up, 'Don't touch that, I tell you. That's Abul's food.'

Motijan broke into her unnatural laughter again. Then she spoke through gritted teeth. 'Rosoi has cooked for him. Why should you worry?'

'What did you say? How dare you?'

Motijan made no reply. She held the plate of rice and curry close to her chest and started eating. She realized that she must not let go of the plate. Her mother-in-law would get the chance to jump upon her if she sat down to eat. So she kept standing and eating in such a way that if Gulnoor attempted to come close she could throw the plate at her. Right at her head. A big piece of fish had been kept for Abul and now, what good luck, it was hers to eat! Or was it something she deserved, after all? That's what Beli *bua* used to say: Claim your own rights. The thought brought a faint smile on Motijan's lips. Ravenously hungry, she kept on eating voraciously without even looking at her mother-in-law. She stole a glance at her out of the corner of her eye. No, she had not taken a single step forward. She realized that Gulnoor was staring at her with dilated eyes. Such defeat was utterly inconceivable to a hard woman like her. Motijan felt within her heart a surge of victory as though the waves of the Mahananda were tearing a path through a curtain of thick mist.

Later in the afternoon she came to the bamboo grove beside the pond. It was a secluded, shady spot. Sunlight failed to reach the ground through the thick foliage. It was as though a solid layer of glue across the tops of the trees kept the light trapped there. The ground was damp and wet, soft and pleasantly cool. Motijan's mother-in-law had perhaps fallen asleep in her room after her defeat. There was no sound from her. She always had to have a nap in the middle of the day; it was her favourite habit. Motijan sat down beneath the bamboos and hummed softly to herself. This was the first time since her marriage that she had felt so happy. The young boy named Budhe had taken the cows to graze on the other side of the pond. He was a very restless child, who couldn't sit quietly even for a moment. He would frequently come up to Motijan and say, 'Why don't you tell me a story, Bhabi.'

'What sort of story? About a king?'

He would nod in agreement. Motijan would tell him a story about a king, about the seven seas and thirteen rivers. Listening to her, the eyes of twelve-year-old Budhe would gleam with pleasure. At this moment, however, Budhe was nowhere to be seen. Motijan felt as if today her heart was full of stories about kings, as if she were travelling across the seven seas and thirteen rivers herself. She longed to tell Budhe about her feelings.

As she left the bamboo groves and approached the house, Motijan met Lokman before the front door. Seeing her, Lokman smiled. He had a tall, slender figure. Motijan trembled when she looked in his eyes. He was Abul's friend and came to the house every so often. When Abul was away for several days, he sent some purchase back home through him. Lokman also went by the house on his way to and from the market. Motijan had never had the opportunity to speak to him, neither did she have the courage to do so. Today Lokman looked surprised to see her at the front door.

'How are you, Bhabi?'

'Well,' Motijan smiled. Her teeth glittered like pearls and Lokman looked somewhat bemused.

'Here – your shopping.'

Motijan reached for the bundle. 'Come,' she said easily, 'sit in the shade. Would you like to have a *paan*?'

The lilting tone of her voice startled Lokman. He wanted to sit for a while. Yet he hesitated and said, 'I have to go now.'

'Do come again, won't you?'

'Yes. I'll come again.' Lokman's face brightened as he spoke. Motijan went into the house, walking with a natural grace and looking back once at him over her shoulder. The rhythm of her movements startled Lokman once more. Was this the same woman he had seen so many times before? It took him a while to overcome his surprise.

Motijan put the shopping down on the verandah and sat there listlessly. Gulnoor was still sleeping. As soon as she woke up, she would open the bundle to check the contents. Motijan was not allowed to open the shopping bag. She never wanted to anyway. Today she felt more at ease, leaving it carelessly on one side. If she could, she would have trampled on that bundle and cast it into the pond. But she did not wish to quarrel needlessly with her mother-in-law. She was engulfed in a dejection that seemed to strike at her like gusts of torrential rain. It was more than a year since her marriage, but she was not a mother yet. The bones in her body grated with her suffering. She was filled with an all-pervading emptiness while Abul was enjoying himself thoroughly at Rosoi's place.

Since her defeat the other day, Gulnoor had been playing a different tune. She tried to provoke Motijan every now and then by her sarcastic remarks and even asked her point-blank, 'Why can't you have a baby?'

Motijan looked stupidly at her. What could she say in reply to a question like that? Once she felt like asking, 'Why don't you ask your son?' But she desisted and, turning her head, went off to attend to her household chores. Behind her back, her mother-in-law raised her voice to complain loudly, 'How can my family lines be kept alive, O Allah?'

The tone of her voice irritated Motijan intensely. She stopped abruptly and turned back, but saw her mother-in-law passing through the side door into their neighbour's house. She came back and sat down on the verandah. Her mother-in-law would now start accusing her of being a sterile woman. Her whole body felt numb. Why couldn't she bear a child, after all? Motijan's eyes brimmed over with tears of anguish.

Budhe came and stood before her. He had brought a load of *jams* gathered in a corner of his *lungi*.

'Have some, Bhabi. Look. I've brought so many.'

Motijan stared at Budhe without saying anything. On another day she would have shouted in glee and said, 'Budhe is a real darling!'

Not hearing her admiring remarks today, Budhe nodded his head understandingly and said: 'I know, Amma has called you names, hasn't she?'

Budhe whispered, 'Don't cry, Bhabi. Amma's very bad.'

Budhe dropped the *jams* on the verandah and ran off. At that moment Gulnoor was telling Noor's mother next door, 'Sister, that daughter-in-law of mine is barren. Otherwise, why doesn't she bear a child?'

Noor's mother giggled, 'What if she's barren? Get your son married again. Be sure to ask for a lot of money this time.'

Gulnoor smiled happily and did not waste any time in repeating it all to Motijan. She added that her life would be meaningless without a child to keep the family line going. Motijan made no reply at all. The word 'marriage' was spinning round and round within her head. When Abul returned home after two days, she mentioned the need to keep the family line going. But Abul simply snarled at her, 'I'll kick the family's behind!'

'But your mother wants it.'

'Go and tell mother ...'

He stopped abruptly and swore under his breath. Motijan was stupefied on hearing the vicious swearing. She felt as though something was moving inside her abdomen and clutching at her entrails. She felt sick. Yet, as she breathed the stench of *ganja* coming from Abul's mouth, she wanted to kick Abul off her. But she restrained herself and imagined Budhe calling her. When the stench of *ganja* hardened inside her chest, she could feel Lokman's tall, slender figure coming within her reach. She stretched her hand trying to touch him, and his body seemed to curl into a small bundle and crawl into her fist.

One day, at noon, the sky darkened with clouds and a strong wind began to blow. There were sudden gusts of stormy wind. Apparently Budhe had not come back from the grazing fields because the lowing of the cows could not be heard from anywhere near by. Gulnoor had gone to Kansat in the morning to visit the family of her husband's elder brother. Before starting she had said that she would return in the evening. Abul had been away from the house for two days. Motijan sat on the verandah with her legs stretched out, embroidering flowers on a handkerchief. She had to do the work on the sly, keeping it a secret from her mother-in-law. She wanted to give the handkerchief to Lokman as a present. She had developed an easy relationship with Lokman. He knew when Gulnoor would be sleeping, when Budhe would not be around, when the sunlight would be filtering through the shadows of the bamboo grove. At such times Motijan had endless leisure on her hand: she could travel across the seven seas and thirteen rivers.

One stormy day gusts of wind blew dust from the courtyard into Motijan's face, blinding her eyes and dishevelling her hair. As she jumped to her feet to take cover, she saw Lokman running across the courtyard to the protection of the verandah. The rains came just at that moment, falling in torrents. Inside the room, Lokman pressed Motijan to his chest in a tight embrace. For the first time, the very first time in her life, Motijan truly experienced the intense sensation of a man's touch on her body. She realized that there was a great deal of difference between Abul and Lokman.

Days roll on, as they always will, following their course. Motijan's days, however, passed differently now. She was going to be a mother. When Motijan first missed her monthly period after that day's incident, she cried out in astonishment. Alone in her room she tried to come to an understanding with herself – to come to terms with the surge of emotions throbbing all over her being, as though all the doors that had so far remained closed were now opening before her.

On hearing the news, Abul looked at her askance. 'So the family line is saved, after all!' But Motijan's mother-in-law was not happy at first. She remained ominously quiet. It was her second defeat, and she had never imagined that it would come so soon. Then she looked obliquely at Motijan and said in a stern voice, 'You must not give birth to a girl child, mind you.'

Motijan said, 'What makes you hanker after a boy child? Your own son does not care for you.'

'What if he doesn't, you slut? You must bear a boy, or you'll suffer the consequences, I tell you.'

Her mother-in-law's hot breath seared Motijan's face. She knew that it was a year of acute drought – crops were withering, fields were cracking up. Her whole body was heavy with a fatigue that was trying to tear at and devour her entire being. She tried to triumph over her physical weakness with the strength of her mind.

In course of time, Motijan gave birth to a daughter. Abul laughed loudly and mockingly, 'So the family line is not going to be saved, after all!'

Gulnoor was grave and refused even to see her grandchild. But Motijan found a release to all the pent-up emotions within her by pressing her daughter to her breast and showering her with love and caresses. Even in the midst of all the indifference and neglect she was subjected to, the ecstasy she felt at the birth of her daughter billowed all around her like the surging waves of the Mahananda. Motijan danced and swung her daughter before her mother-in-law's eyes and sang her to sleep. Gulnoor could not bear Motijan's joy; she became ferocious and threatening. But Motijan grew stronger than before within herself and said, 'If I could, I would give birth to a hundred daughters.' She no longer remained silent but shouted back. This made Gulnoor madder than ever before. Of late, Abul had practically stopped coming home. Motijan came to know that he had left Rosoi and taken up with another woman. He was too busy to bother about anything else. All that made Motijan even more stubborn.

In about a year Motijan was with child again by Lokman and gave birth to another girl. This time Gulnoor remained silent for seven days, then she declared that she was no longer prepared to tolerate a daughter-in-law who bore nothing but a girl child every year. When her son returned home, she would make him divorce this useless wife of his and send her off to her father's house.

Motijan listened silently to her mother-in-law's tirade. She had no time to think of anything else now. She was busy throughout the day with her children. On top of that, she had all the household chores to take care of too. She was nearly always overcome with fatigue and exhaustion.

When Abul returned home after about a month or so, Gulnoor wasted no time in loudly announcing her decision to him. At that moment Abul was very much under the influence of *ganja*. His mother's words startled him. He stared blankly at her for a few seconds, then went out of the house again. Gulnoor filled the house with her angry shouts. 'I'll throw that wretched woman out right now!'

Quite a few of the neighbours gathered in the courtyard. Motijan appeared before the crowd with her two daughters pressed to her breast. Gulnoor was still shouting, the curses flying out of her mouth like fireworks.

Motijan stood her ground. 'Don't you dare swear at me,' she raged. 'I warn you.'

Gulnoor screamed, 'You'll get no food at my house from today. I'll get my son married again. My family line must be kept going.'

Suddenly Motijan burst into mocking laughter, startling everyone. 'Your family line?' she said. 'Faugh! If I had left it to your son, I wouldn't even have got these two girls.'

'What did you say?'

Gulnoor, the hard woman of the village, kept staring at Motijan with dilated, unbelieving eyes. A barely audible murmur spread among the crowd.

Motijan stood there, holding her two daughters close to her. From the safety of their mother's breast, Motijan's daughters glared at everyone before them.

Translated by Sagar Chaudhury

Dilara Hashem

The Immersion

Badal was walking: alone.

He was wearing a new *lungi*; over it was the new polyester shirt his father had bought him before they had left the city. Badal was walking; tripping and running – *lungi*, shirt, trousers – these meant nothing to him. To be unfettered – without clothes – felt most natural to him. This was especially true when his mother tried to pull him away from the windowsill at dusk, when she lit the low-powered bulb in the westernmost room of his grandfather's old, decaying, three-storeyed house in the narrow alley in Narinda. It felt as if the mellow light was pouring a burning liquid over his skin. He would snatch his shirt and *lungi* – wildly tear his shirt, open his *lungi*. His naked shadow on the wall would make him burst into rollicking laughter.

His mother, agitated and sorrowful, would cover her eyes with both hands and plead with him, 'Oh my lovely son, my golden boy, my precious! You cannot take off your clothes now, dearest. You are a big boy now.'

Badal hadn't the faintest notion what growing up meant. He only knew and recognized the sudden fire that blazed between his thighs.

Pressing with both fists that fierce flame, he would stare at the reflection on the wall and burst out in excited and uncontrollable laughter. Exultantly, Badal answered his mother, 'See, Ma – how big I have become.'

As the animated shadow of his penis spread from his fists on to the wall and became bigger and bigger, Badal, in his new untasted ecstasy, stood and trembled with mirth. His mother covered her welling tears with her sari and rushed out, closing the door behind her, mumbling, 'Allah, Allah! Give my child some peace, O Lord.'

Badal could never understand why everyone was so concerned about his peace. He knew where peace was. Peace reigned only in himself.

Through the window of the house he would gaze at the sky all day long. He would see birds flying, clouds, the sunshine; a convoy of ants on the window hinges, squabbling doves, sparrows coming and going. Bubbles of colours would play within him. He would drown within a melancholy tune that would carry him over the vast open wilderness. It was then that Badal would take the charcoal, or bits of broken red brick, and scribble and draw – higgledy-piggledy – many weird strange shapes and forms on the floor.

As a child, Badal had lived by a river. The memory of the golden stretch of the river would sparkle in his breast, and whenever he strained his ears to hear the splashing laughter of the river, Badal too, without any reason, would burst out in merriment. At such moments, if his mother, father or sister Rebecca saw him, their faces would cloud over with sorrow and they would look at one another, exchanging sad and sombre glances. The younger brother and sister playing near by would stop midway in their games, and stare with startled gaze. And at that moment – suddenly – Badal would become aware of their presence, a solemn presence that overwhelmed him with grief. Agitated, he would stare vacantly, and the laughter would come to an abrupt halt, as Badal became absolutely silent.

They did not understand that it was the colours of happiness that sparkled in Badal's soul. It was those colours that he tried to resurrect on the walls of his room with bits of charred wood or pieces of brick. It was only when friends and relatives of his parents stood at his door and stared inquisitively, stifling their sighs, that Badal became enraged. He would stop his laughter and begin to break and smash objects around him.

His mother, anticipating such outbursts, kept the room almost bare. But if Badal could not get anything to smash, he would dash his head against the wall, in an attempt to break and smash it. His mother would come rushing in and, holding him tightly, would offer him an old butter can full of pebbles and marbles. Badal would fling the can on the floor. The metallic clang amused him enormously, and Badal would burst into rapturous laughter, his demon of anger vanishing in an instant.

In that house his 'Ma' alone knew what would make Badal happy or keep him content. The discovery that a can of pebbles could produce such joy was his mother's insight, and she kept this can handy for such violent moments.

Stopping his head-banging, Badal would pick the marbles and stones with both his hands and, placing them on his mother's palms, would say, 'Ma, see, what gems and pearls I have collected! Wait and see what a beautiful necklace I will make for you. Shall I keep these with me, Ma?'

But Ma would never keep the can in Badal's room. She would collect all the stones and take the can with her as she left. Badal's sorrow was that his joy could not bring a smile to his mother's face. Ma would bite her lower lip and with a wan face try to curb her emotion, but tears would spill out and drench both her cheeks. Mother would dampen the *anchal* of her sari and, pressing it on Badal's swollen forehead, intone, 'Allah, transfer my child's suffering to me, give some peace to my little one!'

Badal would press his face against his mother's soft supple breasts, searching for that peace. The mother's body would stop trembling and become rigid and motionless, as she whispered, 'Badal, my love, my dearest boy, you are a big boy now – you don't do that now. Listen Badal – Badal, good boy ...'

Badal wondered where his peace lay and how he would get it. Where would he get respite from the flames that covered his whole being? Would the waters of the golden-etched river provide him with the desired peace?

Twice a day the fierce-faced servant Abdul would march him to the bathroom and pour buckets of water over him. One tub of water was never enough to cool his steaming head and body. Returning to his room, he would once again sprawl naked on the floor and start drawing.

There was so much sky, so many birds, trees and yet more trees that he could draw, as well as the golden gliding river.

The river he had drawn had no water. It only twisted and turned in dark lines. Staring at the barren river – that charcoal-etched river with no water – he would dribble urine over it and be overcome with joy. He watched his pee winding its way, like waves of the river, rolling across the floor. Truly it seemed that the golden river had found its flow. Badal clapped his hands and danced with joy.

But this happiness too made his mother cry. Badal could not understand why his joy made her weep.

On days when his rage went beyond all control and he had broken lots of things, his mother would make the maidservant grind bunches of henna leaves. Carrying this finely ground paste of *mehendi* in a bowl, his mother would come and say, 'Baba Badal, come – let me colour your hair. You love colours, don't you, darling?'

Badal truly loved colours. But if his mother said, 'Come let me put some oil in your hair,' Badal would shake his head obstinately. He hated oil. Once a herbalist had concocted a special oil for him: the oil had a horrible smell. Moreover, the barber, according to the herbalist's instructions, had shaved off a patch of hair from the top of his head. Abdul had slapped on and massaged in the oil on that clean-shaven spot. The stink of the oil had made him throw up all over the floor. The odour of the oil and vomit filled Badal with immense fury. He had lunged at the long mirror on the wall. The splinters of glass cut his hand, and blood spilt all over the place. Ma and Baba, hearing the sound of smashed glass, had run into the room, looking at each other in dismay at the sight. Baba's face was ashen as he asked, 'Shireen, why didn't you remove the mirror from the room?'

Ma, tearing off a corner of her sari with which she tried to stave off the gushing blood, answered drily, 'Badal loves sitting before the mirror. He has never attempted anything like this before.'

Baba's orders were clear. 'Don't keep anything in the room that he can break.'

But Ma knew that Badal needed to smash things occasionally or else his frustrations would ferment. The can of pebbles was her remedy for his distress – no doctor had prescribed it. Every time Badal was enraged, the can of pebbles did not fail to soothe and calm him down.

When Ma was mopping the vomit off the floor, Baba suddenly came close to Badal and gazed directly into his eyes. Badal wanted to hide from his father's gaze. Something turned off inside him, and, as Baba's piercing look penetrated him, Badal wanted to escape. Badal did not want anyone to trespass into his joyous, many-hued, colourful world that he alone inhabited. They would not understand his joy. They only wondered and looked at one another – perplexed, saddened and disturbed by his presence. Badal had seen this happen time and again and had wanted to escape from these searching eyes.

When Badal finally turned his face away, Baba called him in a husky voice, 'Badal!' Badal turned towards his father with anxious eyes. 'Are you in pain, Badal?'

Badal did not speak, but shaking his head said, 'No.'

'What will make you happy, Badal?'

Badal stared out of the window and pointed outside with his fingers. The *jamrul* tree stood against the barred window. Next to the tree was the high wall, and on the other side of the wall was the road. The narrow Narinda lane snaked between the old houses, travelling into the far distance.

Badal gestured with his fingers towards that road.

'You want to go out? I'll take you – you want to go?'

And suddenly as the sharp, putrid smell of oil filled Badal's nose, he started to tear his hair with both hands. He tried to bash his head against the window bars. Baba reacted swiftly and caught and restrained him. Baba seemed extremely distraught and helpless, not knowing how to cope with Badal. With his thin hands, he tried to pull Badal away from the window, and, calling to his mother, said, 'Shireen, come and take over – I can't seem to ...'

Immediately his mother leaped to her feet and came to Badal. Tearfully, but with great tenderness and love, Ma asked, 'Badal, shall I wash your hair? I know and understand how much you hate the smell of the oil.'

Ma was the only person who understood Badal – his likes and dislikes.

Baba interrupted, 'But the doctor has recommended the oil for him.'

Ma never raised her voice in protest. She merely replied in a sad, subdued tone, 'Ask Abdul to bring a pail of cool water. You can see for yourself what sort of help the oil is. Hurry up – go and fetch the water!'

Baba rushed off to get hold of Abdul.

From then on, the sight or mention of the oil would make Badal want to run out of the room.

But he loved having his mother smear henna paste on his hair. The henna cooled his fevered brain, and as his brain cooled, the heat of his body also seemed to subside. Sometimes the *mehendi* would make him fall asleep, and in this sleep he would dream the strangest dreams. He particularly dreamed about the river. He could never see the banks of the river – the river was too wide, an extraordinarily large expanse of water. Badal would see himself drifting on the crest of its waves as the beams of the sun transformed the water into molten gold. Badal felt like a king astride the throne of golden waves as he sailed into the far horizon.

Perhaps it was because he was not usually allowed to go near the water that rivers attracted him so much. He did not like ponds or lakes or enclosed bodies of water – natural, gushing, flowing water had a magical hypnotic effect on him.

But there were no rivers in Narinda. Only the narrow lane outside the window stretched out like a river. Badal spent his days gazing at the road, which seemed to beckon him relentlessly with open hands.

Badal had, on several occasions, managed to slip out of his room, especially when somebody had left the door ajar. He had crossed the lane and walked along it, and once he had become so tired on this clandestine journey that he had fallen asleep in front of a printing press. On another occasion, his frantic father and Abdul had discovered him dozing in front of a sweet shop. No one approved of these outings. Bringing him back, Baba told Ma, 'Shireen, you don't want him locked up because you love him. But do you want to lose him totally because of your love? The streets are full of traffic – what does Badal understand of safety? Imagine if he had fallen under the wheels of a car ...'

Before Baba could even finish his sentence, Ma excitedly held Badal's hands and implored, 'Badal, my Badal, why did you go out without telling anyone, dearest? Why didn't you tell me you wanted to go out? Abdul would have taken you out.'

Baba interrupted her pleas in a voice that echoed with helplessness and dismay, 'No, Shireen, no – do something now! We can't keep a constant watch over him. Don't ever make such suggestions ...!'

Ma silenced Baba. 'Of course he understands – Badal never disobeys me. You are the one who doesn't understand him. Please leave the child in peace! I'll look after him – no one has to worry about Badal.'

Peace! Peace! Peace!

Everyone in the house was so concerned with keeping Badal in peace that they lost their own peace completely!

Lots of friends and neighbours had gathered in the house a few days before. The house overflowed with girls, who flocked together, grinding henna and turmeric into a paste. Badal wondered why they were making the paste. Were they going to smear him with that? He'd like that – he loved being smeared with henna paste.

But no one called him. Outside his closed doors hordes of girls were wandering to and fro, going all over the house. He had not seen so many girls ever before. He wanted to join them – to fix his eyes on their faces, on their breasts, to stare at their bodies.

But for the first time Badal's door was locked – firmly shut. This was the result of an incident in which he had been the central player.

One afternoon, on finding his door open, Badal had wandered into the bride's chamber where a bunch of girls were present. He had crept in and stood right in the middle of the room. The girls had been talking and giggling – the sounds of their laughter reminded him of the gurgling, flowing water sprouting from a fountain. But the minute they spotted him in their midst, the conversation and the laughter stopped abruptly. Stricken faces exchanged glances, and their faces took on an inhuman look, like the faces of lifeless mannequins that Badal had seen in the windows of big shops. Badal felt like smashing these lifeless forms into smithereens. Badal suddenly became excited as he stood amidst these silent wooden puppets.

As long as the girls had been laughing and talking, they hadn't noticed Badal. Badal had also watched them silently – content – as if in a darkened auditorium or a cinema hall, or as if watching a play being performed. But now Badal gaped at a young girl who was standing just next to him. Her sari had fallen, revealing the warm quivering twin orbs of her breasts. Seeing this, something started to tremble between his thighs – he was entranced, enraptured. And it was just at this moment that the laughter and conversation stopped, and the girls gaped at him.

Badal felt as if the dark, congenial, shaded, consoling room had suddenly been flooded with glaring lights. All eyes were on him – how awkward he felt! The girls' looks seemed to fell him to the floor. He pounced on the girls next to him and started to pull them towards him. At once there was pandemonium! Girls ran out through the open door, a cacophony of sounds accompanying them. Abdul, looking like a thug, appeared from nowhere and planted himself in front of him. He was pushed into his room and, for the first time in his life, the door was locked from outside.

Badal could see coloured tents in the courtyard from his window. There was an endless procession of people entering and leaving. A special gate was being prepared. He could see his father with his forlorn face moving from place to place. Ma was so busy in the kitchen that she could not come to see Badal even once. And in the bridal chamber flocks of butterfly-like girls were dressing his sister Rebecca, hennaing her hands.

Badal gazed at his image in the mirror in his room all day long. The mirror showed him a figure with a dark, wavy mane of hair, limpid eyes, aquiline nose, chiselled cheekbones. He kissed this reflection – Ma was right, he really loved the mirror. He had no other companion in the room besides his image in the mirror, who rose with him, laughed and talked with him. The mirror was his friend, his comrade. And if he could love what he saw in the mirror, why could they not love what they saw in him? Why did their faces lose all expression – turn to stone – when they beheld him? Their fear of him, their pale bloodless faces made Badal want to crumple the window bars, break down the door and rush outside and destroy the whole world.

In the evening, Badal saw the girls going for their baths, having spent the day smearing and massaging his older sister – Rebecca Bu – with the henna and turmeric paste. Rebecca Bu was being led from the open courtyard back to her room. Clad in a freshly starched yellow Dhaka sari with a red border, Rebecca Bu seemed to be floating on air. Her hair had been treated with spices, and the smells from her open tresses wafted in the breeze. The aroma intoxicated Badal. Rebecca Bu was the centre of attention – Ma, the maids, the servants, the relatives – everyone was attending to her as though she had suddenly become a queen. No one seemed to remember that there was someone called Badal in this house – even his mother had forgotten him.

What was keeping Ma so busy the whole day? She had not come to see Badal even once. Usually she brought him his lunch, feeding him herself, mixing the rice and curry with her own hands and putting them into his mouth. The delicious smells from the kitchen wafted into his room – but there was no Ma bringing him his lunch. Abdul too was late in bringing his food. His stomach pinched and churned with pangs of hunger, but he was locked inside his room and unable to get out.

There was a bathroom next to his room but in his fury he pissed on the floor. Not finding anything to break in the room, he tore the mattress into shreds, covering the room with flying cotton.

Badal snatched the plate from Abdul when he finally brought his lunch, and flung it on the ground. He hurled the brass glass of water in Abdul's face, which cut his forehead and made it bleed. Abdul ran out of the room, again locking it from the outside.

A small crowd had gathered outside the door. Those bright-faced butterfly-like girls stared at him as if he was a chimpanzee or a baboon. Tearing at his hair, Badal started screaming in a hideous voice.

Finally Ma appeared. She ran in, her hands still smelling of garlic and onion. Badal could see his thin and helpless father go up to his mother and say in a low voice, 'Shireen, the house is full of relatives and neighbours. Tomorrow the bridegroom and his party will be here. Badal is in a terrible condition. We shall lose dignity and face. What will they think? They do not know about Badal. Our daughter's position will be totally degraded in her in-laws' house.'

Baba stopped, and Ma didn't say anything. An elderly man came up and said to Baba, 'Send Badal to the village home for a few days. He will be quite comfortable there. When you have finished with the wedding he can then ...'

Ma interrupted, 'No, never! That's not necessary – I'll control Badal. Ah! I did not feed him this afternoon. He did not see me the whole day, that's why ...'

Baba cut her short, saying, 'You could not look after him today, and tomorrow and the day after will be even more difficult for you, Shireen. Will you look after your son or attend to your guests? Do as the gentleman says.'

The old man went on, 'Don't worry, Badal won't disturb anyone. I will take him to the village myself. It is only a two-hour journey anyway. He will be quite happy there.'

Badal was quite happy to be released from his locked room. Baba first took him to New Market and bought him a polyester *lungi*. He asked Badal anxiously, 'Do you like these, Badal Baba?'

Baba was afraid that Badal might not like the clothes, but Badal nodded firmly in assent.

'You won't take these off and throw them away, will you?'

What did they think of him? Badal felt like throwing his clothes off only when he was locked inside a room, when he was part of his surroundings. Otherwise, would he want to tear off his clothes? He didn't feel that hot then.

On the train, Badal was overcome with joy, even though he had cried when his father hugged him goodbye. Badal was amazed as he had never seen his father cry. Baba's face usually had a sad, pained look, but a half-smile hovered around his eyes. The smile wasn't exactly a smile – it was more like an effort to smile through his grief. Badal was astonished to see, for the first time in his life, this thin, worried, tearful yet smiling man break into tears. His father's face seemed to break into pieces as the tears came into his eyes, just as a reflection on the river broke into a myriad pieces with the stirring of a breeze or the ripple of a wave.

Something stirred in Badal as he hugged his father and started howling himself. His changing adolescent voice came out as a discordant, cracked howl. Wiping away his tears tenderly, Baba spoke as if to himself, 'Baba, I have to send you far away on this joyous day. Be well – you will come home next week, Baba.'

Badal, however, wasn't that eager to return. His room had become a prison, and, now that he was away from it, he felt that he was holding heaven in his hands. Badal wouldn't have cried at all if his father had not collapsed in tears. As the train puffed out of the station, Badal saw his father's figure grow smaller and smaller until it vanished. Badal turned his mind to the scenes around him and forgot all about his father.

This was the first time he was seeing a village.

Everyone craved peace in his home in Dhaka. But peace reigned over the village – why hadn't they sent him here earlier? The cool earthen walls of the mud huts were ventilated with a constant flow of breeze, touched by the surrounding vegetation. Badal fell asleep within these cool and pleasant rooms. He slept deeply for a whole day. When he awoke, he saw a woman, someone who reminded him of his mother. She had a plate with mangoes, puffed rice and sugar cookies. Peeping from behind her was a girl, rounded like a ripe mango. She didn't pucker her face when she saw him, unlike the colourful Narinda girls. She had a little golden ring dangling from her nose over her lips. A black string with an amulet was strung around her neck. She was clad only in a striped sari. Her black, curly, untamed tresses meandered down her back. Her hair looked as if it had never been oiled.

The woman began saying, 'Moina, leave us! Go and tend to the rice on the stove.'

Moina went away but returned immediately, being immensely curious about what was happening in that room. Badal stared at her, mouth open. His eyes scanned her from top to bottom – staring at her healthy, glowing face, her rounded buttocks draped lightly in a neatly tied sari and her heels peeping through the hem of her sari.

Moina's mother continued, 'Badal Baba, come – have a wash and come to eat. Come, let me wash your face.'

Before he could get up, the girl was at the door with a container of water. Without saying a word, she beckoned with her eyes, pulling Badal to the door like a magnet. Badal obediently went up to her and washed his hands.

Moina's mother repeated, 'Moina, give me the pitcher, I'll help him. You go and see to the paddy in the yard. Go and shoo off the birds.'

Moina looked sharply at her mother, and, refusing to hand over the pitcher, she retorted crossly, 'Why should the birds peck at the paddy, Ma? I have kept the stick there.'

Her mother's face clouded at the girl's disobedience.

As Badal washed his face with the water that Moina poured from the pitcher, a tremor of joy ran through him, and he grasped her wrist, which was encircled by a silver bangle. Moina giggled, seductively pushing him off with her elbows. Instantly the heat in his body again concentrated between his thighs. Unlike the other girls, Moina did not freeze at the sight of Badal, and the monster that resided within him did not break its fetters and awaken with its terrible fury. The blazing heat remained imprisoned within him, and he felt agitated. For the first time, Badal tried to control himself, biting his lips in the process. He heard the woman say, 'I am your *chachi* – your father's brother's wife. If you need anything, Badal, just ask, won't you?'

When Badal returned to his room and sat down on the leaf mat, he could see Moina standing at the door. His eyes appealed to her to relieve him from the agony of his pent-up desires. His aunt, understanding the look, glared at Moina, who promptly disappeared from the doorway. Badal was at that moment just about to taste some puffed rice. He hurled the *muri* away and turned his face. His aunt watched these actions and called out to Moina in an anxious and distressed voice, 'Moina, oh Moina, where are you? Come here for a moment. I am in such a mess. Badal Baba, eat up. How will you live if you don't eat? Moina, where are you?'

Badal quietened down and resumed his meal the minute Moina returned. Triumphantly and mischievously, Moina stared back at him. Her mother sighed heavily.

Four days later, the old man, Dada, came to take Badal home. But Badal was determined not to go back and wouldn't budge from the doorway.

'You won't go?'

Badal shook his head vigorously while his aunt stared imploringly at Dada.

'It's not safe to keep him here much longer,' she said. 'I can't control him and look after the house as well, can I?'

There really wasn't much work in the house, and Moina was an efficient helping hand for her mother. But Dada understood the tenor of her objection.

Calling out to Badal he said, 'Hey, Badal, if you don't go, won't your mother cry? Come, let's go to your mother.'

Badal stared at the schemers. Before Dada could complete his sentence, he cried out, 'No!'

'OK. Then I have to leave. I'll go and send your father. He will have to fetch you himself. I have taken the responsibility of taking you back.'

'I won't go! I won't – I won't!' screamed Badal.

Gnashing his teeth, he broke Dada's walking cane into two. Both

Chachi and Dada went pale, scared at this new bout of temper.

'All right, don't go,' said Dada, trying to appease the boy. 'Stay here if you like it here – that's no problem.'

But his aunt's face wore a very worried look.

As the sun reached the meridian, the village lay in a stupor. Sparrows played among the paddy sheaves in the courtyard. Moina guarded the paddy with a stick, waving it and swinging her legs at the birds. Badal tossed and turned restlessly on the mat in the room. No, the fire was not burning through his body – the heat of his flesh did not make him tear his clothes off. But there was another fire, just as fierce, like the fire in the brick-kiln. He wanted to cover the flames of this fire with a coverlet. He wanted to cool the flames, with a nice cool coverlet. His desire for a cool coverlet was beginning to overwhelm him.

Moina peeped into the room just at that moment. Badal felt her like a cool breeze flowing over his body. But he lay still, not even opening his eyes. Moina muttered as she entered the room, glancing at Badal to see what was the matter with him. Her eyes glinted like diamonds in the stillness of the room.

All was quiet – silence everywhere. Badal lay on his mat, tingling with desire, prickly with heat. He could sense Moina as she entered the room on tiptoe, closing the door carefully behind her, coming to stand beside him.

His aunt seemed to be out on an errand. Unguarded as he was for the time being, Badal became as still as a corpse.

A violent, joyous, dream-like feeling seized him. He felt that the slightest breath – a touch – would make him invisible. And Badal held his breath in the stillness of the room.

Moina slowly tickled his back, with the stick to begin with, and then bending lower, she gently caressed his back with her hands. Her warm breath, her soft touch, drew languorous patterns on his skin and inflamed him with desire.

The fire inside him was rekindled and increased in intensity. His body could not contain or restrain the rising flames, which burst and spewed out of him. He could no longer bear the agony. He crushed Moina against him, tearing open her sari and exposing her breasts. He stopped Moina's mouth with his own burning lips. Moina's body felt soft like a pillow, and as lifeless. It was only her mouth that was struggling, trying to cry out – her voice came out strangled but somehow clear. Badal thought that he had finally found the cool shade that would quench his fire. This feeling lasted only a few seconds – and suddenly there was an explosion!

Moina shook herself out of his grasp. Her face was aflame – like a burning stove. She was panting and, without warning, she slapped Badal repeatedly. She hissed out at him, 'Lunatic! Deranged madman! You horrible man! Dwarf – how dare you reach out for the moon?'

With these disdainful words she ran out of the room.

Badal too sprang out of the room like a meteor. His whole body was on fire – his head, his face, his whole being. He remembered his mother – if only she had been here to douse his heat with the henna, if only Abdul had been here to drench the fire with buckets of water. He would have been soothed, the leaping flames of his fire would have been quenched.

The narrow village lanes were beckoning him with both hands, as Badal flew like the wind. He left the neighbourhood behind, passed the bamboo groves, ran through the paddy fields, over the canals, across the holy man's tomb and past the banyan tree. Badal raced on. But the wind only fanned the flames in his body – intensifying them, making them rise higher. He finally reached the banks of the river.

Agony – agony – agony!

Badal flung himself into the waters of the river. And finally, as he had always dreamed, Badal was floating and drifting on the waves. His *lungi* ballooned like the sails of a boat. He tried to grasp the wind with his excited hands. And a voice came out from his innards screaming, 'Moina!'

Calling Moina – and not Ma – Badal surrendered the desires and yearnings of his youth to the depths of his beloved river.

Baba and Dada arrived the following day from the city. Badal was no longer wearing his new *lungi* or his Terylene shirt. He was attired in peace, in quietness – finally at rest. He was adorned in the beautiful robes of peace.

Translated by Saeeda Karim Khan

DILARA MESBAH

The Ballad of Nihar Banu

Nihar Banu, O Banu, what are you doing? A disembodied voice floats up to her.

I'm roaming in the realm of my mind, breathing its pure ether. You understand, do you not, that it is my own realm? Here in its pleasure garden, beautiful plants and trees, the red *champak*, the *beli*, the *chameli*, and the lady-of-the-night waft forth fragrant breezes through the corridors of my mind. In this realm no one wounds another. And here in this world, if any son of a devil dare violate a virgin, I hang him straight away. This is the world of women, the abode of peace. It is not in my nature to praise myself, but still I feel that in today's world one has to beat one's own drum, otherwise no one bothers. That is why ...

So soliloquizes Nihar Banu calmly and firmly. Then she sways gently to her own rhythm.

She is unique and possesses the secret of being able to retreat into her own hidden world. As long as she is in this woman's world of hers, words come cascading forth. She's a beautiful, strong woman then.

But what about the rest of the time?

That's the strange thing. The rest of the time Nihar is a quiet, middle-aged cook. From dawn to dusk, she slogs in a Gulshan kitchen. She possesses a key to an amazing dreamland. In a moment she can fly up to that magnificent world of her mind. Whenever she feels suffocated, she lets her imagination fly on the wings of her much worn, striped sari. She has only to shut the store-room door, assume the lotus position and take deep breaths. She is whisked away to her pleasure palace. Who can touch her there? Who can hold her back? Her body might remain behind in this cursed world, but her mind is free to roam in womandom.

How beautiful and cool the air is in that realm! The garden bursts with flowers. Blue lotuses bloom in the lake. Birds sing melodious tunes. The white marbled floor is carpeted with velvet. The chair is made of ebony. Banu is the sole occupant of that throne brilliantly lit with multicoloured lamps. She holds the title clear, writ in letters of gold.

There is a lot of activity in the kitchen today. *Murgh polao* and pumpkin dessert are being prepared. The guests will arrive soon. The mistress of the house has gone to a beauty parlour to mar the little beauty she has left.

Perhaps the reader thinks that Nihar Banu is an illiterate woman, that she wears her sari any which way like a rustic, that she is just an ordinary woman.

But you'd be wrong. She has learned some rare meditative skills from her grandmothers and has received some education from her father. Her thirst for knowledge is very strong. Very few people see this side of hers. God has given her an innate strength.

Life's garland hangs around her neck. She is a sibyl, replete with knowledge of past, present and future, placed by accident in the shining kitchen of wealthy folk.

Of course, in the world of her imagination, she is a complete woman, self-sufficient, whole, lit by the spark of her personality. She is an uncommon woman, self-educated and proud of her accomplishments.

She is troubled by how women continue to be oppressed and to participate shamelessly in their own commodification. She is tormented by the thought of how men's soft words and touches succeed in trapping women. She invites famous women to discuss these issues. This communication of thoughts is essential for clarity, otherwise there is no hope. She engages in long, lively discussions with Khana. Chewing on her *paan*, she discusses life and love sometimes with the Queen of Sheba, at others with Chand Sultana. Sometimes Begum Rokeya opens the door and steps into the world of Nihar Banu's imagination.

Banu speaks humbly: Sister Rokeya, even a stupid person like me respects your greatness. You were the first person, Sister, to encourage womenfolk to improve their lot. How bravely you fought for them. But, what can I say, Sister? Women have not yet succeeded in improving themselves. They continue to allow themselves to be degraded. They continue to put up with insults. Bengali women are like stone on which moss has been gathering for ages. Sometimes I feel like weeping silently at this.

I am an ordinary woman, but my mind is struck by a thousand thoughts. I dream many dreams all night and all day. I know that even now my countrymen do not grant women their rights. They continue to deceive them. What have they to give? And how can they? They are puppets themselves, slaves of their senses. Barring a few good men, the rest are sick and blind. They cannot see even in bright light. Perhaps I am too small for such great thoughts. Please forgive me.

Banu trembles in the grip of an unknown joy and fear. She feels slightly feverish.

Banu, O Nihar Banu, do you know who you are? The invisible voice blends with the air perfumed by the scent of innumerable flowers. Who asks Nihar Banu this question? Who knows?

Who is this Nihar Banu?

Perhaps she is a special cook to a Mughal emperor or a self-educated and wise beauty of an ancient matriarchal society. Perhaps she is nothing more than a mere reciter of ancient manuscripts or even the eldest daughter of a born poet who has passed her childhood playing with the likes of Kanchanmala, Dalim Kumar, Saiful Mulk Bodiuzzarnan, Behula and Lakshindar.

Where did Banu get her knowledge of history? A woman born with an insatiable thirst for knowledge surely finds her own guru. Perhaps in the clear light of her unconscious mind characters from history flash before her eyes.

Occasionally Nihar Banu suffers from hallucinations. Women are often possessed by evil spirits. Nihar Banu is said to succumb to the spell of jinns. Cook Mubarak tactfully informs his mistress about Nihar's fits. Mubarak and Nihar Banu work together day and night under the same roof. But there is a spiritual aura around Banu that makes it impossible for the cook to exchange pleasantries with her. That is why Mubarak is upset with her. He sometimes gets so angry that his stomach growls. Why should a woman, particularly a kitchen maid, be so mysterious and spirited? Mubarak, a man full of fun and frolic, is given to light-hearted relationships with the maidservants. Up to now, like a second Krishna in Brindaban, Mubarak has had his way with all the women who have helped him in the kitchen. But this woman is an exception. She has no taste for such flirtations. She is a strange woman. Like an earthen wheel. On top of that she is quick-tempered. The slightest touch sets her off.

Is there anyone who can understand Nihar Banu? How is it possible for anyone to understand her? She can see through all of the history of ancient Bengal with her eyes closed. She sees women with beauty and power like lightning in their fists. She sees a life of immense possibilities. In her lie hidden the countless seeds of a bright, mysterious future.

Banu's throat becomes dry in her anxiety. Where is society heading? Life is so difficult. Prices are soaring. What will happen next to the teeming millions of this unfortunate country? Maybe there will be good days in future. Maybe women will some day take charge of this wretched society. When will this dream become reality? When? Banu's temple throbs.

Women are still humiliated. Alas! Will they forever be preserved like crystallized fruit in a glass jar? If they are allowed to breathe free in the open air, will the number of wild beasts increase in this wretched country? These vermin should be poisoned.

It is unbearable. Someone whispers in Banu's ear, Come woman, rest a while in the realm of your imagination. You do not have to busy yourself preparing delicious desserts. All will be ready in time. Your hands are as good as a machine.

After Nihar Banu's marriage broke up, she allowed no one to enter her life. A devil from hell cannot be her companion. She was born chaste and pure. She is nearing forty now. This is an age, of course, when the mind turns to thoughts of piety. Time is relative. The fires of youth are not so strong any more. Still, haven't you some desires left?

Who's asking? The prince of men? Banu chuckles to herself.

How long will I live? This question, too, often disturbs Banu's mind.

Suppose forty more years. The voice comes from nowhere.

N-o-o-o – N-o-o-o – , protests Banu loudly in her heart. One cannot live so long in this cruel world. It's an angry destiny.

Banu, why do you want to leave so early? You suffer from nothing other than a hot temper. It's fine if you want to live on green papaya, greens, mixed vegetables. But you have to have fish and meat sometimes. One also needs to dress up at times. Is it wrong for human beings to have dreams and desires?

Get lost. In the world of my imagination I wrap myself in fine muslin and sip fruit juice. But in this kitchen I am an avowed ascetic. Dress up for Mubarak? A devil from hell? A mountain of sin? He has a hundred and one mistresses. My whole body shivers in disgust.

With whom does Banu gossip?

Is it her fate or her subconscious mind that she speaks to?

No, no, she doesn't speak to a disembodied shadow. It is to her imaginary prince that she speaks. She met him in a dream. Perhaps she considers him her guide, her urban bard. He is not to be found anywhere, not in the lanes, nor in the streets, not in the fields nor in the *ghats*, not on a path through the fields nor on the bank of Sheoria – nowhere. He exists in Banu's eyes alone. Her immortal hero. He hangs like a garland of wild flowers round her neck.

Banu's five brothers and sisters have grabbed all the wealth and assets of their poet-father. This did not afflict her in the least.

Bravo to the independent woman with an aversion to material possessions. We adore you, we salute you.

The other day there was a grand festival in Banu's ethereal world. The city bard sang a song in her praise till late at night. She drew back in embarrassment. The bard sang on.

Applying superhuman strength, Nihar Banu brings herself back to the kitchen and the dessert she is preparing. Meanwhile her mistress's temper suddenly rises. She starts scolding Nihar Banu. She knows very well what sort of woman Nihar is. She knows that the possessed maid is good at her work, but she is moody.

Mubarak has a bad record. None of the maids who help him in the kitchen lasts for more than a year. Then things start to happen. The woman is always the scapegoat. And she has to leave without any justice meted out to her. It is quite impossible to fire Mubarak. Without him, the kitchen would come to a standstill.

All sorts of reports come in about Nihar Banu. That she composes poetry, that she is a mystic, that, closing her eyes and muttering to herself, she can disappear into an ethereal world.

Nihar Banu prepares the dessert carefully. All the guests are delighted with the delicious dish. Some are nostalgic, remembering the days of their childhood.

The guests promise to come again. They will come again to taste this dessert.

The hostess is flattered. It's nothing special. I'm glad that eating it has brought back memories of your childhood. Some day I'd like to treat you to different types of rice cakes.

Oh great, chant the guests in unison. Mrs Bhandaria is a wonderful hostess.

Nihar stands on the other side of the door. She had prepared various types of delicious rice cakes a week ago. Her mistress has no idea how to prepare them. The only thing she can do is gobble up two or three at a time. She praises Nihar, but in a miserly way. Nihar suppresses her desire to laugh.

A young woman says excitedly, I must learn the recipe of your pumpkin dessert one day.

Mrs Bhandaria nods her head. Of course, I will invite you again one day.

The symphony of crystal bowls and spoons continues. The gourmets continue to applaud Dilruba Bhandaria. She flushes in delight. Standing behind the door, Nihar Banu's heart beats rapidly at the falsehoods and lies of this world. She feels uneasy.

Banu feels impatient. Soon she spreads out the wings of her imagination. Very calmly she presents herself before the city bard and unlocks her mind to him. She tells him how everyone had waxed eloquent over her pumpkin dessert.

The bard sighs. This is nothing. People, most of all women, have to put up with even greater lies and deceptions.

Banu asks in a low voice, How long am I to live, O bard?

Why do you ask such a foolish question, daughter? That only the One above knows. Why are you so afraid of life, you free-spirited girl? Is human life so trivial a thing, he asks in anger.

Banu feels something exploding inside her. Her soul experiences a new pain. She feels greatly tempted to set out on a long journey, travelling the world in an endless quest, singing continually a paean to women.

What would happen if the city bard should leave the world of her imagination and descend to earth? Banu's heart trembles at the thought.

Who would share her weal and woe if she had to walk alone on the path of life?

What if there should be no one to accompany her? She knows how to tread the path of life alone. She is her own friend, philosopher and guide.

Translated by Niaz Zaman and Mirza Mamun Sadat

JHARNA DAS PURAKAYASTHA

Barbecue

Motionless, Jaitun stares out at the sky. There isn't much else she does these days than scan the sky. Wait for the sky to become seared by the sun, wait for the rain, wait for a snap of storm to whip out maddeningly, wait for a lash of lightning. Listlessly, Jaitun eyes the sky for a sign.

She stands all day, with her head pressed against the grille, barely touching the morsels that Khorshed the cook calls her to eat up.

And occasionally a gust of monsoon wind sends shivers through her. Not a word from her, tears well to a brim.

The old *ayah*, Rahima, deep in chores, cackles, Hey you, wretch, become a stone, have you? No work for you? And there you go gorging yourself with food. Do you have no speck of shame? Just look how you fat you've become, like a sheep.

Jaitun's mute eyes survey Rahima.

Mehnaz never comes to the servant's quarters. Now, however, she feels a stir, a soft, melting feeling. This girl is her new discovery.

What a terrible disaster had swept over the country. Storms befriended tidal bores, and together they razed huts and houses. The people were virtually washed away. Mehnaz had gone on relief work with her organization. She had found the girl then. Mother, father, brother, sister – the raging waves of the sea had swept them all out. To top it all, the girl's age was a source of worry too.

In the relief camp, she huddled in a corner. A tender face, scraggy hair – her arms folded across her bosom to hide her pubescent breasts.

Mehnaz saw this. Others stampeded for the gruel, made off with relief goods, fought like a pack of hungry dogs over parcels dropped from the helicopters – only Jaitun did not stir.

She would not ask for anything, she would not snatch at the *chira*, dried rice, *gur*, bread – the pale-faced girl never left her corner.

Mehnaz's heart was wrenched. The girl would starve to death. Blown ashore from Kutubdia, this girl did not understand that only the fittest survive, that the world belongs to the bravest. She would have to wake up to this knowledge. One survives in the world by constantly struggling. Existence is learning how to stick it through. Too, too young, she could not have known this.

Her heart softened with pity. Mehnaz had a huge house. She dwelt in the posh residential area of Dhanmondi. Her Lepchu dogs were fed on cooked bone *khichuri* twice a day. She had a luxuriantly furry milk-white cat, exotic fish in an aquarium. Perhaps she was acquiring one more pet, but the girl would live.

Jaitun stared around her in unabated bewilderment as she stepped into Mehnaz's house. A picture-book house. Not a whiff of dust. She stared around her unblinkingly. Mehnaz's daughters, Nausheen and Khushboo, fluttered around like breeze off a butterfly's wings.

From the Akai belonging to Mehnaz's son, Ananya, blared the sounds of the heavy-metal band Poison, 'Every Rose Has its Thorn'. The whole house quaked to the deafening sounds of the instrument.

Jaitun recoiled in terror. It seemed as though from the four corners of the earth a rampaging gust was about to tear in – just as it had that night. The immeasurable sea frothed. Huts were swept out, people disappeared in the torrent. The night swam before Jaitun's eyes in every detail. Mother, father, brother, sister, all her loved ones vanished once again. She lost consciousness.

On regaining her senses, she felt her innards cramping with hunger. Gradually, Jaitun grew aware of her surroundings.

She had known the sea from the time she was born. Yet it had become unfamiliar and unrecognizable. The barren waste was strewn with the mangled bodies of women, men and children, with carcasses of cows and calves. Some kind of fish smell broke through her stupor. A nauseous feeling welled up in her throat. Since that wild night she had eaten nothing. Her hands and legs had grown numb. She had no strength to sit up. Her sea-washed body was sticky with salt. Had she died?

No, she hadn't. Her breath was still rising and falling. The sharp pangs of hunger and thirst made her want to cry. Still, she knew that she hadn't died. She was alive. Jaitun was alive. The sea breeze rippled over her body. She could breathe that air. She could open her eyes in the brightly lit world and see once more. Suddenly, her eyes filled with salt tears.

Where shall I go?

The salt tears trickled down to her lips. She licked her tears with a parched tongue. Her throat, palate and tongue seemed to get back some sensation.

Her house was gone, her mother was gone, her brother and sister were gone, she had no one left. This thought made Jaitun cry again. Her mother would never again anxiously search for her.

Whoosh, whoosh, a few vultures passed above her head. She shuddered. Her skin broke out in goose-pimples. She seemed to hear the cry of a great desolation. That one storm and tidal bore had ended everything. Why had she survived, struggling all night, fiercely holding on to trees and branches? Her tiny heart was racked with guilt.

Shrieks, groans and wails could be heard on all sides. They were soon surrounded by people with happy faces, with not a care in the world. They walked around looking at the helpless victims of the storm. Numerous cameras flashed and clicked.

The cyclone victims closed in on the visitors, screaming in unison, No photos, no photos. Give us food. The young and robust grabbed all they could: *chira*, bread, anything that came by way of food. Jaitun got nothing. Weak with hunger, in the pitch-dark night she felt something hard in her hand. With great difficulty she strained her eyes open. She found herself holding a piece of pumpkin. The water had made it soggy.

Still, it was food. She scooped out the soggy flesh of the pumpkin with her nails and stuffed it into her mouth. Her tongue recoiled at the blandness, but she continued to eat. Ever since the storm she had been wandering about without a grain of food.

Putrid or pulpy, it was still food. The famished girl did not have the heart to throw it away. Tears rolled down her cheeks. She felt somewhat stronger. The pumpkin in her stomach made her sleepy. Sometimes a chilling wind blew across the desolate expanse; at those times she felt the scorching heat of the sun, and her limp body was caressed by a drizzle that felt like a fistful of *jui* flowers.

The blue sky was her roof above, the sand was her bed below. Days dawned and nights passed.

One day two naked children came up to Jaitun. They had matches and candles in their hands, pickings out of the airdrop by helicopters carrying relief goods. Some kind people had given them a bit of *chira* and *gur*. The two brothers had had to fight to keep these for themselves.

They became quite a nice family. The two little ones had grown weak with hunger and thirst. Walking along the shore, they came across a dead fish. Jaitun recognized the fish.

She built a fire with scraps of paper and dead leaves. Gusts of wind blew out the fire.

The three circled around the fire to keep it going. If only the fish could be grilled over the fire. Dry *chira* and *gur* and wholemeal bread stuck in their throats. The water spewed bodies and carcasses, it was no good for drinking – it made them want to throw up.

There was a scarcity of water all around. People from the city came to advise them to drink purified water. Here you are, water purifying tablets. One in a pitcher of water will give you water clean enough to drink.

Oh Allah, Jaitun wished to scream – water, pitcher – what are they going on about?

And then the fish was half-broiled – enough to make three pairs of eyes gleam. Jaitun pulled at the half-broiled fish with two fingers, putting the tiny pieces into her mouth. The two little ones also ate. Unsalted, with not a drop of oil, it was still heavenly to eat!

The little boy said to Jaitun, You have had yours, this is mine.

Jaitun's eyes filled with tears. With her hunger quelled temporarily, they were tears of joy.

Countless people came to look at them as though they were watching a movie. They took pictures, talked to them. Words, hard and difficult to understand, deafened Jaitun.

Gorky, typhoon, cyclone, hurricane – Jaitun had never heard these words before. Now she knew. When people drowned, when human corpses and carcasses of animals lay side by side, when countless people, animals, birds were wiped out, when villages disappeared, when the coastline was emptied of all life – then people from the city would begin to troop in. They would come in droves, taking pictures countless times, saying hard, incomprehensible things.

Suddenly a chapped hand shakes Jaitun awake roughly, tugs on her tangled hair making her sit up. She stares dumbly.

Rahima laughs loudly, Why, you wretch, sleeping like a queen, Why are we never this lucky?

So she has been sleeping on the floor all this time! The days in the old storm were a dream. The dream hadn't seemed like a dream. It had seemed all too real!

Ananya's Akai had stopped playing 'Every Rose Has its Thorn' quite a while ago.

The house has been looking festive since the morning. The whole house has been done up. Flowers have been arranged in vases, music is playing on the Akai.

Jaitun stands apart and stares with fixed eyes. Precious items, stored away for special occasions, have been taken out. Beautiful accessories line the walls, dazzling the eye.

Towards evening, garden chairs are put out on the lawn. The whole lawn has been lit up with countless party lights. What an incredible night!

There's not a spot of cloud in the sparkling blue sky. The moon hangs like a silver ball.

What's going on? Jaitun asks slowly.

Busy Khorshed looks at her, Who knows what you stare at all day? Can't you understand anything? There's a barbecue on tonight, a barbecue.

Barbecue, barbecue, Jaitun repeats this hard new word over and over again.

Mehnaz busily makes for the kitchen and asks Khorshed, All taken care of, Khorshed?

Yes, Ma'am.

The chickens are prepared?

Yes.

Bring the charcoal and skewers to the lawn.

Mehnaz's eye catches Jaitun standing in a corner. Motionless as a picture. Her heart goes out to the girl again. The organization's president, Flora Ahmed, had said, If we don't look after them, who will? You are so generous, Mehnaz.

The recollection makes Mehnaz smile serenely. She ruffles Jaitun's tangled hair.

Mehnaz's pink silk sari, embroidered with glass sequins, reeks of 'Cobra'. Jaitun draws her breath in sharply. She feels as if she is in a fragrant garden.

Barbecue, barbecue.

She repeats the word to herself. Difficult words like this make her heart stop. Something tells her a storm will come again, another upheaval. The neat houses will crumble and be washed away. A little later, an uncontrollable squall will rise. The sky will break into torrents. The sea will begin to hiss.

She wants to hear more difficult, incomprehensible words. The century's most devastating storm will return! All these carefully decorated houses will collapse. Children playing in the fountains of joy will be flung about all over.

These horrors don't intimidate Jaitun any more. She laughs to herself. What does she have to fear? She has nothing more left to lose – she is all alone in the world. In this whole world there is no one she can call her own.

She slowly walks towards the lawn. A huge mass of chicken lies on one side. Uncountable skewers wait beside red-hot charcoals. Some pieces of marinated chicken broil on the coals.

Jaitun looks on quietly. The memory of a half-broiled *taki* fish eaten on the shores floods back to her. Her heart begins to throb.

What's going to happen today? A storm – a typhoon?

Her tiny heart fills with delight. Everyone's pots and pans will be washed away. Pot hangers, mirrors, coloured glass bangles, red ribbons – everything will be swept away by the storm, not just Jaitun. The storm will make everyone homeless. A troubling thought strikes Jaitun. She has heard of Gorky, she has heard of hurricanes, she has heard of typhoons – but she has never heard of a barbecue. Perhaps this kind only demolishes city houses, made of bricks, timber and mortar.

Let the storm come, let it destroy the world completely. The storm showed no kindness to her, did it?

Jaitun keens: O you orphans.

She weeps until her tiny heart is set ablaze.

Let it all go, let it all be destroyed. If the Jaituns of the world can be washed away innumerable times – have to build homes anew – why shouldn't houses made of brick, wood and mortar, with red-carpeted drawing rooms be washed away? Why shouldn't the decorated walls collapse?

Was God to destroy only the huts of Jaitun, Nabitun, Sabura, Halimun, Batashi and. Mariam?

She laughs with cruel pleasure.

But what is the blazing charcoal fire for?

What are they going to do with so many chickens, so many skewers? A feast for everyone, before the storm, was that what it was?

Why isn't the storm coming? Jaitun sobs piteously.

From the lawn float sweet chimes of laughter, tinkles that sound like the breaking of glass bangles.

Mehnaz's two daughters, Nausheen and Khushboo, are laughing. Jaitun looks up at the sky again. Where's the cloud? There's not a speck of cloud anywhere. Instead, the heavy smell of chicken roasting over charcoal spirals into the sky. The air is filled with the scent of tuberoses in Jaipuri vases.

One guest bursts out in raucous laughter, Quite a primitive affair, isn't it? Many thanks for returning us to the days of cavemen.

Everyone relishes biting into the barbecued chicken. Flora rocks on the swing. Mehnaz sits seductively under the large canopy.

Isn't the barbecue coming? Isn't there any storm or typhoon in the city? Jaitun's eyes grow pensive. Why do storms and tidal bores come only for them?

Their dreams are very simple – all they want is a small dwelling, that's all – nothing more. A bit of steaming rice with onions, chillies and potatoes mashed with tangy mustard oil in the mouth is tastier than anything else in the world. Washed rice with tamarind – that's also great.

Then why must the dreams of Nabitun, Sabura, Halimun continue to be devastated by heartless storms?

At one end of the lawn, a couple of young boys sing Phil Collins songs.

Suddenly a low muttering sob is heard. Who is that whining? Crying so piteously? Who is interrupting the heart-pumping music being played in the garden? The carefully planned barbecue is upset by the whining.

Go to hell, Mehnaz's eyes look red. She screams, Khorshed, Bua, Ayah, Rehan, Ananya, Rahima – who is crying?

Hasan is disconcerted when Mehnaz gets excitable like she is now. Dear, don't be so perturbed. You are not well. Your blood pressure will start fluctuating.

Dr Yusuf enquires, Who is crying? Jaitun? Oh, the girl Mehnaz brought from Kutubdia? The girl didn't talk. I suppose she's crying today. This is a very, very good sign.

Everyone gathers around Jaitun.

How strange! A barbecue is on in the house. There are heaps of chickens being roasted. The guests smack their lips in relish. In the middle of all this, why is this starving skeleton wailing?

Khushboo loses her temper. Mummy, why did you have to bring this girl? Send her away, anywhere she pleases.

Ah, Mehnaz serenely replies. Don't say things like that, Khushboo. Here, you, what's wrong with you? Why are you crying? What's wrong, what's wrong? Someone has said something perhaps?

Why isn't the storm coming? Jaitun gasps between her sobs.

Nausheen rolls with laughter. Oh, why isn't the storm coming? Is that what all this is about?

The two sisters, Khushboo and Nausheen, laugh their heads off.

The music of accordions and drums, the party and fun, the roasted meat, the perfume-sprayed sari *aanchals* fluttering, a moonlit barbecue – Jaitun's question turns all of it into a huge lie.

Translated by Niaz Zaman with Nuzhat Amin Mannan

NIAZ ZAMAN

The Daily Woman

The thought of the other child would come at odd times. Like when she was picking the rice, or sweeping the floor, or grinding the red chillies that made her hands smart. At the beginning she had thought of it – her, really, but the child had been taken so early from her that she rarely thought of it as her – when the little one who remained strained at her thin breasts. There had been so little milk for even this one that she had none to spare for the other. This one was a boy. Everyone said boys were better. They would look after you in your old age, they said. That is, if the daughters-in-law let them. Also this one had been bigger. More chance of surviving.

Every year for the last five years – she had been married one year before the first one was born – she had given birth. Not one had lived beyond a day or two. And she had thought that she too, like Fatema, was cursed. And then, she had the two together. Together, they were only a little bigger than the little ones who had died. How long would these two live, she had wondered. Would they too die after two days as the other little ones had? But three days passed, and they were still there. Only one had seemed smaller and weaker than the other. More like a wrinkled old woman. Then the two white men had come to see her with Abdul. And almost before she realized it, there was only one child left.

She did not pause as she ground the chillies. *Ghater ghat, ghater ghat.* The heavy stone roller smoothed the dry, red pods into paste. One did not have to think when one ground chillies, so one could think about the other things one had no time for. A few dabs of water, and then off again, *ghater ghat, ghater ghat*, as the soft, red, paper-thin skins melted into the flat, yellow seeds and merged to form red paste. A pause to stretch her back, and then another dab of water, and the roller started going back and forth on the smooth grindstone. She must tell them to have the stone pricked once more. The pockmarks all over had disappeared. The auspicious fish design on top had also completely faded. It was really too smooth to grind the chillies. Most people had started buying powdered chillies, but there were some who liked their spices ground fresh every day, so there was still some work for daily women like her who could not work *bandha*.

She washed the grindstone. Put it back in its place under the sink. What was it like to work *bandha*, she wondered. To leave husband and children and remain in other people's houses. At least for people who worked *bandha* there was a dry place to sleep in at night. In the hut, during the rainy months of Asharh and Sraban, everything got wet. One's clothes, one's floors – everything. The smooth, hard floor, which she smeared with a mixture of cow dung and mud so that it was almost as nice as Khalamma's floor, turned to muddy paste. But people who worked *bandha* slept inside. There were some even luckier. Like Ali, who got a room all to himself, next to the kitchen. It was small, just big enough for a narrow *chowki*, and when there were guests, the drivers would be given food in his room, so he was expected to keep it clean and just as Khalamma wanted it. But Ali could stretch out there after his fourteen- or sixteen-hour duty – not like some others who could not go to sleep until everyone else had gone to sleep, because one never knew when the guests would leave or who would want to come into the kitchen for a glass of water or a cup of tea.

The bundle on the ground stirred. Even before the tiny eyes opened and the mouth started its fine wail, she had scooped it up and put it to her breast, covering it modestly with her sari *anchal*, so that the head of the baby was inside the *anchal*, and only the ragged *kantha* with which she covered its frail limbs was visible. She had promised Khalamma that the baby would not disturb anyone. Khalamma would never hear it cry. The nursing soothed the baby, and it was hardly a moment or two before it went back to sleep, its hunger satisfied for the time being. She waited a moment longer to make sure it would not wake up and fuss as soon she put it back on the ground. Satisfied that it was asleep, she put it back, tucking the soft *kantha* round the little body so that it would think it was still being held to her breast. She was fortunate that she could bring the child to work with her. Not like Fatema who had to leave her baby at home. Fatema had not been able to give up her job because she had a paralysed husband who couldn't work. And she hadn't been able to bring the baby with her to work. The baby had to be given a bottle because Fatema could not always come back to feed it. And when the baby died, the health worker said the milk had killed the baby. And now Fatema's husband too was dead. It was true that in a way Fatema was better off without a paralysed husband, but what woman would rather work than have a family? And who would marry Fatema now? A woman who had killed her husband and child? A black-foreheaded woman? But weren't all women black-foreheaded? Well, not all. Not her Khalamma. Every day a fresh sari and shoes the same colour as her sari. And she smelled nice all the time. Sometimes like roses. Was this what Paradise must smell like?

Ali handed her the fish and explained that it had only to be scaled and its insides cleaned out. Not cut. Khalamma wanted it to be made into a *bideshi* dish, so she must be careful with it. And leave the tail whole. Be sure not to nick the tail the slightest bit. After it was cooked it would look like a fish – only its scales would be golden because of the carrots. Occasionally, when she had cleaned the fish, she had slipped one or two pieces of fish into her waist knot, but she wouldn't be able to today, she thought. But the insides she could keep. They never had any use for them. Even Ali scoffed at her for eating what she was sure he ate with relish back home. The oil was particularly good to cook with *sag*, made it special. Perhaps Ali would let her have some of the cauliflower leaves that they threw away. These rich people did not know how to cook. They threw away chicken skins as well. One hardly needed anything more than a pinch of salt, a dab of oil and two pinches of *haldi* and chillies to make a tasty meal out of chicken skins. They never ate the feet either. The first day she had come to work, she had cleaned the feet and put them in with the cut and cleaned chicken. Ali had scolded her. Since that day she had kept the feet aside to take home with her. After removing the feathers carefully, she had enough skin to make into a dish for two meals.

Fridays were bad days, because that was when the weekly bazaar came and everything had to be cut and cleaned and put away in the cold box. Khalamma would be rushing in and out of the kitchen because that was the day Khalu would have lunch, and no matter how late the bazaar came he had to have it by one o'clock. In most houses the men went to the mosque for Friday prayers, but Khalu didn't. On Fridays her back hurt with all the cutting and cleaning, and she could rarely make it home before *asr* prayers. But Friday was also a good day for her. Because she could carry home all the *bashi* stuff, like the old vegetables that had been kept in the fridge and gone a little stale and dry. Fridays were also the days after their parties, and there would be *polao* to be scraped up from the *hari*, in addition to the *khabar* that Khalamma always kept for her. Nice things like chicken *korma* or beef *kupta*. Once or twice there had been *biryani* and pieces of chicken *musallam* with *badam* and *kishmish*. And of course there were always sweets. Especially *roshgulla* and *shandesh* and *laddoo*. And *halwa*.

The clothes were already soaking in a pail of warm, soapy water. She had learned this new way of washing from Khalamma. When Khalamma had first poured the soap powder into the pail and told her to wash, she had been perplexed. How was she to wash the clothes without rubbing them with soap and then beating them on the *pucca* floor? Then Khalamma had shown her how the water was full of soap and all she had to do was to rub the clothes against themselves or each other. There was no need to beat the clothes, just go rub, rub, rub, dip once more in the soapy water and keep aside. After the white clothes were all out of the soap water there were a few more clothes – red, yellow, blue – that had to be kept dry and then dipped one by one quickly into the water so that the colours did not run into other clothes. Then she could throw away the discoloured water and fill the bucket with clean water to rinse the clothes. Once, twice, thrice, so that there was no more soap left in the water and the water seemed as clean as fresh water. Then squeeze all dry, all of them, except the nylon ones. Those had to be hung until the water had all dripped out and then hung out smoothly so that there were no wrinkles in them. And then she could have her *chapati* and hot tea. It was always a pleasure to have sweet, hot tea. Two spoons of sugar in the tea – though Khalamma herself always had tea without any sugar. How did they drink tea without sugar? She grimaced at the thought of the sugarless tea that Khalamma drank.

Ali explained to her that Khalamma was afraid of getting fat. All *barolok* were afraid of getting fat. That's why she did not have sugar with her tea. Nor rice nor potatoes. Sometimes she would go on what Ali called a diet. Then she would have nothing but tea and toast in the morning and cucumber in the afternoon. At night, however, she would eat with Khalu – a spoon of rice only, however, or one *chapati*, the small *chapati* she had Ali make for the table, not the big, fat ones that Ali made for the kitchen help and himself. They were allowed three of the *chapatis* with their tea. One she ate sitting in the kitchen, but the other two she took home with the leftover *bhaji* or *jhol*. In that way she only needed to cook a pot of rice for him.

Sometimes she wondered whether, if she had this job when the babies were born, she would have given the little one away. But she could not have brought both with her to work. Of that she was sure. And then it was only after the babies were born that she had met Abdul when he came with the *bideshis* and afterwards got her the job at Khalamma's place. Ali was from the same village as Abdul. That is how Abdul had known that Khalamma was looking for a daily woman to help in the kitchen. He had come with her and told Khalamma that he knew her – though he really didn't. But he had to say it otherwise Khalamma would not have given her the job. And after that day she had never seen him again. Rahima had told her that Abdul must have got a lot of money from the *bideshis*. But she could not believe it. Why would they give the money to him and not to her?

She didn't know whether Abdul had got money, all she remembered was that those had been bad days. The days that they had first come to Dhaka from the village because the river had taken away the last bit of their land. She shivered, remembering those days. Everyone had told them how easy it was to get work in the *shahar*, and they had believed what they heard. There were always roads to be broken or built, and houses high as the sky, sprouting like frog umbrellas after the rains. And if one didn't get work as a day labourer, there were always rickshaws to pull in the city. Sometimes people said there were as many rickshaws in Dhaka city as there were people. One could keep all the money one earned after deducting what one had to pay to the *mahajan*. People in town didn't walk. So there was a lot of money in pulling rickshaws. But rickshaw pulling hadn't been easy. His legs and arms had ached and she had to heat mustard oil and rub him down. And then he had fever for three days, and she had to buy medicine for him. And during the rains no one wanted rickshaws, because everyone stayed home and there was no building either and they starved. Then they had to pay for the *chhapra* – something they had not reckoned with. Two hundred for a place hardly big enough for the two of them to sleep in at night. And always the rain coming down, making everything wet, making the floor into mud. Then the fever had come back, and he had coughed until she thought his eyes would jump out of his head. His body had felt like fire, and she had prayed that he wouldn't die. She had promised that if he lived she would fast seven days so she had fasted and the babies had popped out before the ten months and ten days that babies took to be ready were over.

How hungry she had been, and the two babies crying together were enough to make her go mad. No one she knew had ever had two babies together. No one in the *para* had seen two babies together, and everyone had come to see her and the babies. The white men had also come with Abdul to see her. The man with the red beard had explained to her – sometimes himself – but when she could not understand the way he spoke, Abdul had explained that the other white man wanted to take her child, if she would give it up, seeing she had two. The man wanted to take a Bangladeshi child because he had stayed many years in Bangladesh as a child. Now that he was grown up, and his wife and he could not have children, they wanted to adopt a Bangladeshi child. Abdul explained to her that the white man would look after the child well. Then too she must realize that she had nothing to eat herself. How could she feed one child, let alone two? So she had said yes. God who gave her two children who lived would give again some other day. The white man who wanted the child said he would bring his wife the next day. He wanted the child to be a surprise to her. That is why he had not brought her. He wanted to see the child first himself. They had been disappointed earlier.

She had looked at the girl child for a long time the next morning. But she had felt nothing in her heart for the child. She did not even feel a sense of relief that the child would have a future. Amrika was too far away for her to know anything about it. All that she knew about it was that these tall, pinkish-white people came from there. She didn't believe it when Rahima told her that black people also came from there. She had seen no black Amrikun. Only these pinkish-white people in their big cars, driven by smart drivers like Abdul. Rahima told her that she was doing a bad thing and God would be angry with her. In Amrika they would make her child pray to Jishu. She would surely go to hell because she let her child go with kristans. But Amrika and kristan did not make much sense to her. All she could remember was how hungry she had been all the time, and if it had not been for the scraps of food that Rahima gave her, surely she herself would have starved and the babies too.

The two men had come the next day, and the white woman with them. She looked old enough to be the man's mother. White hair and wrinkles near her eyes. And thin. No breasts. Or behind. Flat as a dried fish. Her arms were like jute stalks and the big round bangles made them look even thinner. Everyone gathered round their *chhapra* to look at the *bideshini* who had come to take her little one away. The man with the red beard explained that there were some papers to be signed – a *tip shoi* would also be all right, if she couldn't sign her name. Just to show that the baby had been voluntarily given up by the parents, not stolen or kidnapped. Some papers were in English, some in Bengali. The same thing in both. One for the authorities in Bangladesh, one for the Amrikuns.

The *bideshini* held out her arms for the child. As she put the thin, wrinkled old woman into the white woman's arms, she had thought how dark her little one looked next to the white woman's skin. The woman saw her looking at her arms and muttered something to her husband. The man took the child from his wife and stared at it as if he was seeing a baby for the first time. The wife took off her shiny, golden bangles and slipped them on to her wrists. She had not wanted to take the bangles. She was not selling her child for gold, but because she could not feed it.

The woman bared her grey teeth in a smile and patted her arms.

After the car drove away, the people continued to crowd around them. She went back inside her *chhapra* where there was only one little figure now, sleeping peacefully, undisturbed by the departure of the sister he would never know. The child stirred, and she picked it up, just to feel it was there. One at least. Proof that she was a mother, not like the *bideshini*, who, despite all her gold, could not be a mother. The golden bangles glistened against her dark skin. And, despite herself, she wondered how much they were worth. Enough to feed them for ten years, surely. How was she to keep the bangles safe so that no one stole them? After all, the whole *para* had seen the *bideshini* giving her the bangles. She would take the bangles off at night and tie them into her waist knot so that no one could steal them without her waking up.

When Rahima came in late that night after her work, she showed her the bangles, somewhat embarrassed, lest Rahima think she had sold her baby. But Rahima had laughed. Those are not gold, she said. They're brass. She drew her arms back from Rahima. No, she had not sold her baby. But she could not believe that a *bideshini* would wear brass, much less give brass to a poor woman whose child she had taken. I have seen gold, said Rahima, if you haven't and I know what is gold and what isn't. Go with me to the goldsmith tomorrow if you don't believe me.

So the next day she went with Rahima to the goldsmith and tried to sell the bangles to him. But the goldsmith had laughed, yes, laughed. Not asked her where she had stolen the bangles from. He didn't buy brass, he told her. She could get maybe twenty takas from the *bikriwala* for the bangles, maybe even twenty-five depending on their weight. But not from him.

She sighed and drank the last of her tea. So that was what a Bangladeshi girl child was worth. Two brass bangles. She picked up the boy. Would he have been worth four brass bangles?

SYEDA FARIDA RAHMAN

Roots

You're Manosh. I'm Shyama. I remember the 1.20 flight taking off from the Old Airport. Whooshing up to the sky, carrying you inside. How close we were once. Stringing words together endlessly, talking of ourselves. How easily time would pass, as if we had all eternity to ourselves. Our feet never touched the ground when we were together – we would fly on golden wings. You'd ask me to meet you at the canteen – I'd be there. You'd tell me to be at Ramna – the moments we shared sitting by the lake in the park, having coffee at the restaurant, sipping a soft drink – I can remember everything. Gliding over the Buriganga on a boat – always wanting still more of the blue sky above and the green of nature far away. You'd take the oars and row the boat quite easily, yet you wouldn't fit in – too handsome to be a boatman. The boatman would laugh, so would I. I couldn't swim, the waves would frighten me – you would laugh at me. You were a good swimmer – laughing, you'd rock the boat.

We were both students at Dhaka Medical College. You would run to the classes. Stand close to me during the practicals. I'd jab you with my elbow, you'd push back with your chest. Laughing and teasing while dissecting male and female bodies, neither ashamed nor embarrassed.

Then one day we were both doctors. You came and told me you were going to Iran – to make me say that I would come with you. You were hurt when I refused, you offered marriage. – Oh Manosh, was I born only for you, wasn't I a person in my own right? And wasn't that person special to you at all? I avoided your proposal or perhaps I was forced to. You thought me cruel. In the end, you didn't go – for some other reason. You always thought of yourself as the victor – triumphant – you never could accept losing.

It was decided that your family would settle in India. Your brother was a doctor – so was your sister-in-law. So was your father. Our dream was in tatters, Manosh. You left for the other side. This Bengal and that Bengal – two Bengals under the same sky. The sky, the air, the light – these had not been divided in '47, just the borders. There's no Pakistan now – just Bangladesh.

I was left on this side of the border – you crossed to the other side. You found security there, though you didn't make a name for yourself. Taking revenge on me? Perhaps people are vindictive when they have the power to avenge themselves. But unless you're empty inside why do you still write to me? I can feel your yearning in your words. What is it that you lack, Manosh? You were the prince of Dhaka Medical College. You performed your duties with joy in the corridors, the passages, the rooms – so alive. Are you a prisoner in a gilded cage today?

You misunderstood me. You knew we lived in Shankharipatti, my parents, my brothers and sisters. We returned from West Bengal after the Liberation War was over, looking for my father and my widowed elder sister. Mother had been able to escape with my younger brother and sister. My elder sister wouldn't leave our father behind. Her tattered sari was found hanging from trees and shrubs, caught on the branches. A shopkeeper had seen her being taken away. Those animals must have ravaged her beautiful body first. Then jackals and dogs must have eaten what was left of her. After a year, there was nothing left to cremate even if we could have identified her. All that we could find after searching the ashes, the burnt heap that was our house, was the iron frame of my father's wheelchair. We didn't have to have him cremated. Their tortured spirits still live in the wind. Everyone said that I'd better stay on in West Bengal – I couldn't. I dislike being a burden on anyone. When we returned, we

started to live in the windowless, doorless, burnt-up skeleton of our house.
I had no regrets; I had you, my country – we were free – and there was
Bangabandhu – our beloved leader. No, I was never involved in politics,
but love for one's country – that is something innate.

Only once in my life did I get to meet the greatest leader of our nation
face to face. I had longed to see him up close. He didn't want to know
my name, caste, religion or anything. When he heard I was a medical
student, he put his hand upon my head and blessed me, 'Be a doctor and
serve your county, my dear, you are the wealth of this country, the pride
of this nation.' And a leader like that was murdered. Our future became
silent – darkness descended.

It was then that you came, wanting to leave for Iran. You left, and I
was alone – soon very alone. I had been offered a scholarship then. I was
wondering whether to accept or not. I was to study in London, leaving
my country behind, for three years. All of a sudden, a colleague, Shahana,
showed me your wedding invitation – it was as if someone had sawed
my heart in two. I didn't delay any longer. I flew away over the seas, to an
unknown country.

Later I heard from Dr Kamal that you wanted to jump off the roof
when you heard I had left. But why? I wasn't burning with jealously or
revenge – your rejections were what pushed me ahead in life. I work at
the Holy Family Hospital. I check the patients' pulses, check their eyes,
push my stetho up against their chests. I free babies from their mothers'
wombs.

Nearly twelve years have passed since then. That chapter of my life is a
pale memory – even memories of you are fading. What else could I have
done? Life is a hard road to travel on. I put down the paper I'm holding,
and you're standing in front of me like a dream. I am surprised. You roam
all over the house, looking at everything, but your eyes never leave me.
You ask for my forgiveness again and again. You ask me desperately, do I
still love you? Why is there no vermilion in the parting of my hair? You
will end my loneliness. You will come back and marry me. Emotions were
what controlled your life – they still do. Don't you understand, Manosh,
how deep my roots have spread into this country? Can love ever end? At
all stages of life, one must embrace love – in the empty spaces – in the
deep recesses. That is the essence of love.

You want to take me to your ancestral home in the village, just to look at it. We hit the road – the two of us. We board the ferry at Aricha – seeing the Padma as we go on our way – you eat some crisply fried fresh *hilsa* with relish. You used to love beef once. We get off at Daulatdia. Then continue on a bus. When the bus reaches the end of its route, we take a boat. The boat glides along the river. We can see the villages on both sides. The river is the Kumar. Farmers bathe their cows on the riverbanks. Boys stop splashing about in the water. They watch you – they watch me too. Maybe we are glittering in the sunlight. I peep out from within the boat, you sit outside, like a prince. You eat chips from a packet you are holding. You do like eating.

After the boat journey, we take the grassy path through the village. There are trees on both sides. You pass swiftly over the field dividers. I stumble and trip forwards. It's getting late. You look at the mango grove and say, 'Do you remember, Shyama? I say "Mother" and my soul cries out.' I laugh at you trying to be poetic. A cuckoo trills from within the bamboo grove. You say, 'Shyama, why don't we spend a night here?'

I say, Why? – to comment on the moon rising over the bamboo grove? Or to watch it silently?

You tell me how a boy you knew, Nayan, would play the flute on moonlit nights – his music could steal your heart. Nayan died in the war. As we pass by a yard, you tell me, this was Shona Mia's house. He was so young and strong. He never came back from the war. This house used to be so alive. We reach a narrow path through the meadows – date trees line the path on both sides. One of the things you loved doing when you were a child was to steal the pots collecting sap from the date trees late at night and drink from them. Even the winter nights were filled with the fun of those stolen pots of drink for you.

But Shyama, you don't know that stolen food tastes better.

You cross the bamboo spanning the canal without stopping, talking all the while. I inch along fearfully. When I finally reach the other side I find you embracing a young man – Nawshad, a childhood friend of yours. He's a teacher at the village school now. He wants to take us with him, but you say, Later, I want to see my home first. His face lights up with joy.

Some young boys come towards us, knotting their *lungis* round their waist – they sing in their cracked voices, My Golden Bengal, I Love You.

They can't hold the tune – but they sing anyway. They stop when they notice us. An old woman hobbles towards us leaning on a stick. You say, Aunt Sharoda? I'm Manosh. Don't you know my father? Dr Bhabani Mohan Das.

The toothless old woman smiles, showing her gums – Oh, you're Bhabani's child? How can I recognize you, son, you've grown up so? You look like a prince – is this is your wife? Oh, as pretty as a picture.

I look away. Thank God, I'm wearing a large red dot on my forehead, or perhaps she would have asked a lot of other questions. She probably hasn't noticed my unreddened hair parting because of her obviously weak eyesight. The old woman asks, Where will you stay? You've sold your house and gone off to Hindustan. I live in a reed shack – clinging on to this soil – such love for this bit of earth! Your mother was a wonderful person – she gave me so much.

You reach into your pocket and push some money into her hands. She smiles her toothless smile, blessing you.

You try to think of other things. A palanquin carried by four singing bearers crosses us. You ask me, Have you ever seen a palanquin? Look over there. My grandmother – my mother – used to ride in a palanquin when visiting her father or returning to her in-laws. The palanquin climbs noisily up the canal bank and moves out of sight. You say, Every Baishakh there used to be a fair in that field, over there in front of that Shiva temple. You point with your eyes, even further away – See that smoke rising there? That's the cremation ground. The Arial Khan used to flow by that bank. Now the river has moved far away – the sandbanks have risen.

You look sad. I can see your home, two-storeyed and white, through the coconut and betel nut trees. Water lilies bloom in the large pond, ducks glide about. The concrete *ghat* is large and overgrown with moss. This is where you would bathe as a child – if you felt like it, you'd go for a swim in the Kumar. There's a huge Kali temple just beside your home. Your mother and grandmother would do the *arati* there every evening and pray for your well-being. There would be a huge *mandap* at each *pooja*. What fun you used to have. Everyone would eat of the *prasad* – caste and religion didn't matter in your village. That Shonamukhi was a golden village!

The cowherds return home with their cows. The village brides walk home slowly with their water-pitchers held to their waists. A flock of birds flies overhead. The conch sounds mournfully, the bell rings at the temple – it feels as if we are totally alien here. As if we have come back to the banks of the Dhanshiri in the guise of birds, the *shankhachil* and the *shalik*. But here is the banyan, under whose shade the weary traveller rests, where the cowherd falls asleep allowing his cows to stray into the fields. That boy, Nayan, would play the flute late into the night. The *baul* would sing, strumming his *ektara*. The *Vaishnab* and *Vaishnabis* would sing here in groups. The barber would shave people and clip their nails – there was no question of caste or religion. This banyan is a witness – to time and to love.

The enormous tree spread its roots, occupying a lot of land – no one objected or resented it. Why, the tree was an ancestor more ancient than our fathers or grandfathers! A tree as revered as they were! The old tree, uprooted, lies like a mountain, closing the path to Manosh's home.

You sigh. Tears drop from expressionless eyes. I am silent too. The sun says farewell to all nature – just as people say goodbye and become distant – so distant.

Translated by Shabnam Nadiya

PARAG CHOWDHURY

Why Does Durgati Weep?

The sky'd been sombre since dawn. So late into the day now and still no sign of the sun. It rained cats and dogs last night. All night the water drip-drip-dripped along the rotten thatch roof. The two of them moved the bed two or three times. This corner, that corner. But it was the same everywhere. The thatch full of holes all through like a sieve. Put up ages ago, when Ma was still alive. Could Jamila afford to have it thatched again then? Meantime, her sleep disturbed, her stupid daughter began to weep, then calmed herself.

Jamila felt lazy in the heat. As if her body wanted to drop off at the joints. She felt like spreading her body on the cool floor and sleeping. But was there time to laze about? Her housework was done. Now she had to go and finish her work at the Mia's place. They were cutting the wheat and threshing it. Her job was to sift and separate the wheat after the men had threshed it. She wasn't fortunate enough to be able to laze around. By this time Elder Wife's screams must be burning up the beams of the ceiling. Before she left the house, covering her head with her *anchal*, Jamila looked into the house. She saw that her daughter still hadn't stopped whining and crying. These few days there was only one song she'd sing – She's gotta have a red sari like Shanu. Jamila's body was burning. She felt like crushing the girl's skull with the wooden stool. The next moment she felt tenderness. Slow-witted dumb girl. She called out in a tender voice – Durgati, O Durgati, don't cry, honey. Get up. Eat the *panta* and then take the chickens ...

– Won't eat the *panta*, won't do no work neither. Durgati felt the tenderness in her mother's voice and fumed. The distress in her listless voice seemed to grow.

– Listen. Listen to me. Jamila appeared conciliatory. Listen to what I'm sayin'. Soon as the chicks are a bit bigger, I'll sell 'em off. Then I'll be able to buy you your red sari, silly. Else who'll be givin' me the money?

Durgati's eyes sparkled. One look into her eyes'd tell you that the girl didn't have much sense to speak of. As if her eyes were the waterhole behind the house. Or a bowl of dirty water. There was no shadow of anything. Never had the shadow of the blue sky fallen within. So dopey and dim-witted. Some sunlight glinted within the dull calf eyes.

– Really, Ma. Will ye buy it fer me? Don't be too late today. Then I be cryin' again. I be cryin', Ma. I say I be cryin'.

Yup, Durgati sure could cry. Her habit of crying came at birth. Any excuse she'd get, she'd start crying as if a beetle were humming away. People had so many different kinds of fancies. Crying was perhaps what she fancied. She'd cry all by herself. Then she'd calm herself as well.

Jamila left the yard and went into the house. Durgati was lying on the floor crying. Jamila bent over and tried to pick her daughter up. She couldn't. The girl had grown heavier. New splendours had sprung up on her body – front and back. Her mind was like a six- or seven-year-old kid's. Her body that of a ripe young woman. How old was the girl really? Jamila thought about it. She remembered Mia Sa'b. Two days ago they were chatting in the yard.

– Y'see, Hasina Bibi, the country's been free fourteen years now. Saleha was married even two years before that. She still don't have no children ...

Jamila calculated. That meant Durgati was thirteen. Jamila's heart flew back to thirteen or fourteen years in the past. Back then Jamila was Jamila the Pretty. A luscious, full-bodied young girl. Her skin wasn't as milky white as Durgati's. It was slightly dark and sweet in colour. She was so vain about the face that she could see in the broken mirror.

Karim Bhai used to say – Jamila, your face looks as if you've washed it with the caress of a moonlit night. It makes me want to touch it.

It was true. Even looking at herself in the mirror a thousand times never satisfied her. She'd touch her own face again and again. But she never let Karim touch it. She had been sinfully proud. Despite running after her day after day, Karim had never been able even to touch her hand. In the end, suddenly everything changed.

One evening Karim came to her as she was sitting underneath the lonely mango tree by the pond. His face half gloomy like a dirty lamp.

– Probably won't see you again for a long time, Jamila. I've come to say goodbye. I journey for the border tomorrow with Shahid Bhai. There may be a big fight with the Punjabis.

Jamila laughed suddenly.

– Fight? You? With who did you say you be fightin'?

– With the Punjabis.

– Who are they? From which country?

– Silly girl. They're the West Pakistanis. Tall and strong people they be, hard inside and out. They're attacking us Bengalis. You haven't heard nothin'?

Jamila felt scared listening to Karim's words. The Punjabis seemed like the demons of legend. Jamila had been too busy with herself to hear anything. But she had seen Elder Brother and Younger Brother worrying over something all day. They would stare at one place as if meditating. Ma would yell at them. Get angry. Instead of working, the two brothers would whisper about something together. A sudden fear thrummed through her breast. There were goose-pimples all over her body.

She said – There's no need for you to fight.

She felt hot because she didn't know the whole story. She was up to her neck every day working in the house with her mother and in a hundred different household troubles. Didn't know nothin' about the world. Didn't know nothin' about what went on around her. Her face lowered, Jamila jabbed at the bark of the mango tree with her nail.

– You really forbiddin' me to go, Jamila? If you truly forbid me from your heart then I won't go. You really forbiddin' me to go? Karim grabbed her hand.

Jamila became befuddled. No words came out her mouth. Karim had perhaps said a lot more; she hadn't heard. There was a hot blast of air coming out of her ears. Her body trembled. What could Jamila tell Karim? She bowed like a gourd plant at midday. Karim left, touching her milk-washed cheek, saying goodbye. The wish to forbid Karim thrashed its wings inside Jamila's breast. Yet no words came to her lips. She couldn't remember how long she stood there like that. In the end she could hear her mother's rasping voice.

– You stupid girl. Why're you standin' in the dark like that? I'm turnin' into a bloody cripple from runnin' around workin' and her royal highness looks for fun out yonder. Get inside the house, you stupid girl.

Bending down, Jamila picked up the hatchet and entered the house. There was a surging within her heart. As if there had been something held in her palm. Just slipped out of her palm like an eel because she wasn't paying attention. Her breast felt empty somehow. Bothered. As if she would've felt better if she could have sat down by herself somewhere and wept. The stile could be seen through the half-open back gate. A young man strode down that road there a while ago. The blades of grass hadn't yet been able to raise their bowed heads.

In the end, one day both her brothers left for the border over that stile. Early at dawn Elder Brother said to mother – Ma, we'll be goin' for a while then. All the young men of the village have left to fight the Punjabis. It's a shame now to stay at home. You understand. Take care of Jamila. If you hear the Punjabis have neared the village, take the North Deep to Uncle Kasem's house right away. Uncle will look after you, it's all been arranged.

Then the two sons touched Ma's feet for blessing. Ma was probably prepared beforehand. She handed them packages of pressed and puffed rice and whispered her prayers.

Then one day there arose a hubbub of shouting and crying throughout the village. People were running around without aim or purpose.

Ma called Jamila from inside the kitchen – Jamila, get the bundle of money 'neath my pillow and get out quick. They're here. Oh Allah! Where should we go?

Jamila's heart thumped. She hunted through her mother's bedding.

Had the bundle of money run away some place?

Ma's broken voice called out to her again – Jamila, you stupid girl. Get outta the house quick. The Bagdi houses are on fire.

Jamila's arms and legs shuddered. It took her some time to find the bundle. Frightened, Jamila didn't know which way to turn. She heard the sound of people's crying shake the skies before she even left the house. Bamboos crack-crack-crackled open in the heat of the fire. Even heard gunfire. And she heard the cows and the calves hollering like anything.

As she was coming out with the money, she bumped into a wooden stool and fell down. When she somehow managed to stand up, she saw no Ma in front of her eyes but two enormous men like pythons were standing there. They were wearing police clothes, guns in their hands. This was the first time that Jamila had seen guns. That was why no scream could come out of her throat. She looked around for Ma with her brimming eyes. Saw that the two python-like men had grabbed her. Ma's keening flew through her ears like river water. As if Jamila were dying out of fear. Oh Allah, Oh Allah. Jamila didn't remember any more. Jamila had opened her eyes again. Felt as though the torment of the grave had already begun for her. Jamila couldn't stand it. Every sin she had committed from birth jumped right out in front of her eyes and moved away. She didn't know what sin this was that she being punished for. Inside her heart, the barren rice fields of Chaitro stared at an empty sky. Thirst wanted to burst her chest right open. As she drowned in the pain Jamila cried out. Like she cried once when she was a child watching the brawling of vultures. Saw how vultures fought over sharing one cow. The cow was dead. Didn't move none. The vultures tore at shards of flesh with their filthy beaks. Felt as if the cow's soul were standing near by, watching the show and crying its heart out in humiliation. Jamila could bring no other picture to mind. In fact, Jamila don't remember nothin'. She really couldn't remember? Jamila fooled herself. If Jamila could've hung herself on the electric fan that day, then she needn't have carried this deadweight around her neck.

Durgati pushed Jamila, surprising her out of her reverie. What good would it do thinking about all this? It was getting late.

She called her daughter and said – Take care o' the house now, child. I'll be off to work then. Won't be back at noon. You ask Aunt Khushi, she'll give ye lunch.

Jamila climbed out of the yard quickly.

She heard Elder Wife's screaming as soon as she crossed the broken threshold of the Mia homestead. Jamila didn't answer. She placed her stool underneath the shade of the mango tree and got to work as she did every day. The sound of the *dheki* rose from the cookin' house – thump, thump. The same sound had thumped in Jamila's breast that day. With three other girls who were imprisoned with her, Jamila broke open the lock and ran away. Jamila reached home by asking directions from people again and again. She came back and found Ma half crazed. Her two brothers had come home to bring her some food. As soon as they heard that they had taken their younger sister, they left saying – Gonna eat those Punjabis raw. Never came back. Then the day Durgati was born, somebody brought news that the brothers were a-comin'. Ma watched the stile near the North Deep the whole day long. In the end, Aunt Khushi brought her back home in the evening. It was Ma who named the new baby Durgati. The girl was like a piece of new cloth washed in soap. Milk-white pretty. Still, what things people said about her. Talked of killin' her off. But she couldn't do it, her Ma couldn't do it either. Hands placed around her throat fell away by themselves once the eyes rested on that pretty little face.

Jamila's arm was hurting her. Jamila pushed the *kula* away and sat down to rest awhile. Clad in cheap, colourful clothes, Younger Wife smiled at Jamila and said – Jamil bu', want a *paan*? He got me some scented *jarda* from Dhaka.

Younger Wife's eyes glinted. She spewed out her stories. She laughed while talking and tumbled on to the sacks of wheat. Jamila rose. Tying the mouth of the sack, she started off for the pond. She needed a dip. The sweat and heat were making her feel clammy. She needed a bite to eat in the cooking house after taking a quick dip. It was getting pretty late. Who knows what Durgati be doin'?

Her heart thumped within her chest. It scared her to look at the girl's body. She'd kept watch over her for thirteen years now. Couldn't kill her off. Left her in the jungle then brought her home clasped close to her heart. There was a *champa* tree in front of the mosque. Seemed to Jamila that a tree prettier than that walked around inside her house. All the people's talk, the irritation of the neighbours – still the girl had grown up. But it was only her body that grew, not her wit. And then she had the habit of crying. Any excuse she'd get, she'd start crying. Who knew what her father'd ...? Ashamed, Jamila let go of thoughts about Durgati from inside her head. Let that shameless hussy die.

Jamila rubbed a green chilli in her rice with the eggplant curry. The heyday of the Mia's house was long gone. All that was left was the show. They say that the dog that has no skin ... Else just eggplant curry, not even a whiff of fish! Elder Wife gave Jamila her baby to feed. Told Jamila to watch over her. The girl had no beauty. A flat, dark face. At this age Durgati was like a doll. People would pick her up to caress her, even though they despised her. Now that her body was growing, she would still be surprised at times. Her birth was all wrong but Jamila protected her with all her heart. Seemed to her that even though people said bad things, the girl was not to blame. She didn't choose the pain of this poisoned world. Allah forgive her. Though she felt tender for her daughter, it irked her when she began to cry. Whenever she'd be wanting something, she'd start off crying again. The past few days she'd been asking for a red sari. The sudden memory of something made her hair stand up on end.

Last night she was talking of Mafiz while lying in bed. Jamila didn't even listen properly. The girl said that Mafiz had taken her to the *nailla* fields. He'd given her foreign chocolate wrapped in paper. Gave her some more – God knows what – stuff. She didn't listen properly because she was drowning in her own thoughts. Khalek Bepari, the egg-seller from North Para, wanted to marry her. His wife'd died last month leaving behind four teeny-weeny kids. People said Khalek had whacked her to death. She was a nice one, the wife. Instead of complaining about the beating, she'd just upped and died. He'd sent word in a roundabout way. That he liked Jamila. Evening before, he'd sent a crimson sari with old woman Guji. Said to give her word soon. It wasn't as if Jamila didn't want to be getting married. She felt like it more and more ever since Ma had died. It was when Jamila thought of Durgati that she didn't know what to do. She knew that the day after Khalek married her, he'd kick the girl right out. Then there was the fear of Khalek's beatings.

What difference did it make that the country was free? Everyone said it was such a wonderful thing. No one had to serve the Punjabis any more. But what happened to the Jamilas? Jamila'd sacrificed her life at the

feet of this freedom. It didn't finish her off at one stroke. Oh no. They
had hacked and sliced at her. They were still hacking away at her. This
liberation that had come at such a price.

What had it given Jamila? It had made her a servant at somebody
else's house now that they'd eaten up the small slice of land left by her
father. It had given her the loathing of the people. It had turned humans
into animals. The peace and quiet of life seemed to have flown away.
People just wanted more and more. Wanted money, wanted land, wanted
respect. Jamila's head ached from thinking. She couldn't even think of
Durgati any more.

Jamila finished eating and washed up. She sat down on the stool and
rested. Then she walked to the shade under the tree and started to work.
She started the sweet daydream of getting married when she was young.
Durgati entered even there. If her mother married, where would the
tearful girl go? People wouldn't give her shelter. They'd shoo her away.
More importantly, bad people would be after her. That letch Mofiz had
his eyes on her. What else was there to worry about? Allah, Allah! The
girl didn't understand. Her wit hadn't grown in keeping with her age. If
the letch took advantage of the girl, there would be no road other than
death. Jamila felt tired through all this worrying. She tidied up her *kula*
and other stuff and started for home.

She met Fuji as soon as she went down to the pond.

Fuji soaped her clothes and said – I think your Durgati isn't feeling
so well. She didn't eat anything at lunch. She just lay there and cried. You
should keep an eye on the girl. Even if Allah hasn't given her any wit, he's
sure given her a body to look at. People are talkin' about Mofiz. Haven't
you heard nothin'?

Fuji kept on talking. Hot air came out of Jamila's ears. She heard
nothing. Her feet seemed like lead. The road back to her home kept
getting longer and longer. Jamila stood in the yard calling for Durgati.
Getting no answer, she went into the house. She saw Durgati lying on the
floor on a mat. Jamila wasn't irritated at her crying. Just her heart skipped
a beat. The torn sari was wrapped around her any old how. Her cheeks
were red from the heat of her weeping.

She called the girl in a tender voice: Durgati, why're you crying layin'
like that on the floor? What's wrong? As she sat near her and touched her

hair, Durgati's sobbing increased. At last she took her by the hand and tried to pull her closer. The girl was heavy. She couldn't.

In the end, she herself lay down close to Durgati. She wiped her face with her hand. It was then that sobbing arose in Jamila's heart as well – Do you wanna have rice, Durgati? You hungry? I've brought some rice and eggplant curry from the Mia's house. Want some?

Durgati didn't answer. She sat up and pushed back the hair from her face. She pouted and said to her mother – You're not goin' to get me a red sari, are you? Look, my sari's torn at so many places. Mofiz told me today, he'd give me everythin'. Anythin' I want. He gave me two ice-creams. He was so nice to me. And ...

A hot blast of air was coming out of Jamila's ears again. What was this cry-baby girl sayin'? Then ... then ... Jamila felt as if her head was a melon bursting in the sun. Insect thoughts were wriggling inside.

Jamila controlled herself and sat up. Her eyes burned like coal fire. She reached out and pulled off Durgati's torn white sari. She searched Durgati's body like a blind woman. What people were whispering was true. How could she be her mother and not know? Cry-baby Durgati couldn't be saved from the wolves and the vultures of this free land.

The people of the village had forgiven Jamila, saying that it was the price of freedom. They would not forgive Durgati. Durgati had no yesterday. Durgati had no tomorrow. Durgati's beauty would be handed around to everyone, but she would find no shelter. How could Jamila watch this blight?

How could she see the end of someone whom she'd taken care of for thirteen years with everything she'd got? Jamila clenched the earth with both her hands to cover her pain. The pain broke into slabs of earth within her breast like the riverbank. Jamila pulled the uncomprehending girl to her breast. She wasn't to blame. It was the world that had treated her badly.

Jamila opened her eyes before the morning *azan*. She pushed Durgati awake. – C'mon, let's go to the city, Durgati. We'll go there and all our troubles'll be over. C'mon, let's go.

Durgati was stubborn. She lit the lamp and showed Durgati the red sari Khalek had given her. The girl got out of bed as happy as could be. She couldn't believe it.

Jamlia dressed Durgati in the sari with care. She covered her body and then her head. Her throat hurt to look at Durgati's face. Blowing the lamp out, mother and daughter started off for the station. The big train from the east arrived almost at the same time that the *azan* was called. Durgati couldn't contain her joy. She jumped on to the train, leaving her mother behind. She got lost within the crowd of people. Jamila didn't even move. The train steamed off to the west in front of her eyes.

It was as if Jamila had lost her senses and was just standing there; who knows for how long. Suddenly she gave a start. She looked and saw how late it was. More people were coming and going to and from the station. Jamila was without sense or reason. She saw people standing in lines. The train from the west was whistling and pulling into the station. The riverbank broke off in chunks inside Jamila's breast. Jamila pushed and pulled herself onto the train. The train rumbled off towards the east.

Translated by Shabnam Nadiya

PURABI BASU

Radha Will Not Cook Today

Morning hovers on the edge of night. A cool breeze swirls gently in the dawn.

Reclining in bed, Radha breathes in the fragrance of the white and orange *shefali* blossoms.

Last night was unusually calm, free from the frequent quarrels with husband, mother-in-law, sister-in-law.

Her body temperature is quite normal – she has no fever. There is nothing physically wrong with her, she is not even tired.

It is not raining outside. The sky is clear. A beautiful blue.

It is neither too cold nor too warm. Radha's only child, Sadhan, is perfectly healthy.

Husband and son are still sleeping soundly beside her.

Nevertheless, Radha suddenly decides that she will not cook today.

Radha will not cook today.

Radha calls the sun and says, 'Do not rise yet. Today I will stay in bed for a long time.'

She has no chance to talk to the night. Night had slipped away before

Radha made up her mind.

Radha calls the birds and says, 'Keep on singing your early-morning songs. Today I want to stay in bed and listen to you sing.'

She calls the clouds and says, 'Help the sun. Hide him in the *anchal of* your sari.'

She calls the *shefali* and says, 'Do not shed your blossoms any more. Imagine that day has not yet broken.'

To the dew she says, 'Keep on falling in little drops onto the grass below.'

The sun listens to Radha. For a long time he does not appear in the sky.

The clouds stretch and cover the blue sky.

The birds continue to sing ceaselessly.

The *shefali* blossoms cling more strongly to their stems and continue to adorn the branches.

The dew drops keep on falling and embrace the grass with their loving wetness.

Radha yawns and stretches on her bed.

Meanwhile there is commotion in the whole house. Everyone has woken up late today.

Forgetting his maths tables and his spelling, Sadhan gazes outside.

It is time for Radha's husband, Ayan, to go to market.

It is time for Radha's sister-in-law to go to school.

Radha's mother-in-law has completed her morning devotions and is awaiting her first meal of the day.

But Radha is still in bed.

Radha will not cook today.

She will not cook, no, she will not cook.

Radha will not cook today.

'What's happened? What's wrong?'

'Will everyone starve today?'

'I can't understand what the matter is.'

Mother-in-law, sister-in-law, husband are all amazed.

Radha is unconcerned.

She slowly leaves her bed.

She picks up the water pitcher from its corner and moves leisurely towards the pond.

'Will my son go to work hungry today?'

Radha does not reply.

Her mother-in-law is angry. 'I'm asking you, where did you learn to be so high and mighty? What is the matter?'

Radha does not reply. Her husband is perplexed.

'Sister-in-law, it is time for me to go to school.'

Radha does not reply. Her sister-in-law is sad and surprised.

Radha sits down quietly by the pond and dips her feet in the water. Behind her there is commotion. With her loud wails, mother-in-law has gathered people around her. Radha is unconcerned. She sits gazing at the water.

The small fishes – *puti, bojuri, kholsa, kajali* – come in shoals and gather at Radha's feet.

'Go away, leave me now. I haven't brought any food for you today.'

But the fishes continue to turn joyous somersaults. Radha's presence is enough. They want nothing else.

Radha looks up at the sky. The sun laughs down at her.

'Are you angry?' the sun asks.

'Why couldn't you wait a little longer?' Radha asks, hurt and angry.

'If you look at the fields, you will realize what would happen if I delayed any longer.'

From where she sits by the pond, Radha glances at the wilted fields. Radha is worried. 'Will they survive?'

'Just smile, and all of them will come back to life.'

Radha stands up. Twirling around, she laughs and laughs. She stretches out her arms.

Radha laughs. And laughs. And laughs.

The grain stalks seem suddenly to rouse up from sleep. They give themselves a little shake and stand up tall.

Suddenly Radha finds her husband shaking her by the shoulders.

Her mother-in-law is glowering with rage and cursing her bitterly.

Her sister-in-law stands weeping in dismay.

But Radha is still laughing. Laughing. Laughing. Radha is still laughing.

The wind rustles through the leaves in tune with Radha.
The water of the pond ripples delightedly in laughter.
The birds chirp melodiously in unison.
The fishes dance and float and dive.
The flowers softly nod their heads in harmony with the leaves.
Radha laughs. And laughs. And laughs.

Her angry husband shatters the empty rice pot and leaves for the market hungry.
Her mother-in-law continues to wail and curse at the top of her voice.
Her sister-in-law steals in gentle steps to a neighbour's house.
Her son Sadhan comes slowly to the pond and stands beside Radha.
But Radha will not cook.
She will not cook, no, she will not cook.
Radha will not cook today.
Radha turns her head slightly.
For a moment she wavers. Then, she steels herself.
Radha sits down on the ground. Then she gets up immediately. She is aware that she is not ill. She realizes for a moment that the most normal things in life can make one ill. So she is not afraid.
'Mother, I am hungry.'
The cry is repeated, as if from far away. 'Mother, I am very hungry.'
There is a turmoil in Radha's heart. The smooth sea is suddenly racked by a storm. Holding her son close to her, Radha continues to gaze at the water.
Then she looks up at the sky. Up at the sun.
She looks at the trees, at the birds, at the flowers, at the leaves.

Radha looks longingly at everything around her.
A small crow comes from nowhere and, plucking a small ripe papaya, casts it into Radha's lap. Picking it up with both hands, Radha peels it and feeds her son. Sadhan's hunger is not assuaged.
Radha calls the kingfisher and says, 'Bring me the lotus pod from that lotus cluster in the middle of the pond.'
The pod is huge – it is sufficient to satisfy any hunger. But Radha's son eats only a little of it.

'Mother, I am very hungry. Aren't you going to cook?'

Sadhan is just four years old. He feels very hungry. How is a small fruit going to satisfy that hunger?

'Mother, aren't you going to cook?'

Her heart wants to burst. She almost succumbs.

Still, somehow, Radha manages to say, 'No.'

Radha will not cook.

She will not cook, no, she will not cook.

Radha will not cook today.

Clasping Sadhan to her breast, Radha walks to the orchard. Sitting cross-legged on the grass, she lays Sadhan in her lap. Then she looks carefully around her. There is no one anywhere near. The leaves of the star apple and jackfruit trees move gently in the breeze and create a soft canopy for Radha. Radha gently uncovers her breasts. Her firm, well-rounded breasts gleam in the light of the sun, under the open sky. Radha lifts her left breast and pushes the nipple into her son's mouth. With her right hand she caresses Sadhan's head, his hair, his forehead, his eyes. For a few moments, Sadhan is bewildered at this unusual occurrence. Then slowly, very slowly, he sucks at the budding nipple of his mother's breast. At first he sucks gently, then he starts sucking harder, till he finally tries to suck with all his strength this nectar from his mother's body.

Radha is pensive. Radha is eager. But nothing happens. What is she to do now? Straightening her backbone, stretching both her legs in front of her, Radha seats herself more comfortably. She glances once all around her. She clenches her teeth, she bites her lips. She is asking for something, praying for something. And just then it happens. Cascading like a waterfall, overflowing both sides like a swollen river that floods its banks, causing her whole body to tremble violently, something bursts forth from Radha's breasts.

Radha looks at her son's face.

Sadhan bubbles with laughter.

From the sides of his active mouth the white milk foams in little drops to the ground.

Radha laughs.

Sadhan laughs.

The cloud comes and covers the face of the sun.

The *shalik* bird rests on one leg. A cool breeze swirls gently.
Radha laughs.
Sadhan laughs.
Radha has decided that she will not cook today.
She will not cook, no, she will not cook.
Radha will not cook today.

Translated by Niaz Zaman and Shafi Ahmed

Shamim Hamid

The Party

The hand-cut crystal chandelier threw its glittering light down upon the select group of people sitting on the pastel-hued Isphahan carpet woven in an intricate pattern of floral vines. It sparkled off the diamonds and heavy gold jewellery worn by the women and glowed on the gold and silver of their rich silk saris. It flashed on the brass buttons of army uniforms, and on the spiky spurs of boots worn by the men.

The women sat relaxed and graceful on the floor. Some sat with legs pulled up under their chins and feet decorously covered by swathes of expensive silk. Others sat with backs against walls or conveniently placed sofas, their legs neatly tucked in sideways and out of sight.

It was the men who were uncomfortable in their western suits and full dress uniforms. Their stiff jackets, narrow trousers and spurred boots did not allow them to find a comfortable position. At times they stretched out their legs to get some relief but pulled them up again soon: it was considered rude to be pointing your feet at anyone, and, in the crowded room, it was impossible to avoid doing so. They shifted this way and that to ease their cramped muscles but they had little choice. It was the President's wish to sit on the floor and listen to songs rendered by those present. And those present were the embassy officers, their wives and the entourage that accompanied the President on this grand state visit.

The stiffly formal reception by the host country, which was attended by anyone who was anyone, was over, and the President, feeling he had admirably withstood his share of the day's suffering for his people and his country, wanted to relax and enjoy the rest of the evening. The President was a four-star general who had taken over the country during a military coup. Since then he had regularized his position and established a kind of democracy in order to placate aid-giving western countries who strongly opposed military governments. The democracy was superficial only, and the President had full power to do almost anything he wished.

The Ambassador was a shrewd and experienced government servant who had done his homework on the President and was fully conversant with his likes and dislikes. Also, the Ambassador shared the President's sentiments that after such formal receptions one really needed some distraction. So the embassy staff and the members of the President's entourage congregated at the Ambassador's house where everything stood in readiness for the President's pleasure.

Smartly dressed waiters in white livery with gold buttons and braids bent over double to serve drinks and salted nuts to those seated on the floor. For the President there was the highly special and expensive twenty-five-year-old Black Dog whisky, for he was very discriminating about his scotch and would drink nothing else. A bottle of the rich gold liquid, together with a Waterford crystal tumbler, stood on a highly polished Christofel silver tray on the floor next to the President. No water, soda or ice was needed. The President was in complete agreement with connoisseurs of scotch. The only way to take such mature and smooth whisky was at room temperature, neat and unadulterated. A minor general of the army kept replenishing the President's glass.

The Ambassador's wife also liked her scotch neat but she was not so discriminating. Short of rice toddy, she was game for anything. Today she had indulged a little too much because the tension of the Presidential visit could only be endured in an alcohol-induced haze. For weeks before the visit, her husband, a vicious, rude man at the best of times, had been impossible to talk to and intolerable to live with. He snapped and foul-mouthed everyone from the Minister Counsellor to the gardener. In a way one could not entirely blame him, for if anything, anything at all, displeased the President during the visit, the Ambassador was sure to lose his job. Even so, in spite of the more than twenty years of a shared life, the Ambassador's wife could not stand her husband's boorish behaviour without an alcoholic buffer.

The thought of leaving him had occasionally crossed her mind. But where would she go? What choices did she have in life? She had only minimal education and no money of her own. Her parents were dead and, if she walked out on her husband, her brothers would certainly not welcome her in their not so well-to-do households. The question of seeking refuge with her sister, who was quite well off, of course did not arise. It was not done. She could lay some claim on her brothers though, because hadn't she relinquished to them all claims to her share of the little house her father had built in the village?

She herself, while once very beautiful – which was why the Ambassador had chosen to marry her in spite of her poor parentage – was rather jaded now. The regular bouts of heavy drinking, while helping to dull the pain of seeing her beauty disappear day by day, did little to preserve the very thing that she saw slipping away from her. So who, in his right mind, would want to marry her now?

Besides, she doted on her children and, had she left him, her husband would have been sure to keep them from meeting her. And he would be backed both by law and society. And anyway, life could be worse. She enjoyed the many parties they attended, delighted in the beautiful clothes and jewellery that her husband bought for her because he thought she had to be suitably dressed as the wife of such a senior ranking officer. And if, at times, she found her husband's behaviour intolerable, a bottle from the shiny, well-stocked bar always helped bring things back in perspective. It also helped her overcome her inhibitions about some of the things she was forced to do to advance her husband's career.

However, nothing she ate or drank could dull the stab of pain she felt when she saw the new Third Secretary and his young wife walk into the room. He was on his first foreign posting, and she knew that he had joined the Foreign Service with full faith in a system that did not exist, innocently unaware that, like it or not, he and his wife were part of deadly games where the winner takes all. She knew only too well that the

Ambassador was very skilful at playing these games, for she had seen the outcome in several of their postings, both at home and abroad. She also knew that she herself had little influence over her husband, and even less power to change the causes and consequences.

'Oh, what's the use?' thought the Ambassador's wife, shrugging, mentally. 'What will be will be,' and, giggling, sidled up a little closer to the President.

He ran his hands over her silk-covered thighs and asked, 'Who is that beautiful young thing in purple?'

'Oh, that is just the new Third Secretary's wife,' replied the Ambassador's wife, pretending nonchalance. 'They have just joined the embassy and have been married only two months. Very inexperienced,' she added discouragingly.

The Ambassador, sitting cross-legged on the other side of the President, overheard the exchange and volunteered, 'But Mr President Sir, she sings like the *koel*, a nightingale she is, no less. If you wish, I will send her to the State Guest House tonight, to sing specially for you.'

In spite of her alcoholic daze, the Ambassador's wife tried desperately to intervene. 'But, darling,' she said to her husband in the western fashion that he found so smart, 'darling, it is Zulfia who is the accomplished singer and who should be given the honour and privilege of singing specially for the President.'

Emptying his glass and squeezing the Ambassador's wife's knees, the President asked, 'And who on earth is Zulfia?'

The Ambassador's wife pointed to a slim woman who was laughingly pretending to protest about someone's arm round her waist. The end of her black chiffon sari had slipped off her shoulder and fluttered to the floor. She made no attempt to pull it back up to cover her décolletage exposed in a provocatively cut blouse.

'Her husband is the Economic Counsellor. See, there he is, asleep in the corner. He has no head for drinks,' giggled the Ambassador's wife, pointing to a bald man with a generous paunch who was sitting slumped against the far wall, snoring gently.

'Well, she is nowhere near the Third Secretary's wife in looks, but she seems willing to play ball,' observed the President shrewdly.

'Sir, Mr President,' interposed the Ambassador, immediately sensing the President's interest in Zulfia, 'I shall personally order Zulfia to sing for you tonight. But tomorrow night our little *koel* in purple will pay you a surprise visit.'

Once more out-manouevered by her husband and feeling sick to her stomach, the Ambassador's wife turned blindly to the Colonel sitting by her side. Pressing herself against him she said, 'Why don't you get me a fresh drink, hm?'

Sitting cross-legged on the carpet in front of the President, Zulfia pulled the box-like harmonium to her. She ran her right hand up and down the keys, and with her left hand pumped the accordion-like bellows of the instrument. She began to sing in a clear voice, popular classical songs and ballads whose lyrics sent the men into paroxysms of frenzy and making them repeatedly call for encores. The cries of '*Wah, wah*' and '*Shahbash*' wafted out into the garden twinkling with garlands of miniature lights, which had been put up for the occasion.

To provide Zulfia with some respite, one or two of the men sang songs of Rabindranath Tagore, but they sounded dull and slow after Zulfia's enthusiastic rendition of *gazals*. Even well-known film songs sounded muted when sung by others. The Third Secretary's wife was also pulled into the centre of the circle. With her husband beaming proudly at her, she sang in an appealing, but untrained, voice, a ballad written by the great Bengali poet Nazrul Islam. But over and over again, the harmonium was pushed to Zulfia, and, over and over again, she rose to the occasion and belted out songs until the very rafters rang with thunderous applause.

At last the President stretched out his legs and announced that he wished to retire for the night. In a flurry of movement, soft rustlings of silk and harsh jangling of spurs, everyone got off the floor with as much semblance of sobriety as individual conditions allowed. The President stood up, swaying on his feet, and was quickly supported by his aide-de-camp on one side and by his favourite general on the other. All three entered the gleaming Mercedes Benz limousine which, with flags flying rigidly on either side, swished out of the driveway. The Mercedes was accompanied by outriders on motorbikes, a whining police car leading the convoy and another bringing up the rear. The Ambassador and his wife followed in another Mercedes, while the entourage scrambled to find their transports, everyone in a rush to reach the State Guest House, if possible, before the President arrived, so that they could be there to receive him. Zulfia and her harmonium followed in the embassy staff car. Oblivious to the world, her husband slept on in the corner of the now empty sitting room.

Next morning the Ambassador called the new Third Secretary to his office and told him that the President had especially praised his wife's singing and had mentioned that he would like to hear her sing some more. She should therefore be ready to go to the State Guest House tonight, immediately after the bilateral dinner that was being held at the ambassadorial Residence.

Flattered and pleased at the attention, the Third Secretary said, 'Sir, I will immediately arrange for the staff car to take us to the State Guest House tonight.'

The Ambassador looked at him coldly and in an exasperated voice said, 'Don't be a fool. She will go alone.'

That evening the long dining table, which seated twenty-four, was covered with a stiffly starched, white damask tablecloth. Earlier that morning the butler had ironed the massive tablecloth and stored it in a roll to prevent unseemly creases. The heavy, intricately carved silver gleamed from the extra-special polish it had received for the occasion, and the Bohemian hand-cut crystal gave out rainbow sparks whenever the pendulous chandelier trembled in the breeze. The formal china with the official crest and seal sat imposingly on the table, while an extravaganza of roses, chrysanthemums and lilies added colour to the white, silver and crystal display. Tall, antique, silver and crystal candelabra complemented the chandelier and cast a warm glow over the august gathering.

Only one place way down at the bottom of the table was empty. It was a little awkward for those sitting on either side of the empty chair because when his only neighbour was talking to his neighbour he had no one to talk to and had to sit looking intelligent and pretend not to be bored. The Ambassador noted the empty seat and looked round the table for the Third Secretary. He was sitting at his designated place with downcast eyes, staring down at his plate and not speaking to anyone.

The dinner commenced, and one course followed another with easy grace. The Ambassador's wife was a past master at choosing menus and arranging parties to suit every occasion. The cook outdid himself, and the waiters performed faultlessly. The Ambassador's wife did not have to lift her eyebrows even once to indicate her displeasure at some lapse in serving etiquette that she had been drumming into the staff for the last week or so. Toasts were drunk, and the President expressed his great pleasure at the success of his visit. He complimented the Ambassador on his superb diplomatic achievements and the Ambassador's wife for her excellence as the perfect hostess. Nothing marred the evening except the one empty seat.

The next day the President left for his own country, and the Ambassador heaved a sigh of relief for a visit successfully concluded. It was no mean achievement even if he did say so himself.

The following Diplomatic Bag brought three letters for the Ambassador. One informed him about a promotion for Zulfia's husband. The second was a transfer order of the Ambassador to an obscure post usually covered by a Chargé d'Affaires. The third was a letter dismissing the Third Secretary from the service, quoting an obscure military regulation which in special circumstances was applicable to civilians as well.

The President could not abide anyone who could not fulfil a promise, even if he was a successful diplomat and did his job well. In fact, it was only the overwhelming success of the visit that prevented the President from dismissing the Ambassador outright, even if he was personally inclined to do so. However, no such considerations stood in the way in the case of the Third Secretary. The President despised even more those upstarts who either pretended not to understand the subtleties of games played in high circles, or had the gall to defy the implicit orders of a Head of State.

SONIA NISHAT AMIN

Under the Lemon Tree

I'm going to visit my birthplace. It'll soon change hands and become the property of another family. Probably be auctioned off to make space for a new shopping complex. Or an eye-shattering apartment building. The old colonial house will no longer stand alone with its sad, decayed aristocracy. Chittagong is still two hours away. The amber light of the train is spreading a soft glow everywhere.

When she heard of my sudden decision to go to Chittagong, my colleague Deepa had asked, 'There's so much to do at the office, what with this special edition of the magazine ... Why suddenly Chittagong?'

I accepted her bossing me around in good grace and replied, 'There's something I have to do there.'

'What?'

'Can't tell you that. It's personal.'

'You're going to see someone?'

'No, I'm going to see a place.'

'A place you've never seen before?'

'Of course I've seen it. I was born there.'

Where I was born. Where I began. On a winter's night. But I am not
the main character of this story ...

I stare at the lifeless house. How long have I been standing here? Ten
minutes? Fifteen? I could feel my cousin Mukta fidgeting beside me.
'Why don't you go down to the market and buy a couple of saris – it's
not far from here.' Why buy saris now, she wanted to know. 'One for you
and one for me. I didn't get you anything on your birthday. And I feel like
wearing a new sari.'

'You'll be all alone here. It'll take at least an hour.'

'It doesn't matter. See that bench underneath the lemon tree? I'll rest
there for a while. There's a tea-shop close by. It's been such a long time
since I've had *bela* biscuits dunked in tea.'

I got rid of her.

Number Twelve Gazi Dewan Lane. Soon there'll be a shopping
complex here. Grandma had lived in one of these octagonal rooms,
Grandpa in the other one. A wide verandah in between. When I was a
child, I used to find words pencilled on the verandah walls – letters formed
perfectly in Grandma's handwriting – written in the interim between
sanity and madness – 'Poison in the milk' or 'I plunge into fire, yet I do
not burn. I jump into water.' And sometimes there were cooking recipes
too – *halwa* for breakfast, raisin cakes. Grandma had been famed for her
cooking, famed for her beauty. Perhaps I had eaten food she had prepared
– at some festival or other in the family. She had made the round *kababs*
herself – the aroma of *polao* was everywhere. But I can't remember the
feast ending smoothly. Probably because Grandma had left the cooking
half done to get 'lost' behind closed doors. I've read somewhere recently
that an illness called 'Chronic Depression Syndrome' has been identified.
Patients suffering from this can't even find the energy to get up and do
their hair. Grandma had refused to open her door that day, despite all
the pleas and entreaties. I saw her do this again and again. She had been
an extraordinary woman. As soon as she closed that door she was easily
transported to another world – and there was no way of knowing from
the outside whether she was dead or alive. Perhaps that was when her
brain cells began to deteriorate. I don't remember how the guests were
fed that day. I was so very young then!

Grandma had had the sort of upbringing that wives and daughters used to have traditionally. But what good did it do? It couldn't save her in the end. Sewing, cooking, religion, reading, writing – her father had arranged all kinds of lessons for his beautiful daughter. This daughter of his whom everyone called the rose-bride – he gave her away to a good husband. But nothing worked. Nothing came of nothing. She did up her living room in the latest fashion after her marriage, crocheted sofa covers, round tables in the corner with lace tablecloths, brass table-lamps, flower vases. Two embroidered pieces framed on the wall – one, a heron done in gold thread, on a black background, the other, the legendary fox underneath the grapevine. I used to tiptoe into this neat and tidy room and stare at the pictures. Grandma's bedroom was next door. She would ask me in a rough voice, while lying in bed, 'Well? What do you want?' I would leave quickly.

No, Grandma, you never spoke to me kindly, with love. You couldn't. That was your inability. I understand now. I'm a bit like you. I can't take too much of the world – I have to lock my door too. But mercy and compassion – Gautama Buddha's virtues – these I have mastered. You couldn't – but then how could you? – your inability was a creation of your time.

You wouldn't spend all your time in bed. Now and then you'd shepherd us together – a bunch of your granddaughters – and say, 'Come on, get ready, quickly. We're going to the Bioscope, and lunch at a restaurant.' She had a huge trunk stuffed with saris – gorgeously embroidered sheer organdies – sky-blue, lemon, white – *Dhakai* saris, onion-coloured *Banarasis*. Each sari neatly folded with matching blouses. Grandma would go into the bathroom with one of them slung over her arm – and come out transformed. We would look on with awe, as though at a fairy-tale princess. A princess sans Prince Charming, of course. But we'd be most astonished when she would delve into her trunk and bring out wads of money. Scented, newly minted notes. She'd say, 'My father sends me money every month. I don't touch a dime of your grandfather's.'

Later we found out that the money was actually Grandfather's. But she had said that she wouldn't accept any money from her husband – so those notes were magically transformed into 'money my father sent me' in the darkness of the trunk.

We'd take a rickshaw down to the rail station to the restaurant Mescaff.

Anything we children wanted to eat – chops, cutlets and puddings. It was a free-for-all. Then the cinema. Those of us who were a bit older were by now impatient for this part of our day out. By now we had a shadowy idea of love. So, along with Grandma, we'd gulp down *Rajlakshmi and Srikanta* avidly. I would fall asleep while listening to Suchitra singing on the silver screen. I remember Rajlakshmi beckoning Srikanta towards eternal love, and me drifting towards eternal sleep ...

We'd return to Gazi Dewan in the evening. My all-enduring Grandfather would ask with a smile, 'So, you're back?' Grandma would ignore him and re-enter her octagonal fortress.

Grandfather would call us to him fondly and treat us to bread with British marmalade. He was well known as a moral man, an important officer; he had protected himself from all the trials and tribulations of colonial Bengal by erecting a wall of morals and ethics around him. Now I can understand that he could feel love and affection, but there was no fire in him. Towards the end, he had begun to arrange his own meals – bread, Horlicks, tea biscuits. At some point, the kitchen had closed down, and the servants started leaving one by one. Grandfather would sometimes go to his brother's place (which was at the top of a hill) for his meals – Grandma didn't even feel the need to do that. My father and mother would ask her to come and take her meals with us, but the social values of the day did not permit dependence on a son-in-law for food.

And Grandma probably didn't need to eat anyway. In the last days of her life (I was abroad then) her door would always be locked. Day after day, bread and water would be left in front of her locked door, as if for a prisoner – sometimes she would eat it, sometimes she wouldn't. It seems that the last few days her door was locked all the time. She died behind those locked doors.

This was an old problem – of locking doors. We would come for a visit and hear that she had locked herself inside again. If we were lucky, she would open her door to us. We would go in. She'd talk. 'When you're older, Shamu, you must read Bankim.' She could quote line after line of dialogue. What a memory she had! When it was time to leave, I would find her sitting by the window in her octagonal room, looking away with vacant eyes, saying, 'Traveller, hast thou lost thy way?' That was her favourite line, 'Traveller, hast thou lost thy way?' After I'd grown up, for a

long, long time, I couldn't make myself read *Kapalkundala*. I would pick
it up and put it back on the shelf unread. I avoided the book, making first
this excuse, then that. I had already had a different reading of it – long
ago.

The lemon tree under which I was waiting for Mukta had decayed.
Yet once it had stood so proudly in the yard, with its spreading branches
– filling the compound with its fragrance. Grandma's fantasies were
entangled in its branches. I was doing my multiplication tables in her
room one day, when she said, 'Would you like to hear a story about a jinn,
Shamu?' I agreed at once, of course. Rahim Buksh. Tall, fair, with a good
figure. A handsome figure. On moonlit nights, from under the lemon
tree, he would walk away into the horizon ... Traveller, hast thou lost thy
way?

A long time afterwards, when I was grown up, I was talking to a
distant cousin of Grandma's, and I told her, 'You know, Grandma used
to tell me stories about this jinn. I never knew whether to believe her or
not, they sounded so convincing. I even remember the name of the jinn
– Rahim Buksh.' I saw my relative laughing in a strange manner – looking
at me obscenely with her cataract-dimmed eyes.

She asked, 'Don't you know?'

'No. What?'

'There was no jinn. Your grandmother wasn't very ... well, let's just say
that there were certain questions about her character. I even remember
hearing about a scandal involving some man. She'd go off to different
places, whenever she felt like it. Said she felt *"bechaeen"* – restless,
agitated. She'd take the train and leave for a couple of days, saying that
she was going on a pilgrimage somewhere.'

'Alone?'

'I don't think so. It was a long time ago – and I only know of it by
hearsay. There must have been servants with her. After all, your grandfather
was an important officer.'

She was right. I remember hearing that word '*bechaeen*' when I was a
child. She was feeling '*bechaeen*' – she must go out for the day with her
granddaughters. Not to the Bioscope or restaurants this time; perhaps to
visit a *mazaar*.

I remember a range of green hills, and steps going upwards through them. Chittagong was a quiet city then – sparsely populated. I was climbing the steps behind Grandma. I don't remember what holy place we were visiting at the top of the hill, but, strangely, I do remember Grandma washing her face and hands with cold water again and again, whether to do her *wazu* prior to praying or to cleanse her body and mind of some invisible dirt – or hoping for some salvation or release ... But there was no peace in her face – only sorrow and pain. Impatiently I stood beside her, like a block of wood. I didn't understand the meaning of prayer then – all I could think of was, why come all this way to this solitude? But that sorrow, that bewildered search must have touched and entered my subconscious mind, or why should I remember this now? A grave was being dug in the mountainside, near the *mazaar*. Birth, death, spirituality – these had not touched me yet – but I had shivered seeing the sad, red earth – an unknown fear and melancholy hung heavy in the air.

Back home Grandma shut her door again. Next day I returned to my own home. It was said that Grandma would read the Holy Koran behind her locked door. That's what she told everyone when she finally emerged. For some reason I couldn't believe her. She had looked for refuge in religion and hadn't been able to find it. What other shelter could a woman find?

She stopped reading Bankim. The fancy organdies were set aside. In her last days, all I ever saw her wearing were filthy, torn saris. She emptied her trunk, giving away everything. Father had been transferred to Dhaka then. Grandfather had died – at his brother's house. Grandma hadn't gone to see him – not even at the very end. Mother brought Grandma over to Dhaka. She wanted Grandma to live with us. She bought her new saris and blouses. Gave her a separate room, told her no one would disturb her. She could have anything to eat that she wanted. An *ayah* was hired to prepare her *paan* for her. The first few days she went around looking quite happy. She blessed my father time and again. Father said, 'We'd be happy if you'd stay on with us. I've only two daughters, and this huge house seems so empty.' Grandma smiled, nodding. A few days later, she stopped talking. Then gradually she gave up eating. Then she began locking her door. A doctor was summoned. The doctor said, 'Melancholia. Keep her happy, keep her surrounded with people.'

That evening the ugly incident took place. In the evening Mother made Grandma come and sit in the garden, among the winter blossoms – dahlias, pansies, chrysanthemums. Suddenly, still sitting in the chair, she started swearing and cursing in a loud, horrible voice – terrible, ugly, obscene words. She cursed everyone – beginning with Grandfather and then going on to even my father and mother – all in a terribly cold voice, her face normal and calm. I was reading a book. Rabindranath Tagore's *Jogajog*. I felt a strange, perverted fascination as I left my book and went and stood in the garden listening to it all. Stunned, my parents told me to leave. Mother tried to stop her and, after repeated requests and protests failed, left crying, to phone my aunt. I stayed and watched the enormous tragedy that had taken human form in anguish before me. The curtains were raised for a few moments from over an enormous darkness. Somewhere I had read, 'This sorrow has no grace, no beauty.' This was the same type of sorrow.

Mukta is taking a long time. Perhaps the range of Tangail saris in Chittagong isn't that good. I have no problem with that. I can sit under this lemon tree until evening. That's why I came. To sit in the shade of this tree, under which a handsome jinn named Rahim Buksh would walk on moonlit nights. 'Does he ever speak to you?' I had mustered enough courage to ask Grandma once. She was in a good mood. She laughed and said, 'Yes, he does – he tells me a lot of things.' Suddenly I think I hear the shutters of the closed windows of the octagonal room rattling. Probably the wind. If I close my eyes, I can imagine Grandma's shadow standing beside the window. Lips trembling – I can almost hear her from under the tree. What is she saying? Traveller, hast thou lost thy way?

No. I almost lost my way – but didn't in the end. I realized something that day. That day in Dhaka, when, Grandmother, you ranted madly for a whole hour. All you would say was, 'Take me back home.' The addiction to darkness had soaked through to your marrow. The intoxication of solitude. The intoxication of locked rooms. You couldn't live without them. Your sad world would beckon to you. Even darkness can blind one's eyes. I couldn't bear it. That day I realized that even sorrow must have beauty. I promised myself that I would never let my sorrow be without grace.

I don't know if I've succeeded ... It's a difficult vow to keep ... You were brought back to Chittagong. Who was to go with you? You said, Only your lost jewel. That son of yours whom you had cared so much about – the one who had gone abroad and lost his job and was leading an eccentric life. A telegram was sent and he replied he would come, to take care of his mother, look after his father's property.

Every day you would wake up with new hope. At last your son arrived on a plane. Who can tell what curse had touched this family? One look at him and we could tell, his life was near its end. I don't know whether your dream of happiness with your son came true. I don't know whether he took care of your property. I was abroad for a long time. I only know this – Uncle sold off all of Grandfather's properties one by one – until all that was left was this house, our homestead. Music was Uncle's hobby; so was homeopathy; and astronomy; and religion; and literature. He would sing a line or two and then go off on some errand; books were bought but never read; he would sit in front of the canvas with brushes, but the canvas was never marred by so much as a single stroke of paint. Religious rules and rites were carried out with ostentation, but God never chose his heart as a dwelling place.

Gradually Grandma slipped back to her old routine. The world inside her room became her only world once again. That was her shelter till the very end. The mad son of a crazy mother – that house must have acquired a bad reputation. I had heard it whispered later on. But whispered gossip is just another name for cowardice, even though we pass it off in the name of protecting decency and respectability. No grace, Grandma. So I'm telling it all, writing it all. What beauty does secrecy have? Ever since I was a child, I've seen how secrecy weakens people, makes them small. Gives others the chance to sneer and jeer and taunt. That's why, no matter how shameful, sorrow and pain should be brought out into the daylight, to heal in the light and the air. Then innuendoes and insults can no longer touch you.

Walt Whitman was a contemporary of yours. But in your time, there was no way women could read his poetry. Then you would have known that men and women can contain multitudes.

In the end, nothing is dirty or ugly if people contain the pain within themselves. That Uncle was found dead in an unknown hotel isn't an ugly fact either.

On a visit home from abroad, I was talking to Father about Uncle's death, while sipping tea. Mother was sitting beside me. 'It seems so sad and strange that the one person Grandma felt so deeply about hurt her the most. If her son had been with her, she probably wouldn't have become so unbalanced.'

Mother poured out another cup of tea but remained silent. Father said, 'Do you think your grandma loved her son so very much? That she spent her days waiting?'

'Well, didn't she? Uncle's photograph would always gleam. Everything else in that house was covered in dust. That picture was cleaned every single day.'

Father sighed and said, 'By then it had turned into a habit. What you saw was the empty shell of the love of a once normal human being. There was nothing inside. It had died long ago. In the end, she just went through the motions.'

'But she would lament for him night and day!'

'That was habit too.'

I listened, stunned. We console ourselves about the tragedies of life by thinking up alternatives – if things had been like this, that might not have happened. The connection I had imagined between mother and son had been shattered. My mind, searching for normality, could find no consolation. I really couldn't understand (because I had made myself walk on the humdrum road of life) that Grandma was the inhabitant of a stony, lonely island. Golapbanu Begum – that is her final identity. No imagined alternative saga can soften this truth.

In the last part of the *Mahabharata*, when Vyasa shows Yudhishthira heaven and hell, he tells the angry, broken-hearted, disillusioned Yudhishthira, 'There is no heaven, there is no earth, there is no hell. This was your last illusion. Now you are freed of that too.' The last illusion is gone too. This is one of the many profound, eternal verities of the *Mahabharata*. But who can face truths like this? Me, sitting under a lemon tree in Gazi Dewan Lane? What was it that made me come all this way in the middle of the busiest season at work? This house has no beauty, no life. Memories grimace at me through the skeleton bars of the broken windows. Still, I was born here once, on a winter's night. In this unhappy house, where the octagonal rooms pulled us in parallel lines to different ends – not letting one life join with another.

The paint has flaked off the windowsills. It used to be a yellow house with green windows. Grandfather, Grandmother – buried in a cemetery in the suburbs. I went there once. It was covered with weeds all over. No one tended the graves. Who was there to do so? The last of their line lives in Dhaka. I thought that there was probably a village near the cemetery.

Grandma would talk of her father's house sometimes. 'My father's house was at the very end of the town. A huge pond, a bamboo grove, a cowshed. Our palanquin was kept there. It was such a beautiful palanquin. Embroidered and curtained. We would travel in that. Cows chewed bran as they stood there. I had a white cow. I named her "Wild Deer".' (Here Grandma giggled.) 'I didn't have a real deer, did I, Shamu, like Shakuntala? The pond was full of big fish. When father asked us to cook, it was usually my elder sister who would do it. I would read novels. Weave garlands of *bakul*. The night air would be filled with the scent of the lemon blossoms. Wasn't there a poem, "I can't sleep for the scent of flowers, I lie awake alone?"'

It seems as if I can smell the lemon blossoms faintly now as I wait for Mukta. Perhaps Grandma had planted the tree. The windows shudder in the wind. Any moment now some voice will ask, 'Traveller, hast thou lost thy way?'

I think that Mukta should be coming back any moment now. She walks into the yard, carrying shopping bags. 'Sorry, I'm late. The shops were so crowded!'

I say, 'Let's go.'

Translated by Shabnam Nadiya

NAHEED HUSAIN

The Deal

Cul-de-sac – a blind alley. At the end of the alley some wooden chairs lie scattered. The notes of a popular Hindi film song emanate from a much-used cassette player placed on a chair. Sunbeams of the dying day spread across the alley from corner to corner. Some crows hover in hope of food. Beside the chairs, a wood fire burns over a makeshift stove. A large pot full of *biriani* is cooking over this fire. The chief cook and his helpers are busy. A fat dark man, perhaps returning from some errand, comes out of the house and sits on a chair that creaks under his weight. He turns down the music and yells.

Hey, Kawla! How much longer? You'll finish me, man! I've told the boss that the stuff'll be ready by five. It's five past already.

The cook replies, Coming coming! I'm just putting some charcoal on the *biriani* and starting the chicken. Don't worry. Gosh! What firewood! Wet – as if it had a swim in the river!

Tempted by the aroma, some street dogs sniff impatiently around for food. The man, unconvinced, gets up to remove the lid and inspect the food.

Inside, the atmosphere is different. It is a dingy old building. Though it had been cleaned that morning, it could not be made to look clean and festive. Damp, moss-covered red bricks peep through the cracks on the walls and floors, laughing at all their efforts. But on the doors and windows there hang new curtains. This family had not been so particular about cleanliness even a few years ago. But the daughter of one of their neighbours had failed to get married because of the tattered gunny-bag curtains hanging on the doors.

After that, the merchant family had corrected their mistake. They too had to get their daughters married. Not one, but three of them. Today is the eldest daughter's engagement: hence the festivities. The female matchmaker or *motasa* (as they are called in old Dhaka) is busy, bustling in and out of the houses of the two families. She had come by this morning to discuss various details about the marriage. She is back this afternoon and announces her presence. Oh Aamirun's mother, how are you? From today you're the bride's mother – how are you?

The bride's mother replies, Don't ask, sister, my backache is killing me. Such a big event, and our very first – I am dead-beat already. Hey, Falna's mother, bring me the what's-its-name.

A matronly cook comes out with a platter of *paan*. She has been in this family for quite a long time and knows exactly what her mistress means by *Falna* or *Dofna*. The *motasa* pulls the *paan* towards her and starts to relate her news. The bridegroom's family were supposed to come with a party of fifty people, but now they are bringing a batch of eighty for the engagement party. The *kaabin* or *mohrana* will be the same – two lacs and one taka as it was fixed earlier.

But another thing, they want the dowry money right away. The bridegroom wants to invest this money in his wife's name. I told them to take it at the wedding. But they wouldn't hear of it, the *motasa* reports.

The girl's father calls the mother into the adjoining room. Whispering, he tells his wife to agree to the proposal. He has already made arrangements to cater for eighty people. And he has already drawn out cash for the dowry.

Sounds of female excitement float down from the first floor. Lucky, the youngest daughter, is vehemently debating with the Ustad-ma from next door.

It had been a tough job arranging Aamirun's marriage. Ustad-ma had brought an amulet to be tied to her hair. It has remained in that place since. Lucky is now insisting on taking off that amulet, there being no need for its powers any longer. But Ustad-ma will not allow it. The wedding has been arranged, true, but the engagement cannot be called off at the last moment. This is why they are quarrelling.

They agree at last. The amulet will not be totally removed from Aamirun, but will be attached to a gold chain round her neck.

The younger sisters, Zeba and Lucky, sit down to comb Aamirun's hair. While tying her hair into a bun, the girls chat and giggle. Hit songs from movies, private jokes, dialogues of heroes and heroines – everything is included in their merrymaking. But the bride remains unmoved. No emotion plays upon her dark complexion. She sits upright with no movement.

What else can she do? She has been dolled up to face different prospective in-laws since the age of fourteen! The neighbours stopped her from going to school. And so had begun a series of ordeals – painting her face to sit in front of the prospective grooms and their relatives, hoping to enchant them with her beauty – only to be refused, time after time. What was her shortcoming? Her complexion, which was much too dark for a bride? Well, her father was dark, her mother was dark, how could their child be fair? These incidents, following one after another, had shattered her confidence totally. Perhaps she would remain a burden all her life. But today, after having been approved by the boy's family, she is getting engaged. Still she has her doubts. She will be reassured only after the event. An engagement ring on her finger will convince her of her coming marriage. After that, the ordeal of making herself pretty in the eyes of strangers will be over forever.

The girl's father has his own anxieties as well. He will also be relieved only after the bridegroom's father has put the ring on her finger and the engagement is ensured. The dowry will be paid in cash, to prevent any objections. The furnishings for her house will be sent on the wedding day. Poor girl, she has been refused so many times. He has suffered for his daughter. He agreed to exorbitant demands from prospective bridegrooms. But, despite this, they all turned back after they saw his girl. His heart broke at his child's agony. Once, after a match had been broken, she tried to lighten her complexion by rubbing a pumice stone on her cheeks. Her face bled as a result and was badly swollen and painful for many days. What do they want, those relatives of prospective bridegrooms? I will give them lots of money, I'll furnish their hearths and homes, and yet they only object to my daughter's complexion?

Thinking of money makes the *bepari* ponder about his business. The price of *daal* is dropping and there are many maunds stored in his warehouse. He has not been able to find a suitable customer; he will probably have to sell at a lower price later. A person has been engaged to find a buyer. This man is supposed to have an uncle who supplies foodstuffs to some dealers. The man came to ask for money, and the *bepari* assigned him the task of finding a buyer. He is to come that evening to inform him whether he has been able to pull off the deal. If not, lacs of takas will go down the drain. And the *bepari* will be forced to sell off his sugar permit. This adds to the tension of the *bepari*. Hurriedly pulling on a shirt and putting on shoes without socks, the *bepari* rushes to the spot where the food is being cooked. The clock strikes six.

He yells out to the cooks, Are you through, your highnesses? I'll make you eat my shoes if you don't serve the dinner on time. What! You still haven't finished cooking?

For goodness sake, *Bepari Saab*, don't panic. All the dishes are ready. The *zarda* will be ready in a minute. Chandu – bring me the ingredients for *borhani*. I'll beat the yogurt in.

Outdoors, the sun is setting. The *azan* can be heard from the grand mosque at the Chawk – all the neighbouring mosques resound soon after. Darkness begins to descend over the alleyways. A man comes out with electric wires and a bulb to light up the alley. Just then, two cars stop in front of the entrance to the alley, honking loudly.

Buttoning up his shirt, the *bepari* runs out to greet them. Flocks of children and ladies alight from the cars. Heavy scents pervade the air. Their gaudy, spectacular clothes brighten up the alley for a while. The ladies are taken upstairs to the room where Aamirun is being dressed. When she hears the bridegroom's party arrive, Aamirun flees to her mother's chamber. The future bride trembles with fear; perhaps it would have been better if the wedding had not been fixed. To sit down with eyes closed, in front of all those strangers – she can almost hear her heart pounding. And she can hardly bear to think about the wedding.

She decides to concentrate on what other people are saying in the next room.

Bhabi, we choose a fair-complexioned girl as our Monsur's wife. And look what happened! She became possessed by jinns the very first year after her wedding – fainting fits every minute. What else can I say, sister? So we did not look for a fair bride for Mokbul. If this girl has a skin colour like us, she'll be good enough.

Another voice says, When did you buy this sari? Quite glittering it is ...

Aamirun does not want to hear any more. Tears stream from her eyes. What sort of place – home – family – is she going to?

After dinner is over, the sisters bring Aamirun, all decked up with ornaments and bridal finery, and place her in front of the bridegroom's people. Having eaten to their heart's content, they now come out, toothpicks in hand, to inspect her. The elders look at the half-veiled shy girl and place either money or gold in her hand. Aamirun still has her eyes shut, but her ears are quite alert, listening to scraps of conversation.

Look at her armlet. Fashionable, huh! Everyone is wearing one, these days.

Someone else comments, She has quite good features. But her skin – much too dark.

Betel stuffed in mouth, someone else comments, They served excellent food. One chicken roast per person. Look, Bashir Miah has left without seeing the bride.

No, his business is probably very dull now. How can he see the bride empty-handed, so he left.

A different drama is being played in the drawing room. Now that the engagement ring is safely on Aamirun's finger, and the dowry money in the hands of the groom's father, the *bepari* heaves a sigh of relief. He feels as if he has made an advance payment for his son-in-law. Then follows a series of mutual embraces between the prospective in-laws. The departing children call out to their new aunt, Bye-bye, ta-ta, and hasten towards the waiting cars with their mothers. Having seen off the last guest, the *bepari* slowly returns to the house. Sitting under a fan, he sighs in relief and rests his tired feet. Well, the future of the girl has been secured, at last. Another source of happiness hums sweet melodies in his ears. What is it? What is it? Oh, yes, the nephew of the contractor – he has come by to say that his uncle will buy the whole consignment of *daal* at the present rate. He will pay the advance tomorrow. Imagine, the whole lot will be sold at a profit.

Jumman Bepari brims with satisfaction. He cannot decide whether his sense of relief comes from being able to sell off the *daal* or from being able to get his daughter engaged. He wafts up to his wife's room with two sweet *paans* stuffed into his mouth. Mother of his dark daughter, his aged wife suddenly seems very lovable. He feels like caressing her all night long. But why this sudden surge of happiness? The *bepari* cannot figure that out through the hot summer night.

Translated by Firdous Azim with the author

JHARNA RAHMAN

Arshinagar

Arafat awoke. He sat up in bed.

A zero-watt bulb dimly illuminated the room. Five children scattered here and there on the enormous bed, under the mosquito net. The pungent odour of piss. All three of the younger children peed in bed. Halima was sitting up. Her long untidy hair flowed downwards, covering both sides of her face. But Halima was not busy changing the pee-soaked sheets. She sat as if she was stricken by some bedevilment of the night. She gazed with dazed eyes. Which way was she staring? Was Halima in a waking dream?

Arafat felt as if Halima was watching him.

Halima's face had been bent over the sleeping face of Arafat.

Her hair was tickling his cheek.

It was Arafat that Halima had been watching.

Had the astounding event that happened two months ago created a different response within Halima? Arafat examined Halima intently.

Arafat could tell whenever Halima got up and left his side.

Halima had to get up at least two to four times each night anyway. There was always one baby or another around. They were usually not that far apart in age. Changing the nappies. Preparing the milk. Stopping them from crying. Breastfeeding them – these were the things she had to do. She would lie down again. Arafat could tell what she was doing even as he lay in bed. He would be irritated at having been woken up. Suppressing his sleepiness, he would say in an irritated voice, Why can't you get rid of the girl's habit of nursing at night? She eats rice now as well. What does she need a bottle at night for? The two of them disturb my sleep. One is wailing all night long, the other is nursing. All kinds of botheration.

Halima understood quite well what this 'all kinds of botheration' meant.

One by one she had become the mother of five children. The children were afraid to sleep in a separate room. In any case, although Aklima and Tahrima were eight and six, the third, Sobhan, was still much too young. Four years old. The next two were right on top of each other. Jannat was two and the youngest girl barely six months old. Halima slept in a huge bed with all of them. There was a separate bed for Arafat in the next room. He could easily go and sleep there without having to endure all this botheration. Arafat read for quite some time after the *esha* prayers. The *Neyamul Qur'an*, the *Sayyedul Mursalin*, the *Qasasul Ambia*, the *Tazqeratul Ambia*, the *Fazayale Amal* or the *Fikah Sharif*. The alarm clock was set. He would get up at the right time for *tahajjud* prayers. The prayers were said with absolute absorption in the isolated room. He could place himself at his Lord's feet with a deep sense of sacrifice. Still, this multi-dimensioned bed – the nagging of the children, childhood illnesses, the stench of pee and shit, milk, medicine, sleep, rocking – attracted Arafat. Unless the intoxicating aroma of Halima reached his nose, the night did not seem like night at all.

While Halima busied herself with getting the children to sleep, Arafat had a lot to do as well. He was the owner-cum-manager of the Sonali Printing Press up in town. The accounts, orders, deliveries for the press, the different jobs for the different clients – most of the workers were prone to slacking. Arafat could barely handle it. A lot of times it was Arafat himself who had to check the proofs to ensure timely delivery. Then alongside the toil for this life there was the toil necessary for the afterlife. Devoted, untiring Arafat. When he came to bed after finishing

everything, Arafat's weary body would yearn for conjugal bliss.
Most of the times Arafat would call Halima to his bed.
But that was more awkward. Perhaps the baby would start wailing just
as he was about to climax. Halima would flinch and turn herself off. Of
course, that did not make much difference to Arafat's sexual enjoyment.
But the sweetly pleasurable numbness of letting his sex-weary body rest
on his wife's – that he did not get. The moment he ejaculated, Halima
would disengage herself from her husband. Embarrassed, awkward,
apologetic, she would bunch her petticoat between her legs and shuffle
off to the next room. As she left she would present him with some excuse
in a guilty tone – Khuki's got a bit of a temperature. She won't go to sleep
if she hasn't got my nipple to suckle on. I'll come back at dawn.

It was to avoid all these botherations that Arafat would come to
the big bed. Even if the youngest one awoke while he was at it, Halima
would cling to her husband riding her with one arm while patting the
awakening child with the other with a peculiar expertise. Placing herself
in this simultaneous role of wife and mother, Halima felt bewildered at
times.

Why was this happening? Was sin entering Halima through these
acts? A child. An innocent angel. This thing in front of them ... But
this also was a duty. Husband. Her shelter in both this life and the next.
Whose place was right after Allah's – it was her sacred duty to provide
him with pleasure as well. Halima couldn't think beyond that.

So while her child suckled on one of her breasts, Halima would offer
the other one to Arafat to fondle and kiss. She pondered the mysterious
ways of the Creator as she satisfied both husband and child.

Arafat was very happy.

Halima was such a good little wife. Just what he had wanted. Salt
of the earth. Their family was large, a joint family. Like a phalanx of
unending mouths. Six brothers, two sisters, father, mother, bedridden
elderly grandmother, widowed childless aunt, maid, cattle-tender,
servant, other labourers, all in all a veritable market-place of twenty-two
people. Although his sisters Salema and Fatema were married, they spent
most of their days at their father's home with their three or four brats.

Halima was the eldest daughter-in-law of this household. For the
first six years of her marriage she had been the only one. In the last four

years the number of daughters-in-law had increased to three: Johora and Ambia were the two wives of the brothers Shahjalal and Badruddin. They were looking for a wife for the fourth brother, Nawshad.

Arafat's father, Mowlana Mohammad Zulfiqar Ali, was a very religious man. An elder of the village. Secretary of the village's Mosque Committee. He was an honoured arbiter in the various disputes, judgments, problems of the Dashra village. By the good grace of Allah, he directed the happenings of his home within the confines of his huge house, Ali Manzil, in accordance with the regulations of Islam, the strict discipline of the *Shar'iah*. All six sons were very obedient. Religious. Of good character. Both Shahjalal and Badruddin were madrassah teachers. The fourth son, Nawshad, was a reporter at the *Daily Sunrise* in Dhaka. The younger two were still students. His daughters were as pretty as fairies. So he had handed them over to eligible grooms of reputable families at a tender age. Both his sons-in-law lived in Saudi Arabia. So the daughters spent most of their days in the loving care of their parents. On top of all this, he had this huge house covering five or six *bighas* of land with fruit trees, cattle, poultry, fish. Where was the joy in all this if it could not be enjoyed with grandchildren?

Fifteen-year-old Halima had been bewildered when she first arrived in this enormous, jam-packed household. Most bewildering were the dark, narrow rooms of the female quarters – the *andarmahal*. So many rooms! Like rows of shops! A dining room for the men, a dining room for the women, kitchen, pantry, the grandmother-in-law's room, the parents-in-law's room, one for the cousin, for her sister-in-law, for the grown-up girls, for prayer – rooms for so many different things. Halima had no idea how many rooms there actually were in the outer quarters, not even after ten years of married life in this house. The sitting room, for the *maulvis*, for her brothers-in-law, the *maktab*, for the servants ...

It was rare that Halima needed to set foot in the outer yard beyond the *andarmahal*. Occasionally when she was on a rare visit to her parents, or was suffering from some severe illness or pregnancy-related problems – when she needed to visit the maternal and child healthcare hospital uptown – only then. Other than that, the women of this house, especially the daughters-in-law, were inhabitants of the *andarmahal*. Their mysterious world existed behind the strict veil. The men of the household could at least hear the voices or the sounds of laughter of the daughters of the house; the daughters-in-law never spoke above whispers.

Halima had become so accustomed to this that even when she whispered with her children, she would gesture with her hands, fingers, eyes and head rather than use her voice.

Her eldest daughter, Aklima, would say sometimes – Mother, are you mute? You always speak in gestures! Halima would smile. She would caress her daughter's head and reply – It's not good for women to talk so loudly. It's a sin if other men get to hear the voices of women.

Aklima would argue – Mother, are my uncles, my grandfather, Uncle Dayal 'other men'? They are of our own household!

Still, can we tell from inside here when people who are not of our household come or go? Anyway, if you get a bad habit once, it's no good trying to get rid of it. So you have to practise these things from when you're young. You should speak in a soft voice, gently and politely. You should read the Qur'an in a low voice. So that only you can hear your own voice. You should read your books silently. That way what you study enters your heart. But it is best to read the Qur'an aloud. Always keep your head covered.

Aklima would cover her head more precisely while listening to her mother's words with intense concentration. As if Halima was not talking, as if she was droning the Qur'an ...

Never be without the veil. Do you know, even after death one must continue practising purdah. When a woman dies, no one other than her own brothers, father and husband can see her face. Similarly, the face of a dead man cannot be seen by women other than his mother, aunts, wives, daughters. Women will bathe the dead bodies of women; men will do it for men.

Tahrima would also listen to her mother's preaching with great interest. Because Halima would tell them so many stories in between the preaching. Saddam's paradise, the tale of the angels Harut and Marut, the ark of the Prophet Noah, the serpent staff of the Prophet Moses, the drowning of the Badshah Feraun in the Nile, the magical throne of the Prophet Suleiman, Khare Dazzal and Imam Mahdi – so many different sagas rested in Halima's treasury! Tahrima loved hearing about the *hurs* and the *gelmans* of paradise, and about the fruit of the *Bancchataru*. And she hated hearing about the *Gacchak* well, the *Gislin Falls* and the *Zaqqum* tree of Hell. Whenever Halima began to talk, the children would gather around her one by one, hungering after a tale.

Tahrima shuddered when she heard the rules for bathing the dead – Mother, then how come father has bathed me so many times? He wiped my privates clean when I was naked. Was it a sin, Mother? Father is a man, and I'm a woman, isn't it so, Mother?

Halima smiles – Silly girl. He's your father. He gave you life. To a father a daughter is a gift from paradise. Pray to Allah – Allah, give us another sister. If it were Aklima, you, little Jannat and another little girl, it would be lovely, wouldn't it, dear?

Halima strokes her swollen, seven-month-pregnant belly.

Yes, it would be lovely.

Tahrima opens her palm like a flower. The thumb is Sobhan and the other four – paradise. Four sisters. She says to Halima – What is the thumb, Mother? The one brother? Is he Hell?

Nauzubillah. Halima is confounded.

She would often face these little stumbling blocks while trying to teach the children about this world and the next, fate, virtue and sin. Quickly she said – No, silly. Why should your fingers be Heaven or Hell? You were just counting your brothers and sisters on your fingers. You gave your thumb to your brother, and the remaining four you took for yourselves. One is still inside my tummy, you don't even know whether it's a brother or a sister!

The next moment the solution occurs to Halima.

The thumb is the guardian of the four other fingers. It looks small. But it has more knowledge. Can you hold anything with only your four fingers? Can you pick up a fistful of rice? A pen? A spade? A plough? Why, you can't even pick up a flea! Those four taller fingers – they're totally worthless without that smaller thumb. In the same way women are worthless without men. Hence, your younger brother is also your guardian. Even if he is younger.

Tahrima found it funny. From then on she began calling Sobhan Ole Thumb. The grownups started calling him that too. Pretty soon, the 'thumb' dropped off, becoming Ole Man.

Ole Man was full of life. Running around here and there all the time.

Halima would always be very worried about this only son of hers. But it was just that – a bit of worry. At times her heart would begin pounding. The boy had been out of sight for quite some time. Had he gone down to the pond? Climbed the gate on to the outer wall? Or perhaps walked to the high road? Rickshaws, autos, trucks were rushing by constantly.

But the next moment Halima's worries would lose themselves in the hundred things she needed to do in the house. The cooking fire was constantly alight in the kitchen. Huge pots were bubbling with curry like the food for a funeral. Lentils. Vegetables. Rice in an enormous pot.

Halima's raw gold complexion was turning coppery from her constant exposure to the intense heat of the kitchen fires. During the summer days, her whole body would be covered in a reddish-white heat rash like *kaun* grains. Locks of her hair would tumble down on to her face drenched with sweat. The heat rash on her face would grew red and inflamed from constant itching.

Sometimes a few drops of sweat would drip into the lentils or the vegetables. So Halima always kept her head covered with a bonnet with a sponge border. It made her head very hot. But what else could be done?

During the daytime Arafat came home once, at noon. He finished bathing, said his afternoon prayers and had lunch before leaving for the press again. Her mother-in-law sat in front and tended to the sons' meals. She confessed her bias in favour of her sons quite frankly. She took good care that none of her sons became too attached to his wife's skirts.

Most days Halima never got to see her husband before bedtime.

Work, work and work.

At times it felt as if this vast world of Allah's had only been created to feed humans. From dawn to dusk, all this running around, just for food!

Arafat was without any worries.

No one in the house had any complaints against his hard-working, devout, subservient, simple wife. It made Arafat proud to think that this house could not run without his Halima. There was another secret pride that he had.

Halima was very beautiful. A round, fair face. Large, soulful eyes under deep blue brows – intense and calm like a river. When she smiled, her teeth emerged like rows of pearls. Whenever Halima heard praise from her husband about her teeth she would start smiling and then feel embarrassed, covering her mouth with the border of her sari. By now it had become her habit.

When he first saw Halima's face during the *shahnazar* at the wedding, Arafat had flinched in amazement and fear. Such beauty! She wasn't the daughter of a jinn, was she? Could a human being possess such beauty? Beauty was destruction. A venomous serpent. As soon as he had brought his bride home, Arafat declared that the men in the immediate family would get to see the face of the bride only once during the *bou bhat*. That would be it – forever. This ruling would be in force even for his brothers. Even if sisters-in-law were supposed to be like their mothers, they were *mahrum*. They were 'other men' to their sisters-in-law.

Halima knew only the names of her brothers-in-law. She sometimes saw their shadowy silhouettes. When there was need to talk to them, speech was conducted from behind a door or a curtain in a low voice.

At times Halima felt that even her husband Arafat was unknown to her.

The man was not to be seen throughout the day. The little time they were together – it was as if Halima could not raise her eyes to Arafat's virtuous, bearded face. It was Arafat who would gaze at Halima's face like a man intoxicated. Her whole body would shiver. As if under the gaze of another man.

Halima would grow anxious and say – Why do you stare like that? What are you looking at?

Arafat would kiss his wife's face and reply – At a *houri* from paradise. Allah has given me a *houri* from paradise right in this world.

Arafat's praise would make Halima more embarrassed, resting on Arafat's chest she would scrunch herself up into a ball and say – Allah has given me paradise on this earth as well. You are my paradise.

Now it felt to Halima as if a *zaqqum* tree had taken root within this heavenly garden of happiness. That tree was extending its branches, entwining her head to feet. Engulfing her.

Halima couldn't sleep. She stared at the sleeping Arafat in the dim light of the zero watt bulb. Who was he? A strange shiver ran through her body. Was this Arafat? Father of her five children? An ache began in her heart. She felt all muddled inside her head. As if someone was grinding her brains.

Halima could not forget that unbearable memory of two months ago. Would she be able to forget it in the rest of her life? Not just Halima, every single member of this household, even the people of the village – would they ever be able to forget it? Had anything as incredible as this ever happened before? Only the Divine Being knew what game He was playing with Halima.

Arafat was now a legend of Dashra village. The hero of the story of how God's chosen follower had been resurrected after death. It was still a fascinating story for the villagers – an unbelievable tale.

Two months ago a terrible accident happened on the Dhaka-Aricha Highway. A bus carrying passengers lost control and overturned into a deep ditch about three or four kilometres after crossing Savar Bazaar. Seventeen people were killed on the spot. The rest were critically injured. The villagers nearby recovered the dead bodies and laid them in rows beside the road. The police, journalists, villagers, passersby gathered at the scene of the accident. It was chaotic. Amid all this a journalist suddenly began screaming – Brother, my brother. A moving, heart-rending affair.

It appeared as a boxed news item in the next day's papers. Reporter Nawshad went to cover the massive accident on the Dhaka-Aricha Highway and discovered the dead body of his elder brother. Nawshad had gone to Jahangirnagar University to cover a terrorism-related incident. He rushed to the scene of the accident as soon as he heard of it. There he identified the body of his brother Arafat, who had been staying at the Kakrail Mosque in Dhaka for the past few days to attend a *Tableeg*. He was killed on his way back home. Pictures of the dead Arafat and the journalist Nawshad appeared in the papers.

Everything happened very quickly. The news of Arafat's death reached his home before his corpse did. Arafat was popular because of his honesty, his piety and his courteous behaviour. And he was important because he was the eldest son of Mowlana Zulfiqar Ali. When Nawshad brought his brother's dead body home after finishing with all the hassle of the police, the post-mortem, the death certificate, etc, it was close to midnight. After eleven.

Still, almost the entire village gathered around. Arafat's daughters hid their faces in their grandmother's lap, crying, scared at seeing their father's disfigured, crushed face. Halima took one look at the face and fell to the ground like a cut vine. She lost consciousness. Nawshad babbled on about how good-looking his brother had been and wept. He turned aside the part of the face that was mutilated. Zulfiqar Ali took to bed mourning his son. The sisters stroked his face and beard like madwomen and wailed – Bhaijan, where have you gone, leaving us behind? Open your eyes. Look, your Ole Man is sitting by your head. Bhaijan, please, look.

Ole Man only gazed in incomprehension.

Death he understood only slightly.

He said – Why did Abba come by bus? If he had come by plane he wouldn't have died. There are planes in Dhaka!

Arafat was to be buried the next day after *Zohr*. A piece of land on the eastern side of the pond, bordering the mango-jackfruit grove, was selected as the family graveyard.

Arafat's face was shown for the last time to the women of the house before his *janaza*. Her face on Arafat's face, Arafat's mother began gasping. Aklima and Tahrima were scared of their father's mutilated face. They covered their eyes with their fists, screaming, 'Abba, Abba'.

Salema, Fatema, Zohra and Ambia looked upon the face of their brother and brother-in-law amid silent prayers.

As she looked at her husband's face for the last time, Halima thought – They had spent so many years together, yet it was as if she had never really looked at her husband properly. As if she had never had the strength to raise her eyes to his face without shame. A feeling of needless yet powerful embarrassment, a secret shame had always kept her husband a distant person. Today he had truly gone far away. She would never see him again. Not in this lifetime.

At the last moment, an emotion racked her body, twisting it violently. She clasped at her dead husband, rubbing his *surma* and *loban*-dust-bedecked face with her own. She washed away the preparations for his final journey with her tears. Today no shame restrained her emotion.

A *gandharaj* tree had been planted at the head of the newly dug grave.

The women were reciting the *khatam-shafa* in the *andarmahal*. Halima herself had taken on the responsibility of reciting the *Kalema Tayyeba* twenty-five thousand times.

The Qur'an was being recited in the outer quarters. It was to continue for four days. A discussion meeting was to be held in the presence of the important and respected people of the area. Nawshad became busy with all these arrangements.

The neighbours had brought over food. The cooking fires would not be lit for four days in this household. The elderly women of the neighbourhood were trying to coax the mourning women into eating something.

Around ten in the evening, the news arrived like a sudden bolt of thunder.

Islam, the elder son of the Talukdar household next door, came to deliver the news – they had just received a phone call saying that Arafat hadn't died. He was alive. It was Arafat himself who had spoken on the phone. He would reach home the next morning.

Everyone was dumbstruck for some time at the suddenness of this news. Then the extreme shock made every single person in the household restless. They had buried Arafat with their own hands. His body had been identified by his own younger brother. Shahjalal and Badruddin had gone to bring the body home. The whole village had looked at him for one whole night and half a day. His father, mother, brother, sister, wife, daughters, relatives, everyone was mourning his death. They had turned to stone on seeing his dead body. How could Arafat still be alive? Wasn't there some kind of mystery here? Was Islam sure that he had recognized the voice? The people of the house twisted within a spiral of belief and disbelief, sorrow and joy, confusion and amazement.

Arafat arrived and stood in the front yard at eight in the morning. He called, 'Where's Mother?' in an eerie, broken voice and ran to the *andarmahal*

Amazement! Wonder without limit. It was Arafat who had returned. Yesterday's newspaper in his hand.

The news spread before the wind. First as a rumour –

The man they had buried the day before – that same man had risen from the grave the next day. He had walked to the front yard of his home. Gradually the dramatic colours of the incident began to fade. And the essence emerged.

The next day, again, there was a boxed news item.

Two people with exactly the same appearance. The parents, siblings, even the wife of the living Arafat had believed the anonymous dead man to be Arafat. The true identity of the dead man was yet to be discovered.

On the evening of the accident, another follower of Arafat's *Pir* had suddenly died of a heart attack at Kakrail Mosque. Arafat had to leave for a remote village in Netrokona with the dead body. When Arafat's own household was occupied with mourning and arranging for his funeral, the same preparatory rituals were going on in that other household. Arafat had been busy all through that day with these arrangements. When the burial was over, he heard about the accident at Savar from people. Then he heard about the identification of a dead body by a reporter. The name of the reporter, the name of the village also reached his ears. Worried, Arafat got hold of a newspaper from a local teacher and was astonished. Arafat couldn't find any similarity between himself and the dead man. Except a general similarity due to the beard and the hair. But he became alarmed thinking of what might be going on at his home. At the suggestion of the local people, he went to the police station and informed them of the whole incident and then called the Talukdar house.

After Arafat returned, a different kind of celebration went on in the village for a few days. The whole village poured in to see Arafat. And along came the reporters. Listening to Arafat's life story, exhuming the dead body, re-photographing the dead man, collecting his clothing, attempting to identify him – it all went on. Finally, after six days, the dead man's wife and father arrived from Tangail. The dead man was Abdul Hannan, *muezzin* of the Tangail Jame Mosque. He had been on his way to his sister-in-law's, to visit his sister who was ill.

Muezzin Hannan of Tangail received the honour of a first-class citizen in the family graveyard of Zulfiqar Ali of Manikganj. It was the earth of this place that Allah had destined for him.

In time the furore raised by this incident died down. The story spread its branches, becoming a great tree. A tree of divine miracle. The story was this – whatever one wished to say, it was through Allah's will that Arafat had been resurrected. He was truly a man who had arisen from the grave. Not a man. A jinn.

The joy, excitement, amazement of the inhabitants of the Ali house also died down gradually. But silently another tumult was aroused within Arafat. At first Halima didn't notice. In her joy in regaining her husband, she was engrossed day and night in grateful prayers and counting the rosary.

Amid all this, one day she noticed that Arafat was looking at her with an intent gaze. Halima no longer hid herself behind the veil of embarrassment she had used for so long. She looked at her husband's face with love. Certainly Arafat was also afloat on this tidal surge of new and deep understanding. As if they had been reborn.

One day Halima shivered all over.

Why did Arafat watch her like that? Was Arafat truly Arafat? Or was he a jinn?

Trembling furiously, somehow she managed to ask Arafat in a wavering voice – What do you look at like that?

Arafat said in a strange voice – At you.

Why? Haven't you seen me before? Don't you know me?

Yes, I know you. But Halima, don't you know me? After seeing me for such a long time ...

Oh dear, why wouldn't I know you? You're the person closest to me. Without you ... As she spoke of her simple emotions, Halima lifted her candid gaze towards Arafat.

Arafat's voice changed even more – Then how could you mistake that *maulvi* from Tangail for me?

Halima shivered. What did Arafat want to say! She managed to say – But everyone thought the same. Father, mother, your siblings, daughters, I swear by Allah, I've never seen so similar a ...

A wave of fire emerged in Arafat's voice – Forget about father and mother. They're old. They can't see properly. Anyway, they were distraught on hearing that their son had died. Forget about my siblings or other relatives. No one can sit around waiting to look at the face of someone who has just died. They have to mourn. They have to weep. They have to arrange for the burial. But you? You're my wife! Shouldn't you have been able to recognize me at a single glance?

Halima felt helpless. She could search through the whole world for an answer to Arafat's question but not find one.

Halima truly could not understand how blind the news of her husband's death had made her. Why hadn't she recognized him once she had regained consciousness? Why hadn't she been able to tell that this was not her husband, even after rubbing her face all over the face of a stranger?

Harsh guilt, a deep sense of sin, a terrible fear like a darkness covering the horizon pervaded her senses.

Within her stupor, Halima quickly turned over the pages of the ten years of her married life. There she could not find a single private moment, where she had seen, known, possessed Arafat as her very own, within herself. As if, with all the responsibilities, activities, the day-to-day being busy with the household, shyness, hesitation, fear, respect, Halima was a dweller of a different land.

Arafat placed a tender hand on Halima's back.

What's wrong, Halima? Why are you sitting up? Do you want to go outside? Are you feeling ill?

Halima didn't answer. She gazed at Arafat with unfamiliar eyes. As if she was within a trance. Arafat pushed his wife gently – Halima, what's wrong with you? Have you had a dream? Do you want a drink of water? What are you looking at like that?

Suddenly Halima woke up from her trance. She looked at Arafat with an intense gaze. There was fear in her eyes. Arafat was scared. He took her by the shoulders and shook her again – Halima, hey, Halima?

Inside, he was afraid. His taciturn wife wasn't going mad, was she?

Halima hissed at him – Who are you? Are you really Aklima's father?

Arafat got down from the bed quickly and turned on the lights. He brought her water.

Drink some water, go on, drink it. You've become weak. Neurotic. No more fasting for you.

Halima drank the water. She continued to look at Arafat with the same fixed gaze as he stood with the glass in hand under the bright light.

Arafat stroked her head and her shoulders.

Are you scared, Halima? What's there to be afraid of? I'm here! I'm right here!

Halima asked again – Who are you?

Arafat laughed – You've been dreaming. You've gone off your head. Don't you know me?

Halima's thoughts roamed through the sky and the earth as she slowly shook her head from right to left.

Translated by Shabnam Nadiya

NASREEN JAHAN

Different

The lamp stands in the middle.

On the other side is my daughter's face – sometimes clear, sometimes coppery, sometimes spreading like water all over the room. I see her fully for the first time. I look at her in utter silence. How strange to think that I carried this woman in my womb!

There's a knock at the door. A moment later, my daughter's voice cries out irritably. Does anyone use a lantern in this twentieth century?

I go to the door. My longer leg is numb. I put my weight on it nevertheless and reach for the latch and ask, Who is it?

No one answers.

Who is it?

There is no sound.

This has been happening for some days. Somebody knocks at the door. Day and night, intermittently. During the daytime I have opened the door. It is bitterly cold on the verandah.

Must be the same bitter wind, my daughter laughs.

So it seems, I say as I come back. On the other side of the light, the half-done crochet work is spread out and I look at it.

My daughter says, Whatever you say, Ma, you are a miser. How much does it cost to buy a charger light? Every two days the electricity is off. Everyone has a charger light in the city now. It's no longer a novelty.

It is not a question of novelty.

Why shouldn't we benefit from those consumer goods that are within our means? Why not throw away the TV and the fridge? In many small towns and villages, people still use lanterns, says my daughter. But the lantern is disappearing from the city.

If everything and everyone became the same ... I realize that I have started to lose the argument. I will have to concede defeat in the face of her irrefutable logic. But still, let me carry on. In fact, we must have something of our own so that each of us can be unique.

With a lantern, then? laughs my daughter.

Look at this crochet piece, I say with great enthusiasm. One needs great patience to do this and so the tradition is being lost in many homes. Yes, with a lantern – what's wrong with that? What a mysterious light it spreads everywhere. It is not open like candlelight, which looks like a tongue of flame wanting to devour everything.

My daughter continues to laugh. Are these arguments? Listening to you, I wonder what nonsense you have brought me up on.

Have I forced any of my arguments on you, ever?

Of course. I have to sit here tolerating the lantern. Ma, if you cannot discover anything new, at least learn to enjoy the benefits of today. What is so different about holding on to the old, to what existed in our homes these past centuries?

I go to bed.

I dream that I am running about. My two legs are of the same length. I am ten or twelve years old, much younger than my own daughter. Rarely have I seen such a dream. It would have been more natural to have seen this dream oftener. Must I admit that having one leg longer than another has given me no cause for remorse? I have often thought about this matter. Perhaps, to ward off remorse, I have become so conscious that even my dreams cannot pierce the iron walls of my will. Still, I have always dreamed that I can walk with ease on my legs. Yet, even in my dream it felt strange to be walking naturally. Even in dreams I cannot escape.

Tonight's dream is special. I am running smoothly without stumbling.

On top of it all, I am a child once more. On awaking, I see my legs under the clear light after many years – as if they are two young brothers growing up together. One cannot leave the other. In the midst of all this, the girl on the wall with streaming hair laughs in a strange voice. Why that streaming hair? Why do you keep that photograph? my daughter asks angrily. My well-wishers say that all I do is unnatural, of course. They will say this. In fact, they are hinting at my deformity. I limp – surely that is unnatural.

Once there was such a wail inside me. Such a wrenching pain. Heaven and hell became one. When I became a young woman – Is this my body, my form? Is this the body I have to carry throughout my life? I would not walk. For hours I would sit tight on my bed.

After some time I found an explanation for myself.

I explained that everyone has two equal legs – everyone walks normally. However bad I might look – I am different.

Gardening was my passion. With the spade I was able to produce myriad colours from the ugly clay – red, yellow ...

Many ordinary people have this passion too. The more ordinary the person, the greater the number of flowers that bloom. All the time I wonder, What can I do that others cannot?

Knock, knock.

My heart leaps up. The bright light soaks up the green light of the room. A strange wind blows. I drag myself to open the door – my daughter.

She says in a strange voice, Ma, I have dreamed a bad dream.

I say, It is good to dream bad dreams. Come, come with me.

You always say something strange and different, my daughter scolds me. Why did you close your bedroom door?

Lying on the bed, with my hands in her hair, I say, I don't know what I thought. Last night I thought I was closing the outside door, but I really closed my own.

Bad dreams are good, snickers my daughter. So you believe in superstitions too.

Melting in the warmth of the quilt, I say, I have a reason. I hope you won't argue just for argument's sake.

Ma, your stomach is so cold.

You were in there once.

The way you say it. As if no one else ever bore a child.

For you the world is as clear as water. Actually, the problem is mine. Now that I see you growing into a young woman, you do not seem to be my own daughter.

What do I seem? Your friend?

No, not even that. It seems that you were in my womb for a long time; now you are out in the light and the air and you will never come back. You are someone far away.

Do not speak so, says my daughter, rubbing her cold hands against my warm ones. It makes me very sad. You did not explain your argument about dreams.

It often happens in my case. For instance, I see a beautiful dream – I am roaming in different lands or I have found something valuable. Upon waking, my heart shrinks – to think it is not true makes me sad all day. On the other hand, say, you dream that a murderer is pursuing you, you are running endlessly, and then suddenly he gets hold of your body. Or say, I have died, you are all alone in the house. You have covered my body with a white cloth. Upon waking you will notice that your head feels empty. But all day you will feel relieved to think that all that was only a dream, it didn't happen in reality. What, asleep already?

Secretly, I read a book about dreams. How easily I explained dreams to her. But I really believe in the good and bad influences of dreams. I believe in palmistry. Most of all, I believe in stones.

My gold ring contains two stones. My daughter knows that they are only there to enhance the beauty of the ring. Can I show her, tell her everything?

No, the book says nothing about the significance, good or bad, about a lame girl dreaming about running around freely and easily.

There's a knock at the door. Pintu, from next door, has come around before. My daughter leaves her book in the drawing room. I have taught my daughter that eavesdropping is wrong. She has learned this well. I am myself eavesdropping now, under the pretext of washing my hands at the dining-room basin.

They are very free together. But I know they are only friends. If Pintu ever proposes, my daughter will die laughing. Yet, they are talking about current sexual topics. Pintu is narrating tales of exploits in a brothel.

My ears sting. My daughter has not yet passed the age of fifteen. I feel helpless. I stumble into bed with a severe headache. I try to reason with myself. This is me. I shan't be like other mothers, that is why I have taught her everything since puberty. First menstruation, conception, how the foetus is conceived, love, marriage and everything else. Abroad, they have classes on such topics in school. I see nothing wrong in any of these young children. I have also taught her that everything has its own age, its own phase. Will my daughter remain within the bounds of my teaching?

This, this is her own nature. This is what she is proving now. Who knows? One day she might even bring some layabout hooligan and try to convince me that this is her true mate.

I am afraid. Very afraid. My problem is that no one is attracted to me. That is why, night and day, I focus all my attentions on her.

If I could find any other object for my affections, I could have escaped this poison of love's overflow.

For many years I have been looking for a book. Some biography of a crippled woman in order to understand how she looked on life, to know her feelings. I have read the life story of the blind Helen Keller. She was blind from birth; I could not empathize with Helen's light and shadows.

Then, must I believe that no crippled woman has ever become a writer? After this – a strong determination takes hold of me. This is my different path – I shall write my autobiography. I shall publish it. My growth, my father's abundant love, my mother's sad and weeping eyes at beholding me – what is so different in all this? My parents' deaths, my brothers' separation, my father's getting me married to a useless but propertied man, his death – yes, death hovers around me. We have let out the downstairs apartment. My daughter and I are alive and kicking – so where is the struggle?

I have waited so long, so hungrily for two normal legs, for one handsome man.

No, everybody walks normally, while I alone hop along like a frog. This is where I am different – I hide my face in the pages of my book. What a damp smell! I take off the poster of the desolate girl from the wall.

I plunge into the white filigree work of the crochet, into that deep forest Madhabkundo in whose solitude the icy cold water cascades down the fall. Once, I had pressed my father's finger in delight and exclaimed, Beautiful!

I have not seen anything beautiful for a long time!

I stick another picture on the wall – a man's face with his hair blowing in the wind, but with half of his face covered with a tom-cat. My daughter will surely say to me, Where on earth do you get these?

I leave the house, take a long scooter ride. Then I hobble up the stairs to the third floor.

You? At this hour? Mahmuda's eyes are incredulous.

I sink into the sofa and sit there silently.

Any bad news?

There is a strange breeze in her room. I think to myself, I know this scent. How do I know? The cat in our house had it. Yes, he's dead too. On a cold winter night, he was found dead in a ditch. With a twitching nose, I look for the cat.

I ask her, Do you have a pet?

No, I don't. You know I am allergic to cats.

That's what I thought, I mumble. What smell is this, then? My past and present churn inside me.

I ask her, Do you know any woman who is also a writer?

Mahmuda knows me. She says, I might. Why?

I want to write my autobiography. I wanted to write it myself – I struggled hard but could not find the words. But I can think of everything clearly.

Would it matter if it was a male writer?

You do not understand. I will be giving birth to this child in my womb, and I am deathly afraid. What will it be like? This child will be born with my identical structure. Night after night, what cold fear! It will be born either as a cat or a dog. As soon as the doctor pulled it out of my womb, I closed my eyes in mortal dread. A long time later, when I saw the bright sparkling baby lying on the tray, it still had the scissors attached to its navel. I looked at the two perfect legs with exhilaration. Instantly, I felt mixed emotions – this cannot be my child. The doctor must have switched babies. I had this strange feeling for a long time. Much later, maternal love drew her to me. Will a male writer understand all this?

Mahmuda becomes serious.

What smell is this, so familiar? This happens often. Someone I see seems so familiar. But, after talking for a while, I find out that the person is a native of Kolkata and has come to this country for the first time. This happened to my husband on our wedding night. When he said to me, Your face is so familiar, I answered, But of course, it would be so because we two have something in common – we are both human beings. Perhaps this is human nature; not the desire to know the known, but to know the familiar.

Mahmuda says, The few female writers that I know here are pretty conservative. Their writings are pretty restricted. They describe tyrannical mothers-in-law, adulterous husbands, unfilial children – these are the issues that matter to them. There is probably some reason. They will find it problematic to deal with your complex issues – the foetus and its growth, childbirth. The other day, a writer friend of mine said to me she had written a story about a woman's adultery. Before sending it for publication, she gave it to her husband to read – and the husband was furious. Since then, the husband has suspected his wife of some such sin.

I am very sleepy.

Goldfish swim in the water. I stare at them. After some moments, I whisper, Do you know anyone who can give me an amulet to ward off jinns?

Mahmuda is taken aback. You believe in these superstitions?

Somebody knocks at my door night and day – I know it is a jinn. I don't tell my daughter – she will laugh at me. You do not know – those who are deformed always have jinns with them.

Ridiculous! You are going crazy.

I become angry. How can you say that? You yourself pray five times a day. Islam believes in the existence of jinns. Have I said anything contradictory?

After coming back from her house, I fall on the bed. How content I am. Human beings struggle so hard. They sleep on the streets, barely manage one decent meal. I do not have to struggle for money. If father had not left this house to me, I could have procured money by showing my deformity to the world.

I sigh as I think of my daughter. How smart and sophisticated I wanted her to be. Once, I was besotted with her singing lessons. But she said, Everybody sings.

My words were returned to me. Then this is all you will ever be – only a girl.

Then my daughter said, Let me walk upside down on my head. That will be doing something different.

Now this girl talks about God knows what with Pintu. Have I made a mistake in telling her everything? But a few of her friends – whose parents are shocked and tongue-tied at such topics – are even more daring. When I hear of their forward behaviour from my daughter's mouth, my nerves throb with anger. Some of them have already had sex at this age, some ...

My daughter just talks. Why then do I watch her so? She never hides anything from me. What else do I want?

She could not become anything different, special!

A heavy sigh, heavy as grey smoke, issues from my suffering breast. That is why I look at myself. Since birth I have seen that people stare and crane their necks to look at me, as they look at big, glamorous stars. But their expressions always make me cringe. Some of them give a muffled laugh and mock me with, Ah, ha! I find myself amidst such people still. The more I walk, the more I suffer. I am stubborn. I want to display myself even more. What can I do to make my deformity exceptional?

At one time I had thought that I should cut off my leg to make them both the same length. This feeling used to wrench my heart. My constant thought would be, How can I make the two equal? Once, leaving such bizarre thoughts aside, I had specially made wooden shoes. One had a heel, the other did not. I was walking along, somewhat draggingly, when a youth commented from behind, When did this cripple fix herself? In such situations people are very cruel. I hurled away the shoe and once again became my natural self.

When I think of this, I feel goose-pimples all over me. I feel somebody is walking on the other side of the mosquito net. I hear a sound at the front door. Am I sleeping? I cannot identify the sound for a while. Is it the sound of my own foot? Who is it that threatens me so with fear? Why this continuous tapping on the door? Do I know who it is? I am very afraid.

As I open the door to walk into my daughter's room, I hear breathing in the corridor. I run and fall on my daughter's breast, deathly afraid.

My daughter runs her fingers through my hair and says, You are so alone, it makes me sad. After a long silence, she adds, You could have remarried!

What would have happened to you then?

I would have called that man my father.

I have not done it, that is why you say so today. If I had, you would have punished me.

You do not know me.

I don't know you? I ask incredulously. Some time ago you were a little different. You would cry so much because you wanted to take me to your friend's get-together. You would say, My mother may be broken, she may be a cripple, still she is my pride. If anyone laughed, you would quarrel with her. Now you say, If you went to such places, you would feel sick and uneasy. You would not be able to tolerate so much noise.

Actually, that is not it. My friends say that you are overprotective.

Actually, your world has become much larger, I say, and I admit it readily without pain. Your mother hobbling beside you would only diminish your beauty.

You yourself have changed so much, Mother. I hardly understand you now.

After many years, I feel my own mother's pain. Why did you not die in the womb? my mother always lamented, and so I had always thought her to be my enemy. Actually, everyone's expression of pain is unique. When she was dying she called for me – I had not gone. I understand her feelings now. A child remains the property of its mother for some time. How stubborn I was then! I was just such a problematic property of my mother. Because my mother could not throw me away, she behaved strangely with me. My daughter's slight originality therefore frightens me. When I think of my mother dying and her terrible agony, I weep silently.

I look at the distant road as I sit on the chair on the verandah. This part of the city is still uncongested. This road, this palm tree, they give me solace every time. The house on the right has a verandah on which a young boy now stands. I have never seen him before. There is a magic play of light and shadow – do I really look so remarkable? He is staring at me so strangely. I shrink but then I realize that he cannot see my legs. After many years, my nerves begin to jangle. I think, even if he stands there forever, I shall not get up in front of him to walk back into the house.

My daughter comes to the verandah. I am like a frozen statue. She sits on the verandah with her legs apart. With green, wet henna on her palms, she says, Isn't the boy too thin and gangly, Mother?

I often think that I will write. I cannot paint. I cannot sing. I know Bengali. Through it I will express my feelings. I think in so many ways. So many of my thoughts have the same theme – deformity and decrepitude. I think, I will write a story – a man steals his child from his wife as soon as it is born because it does not have any hands. He runs and runs with it across the green fields to throw it into the river. He stumbles and falls. The newborn babe immediately says to the father, Father, can you not find me? Here I am, inside the paddy fields. This is no story. I tell the woman next door, I really want to write. She says, Exactly my predicament. If I could only write a single line! I take up paper and pen. There are so many incidents in life – I feel like writing.

No! This ordinary woman has the same desire as mine. I relinquish my own desire to write. I tell my daughter, If only I could find myself in you. You still have time, your life is just beginning.

What do I lack? my daughter says, raising her voice.

You are not doing too badly in your studies. That anyone can do. You will get through your Matric – I can't see much more than that.

You got married right after passing your Matric, says my daughter. I want to do my MA – nothing before that. What's wrong with my plans?

I suppress my sighs and say, But did I get married right after my Matric? I went to college, but on the very first day, the students mocked my hobbled gait so much that I never went back.

My daughter displays her perfect legs and says, These should have made you happy.

When evening settles through the house, my daughter silently opens the door and goes towards the stairs. I stand ghostlike on my crippled leg on this side of the door. Someone is coming up the stairs. The smoke of the mosquito coil is so strong, I crinkle my nose. I hear my daughter's voice say to someone, You knock all the time, I know. What a hero! Why do you run away after knocking? If I tell my mother now ...

Someone laughs. I freeze.

My daughter says, Can't you sleep? In the middle of the night too. Are you insane?

Someone says, I will do it even more.

If I don't break Pintu's leg ...

Day follows day in this manner. Time flows on. I bend, I grow cold.

One day, to my excitement I discover the meaning of another dream in my book of dreams. This dream means that chronic ailments will be cured. Last night, I saw this dream. In the light of day I learn its meaning and start to sweat. I do not need to be anyone special in this life. All I want is to stand upon two firm legs on this earth. I convince myself that one day this dream will come true. I count the passing hours. When will my leg become longer?

In the outer room I can hear Pintu's voice. Henna on your toes? Your feet are beautiful as they are.

My daughter whispers, Do you know, Mother is jealous of me.

Translated by Rebecca Haque

SHAHEEN AKHTAR

The Make-up Box

A never-ending funeral march

Looping itself around the cluster of *hijal* trees, a hair-thin line ran parallel
to the river bank, cutting across the ground. Inside the loop were a few
derelict huts, an empty field, a few date palms and the grave of Mallika's
younger sister, Mala. This was where the river's fury was directed. For a
month it had been raging wrathfully, all bristled up. The monsoon rain
had an intoxicating effect. Like a wild bull, it raised its horns and charged
in all directions, biting off anything that came in its way, be it trees or
cultivated fields.

Ignoring the large-scale erosion of the riverbanks, Mallika had buried
her younger sister Mala under the *hijal* tree. She did not know that a
prostitute was not entitled to a *janaza* or burial. She had an altercation
with the undertaker outside the door of the dissection room, after the
post-mortem was over and the surgeon who had conducted the autopsy
left. She might have been a prostitute or a woman who slept with twelve
different people, but after all, Mala's body, as Mallika, the garments-

factory worker, insisted, wasn't an unclaimed one. Why then should she be dispatched to the morgue? And made to rot, huddled with ten other bodies? And then, if what the undertaker said was true, one day, by the divine grace of the Anjuman, she would find a place in an unknown grave. How would Mallika, nurtured in the same mother's womb, live with that?

Amid such logic, Mallika, intermittently, waxed emotional. The droning sound of her sobs tore fissures in the undertaker's heavy stupor (he was drunk up to the gills) in the numbing afternoon. Perhaps that's what worked. The fog receded. A bright sunbeam fell on the undertaker's head dazzlingly. The preliminary altercations over, he no longer said much. After all, it was just one body, he thought, and a prostitute's at that. Normally one's folks did not acknowledge any tie in such cases. Sister or whatever she was, here was one who had, at least, come to claim the body. What did he care whether she tied bricks to the neck of the body and pushed it in the middle of the river or dropped it in the city's garbage dump? On the other hand, even if the Anjuman picked up this one, that would be right at the end, after the last rites of a whole lot of rotting, decomposing offal had been performed. And what mattered most was that he wouldn't be making a penny by way of cuts.

The undertaker made a round of the morgue, spilling over with flesh and blood, and agreed to comply with Mallika's request. Then he, with a few of his cohorts, using a thick cord, the sort used to sew up gunny bags, stitched up Mala's body. Bucketfuls of water were splashed on it to wash it clean and the unbleached length of cloth brought by her sister was wrapped around the frame. The marks of incision, arising from either side of her uncovered shoulders, joined together right at the top of the cleavage, like a necklace. Mallika, not in her dreams but wide awake in the foully reeking dissection room – like a singed bird – could see a locket hanging there. There was blood in the corner of the girl's mouth but the lips seemed to have been coloured with a lipstick. The false mole on her chin made the dead girl look even more beautiful.

Mala had fallen in love with make-up from the age when she had started to crawl. When she was just six months old, Mallika remembers how she would brush a little tablet of red lac dye on Mala's lips to make her stop crying. How she would chortle even as her eyes held back the tears.

Those days belonged to another era and a lost world, where they were happy, once upon a time. When their parents died, the two girls left the village and came to the city, putting themselves up in a city house. Mallika found a job as a helper in the garments factory. She would go out to work at eight in the morning, and, when working overtime, would return only at ten at night. Mala would stay up till her breadwinner of a sister came home, dozing off sitting in front of the wick lamp, but not going to sleep. She didn't cry when she burned her hands, trying to strain the water from boiled rice. Once Mallika had beaten her black and blue after she had secretly put on some lipstick.

A lumpy sigh shook through the centre of her navel, coming up like a dogged fleet of mosquitoes, moving from wall to wall of the stuffy dissection room. It hampered the undertaker's work. But Mallika's drone didn't seem to end.

By the time one had gone through the thousand and one formalities of the hospital, it had got late. Mallika received Mala's anointed body and climbed on to the van. In the dark night of rain, the van, its bell tinkling, moved towards the darkest graveyard in the city. What if this road never ended, wondered Mallika. She was meeting her sister after five years, and this was the first time she was taking her out. She had never shown her around the city, never taken her on a rickshaw ride. Not that she had never thought of doing it, but where was the time? Besides, money was a constraint. Her sister had left home, lured by a make-up box. She had become a whore. Mallika, when she got the news, ran to the crossroads to bring her back. Her companion took cover for the moment. But Mala herself was adamant. The girl who had never said a word when she was beaten black and blue, raised the black make-up box, trying to hit her elder sister on the head. Quite a crowd had gathered at the crossroads to watch the scene.

Mala never came back.

Now it was Mallika who accompanied her sister on the van, in the night of storm and rain. And indeed, the road they had taken did not seem to end. Mallika could not quite figure out if this ever-lengthening road would take them to heaven or straight to hell. The oil in the lantern she held in her hands burned out. But still, like a nocturnal animal, she carried her sister's corpse from one cemetery to the next in the darkness of the night.

Just three and a half feet of earth

Inside the tiled hut of the office room at the entrance of the first cemetery where Mallika stopped the van sat a man wearing a round cap, swatting at the mosquitoes. There were hundreds of them flocking around his black robe. Insects of all kinds banged their heads against the bulb in one corner of the room. 'I don't care if it's the body of a governor, a king, a minister or a millionaire,' the man said, very clearly, as he finished off a few more. Mosquitoes, that is. 'No one will be buried here at night.' But when he saw that the girl, her body taut under the wet clothes, was still standing at the door, his blood-smeared hands felt numb. He asked Mallika to get the doctor's certificate during the day and somehow managed to make her leave. It took the man in the black robe a little time to restart his job of destroying mosquitoes.

That night, it rained in the first hour, the moon appeared in the sky in the second and in the last there was a rumbling of clouds. But even as the strange game between clouds, the rain and the moonbeams were played out every hour, Mallika got the same answer from every cemetery she went to. The van wallah grew restless. After all, it wasn't as if he was driving the *tazia*, the replica of the tomb of Imam Husain, the Prophet's grandson on Muharram Day. He wasn't required to move all across the city through the night. He hatched an unholy plot. When Mallika visited the office of each cemetery, the man, swishing his wet clothes, walked into the dark hole of the adjacent mosque, ostensibly to light a fag. And that's how, before the night was over, the news that the body in question was that of a whore spread from cemetery to cemetery, like wildfire. In the morning, despite the doctor's certificate, the van could not go anywhere near the cemeteries. Mallika could see huge crowds in front of the gates from a distance. The people wore caps on their heads and carried an array of weapons in their hands. They were, Mallika realized very clearly indeed, now that it was day, ready to break their heads, serve a prison term if necessary but determined not to allow three and a half feet of burial space for the dead girl who had been a whore.

Two strangers in the caravan

Now out of the city, Mallika let the van go and hired a bullock cart. She laid Mala's body on the bamboo platform with great care, and then climbed on to the cart and sat with an open umbrella covering her sister's body. Now one could tie a stone around the corpse's neck and sink it in the river. If one was unable to do it personally, going to the nearby villages to try and persuade people to do it was the only option left. That's what Mallika did.

Slicing through the intense silence of the village, the bullock cart screeched and groaned as it proceeded. Now they were five in all, including the two bullocks. Mallika felt slightly more reassured, now that the team had grown in numbers, even if the two new members were simple creatures. Besides, she knew that in villages like these, although it was not uncommon to have one's residence occupied by others, it wasn't too difficult to find space to bury the dead. When her parents died within two days of each other, leaving behind two little girls, they did not have a single grain of food in the house, let alone money. But when they heard the news of the deaths, the villagers seemed to arrive in droves, flying in. The sisters didn't realize from where the shroud, a fresh bar of soap, bamboo poles, perfume and benzene were obtained.

The feeling of horror that had tightened inside Mallika now relaxed slightly. Beyond the fields of paddy was a row of huts where people lived. Once the five-member team reached there, Mallika wouldn't need to do a thing. The villagers, strangers though they were, would come running to lift Mala in their arms. Seeing that a three-day-old corpse was still above the ground and not under it, they would be cursing the educated people in the city, blaming their negligence on their breeding. In the meantime, two able-bodied men would be sent to the nearest market to get incense sticks, perfume and the shroud. This time Mallika did have some money. She would pay for these things, even if she had to force it on them. The eldest woman in the village would put up a mosquito net from four banana trees and wash Mala under it. Then the *janaza* would be read. A silent procession of mourners, bearing the coffin on their shoulders, would slowly proceed towards the graveyard. Mallika would howl and scream in the receding courtyard. She would scream so loudly that she would shake the throne of God with her plaint, demanding to know why her sister had been murdered in her sleep. Her emotions had been held at bay during the last three days, running between police stations, hospitals and graveyards.

Suddenly Mallika started crying.

The sound of her loud wails reached the village. Crowds – young, old, men, women – came running like a swarm of locusts to the bullock cart that carried a corpse. They wanted to find out who among them had been visited by ill luck. There was no house in the village that did not have a member or two living in the city. They removed the shroud and stumbled over Mala's face. In the midst of the tremendous pushing and nudging, the bullocks started to bellow. The cart driver flew off his seat. Mallika was being crushed between people. The pushing and the wailing went on till all the people in the village were convinced that the dead body did not belong to any of their own folk nor to anybody they knew. And then the villagers shifted their attention from the corpse to the others. Well, a bullock cart would have bullocks and a driver, but who was that woman with the corpse? Why had she entered an unknown village with the body of a murdered woman? The men in the village started interrogating Mallika.

Hearing that Mallika wanted to bury the corpse in their village, they became more apprehensive. It was difficult enough coping with the tyranny of the police when there was the odd murder in the village – even birds deserted the place at such times – and now a woman had arrived from nowhere with a corpse. What kind of a childish whim was this that she should want to bury it here? Besides the apprehension, there were sparks of suspicion on their faces. They interrogated Mallika about and were told Mallika's father's name, her postal address, etc. But that place was a long way off. Never in their lives or in that of their fathers had these people heard of such absurd names. Mallika told them the truth about where she lived and what she did in the city near by, but she did not reveal that Mala was a prostitute. They did not – so generous of them – want to know the story behind the murder and Mallika too said nothing. She said there were so many people in the city that it was difficult to find a place to rest one's head in. People lived in railway stations, on the roads, so where was there a place to bury the dead?

The villagers were taken in. A sense of compassion for the city people welled up in some of them because in the village even those who couldn't grow enough to sustain themselves round the year were entitled to a burial space – near the outhouse, beside ponds. And for those who did not have a house of their own, there would be a public plot of land, reserved for burial with due ceremony. The villagers agreed to find a place for Mallika's sister in the community burial ground, but they would send two people to the city for more information.

It was time for the Friday prayers. The chant of the *azan* could be heard. The men of the village sent off two people to the city before joining the prayer at the mosque. The women went back to work after they had had a look at the corpse's face. Only the children remained, keeping an eye on Mallika and her team.

The cart driver had had a long and arduous day. His glance must have fallen on the usher of ill luck when he stepped out to work in the morning. His very first passenger was a dead person, and now the business of getting her buried was causing all the trouble. When did he think he was going to get out of this mess? Sitting under the shade of the mango tree, the driver ruminated, resting his cheek against a hand. At a cue from Mallika, he started harnessing the bullocks to the cart. Mala was lying on the bamboo platform just as before. Mallika climbed up and sat beside her, umbrella in hand. The cart started moving even before the children became fully aware of it. The bullocks had not had a very good time in this village. They had been pushed without reason. Now they started to gallop fast, like horses, leaving the children behind.

Make-up man, magic box and a young woman

On the second night, the make-up man who worked in the brothel joined the caravan. He was one of the people – pimp, grocer, shop-owner, prostitutes and the madam of the brothel – whom the police had picked up for interrogation after Mala's murder. Since his release from police custody, the man had gone looking for Mala's body in hospitals, graveyards and elsewhere like a man possessed. Two days later, he could see the bullock cart, like a small meteor, rushing towards him like a streak of light, cutting across the dark breast of the village. The man was forty, blind in one eye, and constantly snivelling. Looking at the huge black make-up box in his hand, anybody would have thought that he was a great physician or a magician who could make the impossible happen – even revive the dead.

Mallika started when she saw the man's blind eye. Three days had passed and her sister had not been buried yet. Was this the custodian of graveyards, blind in the right eye then? Had he, not finding the dead body where it ought to have been, come this far to ask for an explanation? Frightened, she moved a little to make room for him on the cart. And the man, to her utter surprise, started whining as soon as he was on board.

The bullock cart moved towards the river. From a distance, they could hear the deep thumping sound of the land breaking off along the river. Mallika wondered what kind of danger awaited them in that place of fearful devastation. The man, she knew now, was not the custodian of graveyards; in fact, he was no one to this cruel world. But there was no saying that he wouldn't be useful, she thought.

Throughout the journey the make-up man had tears rolling down from his lone eye. 'She was my sister, my mother. Now I am an orphan.' Mallika had tears in her eyes for the second time since that afternoon. So there was a mother's heart inside the body of the small self-centred girl, after all. Why, she hadn't known that in the twelve years that she had brought her up.

'You wouldn't believe it, sister,' said the man, suddenly catching hold of Mallika's hand. 'You see, I was not married. Sometimes she would call me a provider. I was the husband and she my wife.' In other times, Mallika would have yanked the make-up man's hand off her and given him a severe scolding. She would have shut his mouth forever, like the closed eyelid on his blind eye. But now, to her, the man was like a long-lost relative, her only sympathizer. And what mattered more than all else was that, three days after the woman had died, this was the first time someone was mourning her. Mallika joined him in his lament, crying in tune with him.

With a little indulgence from Mallika, the memories started running this way and that inside the make-up man's heart. They would then stumble and fall out of his lips. 'I taught her how to tie a brassiere.' Stretching out his palm, he curled his fingers like an eagle's beak. 'Tight, pointed brassieres, like this,' he said. Did Mala turn a little in the darkness? In the last five years, the man had applied colour on her lips and cheeks. He had tied her hair into a bun and taught her to stick artificial flowers in it: 'These are the places to plant them in and that's how you do it.' He had told her many times how to wear the sari loosely, with her breasts outside the cover, and send out a ripple across her waistline when she was standing. As the make-up man went on, Mallika could almost see her adolescent sister turning into a full-blooded young woman. She forgot that the body lying in front of her – whose foul smell was difficult to ward off despite the half-dozen incense sticks burning away – the body that would be buried beside the river in a few hours, was that of her dead sister, Mala.

… You break one to build another

Mallika went back home after three days. Only three days away from her room, bed and furniture, yet they appeared unfamiliar. She felt as if these weren't hers but someone else's. Despite being extremely tired, Mallika was unable to sleep at night. It seemed as if she had hidden her sister under the earth, so that the villagers and the lathi-wielding guards employed at the cemeteries could not find her. There was no witness to or evidence of the act. Not even the man who had groomed Mala for five years, helping her to come into her own – the make-up man in whose colourful descriptions her sister was still alive. As soon as they reached the river bank, Mallika made him leave with his make-up box, along with the bullock cart and its driver. The man did not get to know that the beautiful woman he had sculpted – the girl whose *janaza* was left unperformed and whose body was not covered by a shroud – had not floated away in the river, draped in her sister's sari. She was lying in a grave under the *hijal* tree. Strangely enough, within an hour, small *hijal* flowers began to drop all over the grave covering it like a pink blanket.

The next day Mallika did not go to the garments factory. She left her rented room in the city and took shelter in a derelict hut near Mala's grave, beside the river. Now her only occupation was to guard her sister.

Five years before, when Mala had left home, Mallika was busy, looking for a means to earn a living. Now she was rid of these concerns. Journeying through the harsh terrains of the world with her sister's corpse, Mallika had forgotten about hunger and lost sleep. Now, standing in the middle of the raging river, the rattling riverbank and the tearing gusts of wind, Mallika could well think of herself as one who did not belong to this world. Mala and she were the residents of a momentary island, one that the river had claimed by marking out the boundaries. The difference was that one of them lived on the surface of the island and the other below it.

Although she knew how rivers built and destroyed the land as a matter of routine, Mallika couldn't see the hazy line of alluvial soil across the river, even once. Sitting in the middle of collapsing river banks, she began picking up the *hijal* flowers from the ground, stringing them into a garland, long like an elegy.

Mallika and Mala had all the time in the world.

Translated by Chitralekha Basu

PAPRI RAHMAN

The Rainbow Bird of Slumber and Dreams

Sorman Sheikh bent a little further over the well. The water was almost up to the brim. His head bent lower, as though the water was pulling it towards its centre. At that moment, a medium-sized fish fell on Sorman Sheikh's feet. Suddenly he felt the touch of a cold hand! His whole body shuddered terribly. All this time, a cold squiggly earthworm had been crawling up his spine. When the fish fell, the earthworm started creeping on to his neck. The extreme discomfort stiffened his face as he stared at his still reflection in the hazy mirror of the water. Sorman Sheikh stood upright, shoving aside the cold feeling, the disgusting earthworm, the fear. And at that moment his reflection in the water shook, and Monowara's shrill voice penetrated his ears.

'That greedy old man! All he wants to do is eat! His hunger is never satisfied! And you are up to new games now! Don't you feel ashamed to ask other people for food? Are you a beggar – begging for food, being greedy?'

Monowara's pent-up anger seemed to rip through her voice. The two crows resting on the bamboo twig cawed loudly as they flew away to sit on another shoot. The young branch bent low over the well under the weight of the crows. Sorman Sheikh alone watched this interaction between the supple bamboo and the crows. His feet seemed to be pinned to the ground, and all he could do was stand there, a silent spectator. His legs were frozen and all his efforts couldn't move them. Sorman Sheikh had no choice but to bend again over the shivering mirror of the water, ruffled by tiny waves. Sorman Sheikh's reflection rippled through the water with the playful waves and glided to the sides of the well, where it seemed to get stuck.

Gradually the broken waves came to a standstill, and Sorman Sheikh gazed hazily at his reflection – the clotted grey beard, white rough hair and ruined face. Sorman Sheikh was overtaken by melancholy as he stared fixedly at this image. The fish – a *rui* – was lying at his feet. Monowara's voice kept up its harsh reproaches.

'This old beggar refuses to die! He tortures me to death! He has finished off his wife! I wonder when this old crock will die!'

Despite all Monowara's efforts to send Sorman Sheikh to the next world, he was not going anywhere – at least not on that day. He wasn't going to go anywhere before he had filled himself with steaming rice and fresh fish curry. Sorman Sheikh moved away from the well quietly, wondering whether to proceed towards the food. The plant at the doorway of the house seemed to touch the sky. He stood silently in its shelter, trying to measure the distance of the far sky with his old eyes, which seemed to get lost between the loose folds of his skin. He failed to measure it ultimately and, to hide his failure, he started following Monowara's movements.

Monowara took the fish by its tail and sat down on a stool. With an experienced hand, she sliced off its head. The damp soil seemed to become damper as the blackish blood glided down the gutter. After cutting the fish, she threw the waste on the ground. The entrails fell on the nearby slope. There was a cluster of bamboos along the slope. The young twigs seemed to spread their arms generously to cover a large portion of the well. The crows sitting on one of these branches jumped on the thrown waste at once and happily started playing with it. They seemed to be having a friendly duel – without much bother, no quarrelling or fighting – a playful tussle for the food. Monowara didn't notice the food being divided up neatly among the crows, as she was totally engrossed in cutting fish. Grimly, she counted the plump pieces of fish. A sudden ray of happiness lighted her face as she reassured herself, 'Good – we can have two good meals today!'

As she stood by the well with the earthen bowl full of fish, the ray of happiness continued to touch her face. Singing softly, she let down the rope and swiftly pulled up a bucket of water. Sorman Sheikh could tell what she would do next, even without looking – Monowara would rub the fish against the bowl to get rid of the odour. She would sing the ballad of Leelabati while washing the fish in the water. This would greatly enhance its taste. The sweet song mixed with its magical echo among the bamboo leaves would create a mysterious melody that would soothe her bad mood.

I was asleep – drowned in the night
A thief entered and stole my jewel ...
I am still in search of that gem
I cry through the night – in sorrow and in pain.
My eyes are blinded with tears
To what far land has my caged bird flown?
I have no wings to fly
Or I would have flown to meet my friend.

Sorman Sheikh could not wait any longer. The scorching sun seemed to burn through the leaves, and the oil on his head trickled down the sides of his ears as the huge umbrella-like shade that had been protecting him moved away. He still had a lot to do. Looking at the cooking and food arrangements, he felt that he had to pamper himself. He needed a good bath, he felt. He knew that Monowara was in a bad mood and therefore would not fetch water from the well for him. The pond was his only resort.

When the sun was at its peak, Sorman Sheikh moved away from the doorway. The roof of the verandah was made up of four rusted pieces of tin. There was a long stool on the verandah for prayers. Its legs had become wobbly, having been left at the mercy of the sun and the rain. Sorman Sheikh would hide a sweet-scented bar of soap under this stool. The last time he had used this bar of soap was about five days ago. He desperately searched for that small bit of left-over soap, but it was nowhere to be found. It seemed to have vanished into thin air. Dulu Mia was responsible for this. His grandson couldn't resist these pieces of soap, blowing bubbles and balloons with the foam. The bubbles would disintegrate in the breeze, but Dulu Mia would persist. He kept on making bubbles, blowing them again and again as they burst and vanished into the air.

Sorman Sheikh was disappointed not to find the piece of soap just when he needed it. This was certainly one of his bad habits – this desire to be trim and spruce when a good meal was being served. He liked spending time on himself – preening his body and rubbing his skin with a scrub until it stung. The black marks on his body became a little paler with this sudden scrubbing. But not being able to find the thin slice of sweet-scented soap, Sorman Sheikh reconciled himself to the idea that the banks of the pond would not be suffused with the sweet smell of his bath. However, he might still find Dulu Mia if he was lucky. Dulu Mia was equally scared of Monowara's temper and fled the moment he knew that his mother was in one of her bad moods. During these bouts of ill temper, Monowara would lose all control and beat him mercilessly.

Sorman Sheikh didn't waste any more time looking for the soap. He started off towards the pond with the dirty faded towel and *lungi*. These days he felt weak and tired and had trouble walking. His body was a source of great suffering – his head bent towards the ground when he walked. His erect backbone had begun to rust a long time ago. Old age dragged at his knees, saying, 'You have walked far enough, old man! Take some rest now.'

Monowara's temper – justified or not – created problems for Sorman Sheikh. He could not step over the fence that Monowara's stubbornness had created. While in a good mood, she took good care of her father-in-law – fetching his bath water in the bucket, handing him oil or clothes and so on. However, under these circumstances there was no possibility of getting such treatment from her.

Sorman Sheikh bumped and stumbled his way to the pond. No matter how painful the journey to the water, his eyes lit up as he beheld the water of the pond – it seemed to reflect all the colours of his life.

The surrounding green of the trees made the water even cooler. A large tree had spread its branches over the pond, creating a canopy, while other branches spread upwards, seeming to touch the sky. Creepers and smaller trees stretched past the bushes that huddled against the thick trunk of the larger tree. One mystery was beyond Sorman Sheikh – that of the two kingfishers he always saw on the banks of the pond. All they did was sit and doze together. How strange! All they did was sleep, instead of leaping around and looking for fish. What did they eat? How did they feed themselves?

The water of the pond had brimmed over as it was the rainy season, but it still hadn't flooded the surrounding area – only up to the bushes. Sorman Sheikh was easily scared these days. Age was creeping up on him, and the growing dimness of his eyes was a source of worry. He felt he could easily slip and drown in the deep water of the pond. He looked around in the hope of finding Dulu Mia, but he was nowhere to be seen. The kingfisher couple spread their wings lazily and then went back to sleep. Clambering down the bank, Sorman Sheikh paddled carefully in hip-deep water. He dipped into the water without wetting the top of his head – just half-dips. But he felt as if he had immersed himself deep in the water – under the depths of the seven seas. He quickly struggled back to the bank of the pond. Actually it was the thought of the fish curry that was making him restless. The water made small ripples as he hurried past the bushes.

Beyond the Chowdhurys' pond lay the trodden path. Grass fields bordered this path, which glided snake-like over the land, and in the rainy season the place was sticky and muddy. The monsoons spoiled Sorman Sheikh's undiluted pleasure in his bath, polluted by the stickiness and the mud, which stuck between his toes, forming horrible lumps. But for the time being he did not think of these factors – all he could think of were the large, juicy chunks of fish.

A bundle of bamboo splits lay in the courtyard of the house. Sorman Sheikh spread his wet *lungi* and tattered towel on this with his feeble, trembling hands. He tried to focus – bringing out his eyes from under his sagging old skin. The sun's glare had reduced a bit. It was difficult for him to tell the time with his weak eyesight. He would have to sense the time of day, guessing whether it was night or day. The scorching rays of the midday sun and the heat seemed to burn his wrinkled skin as he tried to tell the time. A mild heat pricked him, and his mind was lit by an orange flame.

He silently crossed the courtyard. He sat on the stool on the verandah, clearing his throat to attract attention. This declaration of hunger was of no avail, however. Nobody was around. Where had everyone gone? Suddenly, after about fifteen minutes, Dulu Mia appeared out of nowhere. Without giving him a chance to say anything, Dulu Mia started pulling at his hand, 'Come on, Grandfather. Don't you want to eat? Mother has cooked fish curry. Why are you so late? My stomach is churning with hunger.'

Dulu Mia took his grandfather's rough hands and put them on his stomach. Sorman Sheikh pulled his hands away and sat tight, as if to say, 'You monkey! Where were you all this while?'

But he couldn't keep up this pose for long in front of Dulu Mia. His intestines were melting with hunger, but he had to bide his time a little longer, trying to gauge Monowara's mood. How could he blame her for her ill temper? A woman whose husband was a vagabond couldn't have much peace of mind. Even as a father, he couldn't explain why his son had decided to leave his home and live the life of a vagabond. Everything had been fine in the beginning. Dulu Mia had been born, lighting their world like a moon. It was after that that Armaan seemed to lose interest, and even Dulu Mia's infant cries couldn't make Armaan return home. Sorman Sheikh had almost given up hope of his son's return. And it was just then that Armaan had come home, during the *baruni* fair. That was the only time of the year when Armaan was seen. Those days were like Eid for Dulu Mia. He would forget the pain of not having his father all year round as he played with the earthen horse, the kite and the other presents his father gave him. Armaan would also devote all his time to his son. But after a few days of this domesticity, he would be overcome by the old feeling and flee from his family. Sometimes he would send some money. Sorman Sheikh had no idea what his son did or where he lived during his absences. Monowara remained depressed – struggling with her husband's vagabond life and the constant poverty. The heat of her temper burned into the soul of her old father-in-law.

By the time he sat down to eat, Sorman Sheikh had forgotten the horrible show of temper with which the day had started. Monowara had spread a mat on the floor and carefully laid plates for grandfather and grandson. There was hot rice, fish curry, mashed beans and *daal*.

Monowara was an excellent cook. The moment he put some rice with the fish curry into his mouth, his stomach started rumbling and making sounds. But he could not get up as the two pieces of fish on his plate were too tempting. He looked at Dulu Mia through the corner of his eye. Dulu Mia was amazed at the way his grandfather was eating, so much so that he even forgot to eat himself. Monowara gathered the last bit of rice from the pot and put it on Dulu Mia's plate, saying, 'No more rice today, son, finish this.'

Sorman Sheikh ate on. At the sound of Monowara's voice, he hid his head between his knees. His stomach still felt empty. What could he do? Perhaps his daughter-in-law would have to go without food again. This happened all too frequently. But what was Sorman Sheikh to do? The hungry monster in his stomach went crazy at the sight of food, and he couldn't help himself. The uneasiness in his stomach increased as he finished his meal. And just then Monowara remembered the unpleasant incident of the morning. She berated him, 'Did you really ask Atarjan for food? How could you do that? How could you be so shameless?'

With the taste of the fish still lingering in his mouth, Sorman Sheikh was in no mood to answer this question. He knew he had done something wrong. With age creeping up on him, he had lost all self-restraint and could not ignore his desire for a good meal. But he felt he hadn't committed that big a crime. Asking for something from Atarjan – who was after all a distant relative – could not be that shameful. Atarjan was married into a well-off family. She was visiting her father's house for a few days. Knowing this, Sorman Sheikh had blurted out his desire for fish. That was it! Monowara would not ask anyone for food, even if she were starving to death. Poverty had hardened her, and she was not about to become a beggar. It was Atarjan's present of fish that had put her into such a bad mood. Monowara asked again in a softened tone, 'Why don't you say something? You wanted to eat fish?'

The rumble inside Sorman Sheikh's stomach had reached its peak. He somehow nodded in reply to Monowara's inquisition and ran towards the well. He sat behind the dry banana leaves, trying to release the uneasiness in his stomach.

Dulu Mia looked for his grandfather all over the house. He called out for him, but his young voice could not reach very far. Finally he approached the pond. Dulu Mia's lively eyes found Sorman Sheikh sitting behind the bush in knee-deep water in his wet *lungi*. Maybe his grandfather hadn't been able to dip in the pond. As Dulu Mia approached him, Sorman Sheikh gestured to him to stay quiet.

'Hey Grandfather! What are you doing there?'

'Oh, shut up!'

'Why? Haven't you already had your bath? Why have you come again?'

'Didn't I tell you to shut up?'

'Why?'

'Look at the branch.'

'What? Is there anything new to see?'

'Look at it first.'

Dulu Mia couldn't see anything special. Just three pairs of kingfishers displaying all their colours on the lower branch. Their bright colours melted into the water of the pond. Sorman Sheikh watched in wonder as two of the kingfishers dived into the water and returned to the branch with a big fish between their beaks.

He had been watching them for so long but had never seen them catch fish. He turned his thoughts from the kingfishers to Dulu Mia.

'What have you been doing here for so long?'

'Watching birds.'

'Haven't you seen birds before?'

'Can't you see, they have some visitors today?'

'How do you know they are guests?'

'They are catching fish for the guests.'

'How does that matter to you?'

'Not at all. Just that everyone wants to eat good food.'

'Rubbish. Fish is their food.'

'Then why were they dozing all this time?'

'I don't understand a word of what you are saying.'

'You don't have to understand. Go home.'

'Come with me. Why are you sitting in the water? Do you want to catch a fever? Did you dirty your clothes?'

'I don't know how it happened. Can't seem to control it.'

'Mother will be furious. Can't you eat less if your stomach is upset?'

'Don't tell your mother.'

'Ok, I won't. Now let's go.'

A foul smell filled the air as Sorman Sheikh emerged from behind the bush. Dulu Mia held his nose with his fingers and, even though he felt like throwing up, he was extremely sorry for his grandfather. Still holding his nose, he said, 'What have you done? Mother will kill you when she sees this.'

As the afternoon sun went down, Sorman Sheikh reached home with Dulu Mia.

Caged birds do not have to fend for themselves in forests –
How can you ever forget the care given to you?
Those who cared for you with puddings and pies
How can you ever forget their care?
All that love and care –
And what did she say when she left?
Naming some country she departed –
I am sure you birds know a thing or two.

Monowara hummed softly as the sun went down, her song floating clearly through the air. She had seen the performance of the ballad of Leela and Kanka a long time ago with Armaan. How happy Armaan had been after the show! Monowara flushed with pleasure remembering that scene. Sorrow had now become her constant companion, and Leela's sad song echoed through her voice. Tears flowed from Sorman Sheikh's eyes as the music of the song wafted to his ears. He understood her sadness – the sadness of a woman abandoned by her husband, unable to fly to another world and another life. Her wings had truly been cut.

Monowara's humming stopped when she saw her son and father-in-law coming home with dripping wet *lungi*. Nothing could evade her keen eyes. She really lost her temper at this sight – the old man had no control over his appetite, and then would start this disgusting behaviour.

'Have you dirtied your *lungi*? That's all right – but why did you have to go to the pond at this hour? Do you want to break your arms and legs?'

Sorman Sheikh stuttered, 'Actually I didn't understand – I didn't know what to do.'

Monowara shouted. 'You are getting old. You have to eat sensibly.'

Head bent in shame, Sorman Sheikh stood helplessly in front of his daughter-in-law, silently bearing the brunt of her anger. Monowara was really disgusted with the old man – she had had enough! He had wet both his *lungis*. What was he to wear now?

As a last resort, Monowara brought out a torn and faded old *lungi*. Handing this over to her son, she called out to her father-in-law, 'Go and change. We'll have the added job of looking after you if you catch a fever.'

No words came out of Sorman Sheikh. As he dropped his own *lungi* on the floor, a foul smell filled the room. Monowara threw up as she held the soiled *lungi* with two fingers and took it to the well. As soon as she stopped vomiting, she called out a warning to her father-in-law, 'Don't even think of dinner. You gobble down the food, and we have to pay the price!'

Monowara's warning made Sorman Sheikh's heart skip a beat – no more fish for him that night – after having wheedled the fish from Atarjan. Why was Monowara so hard-hearted?

Evening had already set in when Sorman Sheikh came to the pond for the third time with his faded *lungi* and wet towel. In that pale light, the three pairs of kingfishers were catching fish and eating them happily. Sorman Sheikh watched them – with sadness in his heart. He knew that Monowara would not give him anything to eat that night. The thought sent a paralysing shiver down his body. Holding on to the trunk of a stocky tree, he washed himself up to his hip with difficulty. He tripped several times on his way back home. It was dark – all the light was gone when he finally crawled into the courtyard of the house. He didn't want to be accosted by Monowara's cross face, so he stood outside, leaning against the bamboo shoots, lost in thought.

Night fell. Fireflies danced in the darkness, frogs croaked and crickets chirped. The nightly music and dance proceeded apace, but nobody came to look for him. Hurt and disappointed, Sorman Sheikh dragged himself towards the verandah of his house. He waited eagerly to hear Dulu Mia call out for him. The little boy would never sit down to eat without his grandfather. His wet clothes made him shiver a bit. But neither Monowara nor Dulu Mia came to call him. Well – mother and son would eat heartily together!

The moonlight spread like a flower over the night. Sorman Sheikh slept in the moonlight with his hands on his stomach. He just couldn't stay awake – maybe he was tired after his three trips to the pond or perhaps it was his mind that was exhausted. His eyes closed automatically under his sagging old skin. He shuddered a few times in his sleep. Dulu Mia was a great fan of his grandfather – perhaps he had called him a few times, but he hadn't heard as he was so sleepy. He would have liked to stay awake nursing these false hopes – of food, of Dulu Mia's call. Dulu Mia definitely knew how his grandfather craved for good food – for a good fish curry. Dulu Mia would be really disappointed if his grandfather didn't answer his calls.

His eyes shut, the waves of sleep making it impossible to keep awake. He couldn't distinguish anything – whether this semi-conscious doze was only an illusion. The white-breasted kingfisher couple penetrated through this haze and flew towards him along with two pairs of guests. And who knows why, they threw heaps of fish as they flew over Sorman Sheikh's head – all kinds of fish – *rui, koi, pabda, chitol, shoil.*

The perfume of the moonlit night blended into the terrible scaly smell of fish. As Sorman Sheikh sank into this bottomless maze, Monowara's sad voice wafted through the air.

Birds fly on their wings
One day my friend, our paths will cross
We shall meet each other.

Translated by Firdous Azim and Shagufta Hyder

NUZHAT AMIN MANNAN

The Wardrobe

Grandmother Meher had a thing for furniture. She had brought a few pieces from her father Haji Wares Billah's house – among them a huge mahogany four-poster carved with swans and lotuses. On moonlit nights the swans came out alive, gleaming white. On pitch-dark nights, they rippled along a mahogany-blue stillness, looking wet and lustrous among the lotuses. When her husband Sattar, a rubber-shoes merchant, was snoring in time with the clock ticking noisily in the adjoining room, Meher would be clutching at the ends of her freshly starched pillow, watching the swans preen and glide through the foliage. She spent considerable time each day, rag in hand, polishing the pride of her mahogany exotica, which contrasted wildly with the other objects in the room. There was a pink steel almirah with yawning doors that convulsed every time it was wrenched open. There was a battered black-and-white fuzzy television set perched on a Formica chest of drawers that Meher's youngest son had cleared out of his room when the dowry sent by his new in-laws arrived. At the furthermost end of the room was a dressing-table that Meher had also brought after Haji Billah passed away. Her children would have clearly preferred some of the contingent of rickshaws their grandfather owned – but they knew their mother was an aesthete, who fancied things that no one else valued.

The dressing-table, the *singaar*, as their mother referred to it, was once a dainty piece. There were recesses for vanities, one for *surma*, the grey, powdery substance that made women look foreign and mysteriously remote. There was a little recess for hair oil and one for *alta* for women of the house to dye their feet with. An oval brass trinket saver had hairpins, a few buttons and a few scrawny-looking keys that did not belong to anything. Water stains and pocks of neglect had ravaged the piece. The tabletop was stamped with age, and the hibiscus flowers etched on it had chipped and worn away in places. The mirror was speckled with splotches so bad that it required a huge leap of imagination to see a reflection of oneself. Meher did not care to inspect herself in the mirror; it stood blatantly unused; she no longer had use for *alta* or kohl. She was beautiful in an inexplicable way – not one feature she had was perfect. But on the whole she had always looked secure and healthy, her complexion never faded, and when her temples began to show signs of white, she achieved a calm, dignified look, befitting the matriarch of a sprawling family. Draped in fine white *beeti* saris, fetched from Pabna, Meher held herself well. Famous for her *chhaanar jelebis*, when she sat in front of a huge cauldron of boiling milk, she was a picture of domestic serenity. And even though in her dreams she sometimes saw swans swimming, in her waking hours she was a sedately ordinary woman. The dressingtable with its broken hibiscus flowers and myriad careless *alta* stains on it was lovingly dusted each day. Its frail edges reminded her of an unnamed rite of passage from material to possession.

On the odd afternoon when the grandchildren happened not to want her or the servants took their bickering elsewhere or when her husband sat in the verandah watching the clouds gather – a longer monsoon was always good for business – Meher reclined against her pillow and watched the wooden things whisper and heave of their own volition. The lotus leaves trembled, the swans dipped, the hibiscus wilted. These reveries did not last long. As soon as the clanking of iron and the rhythmic battering of bricks in the construction site next door resumed, Meher's siesta would automatically end. The serpentine streets the Mughal planners had made nearly four hundred years ago had now reduced to claustrophobic alleys. Every day a parapet or rooftop or a balcony or a cornice to fly kites from trembled, crumbled and gave in to the vicissitudes of time. Every day, electric and telephone wires multiplied. Every day once noble-looking houses sank, fighting nature, filth and modern renovations. As rickshaws hurtled and joined cars in blind jams, Old Dhaka went on with its criss-crossed harlequin existence. Here something was old and crumbly, sad and beautiful. And then again many things were brash and loud, merry and bustling. Vivacity reigned here. As children trampled mud and skipped over drains on their way to school, as a cacophony of voices melted together, Old Dhaka came to life – no matter what. Standing on the banks of a slushy river, the city's greying old quarters never found life dull.

Even though occasionally you had to remind yourself which century you were in – so many centuries held together in Old Dhaka – it was hard to miss what time of the day it was. The cannons at sunset in Lalbagh Fort had not boomed for centuries now. But the five prayer calls went trilling from star-etched minarets, invisible behind curtains of live electric wires that were frequently roosts for pigeons. Stroll into a *qasida* soiree during Ramadan, and the precincts of Ahsan Manzil boomed with fine voices singing melodious *ghazals* and lyrics in praise of the Prophet. Meher listened from her window, the menfolk sat in a trance, the fervour of the *ghazals* melted into the night. For centuries, the old quarters had been the commercial artery of the city – kept alive by sowdagers and beparis with their Urdu-laced Bangla scintillating through their *paan*-glistening humour. The beparis and sowdagers had maintained tradition; they had perfected an inimitable lifestyle. Their VCRs blared but their hearts were soft and decent. Trust a Dhakaiya, an original settler of the old city, to be more generous than is good for him, to be more boisterous than he need be, trust a Dhakaiya to trade in banter and witticisms, to make his seriousness about money look like a shining ethos. Filled with a zealous sense of ancestry, the Dhakaiyas, famous for their love of pomp, lavish display and hospitality, would rather die than be outdone. Dressed to the nines in finery, the Dhakaiya loves doing what one was meant to do in life – enjoy!

For Meher and Sattar's fortieth wedding anniversary, the children had planned an elaborate banquet. Goats were bought and fattened on fresh young grass. Pure ghee came from Bikrampur, bags of spices came from Brahmanbaria Store, and their eldest son had got Basmati rice from

Pakistan and pure saffron in a glittering golden box dispatched by his brother-in-law who worked in Riyadh. The marquee went up on the roof. Wiry-looking, unfed men in unwashed whites were hired to play the band. There was a mighty commotion as mikes blared, sonorous film songs boomed, children ran up and down the stairs in a frenzy, ladies swished past one another like butterflies in their resplendent saris. The cooks had spent the whole day cooking *biryani*, chicken roast, mutton *rezala* and fresh curd. The aroma lingered for days – no one was able to touch a cake of soap or a towel that did not smell of that divine meal.

Sattar could clearly see himself as a bridegroom dressed in a white *sherwani*, a *zari sehra* over his face, when he had gone to Haji Billah's house forty years ago to wed Meher. The night before the wedding seemed like yesterday. His friends and younger members of the extended family had enjoyed themselves, eating sweets and kebabs and chewing *paan*, and every now and then someone hollered for tea. The girls sequestered indoors laughed gaily attending to their chores. Sattar was no fool. Being a good-looking bloke, he knew quite a few of the young ladies of the inner quarters felt that their hopes had been dashed. For the anniversary, Meher's husband had shyly ordered a pair of gold bangles, a small token, considering he had fared well during the forty years he had spent with a woman who was by all accounts a good wife – dutiful, undemanding and simple. Meher was a pillar of strength, hard-working, unswerving in devotion. She had not been difficult to please either.

'You needn't have given me the *balas*. You know I hardly wear these things.'

'It's been a while since I gave you something ... who knows when I will be called by the Almighty,' Sattar murmured as tenderly as possible.

'I'd like something very much,' Meher cut in unceremoniously.

'What?' Sattar said, amused but also slightly trapped.

'A wardrobe, one made for me, not something from a shop.'

'A wardrobe,' Sattar echoed, unable to contain his astonishment.

'I want something ... so beautiful that it makes one's eyes water.' Meher's voice began to quiver.

'That shouldn't be a problem,' said Sattar generously but still in some shock.

In the matter of seconds he had sketched out what he had to do. He would call the carpenter, Old Tarakanath, tomorrow, get him to buy some *sheelkoroy* and get to work. In two weeks' time he foresaw the room crowded still further with the inclusion of this new piece of furniture.

'Call Tarakanath, I will tell him what I want,' Meher added, with the poise of one who had been accustomed to reading Sattar's mind for forty years.

'What is all this wardrobe business?' Sattar asked querulously.

'Just something that makes you feel complete.' Meher turned on her side preparing to go to sleep.

Tarakanath was a young lad of fifteen during the Partition when he found himself in charge of marrying off five sisters following his father's paralysis. Poverty was a constant teacher and, by dint of his poverty, Tarakanath had had an extensive education in humility. He held no grudges or grievances against anyone. With sunken, unshaven cheeks and bright dark eyes he took on his share of troubles – he bore his father's paralysis, his bouts of typhoid, the family's mounting loans, the wedding dowries for his sisters, with a humble but unbroken resolve. But none of these scourges had been able to wither the sap that flowed into his knotty fingers – he knew how to saw and chisel and carve. Wood was his mother, he said with satisfaction. Tarakanath had been summoned from Chawkbazar. He held a pencil behind his ear and listened with his eyes moist with cataract and an approaching cold. Eight months later the wardrobe was done. The panels were ornate – there was an extravagant garden with peacocks and pomegranates. Grapevines clustered in wreaths. She had asked for *dolonchampa* flowers to be done in the border. The wardrobe rested on four exquisite lion paws. The side panels were stunning with butterflies and dragonflies, briskly wafting about reminding one of a calm summer evening. Meher had drawn her breath in every time she had passed by to check on Tarakanath's progress – as the shavings of the wood grew, as he whittled slowly, the wood rose to life.

The wardrobe was a spectacle. Even Aziz's Ma who came daily to mop the floors stared at it with wonderment. It was like watching a bioscope. She remembered when they were tiny, they would rush whenever the bioscope *wallah* was heard playing his music. Children and even a motley group of elders would gather and impatiently wait their turns. For an *anna* one got to peep inside the box – there would be slides rolling of Calcutta's Victoria Memorial, of the Bridge over the Thames, of the Taj Mahal, of waterfronts in Mumbai, of Kedarnath-Boddinath, the Himalayan crests and the Shalimar Gardens. To Aziz's Ma, Meher's wardrobe was preposterously 'foreign' beyond the realm of the ordinary. Meher had spent hours arranging her *dhopa*-washed saris shimmering with speckles of *abrok* on them. She put layers of white on top of layers of tapioca, the mint greens went with the light blues and pale yellows. She carefully folded her *garads*, the *benarsis* and the zari-embellished saris her brothers had given her. She stowed away her purses, her jewellery box, a few bottles of rose attar, a few pieces of shawls that she used in winter. And a pearl-coloured *burkha* she seldom got around to using.

Fourteen months later, Meher suffered a fatal haemorrhage. She had lain in the hospital bed for three weeks, unconscious. Sattar and his children were inconsolable. When they spoke of their grief to friends, relatives and neighbours, they frequently used words like 'bedrock', 'an incomparable cook', 'the gentlest ear', 'the best mother', a 'most attentive wife'. After Meher was buried and a semblance of nomal life returned to the Sattar household, someone demurely suggested it was time to divide Meher's belongings. Each of her children would get a piece or memento to remember her by. It was easier to divide her bangles, *jhumkas*, rings and chains. The cotton saris went to her father's *mahallah* to be distributed among the needy. The finer saris the daughters-in-law divided among themselves. Sattar enjoyed the bed until he died. Before long, the family moved out of the precincts of Ahsan Manzil to a newer part of Dhaka – and the four-poster, the dressing-table and the wardrobe went on sale.

SHABNAM NADIYA

A Journey into Night

Anjona first noticed the girl as she was moving towards the door of the bus. It was one o'clock in the morning. They were on their way to Cox's Bazaar. The bus had stopped for the passengers to have a cup of tea, a bite to eat, a moment to stretch their legs. After hours of sitting scrunched up motionless in her seat, Anjona needed it. It was a big bus and comfortable, but with her daughter's head resting delicately in the crook of her neck she had been careful not to move too much. Her daughter was a skinny little girl and needed her rest. With the excitement of the long-awaited trip to the seaside, who knows how much sleep the child would get in the coming days? It would be a terrible thing if they returned to Dhaka just to have the girl fall ill with something – her sister-in-law kept insinuating anyway that Anjona wasn't a good enough mother.

As she was preparing to get off the bus, her husband said, 'Where's your purse?'

'On my seat,' she replied.

'Well, don't just leave it there, go and get it! Do I have to tell you everything? Women!' her husband grumbled. As he looked away, Anjona stuck her tongue out at him playfully, making the children giggle.

Anjona turned around to return to her seat. She wouldn't have noticed the girl at all (she didn't notice people or her surroundings much these days), except that the sudden jerking movement in one of the seats caught the corner of her eye. The inside of the bus was half dark. Anjona looked and saw a figure huddled in the seat with the face twisted away. It was a female figure, a man sitting beside it. The man was laughing and saying something bent over the girl. In that single glance she noted that the two were holding hands. The sound of happy laughter touched her. Newly-weds? Anjona passed them and went for her bag. Maybe they were on their honeymoon, she idly thought, holding hands like that. She had never had a honeymoon. In fact, this was the first time she was going anywhere with her husband. On her way back she thought of turning again to have a better look at the girl, just to see her face, nothing more, but her husband called out, 'Have you found it?'

'Yes,' she said and hurried towards him. The children were waiting impatiently just by the steps of the bus.

'Hurry up, *ammu!*' her children called, 'you always make us late!'

Their father smiled at her, 'Let's get something to eat.'

Her son and daughter were chattering away excitedly between themselves. It was all such an adventure to them. Spending the whole night on a bus, dozing their way to the sea, walking into a brightly lit restaurant at one in the morning. Anjona took her daughter to the bathroom and instructed her husband to take their seven-year-old son. This was the only chance they would have of relieving themselves for the rest of the night.

'*Ammu*, you stand here while I go,' her daughter said. Her eyes looked swollen with sleep, and her long lashes blinked rather slowly as if unsure whether they were supposed to be open at this time of night or not. Anjona felt a deep swirling inside her heart as she watched the frail frame of her child walk into the toilet. She recalled how disappointed her in-laws had been at the birth of this child. Everyone had been expecting a son. All the signs had said that the child was to be a boy. The shape of her distended belly, her morning sickness, the way she walked, the dreams she used to have – it was all there. And yet when the time came ... Anjona remembered cringing inside when she had woken up after her difficult labour to find out that she had given birth to a girl. Not that anyone had neglected the child. No, she was the first grandchild her grandmother had had and had been treated like a princess. It was just the way ... anyway, that probably had more to do with Anjona herself than with the child.

Her daughter came out. Anjona handed her the bag. 'You hold this while I go, OK?'

Her daughter nodded with a serious face. '*Ammu*, the flush doesn't work.'

Anjona held her breath as she went in.

Her father had died when she was a child. Among the other deprivations that this fact entitled her to, Anjona had learned when her family began looking for a groom for her that it also made her less saleable as a bride. She was rejected a number of times because, according to the prospective grooms' families, she had grown up without proper guidance. When she finally did manage to snag a husband it was because of her complexion more than anything else. Well, at least she had managed to pass her fair skin on to her daughter – that would be a good thing when the time came to marry her off.

Anjona came out of the toilet and stood at the basin to wash her hands.

'Have you washed your hands?' she asked her daughter.

'No,' her daughter said guiltily and stepped forward.

A moment's silence, then her daughter said, '*Ammu*, is *Dadi* very angry because we came to the seaside?'

Anjona's hands stopped moving under the flowing water. 'Why do you ask?'

'I think she is.'

Anjona slowly shook the water off her hands and rinsed them. She watched the water as it trickled endlessly out of the tap.

'Did she say anything to you?'

'She said ... well, she said that if you had had better care and came from a better family then you wouldn't go dancing off to places the first chance you got.'

Anjona handed her daughter a tissue, trying fast to think of something to say to her daughter without denigrating her mother-in-law too much.

'She said that to you?'

'No, she was talking to Asma Bua. I was playing in her room.'

Well! Anjona thought. That woman! Saying something like that to the maid ... and then getting angry because servants these days didn't show proper respect. Her daughter was looking at her, expecting some response. Anjona opened her mouth to tell her that her grandmother was old, that old people sometimes behaved strangely ... she began telling her the things that a good daughter-in-law should. And then suddenly she didn't want to. She wanted to be bad and bitchy and tell her daughter that her grandmother was an old hag and always had been an old hag and that the last thing she wanted her daughter to do was to emulate her grandmother in anything she did.

But she didn't. Instead of saying any of these things, Anjona pulled her daughter close and said, 'Here, let me comb your hair, it's an absolute mess.'

'*Ammu-u-u*!' howled her daughter as she twisted away, 'not now, I want a Coke!'

And so Anjona followed her daughter out of the toilet, envying the slickness with which childhood kept unpleasant thoughts and memories out of sight and out of mind indefinitely. It was such a long time since she had been a child.

How dare the old woman say something like that? She was the mother of two children now! And after twelve years of marriage the fact that she had lacked the stern rigour of a father's discipline and that one of her female cousins had eloped still made her a girl from a family with loose morals, still made her less of everything that her husband's family was. Her mother-in-law had made a career out of making Anjona feel less – less nice, less moneyed, less pretty, less decent, less respectable, less religious. Why on earth she had deigned to let Anjona join her family at all was a mystery.

Anjona sat at the table her husband and son had been holding for them and tried not to think. She watched her family as they talked, joked and laughed while they ate and sipped slowly at the cup of tea she had ordered. She was going to the seaside with her family – this was a good thing. For a few days she would not think of mother-in-law or her sister-in-law or about the 'women trouble' (as her husband called her in-law problems whenever she attempted to discuss them with him). For a few days she would be glad just to be alive. For a few days she would feel what it was like to be alive.

But how could she have said something like that in front of the maid, in front of her granddaughter? Anjona couldn't decide which was worse. Everybody was done eating and drinking. 'Are you sure you don't want anything to eat?' her husband asked her. When she shook her head without saying anything, he called to the waiter for the bill. The bus assistant came to their table with a smile and said, 'Aren't you Blue Bird passengers? The bus will be leaving in fifteen minutes.' Her husband nodded and said, 'We'll be out in ten minutes.'

The assistant left. Her son began an argument with his sister about changing their seats. He wanted to sit with *ammu* this time. Her daughter said no and stuck her tongue out at him. Her husband interrupted their argument, 'No fighting – that was the deal, remember?' And all through this, while all this was going on around her, Anjona sat there with a slight smile fixed to her lips and saw and heard nothing. All through this, all she could think of was that, after all these years of making a home for her husband, being a good little wife, after the pain and pleasure of having two children, what was she? No matter how nice she was, no matter how 'good' she tried to be, no matter what care she took of her mother-in-law, Anjona was still the girl whose mother had not taught her properly how to sew because she had once sewn uneven pleats in her mother-in-law's blouse. She would forever be the fatherless girl whose sisters eloped and whose relatives made bad marriages, the girl whose family was not quite up to the mark in terms of character and morals. 'Nothing really changes in life,' she thought to herself sardonically. 'We just grow heavier, older and more wrinkled.'

Anjona left the shiny roadside restaurant with her family and boarded the bus. The honeymooners whose happiness she had wanted to steal a glance at were nowhere in her mind at the moment. Yet when she climbed into the bus, the man's seat was empty and the girl was standing half in the aisle trying to put a bag in the overhead compartment. Her head was covered with a red, heavily embroidered *orna*, effectively hiding her face. Anjona would have passed her by unnoticed this time except for something familiar in the way the girl's slim body moved. As Anjona moved forward, the girl slid into the darkness of her seat and could no longer be seen except as an obscure shadow, the contours of which merged with that of the bus window and the seat.

Puzzled, Anjona followed her husband and children to their own seats, wondering why the girl looked familiar. This time – their disagreement resolved by their father – the son came to sit with the mother, directing a triumphant smile at his sister. Anjona took a scarf out of her bag and handed it to her husband to wrap around their daughter's throat. As the bus resumed its journey, her son chattered to her excitedly about all the things he expected the sea to be, and the crabs he was going to catch and the shells he was to collect, the bus and the journey. Unlike the daughter, who was older, in his intense excitement the son did not require too deep a response to any of his talk, and judicious interjections of hmm and really? from the mother were enough to keep him happy. Soon he began dozing, his head occasionally bumping against his mother's shoulder. Someone snorted in their sleep somewhere at the back. Anjona sat and thought. Throughout the night.

Dawn arrived, peeking through the ragtag curtains spread across the bus windows. An hour at most, and they would be there. People were stirring throughout the bus, waking up to the unaccustomed early light. Anjona watched a shard of sunlight scraping her son's cheek as he slept. His young face seemed to bear a strange imprint of his father's face. He was a good man, the children's father. But that didn't make much difference to her life. Anjona had decided to have a 'talk' with her mother-in-law once she got back home. It was about time. For once she would behave with them the way they behaved towards her. For once she would attempt to be someone.

Her husband stretched and looked at her, 'Haven't you slept at all?'

'No,' she replied briefly.

'I've had a grand sleep,' he yawned, 'but I'm still sleepy.' Anjona moved the curtain and looked out of the window without answering. Her daughter rubbed her eyes and sat up straight. '*Ammu*, are we there yet?'

Anjona didn't answer. Someone at the front called out to the bus assistant, 'Bhai, how long till we get there?' The assistant walked down the aisle holding on to the backs of the seats. 'Half an hour at most.'

'That was fast,' said Anjona's husband.

'Yes, sir, the roads were clear, and our drivers are very good.' The assistant moved to the front of the bus again.

'Are we early?' asked Anjona.

'Oh yes, we're only supposed to be at Chittagong by now. We're almost an hour and a half ahead.' He reached across and shook their son awake, 'Come on, sleepy-head, don't you want to see the sea?' The child sat up and blinked then smiled eagerly at his parents. 'Where is it? Where is it? Are we there?'

'Of course not, stupid, we'll be there in half an hour,' his sister replied with a wise air. Their father laughed. '*Abbu*, can I sit with *apu* now?' asked the son.

'Okay ... but no fighting!'

Anjona's husband climbed out of his seat to let brother and sister sit together. She moved to the window seat; he sat down beside her. He dozed off again almost immediately, despite the low-pitched yet excited chatter in the seat beside them. After a while he asked, 'Aren't you hungry? You didn't have anything to eat in the night.'

'Didn't feel like it,' she replied shortly.

'Is there anything wrong?' he asked.

'What do you mean "wrong"?'

'Well, you sound ...'

'I sound what?' She didn't even let him finish.

He turned and looked at her. 'Look,' he began, 'if I have ...'

'Your mother told my maid that because of my family background I go dancing off the first chance I get.' He didn't say anything. Just looked at her.

'She said it to the maid,' Anjona repeated. 'In front of our daughter.'

Her husband exhaled slowly. 'If *Amma* said ...'

'Yes, yes, I know, you're not to be bothered with women trouble, it's not your problem. It never is.' Anjona moved her body slightly away and looked out the window. Wisely, her husband stayed silent.

Soon they had reached Cox's Bazaar, and they were even treated to a glimpse of the sea, like a trailer of coming attractions for a forthcoming film. Her son was bouncing up and down on his seat in excitement, while her daughter tried to retain her composure in keeping with her elder sister status. But her excitement at the sight of the waves billowing on to the sandy beach was betrayed by the sheer exuberance of her smile. '*Ammu*, did you see, did you see?' they exclaimed. Although this was the first time for Anjona too, somehow she didn't feel as excited as she had thought she would be.

The bus stopped, and people began trickling towards the exit, still comfortably half-wrapped in sleep. Anjona checked the seat pockets a last time and followed her children off the bus. She climbed down on to the road and stood a bit to the side with the children, while her husband went to the side of the bus to see about their luggage. The people who had got off before them had already got their bags and were beginning to drift away – some looking this way and that for rickshaws, some moving purposefully ahead to their destinations on foot. It was then that it happened.

Her husband turned and beckoned to her to come and help him with their bags. Anjona told the children to wait there while she went and helped their father. As she walked towards him, the couple she had thought of as honeymooners were walking towards her carrying a bag each. The girl still had the red *orna* covering her head. As they walked towards her, for the first time, Anjona saw the girl's face. She stopped in mid-stride. It was Sheila. Her mother-in-law's niece. That was why even in the darkness of the interior of the bus Anjona had felt that the girl was familiar, for Anjona had known the girl for the whole twelve years of her marriage. Sheila who was studying history at the university. Sheila whose mother had complained that marrying their boy to Anjona had not been such a good idea. Sheila who was now walking with her hand lightly yet intimately resting on the man's arm. Sheila who was not married.

Anjona felt a peculiar sense of satisfaction, bordering on cruel exultation. Well, well, well. Now where would the good name of the family be? This family whose daughters danced off with men the first chance they got? So this was how Sheila spent the time she was supposedly staying in the university hall studying with friends. Now what would Sheila's mother and aunt have to say about this, one wondered. Particularly to the undisciplined, misguided, coming-from-a-bad-family daughter-in-law?

Thoughts raced through Anjona's head in seconds, vindictive, cold, satisfied thoughts. Then their eyes met, and she looked at Sheila's face. For a second there was recognition in the eyes that were glowing with happiness – and then there was just heart-stopping fear. Ashen white, the girl's face twisted in fear, as if the future had come and suddenly stood right in front of her. Her male companion (he was a boy really, Anjona now saw), not understanding, was looking at her with concern and was asking what was wrong. In about two seconds he would follow her stricken gaze and look at Anjona.

And at that moment Anjona felt as if she could never look into her daughter's eyes again with a clear conscience. She felt that forever after when she laughed with her daughter in shared happiness, or asked to be let in on a secret that only children were supposed to know, there would always be a small place where that sunshine could not enter. And that small piece of darkness she would carry around in her heart for as long as she lived, perhaps longer.

Anjona smiled at Sheila's stricken face. There was so much that she wanted to say in that one smile – so much disappointment, and joy, and love, and laughter was stuffed inside her that it was like a fire in her belly that reached and seared the inside of her throat. Anjona said nothing – for there were no words that could say the things that needed to be said.

Anjona walked past Sheila as she walked past the other people from the bus. She smiled at her husband, a smile as clear and happy as her daughter's, a smile that could swallow misery and turn it into something so preciously close to joy and said, 'Come on, hurry up, you slowcoach, the children are waiting.'

Audity Falguni

Wildflower

[Author's Note: The dwellings of the Mandi people, whom we call Garos in accordance with British terminology, are spread across Madhupur, Tangail and Mymensingh of Bangladesh, right up to Meghalaya in India. Historians believe that almost a thousand years ago a group of men and women spread out across the Tibet–Bhutan–Assam region to Meghalaya and Madhupur through Mymensingh from China's Kideo region during a protracted migration. Although the Mandi people accepted minor elements of the Hindu religion within their own religion and culture with the passing of time, their names, cuisine and legends retained the influence of China and Assam's Bodo–Mongolian tribes. Christianity has been preached among the Mandis since 1872. Currently, about 95 per cent of the Mandis settled in Bangladesh and India are 'Christians'; the remaining 5 per cent continue to be followers of the ancient Shangsharek religion, the original religion of the Mandis. The characteristic that makes the Mandis extraordinary among social systems in the world as well as among other minority ethnic groups living in Bangladesh is their matriarchal social system. According to the legends of the Mandis, the matriarchal system was established to prevent decrease in the population of the war-weary Mandi people on their trek from Assam to Meghalaya and Bangladesh. In 1964, during Pakistani rule, the Mandi people endured appalling state-sponsored riots. Many Mandi warriors fought in the 1971 Liberation War. In 1975, a number of Mandi warriors crossed over to Meghalaya. Although the government increased access for the Mandis in lower-level government jobs in the face of Mandi activism, their overall situation remains frustrating. The Shal Forests of Madhupur are being wiped out, the women of the poor indigenous Mandi people toil in the hair parlours of the capital city, the newly preached religion is gobbling up the old traditions. This story is about how the Achik Mande, the 'Courageous People of the Mountains', detached from eternal nature and religion, are faring in this state with a Bengali majority.]

Pantho dolong ninama rippeng,
Ama asong ninama rippeng,
Ian jokkai rippeng angni asong deng
Fina gitdik dakgobade.
Abri gapa asong-o
Rongthi mithi gisim
Rama riye romachum
Dao de rongthi maini rama – rijang-a
Rippengnara khinna thokbo ne.

[Our mountain river flows just beneath that sky, way over yonder. The mountain village is dead, silent. Yet in the past our villages were like legends. We had the forests and the black stones by the streams. The stones spoke then – in the past they would walk like people. But the god commanded, 'Stone, remain still. Or else how will the grass and the grain grow? How will the people live?']

The *aduru*, the *kal*, the *imbangi* play. The noise thickens in the plateau ...

Yes, how long ago it was when Mihgram Sildareng and his subjects began whetting the *millam* stone to punish the ungrateful Khalkhame Khalgra, and out of fear Khalkhame Khalgra dived into seven lengths underwater and herded back seven crore swallows to destroy the rice fields of Silderang. Or when Sisi Thoppa played on his own belly like a drum,

Nahsudanga played the flute with just his lips, and roly-poly Fokkaronda and short-legged Daling sang and danced naked in the half light, half darkness of the underwater palace, engaging in pleasure, forgetting days–months–years ... it was then or a few days either side of then.

There is noise in the plateau.

The festive procession moves forward. In front are the *toktengfa*, the ironmongers, with long iron *millam* swords, thick rhino-skin *sfee* shields, joyous *jattha* spears with bloody *wak* pigs impaled upon them and *mongreng* axes on their shoulders.

Next in line are ten young warriors carrying the *khumba* statue of the last *nokma*, the last village chief, wrapped in bright *cheena giccha*, in bright red cloth. In the third row all the unwed young men and women of the five *maharis*, the five tribes – the *Ambeng*, the *Chibok*, the *Dual*, the *Brak* and the *Attong* – dance the *Grikkadoppa* wardance. The young men all wear narrow *gando* of yellow cloth, making visible their slender buttocks, lean thighs and the vigorous angularity of their genitals. The young men have wrapped red *khofing* turbans around their heads, some have *jakchhap* jewellery encircling their wrists. The young women wear striped *ganna* draped around their bodies from shoulder to knees, silver *nathek* and *penta* in their ears, silver *shangdap* around their waists, *kokhashil* on their foreheads. The married women walk with *kok* grain baskets slung on their backs filled with *mimittim*, *misimi* and *mimande* paddy, *billik* and *kharek* beans, and *thamandi–thabolchu–thaja–thamlang–thahicchak–steng* – six types of potato – their babies bound to their chests and conch-shell *ribok rubbok* wound around their necks. The married men carry twenty enormous *dikka* wine barrels filled with a rare *chu* liquor of *khamir* grain a hundred years old. Weary boys and girls walk along the road sucking on bitter *antri* fruit. Dozing old men and women walk right behind the children; despite the difficulty, they are calmly pulling along forty large brass *rangs*, forty large tubs. Most of the *rangs* are empty, but *sasatsu-a* incense still burns within a few. Until now the elderly have had a good time of it, sitting around at the thatched *ballim* pubs of Jogigopa Dumri, south of Misikhokdok, guzzling *chu*, grain-alcohol. But now, in accordance with the orders of the five chief *khamal* priests of the five tribes, they are having to bear the heavy brass *rangs*. The five chief *khamals* walk right behind the old men and women;

on their shoulders rest the idols made of *aret* leaves, *kash* fronds and wood of all the leading deities – *Tatara Rabuga* the creator, *Saljong Middei* the sungod, *Baguba* and *Rakgusi Middei, Rongsri Middei* the harvest goddess and *Shushmi Middei* the moon goddess. Beside them, with bowed heads and unhurried steps, as is the custom, walk the *jikmamong*, the head wives of the *khamals*. The *jikmongma*, the senior elephant wives, and the *jikgidi*, the concubines, all wear *dokbanda* of a soft weave. Encircling the *khamals* and their wives walk twenty assistants, about twenty-five to thirty tied up wild fowl in their hands for the *middei amoa*, the prayer sacrifice.

Right behind the *khamals* walk the seven *nokma* of the seven villages left behind on the Jogigopa Dumri, their hands crossed over their chests, their faces impassive. In the last line, behind them all, come the musicians. The *damma* drummers walk with the huge *khram* drum hung around their necks with *masu brigil*, cowhide twine. The blow-holes of the *aduru*, the *kal* and the *imbangi sanai* are pressed to the lips of the *bomsikka* flutists,

Himma, dolma, bilma, bisnoma,
Sikme, doles, ulonga, uongi,
Asong tibbet groin
Chiza apil jangsani ...

The notes of the *aduru*, the *kal*, the *imbangi* come to a halt. Only the *khram* continues to play. The beat of eight huge *khrams* resounds ...

Yes, how long ago was it? Achik Mande, the people of the mountains, as powerful as wild eagles, before they became as cowardly as the people of the plains ... they used to build *borangs* and live in the highest boughs of the trees – their feet entangled with the *sithri* vines, the Achik Mande, people of the mountains, they walked such long roads! Like the small town of Kideo, quite tranquilly sitting between the Salwin and Chinduin rivers, a little to the west of the Hwang Ho, but when the curse of the ancestors hit the serene town of Kideo, and there appeared a scarcity of grain and land, then the Mandis walked with their feet entangled in the *sithri* vines. Hawks pecked out the eyes of dead children in the streets of Kideo, and the road to survival lay way over to the east, straight as the crow flies, where the Garo mountain of Tibet hides all the tunnels to the underworld. Tibet was beset with ice, there were almost no rivers there at all, so the crops did not do well. But then the valiant Jagfa Jalinofa and Shukhfa Bonggifa raised their heads. They took the Achik Mande with *millam* swords in their hands and crossed Mech, Rava, Mikir, Naga, Mismi – all the rivers of all the people – and they dug through all the mountain peaks of Sikkim and Saura – their feet entangled in the *sithri* vine. It was so long ago that the Mandis went beyond the mouth of the Menam River and came to the land of Rongdu Gahal Kho, Kamrup. In wars one after another, Achik Abrasen and Abanonga acquired the mountains of Tura and Nokrek, Jogigopa Dumri.

'Asong nonoini ...' Jobang Ambeng, the finest of the khamals of the five tribes flings a handful of *sasatsu-a* incense to the sky. '*Chiga nengkhuch (ni)* ...'

The red ants of the *dolagipa* tree in the Bonefani Nok Fanti valley continue with their own silent comings and goings. Behind them rises the sheer Misikhokdok Mountain. The ashes of the *Agalmaka* festival, the Spring Festival, adrift in the wind of the Jogigopa Dumri south of Misikhokdok Mountain, do not reach the winds down here. Before leaving the Jogigopa Dumri behind, the sighs of the *mimang* souls of the recently slain warriors, cremated in the last *delafranca* cremation ground, rise in the air.

Jobang Ambeng takes another handful of *sasatsu-a* from a *rang* and touches it to his forehead:

Nokmani dredang
Saneni sudrangv ...

'We have left the homesteads of Jogigopa Dumri far behind. The last fire of *Agalmaka* has turned to ashes and blown away with the wind. We have picked all the rice, potatoes, *hittang* ginger, *jallik* pepper and *ganasi* beans from our old *jhum* fields, and we have lighted the divine fires of *Agalmaka* in the exhausted *jhum* fields as we are supposed to. Perhaps by now those *jhum* fields have burned properly.

'I swear by the creator *Tatara Rabuga*, I swear by *Saljong* the sun god and *Shushmi* the moon goddess, and by all the great kings born of the Mandis, I swear by this sacred *khumba*, by the valiant Shojinofa, whom we lost in this winter's war, who became a true king from just a simple *nokma*, who united the five warring tribes of Jogigopa Dumri … Today when the Mandi men are almost destroyed from the various wars, I, Jobang Ambeng, having paid homage to the Tura Mountain and the Nokrek Mountain in the west, the flowing Mother Songdu, the river Brahmaputra, in front of us, the *mimang* souls of the thirty soldiers who died for the Achek Mandi this winter, I declare –

'As of today, the familial and tribal lineage of the Mandi tribe will lie with the mother. Henceforth the women will inherit. From today, the *she* husband will move to the house of the *jik* wife, the *jik* will never move to the house of the *she*. The men have gradually lost control over the *jhum* fields and the animals because of constant war. So from today onwards, all ownership of grain, household, cattle and children will lie with the women. All *acchu-ambi*, all elderly men and women, all *afa-ama*, all fathers and mothers and the middle-aged, all *achik-michik*, all boys and girls present, do you abide by this decision?'

Although there have been rumours for some time that something like this might come about, this unexpected declaration makes the perspiring faces of the weary women flush in enthusiasm. Joyously, they raise the children bound to their breasts and the grain-filled *kok* baskets up to the sky. The men, many of whom have just recovered from war wounds, subjugated by hard work, pledge support to the *khamal*'s decision by touching their hands to the *millam* with impassive faces.

The fire grows under the shade of the *dah miljang-a* tree. The *waks* impaled on the *jatthas* are thrown on to the fire whole – *chu bicchi* alcohol is poured into small gourd *fongs* and handed around. After eating, they journey about a quarter mile upstream of the Songdu River, where awaits Indrajalinofa, friend of the dead king Shojinofa – it is he who will take the Achik Mandi to the new settlement thirty miles upstream of the Songdu against the course of the Siju River.

… *Actually Mrs. Shing had seen the dragon guarding the grave and the crown of Confucius, which was the cause of Salnima's bleeding.*

And Molita falls asleep while wielding the hair drier on a customer's head … when the purple sun plays on the mosaic floor of Shing Hair Parlour. Heavy drapes hang over the opaque windows – still the wayward purple sun plays in the scattered, discarded piles of hair. The Achik

Mandi move forward with their soaked clothes, soaked weapons, soaked grain, journeying thirty miles against the tide of the Siju River upstream of Songdu. They walk through the outer slopes of the Tura Mountain, when Molita falls asleep wielding the dryer on a customer's head. Or perhaps her name was Salnima. Still, to learn why all governmental documents continue recording her as Molita instead of Salnima, it is essential that we read the *Father Tree*, and it is also important to read the *History of the Sisters Maria Born of Light*. But we cannot move on to that topic immediately. For Molita picks up the hair drier after mushing the customer's hair with Palmerson and Pantene Pro-V shampoo. On the wall of Shing Parlour chafed by the purple sun, the Price List swings in the gusts of air raised by the fan:

Ring Bun – Taka 200
Onion Bar – Taka 220
French Braid – Taka 180
Pakistani Braid – Taka 180
Sixteen/ Sushmita Chignon – Taka 200
U Cut – Taka 100
Three Steps – Taka 100
Curl Roll – Taka 500

Molita is not exactly sure, is she Molita or Salnima? This profound uncertainty never left her before or after her death. Yet before she even picked up the hairdryer in her hand, probably while she was rubbing in Palmerson, she had fallen asleep. Because, long before she had fallen asleep, Molita had died – and many times, before the numbers of the daily and the money-making chores – which are typically identified by the verbs 'living', 'awakening', 'arising'. In truth, human beings can continue to walk about in their physical manifestations time and again even after death, they can work, make money, wear nice clothes, go on to marriage and even sex and in the end can even sleep many times. Without any apparent decay or stink of infection.

How long ago was it? When the whole of Shing Parlour was fast asleep in sleep of different dimensions. Intense and light. Sorrowful and without care – all kinds of sleep. Dipti – Kushum – Mukti – Purnima (... to know why their names sound like those of Bengali Hindus, the *Father Tree* and the *History of the Sisters Maria Born of Light* should be read immediately) – all the employees of Shing Parlour were more or less dozing with scissors in their hands. Even Mrs Shing – she who goes on counting bundles of money with her broad yellow hands eighteen hours a day in front of the huge dressing table. Asleep were the young and old women customers desiring beauty, their vacant eyes gazing at the mirrors. But the work continued alongside the sleep, without pause … the continual rasping of the scissors, the mounds of hair cut in the same rhythm, the stifling air of the parlour made stuffier with hair spray. And how unfortunate! It was at that moment that the ancient festive procession of the Mandis came towards Molita playing the *khram-imbang-aduru*. As a result, the hair of the tired and silent young lady who sat quietly under the dryer with her hair laden with Palmerson and Pantene Pro-V shampoo continued to entangle and tear in the drier's vents. The so far impassive Shing Parlour shook itself awake to the smouldering stench arising from the electric dryer … (it was at this moment, when Molita was embroiled in three immense Sleeps even after her death, and the narrative of this story revolves around Molita's Third Sleep) … and the counting of money by the broad yellow hands halts for a few moments. What happened then, people close to Mrs Shing know, for the owner of the busiest hair parlour, Mrs Shing, is a very compassionate woman. If anyone saw Molita Murik that evening, lying covered in blood on the floor of Shing Parlour, they didn't know that the tired young client, whose hair was torn by the dryer, had left, calmly paying the bill and asking Mrs Shing to cool down. Yet if she had remained hostile for some time like other customers, if Mrs Shing had had to apologize again and again, then the impossible duration of living, which does not seem to end even with the all-day scrabbling around of business – a few moments of that might have erupted into some kind of drama! It was merely to expend the prolonged moments of living that Mrs Shing had stabbed the air with her high heel plated with Shanghai steel – the air that only contained the deeply dark earthen grave, the grave that was guarded by an enormous dragon with a flickering, flaming tongue, sitting at the head of the grave, on the other side the crown of Confucius bright in the overturned expansive blue sky.

The Shanghai steel heel had only split open Molita's nose and lips.

The Father Tree and the Sisters Maria Born of Light
'For thou wast slain, and hast redeemed us to God by thy blood out of every kindred, and tongue, and people, and nation.' – *Revelation* 5:9
Segment of speech given by Father Paul Massang at the Ranikong Catholic Mission on 25 December:
'My Mandi brothers and sisters gathered here, today, on the birthday of the Lord, may all receive refuge at His feet; let the world be bathed in the love of the Father, the Son and the Mother.
'Today it is 1987. Remember, that holy day in 1872, when Radhanath was the first Mandi to be baptized into Christianity by the Bangali priest Krishnapal. Today, ninety-five per cent of the Mandis in Bangladesh and Meghalaya in India are Christian. The Mandi religion, Shangsharek, so full of superstition, blindness and ignorance, is almost extinct. Let your hearts be filled with great gladness: under the Lord's mercy, on average about seven hundred Mandi baptisms are being performed in Bangladesh today.
'Mandi people! Remember the holy Fathers, who have ignited the fires of Christianity among the Mandi tribe from the Shal forests of Madhupur to Meghalaya, enduring such pain and torment. History always shows us, it is as if the Holy Father has sent the worthiest of preachers and the Sisters Maria Born of Light to the small tribes roaming the forests. Remember the noble Belgian preacher Father Levens, who lighted the flame of Christianity among the Munda tribe of Chhota Nagpur of undivided India. Who baptized nine thousand children within the span of three weeks and arranged for Bible instruction for fifty thousand adults.
'... Remember the Belgian preacher Pastor Bian, who established the First Victoria Baptist Foreign Mission in Mymensingh town. Remember all those Bengali Christian preachers: Gangacharan, Ramkanta, Upendra et al. and also remember that first brave Mandi couple, Jambang and Miksai, the first Mandi couple who surrendered themselves to the feet of the Christ. After becoming Christians, their names were Chandramohan and Chandomoni. And the local trio Acchu Pishi Nol, Govinda Daring, Kanailal Sangma and Jainath Kubi, who gave their lives in endless toil to extend the Kingdom of Christ. And let us not forget the contributions of Father Francis of our Ranikong Catholic Congregation.
'I call on the Mandi women to follow the ideals of the Catechist sisters.

In Mymensingh on 18 March 1933, the Sisters Maria Born of Light, the Catechist sisters, who, without longing for husband–child–home, have pledged their lives to the benefit of humankind – learn from their lives. Now, let us move on to another subject. In recent times, some foolish young men ask, what will happen to us, as we are about to forget our traditions and culture by becoming Christians? To answer these foolish questions, I have myself composed several songs on the occasion of our ancient harvest festival of the *Wan-gala*. These songs you will hear when I have concluded my sermon. In places I have added lines to our ancient songs praising Christ where the praise was for the festival; in places where the songs glorify the ancient deities, there I have replaced "god" with "devil".

The whole thing happened in the past ... on the day that the Buddhist goddess Bhuga Rani jumped off the Ranikong Cliff – the morning in 1909 when Bhuga Rani met the white preacher Father Francis, when Bhuga Rani screamed in deathly sorrow, "This land is tainted! We can no longer live in this land." One morning in 1909 a yawning black abyss was created in Ranikong, which is the only future happening of the inhabitants of the Birishiri Vale. When the yearned-for and mystically poignant rainful Sravan days arrive in Birishiri – those Sravan days, when the whole planet overturns and all of the past remains motionless within that overturned planet, when not a single person in Birishiri ... yes, not a single Shangsharek remains in Kalmakanda apart from the old *khamal* named Misa Attong; Father Paul Massang turned even the old wife of the *khamal* into a Christian at the conclusion of his 25 December sermon by dousing her in baptismal water – still the converted Mandis of Kalmakanda retained memories of the Buddhist goddess Bhuga Rani's abyss – that black cavern, the tunnel through which Bhuga Rani returned to her birthplace, Bhutan. So when the yearned-for and mystically sorrowful Sravan days return, Mridanga Chisim, son of Sonali Chisim, Kalmakanda's handsomest young man – the fixed candidate for the role of the hero Waljan in the love story *Sheranjing* – takes Molita to the black abyss of the overturned Ranikong Cliff. Or the girl may have been called Salnima ... I don't remember very clearly.

How long ago was that? When the stones moved around, when they spoke like human beings? When the good winds like the pink petals of the *maccha jaseng* blossom shook the mountains? The past continuously weaved its pulsating events, and the old *khamal* Misa Attong coughed: 'S-a-l-n-i-m-a! S-a-l-n-i-m-a!'

Ambi Adra Murik, whose name after 25 December became Nirmala Murik (to know why the names of converted Mandis sound like those of Bengali Hindus, it is essential to immediately read the *Father Tree* and the *History of the Sisters Maria Born of Light*; the Ranikong Catholic Mission will provide that information quite quickly), touches the cross recently hung around her neck to her forehead and shouts in a tinny voice, 'Don't call Molita by the name of those devils and demons again!'

'A big Christian you've become! Yes ... a seven-day-wonder Christian! S-a-l-n-i-m-a!' The old man raises his voice again, 'Bring my medicine pouch ...'

'You're going to do that *amoa*, that healing through certain prayers and meditation, again? Why, your *amoa* couldn't heal me of my sickness! It was the Father's medicine that did.'

'You've become a Christian like your daughter and her husband, good for you. But don't badmouth the *amoa*.' The old man roars and trembles, 'You must have neglected to call upon the goddess Shushmi with all your heart! It's not the fault of the *amoa*, it's your fault. The power of the *amoa*, is it something you can joke about? Why, didn't this same Misa Attong bring back Eugina Murong right back from the tiger's belly through *amoa*? Eugina Murong, daughter of that Christian Francis Murong? The time when Eugina Murong was five or six ... the girl was taken by the tiger in front of everyone's eyes. I did the *amoa* for two days and two nights – on the morning of the third day, the girl came right back, walking with a *bipang* tree branch in her hand. The smell of tiger all over her body ...'

The old man jabbers on and walks with his hand on Salnima's shoulder: 'Salnima! For some reason I have a lot of hope in you. You're not just any other girl, you are Salnima, the mother of the sun god Saljong. The god Saljong told me this in a dream. Look carefully ... this mountain, these stones and the stream – it is all being destroyed. The best of the Mandi people! I will teach you all the stories and songs of our gods, of our old Shangsharek faith.'

The old man pants, sits down on a stone. 'You will do one more thing for me, Salnima, promise me. When I die, there will be no one in all of

Kalmakanda to offer the *ampengni* potato to the god Saljong during the
Wan-gala harvest festival. After my death, every winter, on the day of the
Wan-gala, you will give offering of at least one *ampengni* potato to him.
And you will chant this prayer:

Saljong mite mingipa dong-ana
Sreng Ampengni palo mika chana
Mibitchriko jena kaseyi gunana

[There was a god named *Saljong*, the Sun. He came to us to eat the
ampengni potato. We offer this *mibitchriko* wine in the name of that old
man of ages past.]

Molita quivers in suppressed and numbing moans, like an animal
decapitated by the sudden blow of a razor-sharp *jattha*: '*Acchu! Acchu!*'

An enormous purple sun plays on the floor of the Shing Parlour
... the blood on Molita's nose and lips is purple, but blood is such an
impossibly trivial thing, which proves nothing. Because Mrs Shing is a
very compassionate woman, who gives her employees new clothes on
Eid–New Year–Christmas, three festivals a year, no less!

More recently, Bengali women have entered the hair parlour business,
so she has lost the monopoly that she had, and we are quite certain that
at least her Shanghai steel shoes were not responsible for the occurrence.
For even after death, Molita traversed three gargantuan Sleeps – like an
eternal autumn afternoon, the silence of a world past its youth. Although
the narrative of our story focuses on Molita's Third Sleep, if we are to search
for the source of the purple blood, then we must go back to Molita's First
Sleep. When a pot full of blood-red carrots was burned to coal. For the
mistress of the household – the Bengali Christian household where Molita
first arrived in Dhaka to work as a maid – had given her the responsibility
of cooking carrot *halwa* that day. The air had turned loathsome that day
with the pungent smell of burning, as she stared unblinkingly at the pot
and slept. Consequently, the mistress of the household had been forced
to leave the VCR and enter the kitchen and pour the boiling hot water in
the pot on Molita's body. When the mistress of the household saw that
even that failed to wake her up, she heated the metal ladle in the gas fire

and pressed it again and again against Molita's underarms, her adolescent breasts and loins. Yet the music of the *khram* and *imbangi sanai* reaches Molita's ears ... when the mistress of the household skewered her clitoris with the handle of the hot ladle, she fell to the floor with quite calm a mind. The finest *khamal* of the five *mahari*, Jobang Ambeng, stooped over Molita's immobile body with the herbal root of the *dolagipa* tree held between his teeth.

The Mandis row their boats upstream of the Siju River thirty miles against the tide of Songdu.

'*Acchu! Acchu!*'

'Do not fear, Salnima, Jobang Ambeng himself will look after you.' The voice of the grandfather can be heard clearly.

How long ago was it? When the good winds like the pink petals of the *maccha jaseng* blossom would make the mountain quiver?

The past continues to weave its living events ... for instance, on 25 December, Father Paul Massang of the Ranikong Mission works on the lengthy *Father Tree*, detailing the preachers spreading Christianity among the indigenous tribes.

On the days following 1981, the mystical rainy days of Sravan arrive on the outer slopes of the Birishiri valley like a goddess awakened before her time ... The Rong Forest goes quite a long way through the outskirts of Kalmakanda. Recently, of course, the density of the Rong Forest has begun to decrease – if someone with courage starts walking half a mile or a mile into the heart of the forest, they will come across the 'Ministry of Forest and Environment, Government of Bangladesh: Structural Adjustment Program, Sponsored by World Bank' signboard.

As in the past, in the beginning only the process of structural readjustment is initiated. For instance, the local forest range officers come with yellowish-brown tape-measures in hand to measure the land; some nights three to four non-local woodsmen appear suddenly in trucks. The trees are cut down with half human, half machine technology throughout the night. One day the whole of the Rong Bazar Forest disappears – the Mandis never even know. Even if they did know, there is nothing they could have done, so the Mandis of Birishiri say they know nothing of what is going on in the forest these days ... They put their lips to gourd *fongs* swigs on *chu bicchhi* and live in the world of fables, the world which one day exiles itself from them of its own will.

At times, the enormous black stones walk or crawl to old man Misa Attong. They complain, 'Not a single person is alive in Birishiri. Then why should we remain still? Let us move again.'

The last *khamal* of Kalmakanda, Misa Attong, bows down in front of all the stones of the Rong Bazar Forest, pleading, but the god commands: 'Stone! Remain still.'

Before the mystical rains of Sravan have settled in, all the leaves of the *bipang* trees flutter in the strangely yellow, phosphorescent light of the sun. There's a small, grassy brook running towards the east through the mouth of the Rong Forest. Just across the brook, the Mission rests on a hillock. Around twelve noon, Molita almost flies in the rain-washed strange yellow, phosphorescent sunlight: 'Father, my *Acchu* is very ill.' Sitting at a desk in the Mission garden, Reverend Paul Massang is preparing the *Father Tree*. He leaves his pen and paper and stands up: 'Where? Let's go.'

Misa Attong lies flat on his back on a motionless black stone beside the stream. Old yellowed skin hangs from his collar-bone, his eyes are barely open but gradually becoming motionless... Reverend Paul Massang bends over him. 'Misa Attong, do you repent the sins of your long life? Do you want the shelter of the Son? Do you want baptism?'

Only the red ants ascend and descend in lines on the *dahmiljing-a* trees. The Reverend's assistant proffers a bowl of water, and the Reverend sprinkles the water on the lips of the unconscious Misa Attong. The last idol worshipper of Kalmakanda has taken the shelter of the Holy Trinity. He has become a Christian before his death. Today Kalmakanda is free of the false Shangsharek faith.

A *dobaski* flutters its wings and hops around absent-mindedly. A chorus echoes in the church: '*Wan-gala Wan-gala Wan-gala/ Gitel Christo rojana hai Wan-gala*. The *Wan-gala* has returned after a year because of the pity of the Lord Christ.'

Deep white letters etched in broad wooden plaques in the main entrance to the Ranikong Mission bear witness to two years of labour of the Reverend Paul Massang:

The Father Tree

1911–1918 AD
1. Adolf Francis, CSC
2. Matthew Kearns, CSC

1918–1921 AD
3. Charles Finer, CSC
4. Joseph Harrell, CSC

1921–1927 AD
5. Christopher Brooks, CSC

1927–1928 AD
6. Morris Norker, CSC

The *Father Tree* is lengthy because the *Tree* details the names and descriptions of all the Fathers who worked there in the past years such as 1998, 1997, 1996, 1977, 1964 or 1872. The *Tree* details the names and descriptions of the Fathers of the remote past, such as 3014, as well.

Structural Adjustment, which is primarily a description of the Second Sleep
The line of bald acacia trees nod. One can't hide in the acacia bush. Once, a *matmatchi* porcupine, about a hand's breadth in length, brought some warriors of the Naderia Troop right through the mountains of Meghalaya into Birishiri. The *matmatchi* wanted the warriors – Prabeer Chiran, Parimal Marak, John Murik, Kishore Areng, Khhosru Ali and Bibhas Ruga – to hide through the night in the Rong Forest in the shadow of the tall *chambil* tree. They would attack the Kalmakanda police station at dawn. But, what a surprise, when the *matmatchi* brought the six warriors to the Rong Forest with rocket launchers and LMGs in hand, it found that there was no place to hide at all.

The thick leaves of *chambil* tree heavy with fruit or the secret hollows of the *thablochu* potatoes, of which only the *matmatchi* knew – nothing was there. Torn, pallid, crumbly earth and new species of dwarf trees. No leaves, no life in the boles – the pale, dusty trees stare at the darkness of the night, baring their broken teeth. Although it was night, the stars had thickened in the sky, so the Naderia warriors could not figure out how they were to hide themselves. Yet it was necessary to remain within the borders of Bangladesh during the night. What if they could attack the police station at dawn? So they lay down in the deforested land. They did not know that the general who covered his eyes with black sunglasses had visited Kalmakanda only three days ago. The general did not think of money as a problem – the military, the BDR, the police, the DFI – all he had bought at steep prices, so the prices for the blood-curdling covert killings were auctioned off at the Bangladeshi army barracks from the lowest of a lakh taka to amounts in crores. The BDR and No. 31 Rifles Battalion in Kalmakanda had been ordered to remain at highest alert.

Although the Mandis of the Birishiri Vale had been saying for quite a long time that they had no idea what went on in the forest these days ... although, their lips pressed to gourd *fongs*, the Mandis would say this often, ever since a pregnant woman named Protima Marak had been shot dead by a forest guard while she was on a regular visit to the Rong Forest to collect fuel-wood; still they had believed that the Mandi warriors who had joined Brigadier Nader Siddiqui's troops and crossed over to Meghalaya, would suddenly appear on this side of the border in the darkness of the night to take over police stations, arms or supplies ... that the Rong Forest still held enough trees to cast shadows that could conceal them.

As in the past, only the process of structural adjustment was begun. For instance, the local Forest Range Officers arrived, yellowish tape-measures in hand to appraise the land. At night the contractors came, bringing woodsmen with them. Throughout the night the trees were cut down with half human, half machine technology – eucalyptus *camaldulensis* – acacia *nilotica* – while stars gathered over the bald treetops.

The Birishiri Mandis knew nothing of this. The elderly continued to drink *chu bicchi* sitting in the thatched *ballim;* the young men and women were absorbed in *kudima*, in kisses and caresses.

On those days the good winds, like the pink petals of the *maccha jaseng* blossom, would make the mountains quake. On the other side, thunder would glint suddenly atop the Tura Mountain of Meghalaya. The rain would start any moment, distending the womb of the *Simsung*, the Shomeshwari River. On those days Mridanga Chisim, the handsomest young man of Kalmakanda, would take Molita to the Black Cave of Bhuga Rani, the chasm where Bhuga Rani met Father Francis in 1909.

'Do you feel sad for your *afa*, your father, Molita? He's a big-shot commander of the Naderia troop! He's the right-hand man of Brigadier Nader. Why don't you sing that song, Molita? I so want to hear it.' The *akashmoni* and *rangeen bipang* trees float down with the waters of the Shomeshwari from the mountains of Meghalaya. In those sorrowful magical days, the leaves of the *Rangeen Bipang* would make the waters of the Shomeshwari as red as tea.

Salni Anthamango/ Simsung chi rikkamo
Asong enba ang-a/ Nangkho gisic rak-a.

[It is evening. I am sitting by the Simsung in the sunset. Oh love! It is you I am thinking of.]

Mridanga exhales and stands up. '*Ang-a nangkho namnika*. I love you.'

Mridanga frees himself after a deep, lingering *kudima* kiss. 'Farewell, Molita. Do you see how many *bipang* have floated down the waves of the Simsung? I must pull out some *bipang*. The mission needs new furniture – Father told me.'

Perhaps this is how the purple blood congeals on Molita's lips, through prolonged kisses and the sharp bites of men. *Kudima* is that prolonged pathway to sleep, where Molita travelled thrice after her death. So when Molita sleeps unconscious, with her arms and legs splayed on the mosaic floor of the Shing Parlour amidst the cut hair strewn all over the room ... purple blood thickens on her lips. Yet Mrs Shing's Shanghai steel heels can in no way be held accountable for this event.

For Salnima was then engrossed in an eternal *kudima*. Oh, Salnima's whole body was overwhelmed in such a prolonged kiss, such a deep winter-sleep! Winter-sleep can blossom even in the seed-vessel and the calyx of a fallen flower (be the flower a zinnia, a chrysanthemum or a dandelion) or even in the maroon-hued fossil of a mare mated with a milk-white stallion, even after death, an embryo is planted in the womb – which is the closure of the Second Sleep.

When Molita took a job at a newly sprouted hair parlour of some unknown Bengali woman in Kathalbagan, the first week the mistress just made her do the housework – sweeping, mopping, cleaning, doing the baby's pee-soaked laundry. When Friday came round next week, the mistress handed her a whole bottle of Sunsilk shampoo: 'Go and take a bath, and shampoo yourself properly.'

When she had completed her bath, the mistress pursed her lips in a smile. When she pulled off Molita's skirt and blouse and wrapped a quite expensive pink towel around Molita, covering her from her underarms to her knees, Molita looked like a girl in one of the cinema magazines. Music played in a slow tempo in the enormous hall room on the third floor. Dipti Areng, three years older than Molita, taught her massage there, under the dim green light.

Pink/ green/ blue/ white/ brown/ maroon: after eight months passed for Molita, wearing endless towels, the yearned-for and mystical rainy season of Sravan approached.

One day when the clouds expanded, covering the *aret* leaves, Mridanga appears. Molita bows and immerses herself in an eternal kiss: 'Then you are alive, Mridanga? The waves of Simsung didn't sweep you away? Oh, the creator *Tatara Rabuga* has sent you to me again.'

As he shivers in the intense cold and sweat of marijuana, Faisal, the yellow-complexioned, beady-eyed Bengali youth, smiles absent-mindedly, 'You speak in the language of dreams. Who knows – maybe I am your Mridanga!'

'Our marriage will take place this winter, Mridanga. The Father has said so.'

The dead Salnima is resurrected in the crimson caresses of *kudima* and *thunapa*, the premarital sexual relationship of young Mandi men and women ... When a living child kicks inside the womb of the dead Salnima, reproductive medicine is amazed. So when reproductive medicine enters an elongated tube into her vaginal canal, alongside the slick and very warm blood, an intact skull of a Homo Sapiens spawn also emerges.

Shilchor Picnic Spot: Long After the Structural Adjustment

Sparkly new luxury coaches ply the roads. The Tourism Authority has built an ultramodern motel leasing the eucalyptus *camaldulensis* and acacia *nilotica* garden conserved under the 'Rongbazar Thana Forestation and Nursery Project'. A small lake has also been created near the motel by damming up an ancient stream of the Rong Forest. Honeymooners, picnic groups from government offices, TV crews with cameras slung on their backs shooting television dramas – a lot of people arrive at Shilchor picnic spot to have a good time.

However, the tourism services in Bangladesh are not that developed yet, complain the displeased Bengalis arriving from far-off towns. The truthfulness of their complaints can be judged as one descends at the bus stop of the newly built highway at the entrance of the Rong Forest. 'Help Freedom Fighter Prabeer Chiran. He played a valiant role in the Liberation War of '71 as a member of the 23rd Platoon under Brigadier Nader.' A mad beggar with a white placard with red lettering hung around his neck often bothered the travellers. The men and women out for a pleasure trip would try and get rid of him in so many ways. Yet how the madman managed to follow them inside the restricted picnic spot, where it was impossible to get in without paying an entry fee of two hundred taka, was a big mystery. He would crouch in front of the bubbling *biriani* pots with a tin plate in hand. Of course, all the Bengali tourists who came for a visit were not heartless. For instance about a week ago two professors from Dhaka University, who were also supporters of the pro-Liberation powers, gave two one-hundred taka notes to the madman. The sociology professor knotted his brows and said, 'Tribal people are free from three major repressions of civilized society: insanity, rape or sexual crimes and thievery. Then why is this man mad? Has the dehumanization process of society and the state reached such a critical level?'

The philosophy professor said with undiluted amazement, 'Oh, so the tribals fought in the Liberation War as well! But – but why is he dumb?'

None of the Kalmakanda Mandis come to the protected acacia *nilotica* forest any longer, although a non-governmental human rights organization has been in litigation at the Land Appeal Tribunal for the past ten years over the traditional *mahari*, tribal rights to land of the Rong Forest. But the truth is that none of the Kalmakanda Mandis come to the protected acacia *nilotica* forest, so the two professors never know that the mad freedom fighter Prabeer Chiran is actually an accursed *mimang*, a dead soul. They do not know that the lake at the Shilchor picnic spot is also a haunted lake. The pebbles gathered in the depths of the lake are the souls of all the male and female demons and fiends of Shangsharek, the extinct religion of Kalmakanda. Misa Attong, Prabeer Chiran's father-in-law and the last Shangsharek *khamal*, bound every stone in the Rong Forest with a strong enchantment. The whole family was accursed.

The night a *matmatchi* brought six warriors from the Naderia troop
to hide among the bald acacia bushes – it was an irony of fate that at that
time it was the reign of that most cold-hearted and cold-brained general
whose eyes were covered in black sunglasses. He never thought of money
as a problem, and every day the auction prices for the covert killings
conducted by the army and the intelligence services leaped from lakhs
to crores. It was at that time that the Kalmakanda Mandis saw the quick
whooshing off of a military convoy with the six fighters of the Naderia
troop, their arms tied behind their backs. Although they were not brush-
fired right in front of the Mandis, still when someone is picked up by
an army convoy for judgment, their fate can easily be guessed. Anyway,
Prabeer Chiran's whole family was accursed. Prabeer Chiran had a very
beautiful daughter, whose fiancé went to the Simsung to gather trees and
never returned. The girl later went away to Dhaka, there she either cut
hair in a parlour or prostituted herself (the two are synonymous) – no
one knows for sure. And Prabeer's wife ... well, these days who can keep
track of all that? The life of the Mandis is fast becoming similar to the
busy lives of the Bengalis ... but probably she went away to Meghalaya, to
some relative's house. The two pro-Liberation professors did not find out
any of this information. When all of a sudden the winter night descends,
they give two hundred taka and a bowl of excellent *biriani* to the dumb
madman and climb aboard the Dhaka-bound night coach.

Not bones or pickings, but *biriani* with good meat ... after so long!
The madman gobbles it up, then falls asleep with his unwashed hand
covering his eyes. Because Misa Attong, the last Shangsharek *khamal*
of Kalmakanda, has bound the souls of the ancient Shangsharek gods
and goddesses through enchantment to every last grain of dirt of the
conserved Rong Forest ... because after the madman fell asleep, all the
stars gathered one by one over the eucalyptus *camaldulensis*, the moon
goddess *Shushmi* emerges in the Milky Way shining with *Shandap*,
Pentha-Rirok, *Rubbok*. She tilts her head to the south once and sees the
dumb madman asleep in the acacia forest. Then she bows her head to the
north and sees Salnima lying in blood on the floor of Shing Parlour. The
goddess *Shushmi* descends to the earth, passing by the stars Krittika and
Rohini, past Andromeda. Suddenly in the early dawn, magical moonlight
floods the floor of Shing Parlour.

'Salnima! Salnima!' The goddess *Shushmi* places her hand on the bloodied cheek of Molita, 'You have nothing to fear. Here, I am wiping away your blood. You are the granddaughter of our loyal follower Misa Attong. It is dawn, Salnima. Today is the first day of *Wan-gala*. What was your pledge to Acchu Misa Attong? You will offer an *ampengni* potato to the god *Saljong* on the first day of the *Wan-gala* each year. Look, I have sown *ampengni* in an empty pot on the roof of the parlour during last winter. Arise, dig out the potato. Prostrate yourself to the god *Saljong* and chant: *"Saljong mite mingipa dong-ana/ Sreng Ampengni palo mika chana".*

Translated by Shabnam Nadiya

Biographical Notes

SHAHEEN AKHTAR is one of the new novelists on the literary horizon in Bangladesh. She has two novels to her credit *Palabar Path Nai* (*No Exit*, 2000) and *Talaash* (*The Search*, 2004) which has been awarded the *Prothom Alo* Best Book of the Year Award for 2004. Her writings are of an experimental and exploratory nature, as is borne out by her collection of short stories. She works for a human rights organization.

SONIA NISHAT AMIN is an Associate Professor in the Department of History, University of Dhaka. She completed her PhD on the history of women in colonial Bengal in 1994, and has been doing extensive research on the modernization processes that effected the lives of women especially during the nineteenth and twentieth centuries. A book based on her historical research, entitled *The World of Muslim Women in Colonial Bengal*, was published by E. J. Brill (Leiden / New Yale) in 1996. She is also known for her creative writings such as *Boston Diary Theke* (*From the Boston Diary*) and her English translations of the poems of Syed Shamsul Huq. She is an active member of the women's movement and the anti-communal movement in Bangladesh.

PURABI BASU is a nutritionist by profession and has published extensively in her own field. At the same time she is also a creative writer with several anthologies of short stories to her credit: *Purabi Basur Galpa, Ajanma Parabashi, Niruddhu Samiran*. Her feminist concerns are reflected in her short stories as well as in her translation of short stories, *Nari Tumi Nitya*. Her short stories and articles have been included in anthologies published in both Bangladesh and India.

PARAG CHOWDHURY is the penname of Dr Sauda Akhter, Professor of

Bengali, at Jahangirnagar University, Bangladesh. She began writing at an early age, and made a name for herself as a teenager publishing poems, rhymes, fiction and non-fiction pieces in leading children's magazines of the day such as *Tapur Tupur, Kochi Kachar Mela*. However her career as a writer was interrupted as she focused more on her career and her family. In recent years, she has been gradually returning to her childhood passion of writing.

AUDITY FALGUNI is a writer and journalist. She focuses on important political and social issues that militate against injustice and inequity. She is one of the brightest young creative writers in Bangladesh.

SHAMIM HAMID works as a social scientist and researcher in an international development organization. She has published extensively in her own field and has also brought out a collection of her short stories, *Zuleikha's Dream and Other Stories*, from which the story in this collection has been taken.

DILARA HASHEM is a novelist and short story writer. She lives in Washington DC, where she works in the Bengali Service of the Voice of America. She has several novels to her credit, of which *Ghar Mon Janala* (1965) is especially well known. Her collection of short stories *Holde Pakhir Kanna* (*The Cry of the Golden Bird*) and *Nayak* (*Hero*) were published in 1970 and 1982 respectively. In 1976, she was awarded the Bangla Academy Award for Literature. She is also a poet and translator.

SELINA HOSSAIN is one of the foremost women writers of Bangladesh. She has retired from a long service at the Bangla Academy. She has several novels to her credit, among them *Hangor, Nadi, Grenade*; *Nil Mayurer Jouban* and *Nirantar Ghantadhani*. She also writes short stories. The story 'Motijan's Daughters' has been taken from the volume *Motijaner Meyera*. In 1980, she received the Bangla Academy Award for her short stories and, in 1981, she was awarded the Alaol Literary Prize. Among other awards she has received are the Philips Literary Prize in 1988 and the Lekhika Sangha gold medal in 1989. Her novel *Hangor, Nadi, Grenade* has been made into a film.

ROKEYA SAKHAWAT HOSSEIN, writer, educationalist and social reformer, was born in 1880 in the village of Pairaband of Rangpur district in Bangladesh. She grew up in the later days of colonial India in a Muslim family before the partition of the subcontinent. She died in 1932 in Kolkata.

As a writer she was very radical and had a sharp and critical insight into the position of women during her times. She had a keen sense of humour, making her a good satirical observer of Bengali manners and mores. Her writings are especially critical of *purdah* which is the main object of attack in *Abaradh Bashini* (*The Secluded Ones*). She also envisions utopian feminist communities as she does in 'Sultana's Dream'.

There is a slight confusion regarding the spelling of her name in English. The prevalent spelling is 'Rokeya', though there is evidence to suggest that she herself used 'Ruqayyah'. We have opted for the more familiar spelling. She is popularly known as Begum Rokeya, though she herself signed her name as R. S. Hossein.

NAHEED HUSAIN teaches English in a government college. She has published her short stories in newspapers and journals. This particular short story was first published in *Ittefaq* in 1991. Later, this same story was published as part of an anthology of her writings entitled *Ekti Katha Chhilo* (*A Few Words*) from Dhaka in 1992.

NASREEN JAHAN started writing from a very early age. Her novel *Udukku* won her the prestigious Philips Literary Award in 1992. Among her other novels are *Jadu Bistar* and *Sonali Mukhosh*. She has also won considerable fame as a writer of children's fiction and won the Alaol Literary Award in 1995 for her work in this genre. She belongs to a younger generation of writers who boldly examine the tensions and contradictions of human relationships. In 2000 she was awarded the Bangla Academy Award for literature.

HELENA KHAN was born in Mymensingh in 1929. She has been publishing short stories since the 1960s, in publications such as the weekly *Begum*. Among the many prizes and awards that she has won, special mention must be made of Bangladesh Lekhika Sangha Prize (1976), Sajidunness Khatun Chowdhurani Literary Medal (1992) and Naz Travel's Gold Medal (1994). She has written short stories, novels, travel books and children's stories.

M. FATEMA KHANUM was born in 1894 in Dhaka. Her collection of stories covers a span of 10 years from 1920–30. This is an important collection, as these stories had been published in journals such as *Saugat, Shikha* and *Juger Alo*. She is also known for her essays, especially 'A Letter from a Muslim Woman'. Her only novel *Saptarshee* was published after her death in 1957.

RABEYA KHATUN taught for some time before devoting herself to writing. Among her books are *Madhumati, Man Ek Swet Kapati, Rajabagh, Kumari Matir Deshe, Ekattarer Nay Mash*, and *Titumirer Bansher Kella*. Among the many honours she has received for her contribution to literature are the Bangla Academy Award (1973) and the Ekushey Padak (1993).

RAZIA MAHBUB taught briefly at a college before starting her own school. She has written novels as well as short stories.

NUZHAT AMIN MANNAN is a teacher of English literature at the Department of English, University of Dhaka. She is a regular contributor to the literary pages of English dailies. Writing both poetry and prose, she seeks to combine both her academic and creative interests in an innovative manner.

Makbula Manzoor has published many novels, including *Ar Ek Jiban*, *Baishakhe Sheerna Nadi*, *Shiore Nioto Surya*. Her novel *Kaler Mandira* won the National Archives and Literary Award in 1997. She also has several collections of short stories to her credit. In 1984, she received the Bangladesh Lekhika Sangha Award for her short stories. Among other awards she has received are the Kamar Mushtari Award 1990 and the Rajshahi Lekhika Sangha Award 1993. She also writes children's fiction and plays for radio and television.

Dilara Mesbah is a professional writer. She used to write essays and features under a pseudonym for the weekly *Robbar* as well as for *Shachitra Bangladesh*. She has published volumes of short stories, novels and poetry, as well as nursery rhymes and a collection of essays. She has also received an award from the journal *Urmi* of West Bengal.

Shabnam Nadiya, who works as a senior director in the Bengal Foundation, a foundation for music, arts and literature based in Dhaka, is a writer and translator. Her stories have been published in Bangladesh as well as outside the country, notably in *Whupping Christ for Hollywood*, *The Beat* (http://the-beat. co.uk), and *Cerebration* (http://www.cerebration.org/index.html). She has also worked as translator for a number of literary anthologies and magazines.

Jharna Das Purakayastha is a well-known writer. She is also a renowned singer and performs on both radio and television. She writes stories, novels and articles for various newspapers and journals. So far she has several volumes of short stories, novels and children's books to her credit. In 1992, the Ragashri Shilpa Goshthi gave her a special citation for her novels. In 1993, she received the Shiri Shishu Sahitya Kendra Award for her children's fiction. She has also received the Sajedunnessa Khatoon Chowdhury Literary Award.

Jharna Rahman has been writing since the 1980s. Her stories and articles are published regularly in journals and dailies. Her novel *Cheleta* (*The Boy*) was awarded the first prize in the 21st February Literary Competition in 1980. She has four collections of short stories. She teaches Bengali in the Rifles Public College.

Nayan Rahman has been writing for many years. She has published several anthologies of short stories, novels and stories for children. She has herself edited a volume of her writings entitled *Kathar Phuljhuri* (*A Garland of Words*). Her novel *Annyarakam Juddha* (*Another Kind of War*) has received the Kabi Jasimuddin Award and the Nattyashabha Award. It has also received a prize from the *Urmi* of West Bengal. She has also been awarded the Ashwini Kumar Dutt Gold Medal for her literary output.

PAPRI RAHMAN has been writing since the 1990s, and her first novel *Shokol Andhakar hey Amaar (All My Darknesses)* is in the press. She edits a literary journal, and has already published two volumes of short stories. Her stories have been published in both Bengals, and she is one of the most promising young writers in the country.

RIZIA RAHMAN writes both short stories and novels. In 1978, she won the Bangla Academy prize for her novels. Her novels include *Ghar Bhanga Ghar, Banga Theke Bangla, Aranyer Kachhe.* Her collections of short stories include *Agni Shakhara* and *Nirbachita Galpa* from which 'What Price Honour?' has been taken.

SYEDA FARIDA RAHMAN is an artist and writer. She is the President of the Banalata Sahitya Parishad. She has published novels, poetry, short stories and a collection of essays. In 1990, she was accorded a special literary reception in Chittagong and in 1992, she won a literary prize from the North Bengal Parishad. In 1994, she was given a literary prize by the North Bengal Theatre World of Jalpaiguri in West Bengal, India, which also awarded her a special reception that year. In 1995, she was awarded the Silver Jubilee Award by the *Urmi* as well as a prize for literature by the Michael Madhusudan Academy of Calcutta.

KHALEDA SALAHUDDIN is an economist by profession and has taught at Eden University College in addition to other institutions. She has also served in an advisory capacity in the Ministry of Textiles. She is closely associated with social work and is an active member of Women for Women, a research and study group. In the midst of all these activities, she has maintained her interest in creative writing and has a number of collections of short stories and poems to her credit. She has received several awards for both her research and creative work. Her research has been published in journals at home and abroad. She writes in both Bengali and English.

NIAZ ZAMAN is Professor of English, University of Dhaka and has published voluminously in both literary and cultural areas. Her published work includes her prize-winning study of the Partition: *A Divided Legacy: The Partition in Selected Novels of India, Pakistan and Bangladesh.* She is also a creative writer and has written a novel, *The Crooked Neem Tree,* as well as several short stories. The title story of her short story anthology, *The Dance,* won an *Asiaweek* short story award and has been included in *Prizewinning Asian Fiction.* Her story 'The Daily Woman' has been anthologized in *Worlds of Fiction.* At present, she is Literary Editor of *New Age,* Dhaka.

Notes on Translators

SHAFI AHMED teaches English at Jahangirnagar University. Apart from academic writings, he has also done considerable work in literary translation.

ZERIN ALAM teaches English at the University of Dhaka. Her interest lies in the area of women and language. She has done some literary translations.

FIRDOUS AZIM is Professor of English at BRAC University in Dhaka, Bangladesh. She has published widely on literary, cultural and women's issues both inside and outside the country. Her critical writings include *The Colonial Rise of the Novel* (1993), as well as contributions on post-colonial and women's writings in journals and edited anthologies. She is an active member of Naripokkho, a woman's activist group in Bangladesh. She is at the moment working on a women activists' memoir project.

CHITRALEKHA BASU is a writer and journalist based in Kolkata who writes regularly for the *Statesman*.

SAGAR CHAUDHURY is a journalist, broadcaster and translator. Born in Kolkata, he now lives in London where he used to work for the BBC.

SHAGUFTA HYDER teaches English at Eastern University. She regularly translates from Bangla to English. She is a fledgling writer who is yet to see her first story in print.

REBECCA HAQUE teaches English at the University of Dhaka. Her area of expertise is twentieth-century British and American fiction and drama. She has published two books, *Commencement Poems and Occasional Essays* and *Women, Gender and Literature*. Rebecca Haque is also a poet and translator.

MD JAMAL HOSSAIN is a fourth-year Honours student in the Department of English, University of Dhaka. The two stories that he has translated for this volume are his first attempts at literary translation.

SAEEDA KARIM KHAN studied English literature at the University of Dhaka and taught for some time at English medium schools. She is a freelance writer and translator and used to write a column for a local English daily.

NUZHAT AMIN MANNAN *See Biographical Notes*

SHABNAM NADIYA *See Biographical Notes*

MIRZA MAMUN SADAT teaches English at East West University. He occasionally tries his hand at translation.

NIAZ ZAMAN *See Biographical Notes*